Genfic

DISCREET INTERVENTIONS

By the same author

Shelley's Boat

*The Discreet
Interventions of*

VERDON
JAMES

Julian Roach

HarBOUR

First published in paperback original by Harbour in 2007
Harbour Books Ltd, 20 Castlegate, York YO1 9RP
publicity@harbourbooks.co.uk
www.harbourbooks.co.uk

UK and Ireland sales by Signature
20 Castlegate, York YO1 9RP
Tel 01904 633633   Fax 01904 675445
sales@signaturebooks.co.uk

ISBN 13:   978 1 905128 11 2

Typeset by Antony Gray
Printed and bound in
Finland by WS Bookwell

For May Roach

Acknowledgements

I must record a debt to my great and generous friend Dr Wolfgang Schaeffer, but for whose peculiar genius, late German High Romanticism – and this book – would be short of a gem far too good to be called a fake, and Wales would be without one of its most beautiful gardens. To Stephen Powell, once again, go my thanks for his patient editing and many helpful suggestions.

The Theatre of War

I have in front of me an item I clipped from a newspaper a long time ago – the date scribbled on the corner is December 1969. It describes a curious piece of theatre.

> The guard was changed last night at Spandau prison. In the searchlight towers, the watchers of one nation handed over their vigil to the watchers of another with the same grim little formalities that have occurred every month for a quarter of a century. One detail only has changed: there is nobody to watch – except each other. Their boots rang on the cobbles and the sound echoed through a thousand empty cells. Rudolf Hess, one-time deputy of Adolf Hitler, the last and only prisoner of Spandau, is sick. They're forwarding his mail to the British Military Hospital. The star of the show – in fact, ladies and gentlemen, the only member of the cast – is indisposed. But the show will carry on without him.

Beside it, because I keep it in the same manila envelope in my makeshift filing system, is a handwritten copy of a memorandum that I wrote in 1945 on the first night of peace in Europe. It was addressed to the Prime Minister with copies to nobody.

Straight away, let me tell you that I did nothing brave or bold in the war and not too much, I hope, that was bloody. My circle of friends, on the other hand, was quite bowed down under the weight of medals and bars. It was lucky for me that modesty and self-deprecation were the fashion among heroes, because there was nothing else I was entitled to wear. Now that such a lot of time has passed, and so many heroes are laid to rest, I'll make a small boast. My little corner of the war was the one part of the field where we –

I mean we British – outplayed the opposition from start to finish. There was some reason for thinking, in my little department, that we'd done a rather good job, but on VE night I went to bed early and alone.

I did not get a night's sleep. There was unfinished business on my mind and, anyway, the noise of a party – somebody rolling out the barrel – made it hard to sleep. At three o'clock, I got up, made a mug of tea with rum in it, and settled down to write my memorandum.

to: *Prime Minister*

from: *Capt. V. James*

However eager the Russians are to have the prisoner known as Rudolf Hess stand trial with the other German leaders, it would be better to deal with him in some other way. Our line of argument might well be that he effectively ceased to be a member of the German government when he flew to this country in 1941. At that time his country was not at war with the Soviet Union. Treaty relations existed between the two nations. There can, then, be no case for submitting the prisoner known as Hess to the interests of Soviet Justice, or to any judicial process in which the Soviet Union may play a part.

Should the Soviets insist, despite this embarrassment, then a valid plea may be entered that the prisoner is unfit to stand trial. His mental state has deteriorated during his time in captivity. He has bouts of depressive illness attended by episodes of amnesia and confusion. Dr Delaney is sure that these are genuinely pathological and my own observations lead me to agree. The prisoner's symptoms may have been made worse by the efforts of mind required by the training and educational aspects of his treatment while in our custody. If a clinical term must be coined for his condition, we may call it Uhlsdorf's Amnesia. A plea of unfitness along these lines should be prepared in terms that the court may accept. The prisoner may thus be dealt with more conveniently without embarrassing the Soviets.

I scribbled in the margin afterwards, in pencil: 'Patients suffering from Uhlsdorf's amnesia are inclined to think they are someone else, and blot out certain contradictory parts of their own memories. There is no point in looking up "Uhlsdorf's Amnesia" in any medical dictionary. You will not find it there.'

When the time came, a submission setting forth the plea that I suggested was prepared and advanced on behalf of the prisoner at the Nuremberg court on the 30 November 1945. I could not have foreseen that the prisoner would then dismiss his counsel and beg leave to address the court in his own behalf. He admitted that he had certain small mental difficulties, but claimed that his previous assertions of amnesia had been lies and that he was, in fact, perfectly fit to stand trial alongside the chiefs of the Nazis still living.

I had better fill you in. In 1940, Alastair McLaren said something vague about finding war work for me to do, but it did not seem to be the most pressing item on his agenda. My detectable asthmatic wheeze had led all three services to decline my offer. As it happens, the wheeze was caused by an allergy to something in carpets. Had anybody known at the time, I could have been sent off in a Spitfire, a submarine or a Sherman tank with as much impunity as the next man. The office in which I sat each day, on the other hand, was laid with an especially insanitary patch of ancient Axminster. The fact that what I did there was write defiant leading articles, and other expressions of the national resolve, for a daily newspaper only added to the anguish. Pacing the carpet must have exacerbated the wheezing. I pestered Alastair. I pestered other people. The best anybody ever seemed to come up with was the name of some new person I could pester.

It was not easy to come to terms with the idea that I might, after all, be quite useless when it came to fighting a war. The morning that I walked into St George's to attend the memorial service for Alwyn Spenser, the idea was especially oppressive, as it seemed that almost everyone in Hanover Square was in khaki or blue. I felt so useless, in fact, that I stayed in my pew as the church emptied afterwards, so that I could wait for everybody else to go. I didn't want to hear the questions, 'What are you up to?' or, 'Who are you with?'

So I stayed in my pew under the pretence of lingering at prayer, listening to the murmur of greetings and conversation outside the church. When I could hear only the traffic, I got up to leave. I found that I was still not quite alone in the church. One other straggler remained. I passed him on the way out but he caught up with me just outside the door.

'You're James, aren't you? My name's Ross.'

We shook hands. I had the impression of having seen him before and said so, apologising for my forgetfulness.

'Friend of Alastair's. Colleague in a way. Are you doing anything for lunch?'

As it happened I was engaged for lunch.

'Can you telephone and put the thing off?'

I looked at him with some surprise. When a stranger suggests with quite that confidence that you break an engagement, he's either a lunatic or he has something serious to say. Ross didn't seem to be a lunatic.

'Can I take a short cut?' I asked him.

'To where?' he asked, slightly surprised.

'To the point in the conversation where you may be about to suggest there is something I might be able to do for you or you for me.'

'At this rate we can probably skip lunch. You've been looking for a job. I might be able to find you something. What do you suppose your answer would be by the time we'd had lunch and I'd told you as much as I was going to tell you?'

'I have a feeling that wouldn't be very much anyway.'

'As it happens, no, it wouldn't be.'

'Doesn't make much difference. The answer would be yes. I want a job to do.'

'There could be an outside chance. We'll have lunch another time.' He put a calling card in my hand. 'Come and see me, ten o'clock tomorrow.'

He turned and strode off across the square, holding his hat against a little flurry of wind.

At ten o'clock the following morning I walked the short distance from my rooms to Vincent Square and rang the bell at the address on Ross's card. Not being sure that the bell was really working, I also thumped with the tarnished brass knocker. The house seemed to be a private dwelling with nothing to distinguish it from the rest of the terrace. White shutters were drawn across inside the windows on the ground floor and the glass was taped against blast. There was a basement with a railed area in which someone had dumped a tangle of barbed wire. The door was opened by a woman in a tweed suit. She had glasses and nicotine stained fingers and didn't pause to listen as I introduced myself.

'Up the stairs to the room straight ahead of you.'

There was no name on the door and it was not a very cheerful room. It was waiting to become somebody's office. There was a brown desk with a linoleum top standing not quite in the middle of the floor. A chair to match it for utilitarian ugliness was lying on top of it. A green filing cabinet stood obscuring part of the window. A telephone sat on the floor at the end of a skein of black cable. The walls were covered in a dispiriting greenish wallpaper, extremely grubby around the light switch. There were no pictures or decorative touches of any sort.

I waited for ten minutes or so but nobody came. I went back out on to the staircase and listened. A certain amount of muttering came from behind the next door along the landing, but I could make nothing of it because a typewriter was chattering away on the floor below. I went back down the staircase and opened the first door I came to and found the tweed-suited woman typing in maestoso style at a black machine not much smaller than a grand piano. She had a cigarette pushed to one corner of her mouth, with her face screwed up to keep the smoke out of her eye. She showed no interest in my arrival.

'I believe Mr Ross is expecting me,' I said.

'Colonel Ross,' she said and kept on typing.

'I wonder where I might find him?'

'Up the stairs to the room straight ahead of you.'

'You are quite sure of that? There is nobody there at the moment.'

'No,' she said, 'that's because you're down here.'

I went back to the room on the first landing. There was still no sign of Ross. The chair still lay on the desk.

I took it down and moved the desk to a more convenient position where it enjoyed what light came through the heavily taped window. The filing cabinet was more awkward to move and had to be waddled on alternate corners to a better resting place. Out on the landing I had noticed a coat-and-hat stand. It looked more purposeful when I had put it in the corner by the door. Once I had hung my hat and coat on it and hooked my umbrella on the thing, it lent a pleasant air of occupation to the room. I wiped the dust from the seat of the chair and sat at the desk. The drawers were all empty, but for one, which contained several sheets of ruled paper and an incomplete maintenance manual for a motorcycle of some kind. The ruled paper I squared up and put on a corner of the desk. The motorcycle manual I passed up as the first offering to the waste-paper bin. If the telephone had only been connected to an exchange, I'd have been ready to set myself up in any business that took my fancy.

The woman in the tweed suit, still wreathed in smoke, had reached a very animated passage of typing when I opened her door again.

'Why does the telephone not work in that room?'

She stopped typing and took the cigarette out of her mouth, which allowed her face much needed relief from contortion.

'They're supposed to have done the telephones last week. You can't say when they'll come. They say there's a war on.'

'See if you can't chivvy them up. And if there's any gas . . . ' I glanced at the far corner of the room where a kettle stood on a gas ring, next to a teapot, 'I should be extremely glad of a cup of tea.'

I looked at my watch, which, by reflex, made her look at her own, confirming that it was time for a cup of tea. 'If you could send one up. No sugar. Milk if there's any. You seem to have rather a lot of chairs.'

A row of bentwood chairs scraped the walls on two sides of her office.'

'We need them,' she said. 'From time to time.'

'Then call on me if you should run out,' I said, lifting the least rickety looking chair and taking it with me.

I now had an office, a desk, a hatstand, two chairs, a wastepaper bin and the prospect of a telephone line. By retrieving the too hastily discarded manual from the litter bin, I was equipped to offer advice on certain aspects of motorcycle maintenance. It was beginning to look as if I might, at last, be able to make a contribution to the war effort. I knew from many conversations I'd had that London was stuffed with people in similar offices making just about the same contribution. The difference was that they had more paperwork to show for it.

The woman in the tweed suit brought me a cup of tea accompanied by two biscuits in the saucer.

'Colonel Ross telephoned. His apologies, but he's tied up. He'll try to see you this afternoon, if you can wait.'

'If there's still a war on this afternoon, I'll wait.'

'About the tea. We have a little fund. To buy the sugar and biscuits and so on. Everybody puts in sixpence a week.'

I gave her sixpence. The tea was disgusting but I drank it on principle. Once you're in the tea fund, you're part of the establishment. At lunchtime I walked up to the Army and Navy Stores and bought a calendar, an inkwell and a blotter. In a bric-à-brac shop near the station I found several pictures. One was a portrait of Admiral Beatty in a quite respectable frame. Another was a stirring depiction of the battle-cruiser *Lion*, steaming full ahead at Jutland, that must have come from the same house clearance. There was also a large watercolour of Tintern Abbey. One of the odd advantages of the blitz was that it was easy to bargain down a price with a man who couldn't entirely dismiss the idea that his stock might be blown to oblivion in the night. I got the lot very cheaply, together with a few nails and some wire to hang them.

HMS *Lion* I put up behind my desk, Admiral Beatty on the wall opposite. I used my shoe for a hammer. Tintern Abbey took a little thinking about. I tried several places and eventually settled for the piece of wall that first met your eye on entering. It wasn't the best light for the picture but the effect was the most congenial and welcoming. When I'd finished, I thought of the Tabriz rug on the floor of Alastair McLaren's more stylish office a mile or so nearer to Downing Street and wished I could throw down one to match it. I couldn't, of course. Some of us have to settle for linoleum.

I was writing a letter when Ross came in. Naturally, he came in without knocking but in an instant he stopped.

'Sorry, old man,' he said and immediately left, closing the door behind him, even before I looked up. I heard his footsteps out on the landing; heard the door to the next office open and a brief exchange of voices.

His footsteps returned and passed down the stairs. The sound of typing was arrested for a few moments and then Ross's footsteps came back up the stairs. The door was opened and it stayed open. Ross stared at me.

'Whose is this bloody office?'

'This morning it didn't seem to be anybody's. This afternoon it seems to be mine. Do come in.'

'Yours, is it? And what do you do in it?'

'I'm waiting for somebody to tell me. Just like half the chaps in London from what I can make out.'

Ross sat on the bentwood chair, threw his feet up on the desk and carried on staring at me while he took a cigarette case from his pocket.

'Smoke?'

I declined.

'Do you mind?' There was a certain sarcasm in his tone.

'Not at all,' I said. 'Use the bin for an ashtray. They don't seem to have supplied me with one yet.'

He lit his cigarette and drew on it a few times.

'There's someone coming to see me in a little while. Someone who doesn't know me. So for this afternoon's exercise, as you've occupied my office, you might as well carry on being me. You're Ross.'

'What's he coming to see you about? See me about, that is?'

'Find out. And don't make assumptions. You speak German, I gather?'

'I read it better than I speak it, I'm afraid.'

'Been to Germany much?'

'Not much, no.'

'Why the German, then?'

'Because there is really no such thing as exact translation. I was reading philosophy at the University and rather a lot of it was turned out by Germans. So I learned German.'

'You read Greek as well, then, do you?'

'I don't suppose that will be very useful in the present emergency, will it?'

'I don't know what will come in useful, but don't mention philosophy too often. The War Office doesn't have much time for that sort of thing. They might decide you're an intellectual.'

'I'm hardly that. Anyway, I ride and shoot and so forth so my disguise is pretty well complete.'

I heard the light patter of a woman's footsteps outside. Then came a tap on the door and I realised what Ross had meant when he advised me against making assumptions. She was striking enough to look at, not at all fragile, well shaped and with an expression that either challenged or invited you to look twice. Without needing to look twice you were aware of the sensual mouth and the abundance of brown hair that framed her face. She wore her clothes with the air of a woman who expected her clothes to be noticed. I remember only that she wore a suit with a slim skirt and that her hat was made of velvet.

I introduced myself as Ross and introduced Ross, with an air of intentional reticence, as 'a colleague'.

'You haven't met, I assume,' I said looking from one to the other. They both shook their heads.

'This is Miss . . . forgive me . . . ' I turned to her.

'Fanshawe. With an e. Diana Fanshawe.'

They shook hands and then she sat on the bentwood chair proffered by Ross and waited. Ross wandered to the window.

'Well, Miss Fanshawe. What is it that you think you might be able to do for us?'

She rearranged her legs and adjusted the hem of her skirt by a millimetre or two, then turned on me a softening look from her brown eyes.

'I thought I was here for you to tell me.'

I was aware of Ross resting indolently against the window-sill and reaching for his cigarette case. I couldn't see whether he was smiling or not.

'Then . . . tell me something about yourself.'

She crossed her hands on her lap, leaned back a little and looked up as if wondering where to begin.

'Don't start too far back. What have you been doing lately?'

'Lately I've been in a long run at the Prince Frederick.'

'Of course,' I said. And of course, I should have known. She was an actress. I could not, though, remember having seen her, or recall what had been playing at the Prince Frederick.

'You had rather good notices in that, didn't you?'

'The play had good notices. I took over from Hermione Street quite well into the run. I imagine you really know all this. The man who told me to come here certainly did, so why shouldn't you?'

'Don't put too much faith in – er – liaison, Miss Fanshawe. We can make no assumptions at all, just at the moment.'

'To be quite honest, when your man spoke to me I wasn't sure whether I was being arrested or recruited.'

I took a leap, not entirely in the dark. Ross had been scheduled to see me in the morning and Miss Fanshawe in the afternoon. The interviews might not have been entirely unconnected. Ross knew, probably, rather a lot about me, but he'd only brought one thing to the surface.

'Do you speak German, Miss Fanshawe?'

'I hope it's not an offence.'

'Not at all. How do you come to speak German?'

'I had a German nanny.'

'And you have spent time in Germany?'

'Am I being investigated?'

'Of course. Everybody in the country who had a German nanny or governess is being brought in and interrogated.'

'It must help to pass the time.'

'You spent time in Germany?'

'You must know all this. I spent holidays in Germany as a child. I have Hessian relations. A Hessian is a kind of German, I cannot deny it.'

'Miss Fanshawe, I'm not suggesting that it is improper to have German relations. Or even to speak German. I'm in rather the same boat, but in my case it's worse. I have German friends. Relations, after all, you can't choose. To have friends is much more suspect.'

'Then why are you talking to me at all? It's such a rigmarole.'

It seemed a good time to invent a reason.

'Miss Fanshawe, you will be aware that very few English people speak German, or indeed, any foreign language.'

'I am certainly aware of that. It seems to be considered rather un-English.'

'You probably know that in Holland, for instance, practically everyone speaks German or French and quite commonly both, as well as Dutch.'

'I believe so.'

'Holland is, at the moment, occupied. But any conversation between Germans is likely to be perfectly understood by any Dutch man or woman who might happen to overhear it. Imagine for a moment that a German invasion were to succeed or partly succeed here. Things would be rather different, wouldn't they?'

She raised her eyebrow to mark that she was following me perfectly.

'Exactly. The Germans could walk about chattering their darkest secrets pretty well with impunity. They could hold strategic planning meetings in the bandstand in Hyde Park. Compared to the Dutch – or even the French – any potential British resistance is off to a poor start. Now do you see why this department . . . ' I waved my hand deprecatingly about the room I had furnished, 'why this department wants to contact intelligent and – er – reliable men and woman who understand German?'

'Yes. Yes, I do.' She leaned forward to my desk. She was following my thoughts quickly, almost more quickly than I could invent them.

'Your talents and training as an actress might be as useful as your command of German. Simultaneously useful, if you can imagine that?'

'I can.'

Ross straightened himself from the window-sill, walked to the door, where I could see him but Miss Fanshawe could not, and shook his head. He made a gesture with his hand that clearly meant I was to bring the interview to an immediate close.

'Then for the moment, Miss Fanshawe, may I say that it has been delightful to meet you and very encouraging to speak to you. This department will be in touch. Thank you for coming.'

Behind her, Ross opened the door and smiled.

She turned in the doorway, very much as an actress would turn, making an exit.

'It has been very interesting, gentlemen. I'm only disappointed to think that you won't be getting in touch with me again, after all.'

'Will we not?'

'No. Because when the bastards do try to invade us we shall kick them where it hurts. They'll never walk into London the way they walked into Paris. Still . . . it seems you know where to find me, if and when you want me. Good-day.'

Ross closed the door behind her.

'Where did all that guff come from?'

'I made it up as I went along. Still, it was rather a good guess about the German, don't you think?'

'Yes, it was.'

Ever since I had begun the interview with Miss Fanshawe, Ross had been toying with an unlit cigarette. He now lit it and clouded himself in smoke and his own thoughts for a while.

'Why don't we have some tea?' I suggested. 'I've put sixpence in the fund, after all.'

Ross looked at me, not very amused.

'I'm not sure what I should make of you, James. You've usurped my office and, either by a fluke or some kind of unhealthy divination, you seem to have absorbed my thinking processes.'

'I just thought you'd be ready for a cup of tea.'

'All that stuff about the British resistance was on the nail. What you said to Miss Fanshawe was a pretty good summary of why both of you are in my address book.'

'Do I win a goldfish or a coconut?'

'I'm not sure what you win. Probably a bullet in the back of the neck. If the Germans do invade we need to have a body of credible collaborators that British intelligence can run. I imagine that Miss Fanshawe might get on to – er – intimate terms with a top Hun. And you seem to be able to worm your way in anywhere. Starting with my office. Sixpence in the tea fund, eh?'

'Look here, Ross, if you like I'll explain why I made free with your office.'

'You needn't bother. I may be in military intelligence but I'm not stupid. You were brassed off waiting, and it was a way of saying you were tired of it and that you really did want a job.'

'Thank you for understanding. The pictures cost me five bob. You can have them if I get a job.'

'You can keep them yourself. You can keep the office, too, though I should think you'll have to share it before very long. You've got a job. Get the tea up and we'll talk.'

Despite my inclination to asthma, it was necessary for me to be subject to military discipline. Within a week, I had the King's commission, despite my unreliable respiration. For administrative convenience, I was put on the same list as chaplains, and therefore immediately enjoyed the rank of captain. The only advantage this rank afforded me was that in the case of any serious lapse on my part, I would have the privilege of being shot by my employers rather than hanged.

Having war work to do was, for the first few days, very like not having war work to do. I went to my office in Vincent Square every morning and before long had given the nicotine-stained Mrs Ambrose another sixpence so that I should have tea to drink. I got on to nodding and greeting terms with the two men who worked in the office next door, without knowing what they did there. Ross brought papers and assessments – that is, guesses about the enemy's plans to invade – that I was to read and digest. I was in the dark about what to do with the information once I had digested it.

'Look James,' said Ross one afternoon, 'your job is either top priority or it doesn't matter a toss. Get your imagination working on ways in which British resistance might be sustained, co-ordinated and directed in the case of enemy occupation. There is, at present, not a lot under this heading on the War Office shelves. Our friend McLaren believed that your mind was fashioned on somewhat oblique lines. What I know of you inclines me to agree. The point being, if meeting the Germans head on doesn't work we may need to resist them more obliquely. *Carte blanche*, dear boy. Let us know your thoughts. Nobody else has any.'

While Fighter Command was fighting them in the air, and Winston was telling us that we would fight them on the beaches and the landing grounds, I was imagining how we might, if it came to it, fight them in the cellars and the sewers and by stealth. It did not take long for this job to seize my imagination and I worked on it night and day. In a very short time I had written thousands of words for a fairly small readership. I defined what I hoped were good general principles and then outlined proposals for the command and control of an organisation that had no command and control centres and many of whose forces would be without military training or under-standing. For this part, if no other, Captain James was better qualified than most. I'll admit to being pleased with the general introduction, which I wrote last of all. It was a short but closely reasoned chapter that I entitled 'The Objects of Resistance'. I began by addressing a fundamental question and my first paragraph was headed, 'Why Resist?' I am told that Mr Churchill tore the pages out and threw them away. 'It is a question we need not answer,' he said, 'because no Englishman will ask it.'

All the same, I'll admit to being so pleased with my efforts that I was almost disappointed to see the threat of invasion recede. This didn't put me entirely out of work: the job was simply turned inside out. I was told to imagine that I had been given exactly the same job by the Abwehr, and to think how German resistance might be organised in the event of an Allied invasion. In 1941 this possibility was so remote that my work could not really have been called urgent. I began to pester Ross for work from a slightly more active file.

'The trouble is finding a niche for you, old chum. You have no military expertise, so you're not going to be much use assessing intelligence coming in – or, more especially round here, going out.'

'I thought the idea was just to stop intelligence going out, not assess it as it went.'

He lit another of his cigarettes and I pushed him the ashtray I'd bought especially to cope with his visits to my office.

'Of course that's what the brass wants to do. Stop anything getting out. But there is another way of looking at it. Imagine for a moment that we have scooped up an entire network of German spies. Then imagine that we are smart enough not to shoot them. Then imagine that they are smart enough to be turned into agents working for us. What have we got?'

'Assuming the Abwehr hasn't rumbled what's going on then you've got a pretty good way of wrong footing the Herman High Command, haven't you?'

'Exactly. You can use this network to feed the enemy misleading information.'

'For so long, anyway,' I said, 'until they realise that it's duff gen.'

'You have touched the thing with a needle, old chum. If all you feed them is duff gen, they'll rumble it pretty damn quick. It follows that you have to feed them a carefully balanced diet. It means you have to let them have some of the real stuff.'

I sat back to think about this. It was a slightly alarming reversal of the ordinary assumptions.

'So, if you had scooped up a whole network of German spies, you're saying you'd want to give them real, valuable military information to pass on to the Abwehr?'

'Yes.'

'Information about our operational dispositions?'

'Yes.'

'Information, say, that might help the Luftwaffe select its targets? I assume that's what spies are supposed to do. How about that?'

He looked at me very steadily.

'Yes.'

'My God.'

'You've hit a very good point with Luftwaffe targets. It is possible that we could, by selective dissemination of intelligence, lead the Luftwaffe to attack a particular target, one particular town, one city, rather than another. Yes.'

I think I may have whistled at the implications.

'It might be phoney information, but they would be real bombs,' I said. Not that he needed me to say it.

'We would be sacrificing pawns. Sometimes more than pawns. But if it protected some more valuable piece on the board . . . '

I stayed silent for a while. So did Ross. He simply smoked and looked at me.

'Do I assume that we have scooped such a network of German spies?' I asked him.

'Funnily enough. Not everybody is quite certain about this, but I am. I know in my bones that we've got them all. We are at the moment running all or just about all the German spies in England.'

'Why do you think that?'

'They had a few chaps in place before the war and we rumbled them. They weren't really very good, but we turned them. One of their chaps has been transmitting quite cheerfully from a fairly comfortable cell in Wandsworth Prison for over a year. The point at first was to know what sort of information the Abwehr was asking for. Tells you a lot about what they're planning.'

'I see that. How is it we seem always to have been taken by surprise, then?'

'Don't be sarcastic, old chum. Not all of us were. And since then, there's been more of an inclination to believe what some of us say. The point is, the Germans suddenly decided they needed a lot of information very quickly before they invaded, so they threw in a lot of agents in a hurry. They all had beautiful papers which they used with the greatest confidence because they'd been forged according to details sent back by their chaps *in situ*. They just didn't know that the particular *situ* was Wandsworth Prison. The beautiful papers made them very easy to bag. They weren't very well trained, they thought their job would be over in a few weeks anyway, and they weren't hard to turn when they'd been picked up. One or two were genuinely dedicated, very tough chaps. They had to be executed, in accordance with the Articles of War. Which, I suppose, only served to make the Abwehr believe that everything was running pretty well as per normal in the spying business. And, by the way, I'm not very sure I should be telling you any of this.'

'I'm still wondering why you are.'

'Because what we have in our hands is an instrument for deceiving the enemy. In the end, when we get a chance to kick back at the bastards, good deception could be crucial to the success or failure of a big attack. As long as we can keep the instrument in tune until then, of course. Now it's up to other people to sort out what kind of real gen to give them. I want you to put your mind to ways, means and ends of deceiving the enemy. Let's start to work on a few essays in deception, so that when we have to do it on the night, we won't be doing anything we haven't rehearsed. Am I making sense?'

'Perfectly.'

'Then let me have your ideas. Not on paper. You remember the day you moved yourself into this office?'

'Yes.'

'I think that's when you got this job. All you did was to arrange the furniture and put up a picture. But when I walked in through that door, it wasn't my office. I was absolutely deceived. In the same circumstances, I think anybody would have been. But all that happened was that some cheap furniture had been arranged to accord with one set of expectations rather than another. Think the same way and call it strategic deception.'

I was in the deception business. I didn't realise at first that I had joined an élite unit. As I began to meet the rest of the department, I was rather flattered. I worked with men who marshalled and deployed entirely imaginary forces, sometimes whole notional armies – there were several of these in the end – and they were among the most able and intelligent officers I met in the course of the war.

I reported to the Twenty Committee. The Twenty Committee was subordinate to the W. Board. The W. Board was accountable to nobody but itself, not even the Joint Services Intelligence Committee. Disinformation is too delicate for discussion. Few regular officers knew of our existence, but among those few we were deeply distrusted. It was as well that not many people knew about the Twenty Committee and how it came to be called that. The Roman numeral for twenty, you will remember, is a double cross.

Sometimes the notional units and forces that we put into the field were pure phantoms of the cipher world of intelligence. Their existence could be inferred from rumour; given foggy substance by decode and interpretation; proved by intercepted radio transmission. They were creatures of the ether. Sometimes the business was much more like putting on a pantomime or amateur theatricals. Sometimes it was all of these things together. Many a night in 1942 I sat with an amiable German spy in his accommodation in Wormwood Scrubs, listening to him as he relayed fragments of information to the Abwehr. I had to be there as now and again he had difficulty reading the careless talk that he had picked up. I have never had the clearest handwriting and he needed a little prompt before picking up the staccato theme again on the Morse key. The following day, a reconnaissance Messerschmitt appeared over certain acres of Sussex. We know that the Messerschmitt pilot found a concentration of armoured vehicles. As he knew where to look, the attempts at camouflage were easily penetrated. Clearly, there was a field of tanks and other motorised units crudely disguised as small farm buildings, perhaps pigsties, and agricultural machinery. In the same cell in Wandsworth, two nights later, I was playing chess with my friend the German spy. I was going to beat him, but he was putting up a more astute defence than I was used to seeing from him. We had to put the game aside unfinished when the time came for him to tune in to the Abwehr for instructions. He was to pay particular attention to gaining information and, especially, possible embarkation instructions of the armoured unit mustered in Sussex. What unit was this? Under what command? Details of armour type? Were the vehicles fitted with desert filters? I'm sure he managed to send back snatches of useful stuff. On the ground in Sussex, a collection of small farm sheds was demolished and farm vehicles were sent back to their proper business the following night. A bonfire was made of an amount of timber and painted calico. A tank flimsily disguised as a corn thresher is hard to distinguish from a corn thresher flimsily disguised as a tank. It depends which you're expecting to see.

In my working hours I was a backstage worker in a rather peculiar theatre of war. In between times I was becoming familiar with the backstage world of Shaftesbury Avenue.

I had been put in a position that made it easy to get in touch with Diana Fanshawe again. If I asked her to lunch – which I did – it was a certainty that she would not turn me down. It helped that she was under the impression that it was her duty to accept. She believed that she knew why I was asking her to lunch and she believed that I was called Ross, so there was a certain amount of unstitching to do. It wouldn't have been necessary, had I not found that I was thinking of her a good deal.

DEAR MISS FANSHAWE – you were kind enough to call in at Vincent Square and talk to me about a long-term theatrical project. It's beginning to look as if the show may not be going ahead but, all the same, I wonder if we might meet to discuss other possibilities. May I suggest lunch any day you like next week?

Yours,

DIANA FANSHAWE

DEAR MR ROSS – I should be delighted. Will I be? Say where.

Yours,

DIANA FANSHAWE

DEAR MISS FANSHAWE – I hope you will be. You deserve to be. The Maison Blanche? Wednesday at one?

It was still possible to dine out well in London. As the war went on and rationing became more stringent, the menu became shorter. The first time I went with Diana to the Maison Blanche, they were still able to offer something passably like the pre-war à la carte. By the war's end we would simply sit down and eat whatever they could put in front of us. The other hospitable pleasures remained, heightened by shortage and uncertainty: the sparkle of white linen, the uncorking of good wine, the easy formality of good waiters with familiar faces, the breeze of cheerful conversation around you, the sound of your own voice saying foolish things.

I began, as I had to, with the confession.

'There is something I must get out of the way. My name isn't Ross. That was a quite meaningless deception, not aimed at you.'

She did not seem in the least put out.

'What is your name?'

'James. That's the second bit. The first bit is Verdon. It's a slightly back to front sort of name. Use any bit of it you like.'

'I think I prefer Ross. Ross was a colonel. Are you?'

'I'm only a captain, I'm afraid. Not a very convincing one, I know, but I am.'

'Captain James, then.'

'Please don't call me that. I am a captain, but I don't even know how to salute. It's just so they can court-marshal me if they feel the need.'

'I can't call you Mr James. It makes me sound like the house-keeper. Verdon will have to do.'

'Thank you.'

'I should tell you that my name isn't really Diana Fanshawe.'

'Is that a stage name?'

'I'd stick to it if I never worked again. It's a great improvement.'

'On?'

'Dorothea Tremlett.'

'Diana suits you better. I'm not sure about Fanshawe.'

'Call me Diana, then.'

'She was the patron goddess of slaves. Did you know?'

'I thought she was simply the huntress.'

'Oh, she was certainly that. There was a special cult of her worship at Aricia, with a temple deep in the forest and a high priest who got the job by slaying his predecessor. He kept it for as long as he was strong enough to avoid going the same way.'

Her eyes lit with delighted laughter.

'I didn't know that. It sounds like an excellent arrangement. One would never have a doddery high priest.'

'I suppose that was the idea.'

'If one were a big enough star, the casting of leading men could be arranged on similar lines.'

'Who would I have to kill at the moment?'

'Do you have ambitions to go on the stage?'

'Of course.'

'At the moment you wouldn't have to kill anybody. I'm not in a show.'

'No leading man at all?'

'None.'

'A high priest anywhere?'

'No. One or two altar boys who turn up occasionally, I think that's all.'

'Diana, I can't quite believe that. London is full of handsome and heroic young men who believe they may be dead tomorrow. They'd fall in love with a town-hall clock if it struck at the right moment. You are not a town-hall clock. You're extremely beautiful and you're marvellous company. They must be clambering over each other.'

She put her hand over the top of her wine, the way someone might who was declining the offer of more. She was silent for a while.

'Yes. A lot of them will be dead tomorrow. Some of them already are.'

'It was rather a crass thing for me to say. I'm sorry.'

She shook her head abruptly and stared at her glass for a while. Her features displayed no emotion. She had the composure you might see in a carving from Egypt and the light that shone from the white table linen, sculpting her face, only heightened the impression. I felt stupid. It's not how you want to feel when you take a beautiful woman to lunch.

Let me tell you about Dieter Maria Uhlsdorf, the dye-stuff sales-man. In 1940 he was working in a prison bakery in the North of England and had become quite an accomplished baker of bread. Dieter Maria's job had been to sell German dye to the English cloth industry and his English was excellent. He had been taken off the street in Leeds and interned in 1939. MI5 was slow to be con-vinced that Dieter Maria was innocuous and he had been inter-viewed intensively. In the end, it was clear that if he was a spy, he was nothing more than a low-level intelligence gatherer, like any other businessman. He was punctilious and obliging, and an unshakeable admirer of Adolf Hitler. His faith in the inevitable triumph of the Third Reich ran to complacency. It made him laugh to reassure his jailers that he would put in a good word for them after the British surrender. It made him laugh, but he was not joking. Apart from that, he had not much to say that was amusing or interesting. The most interesting thing about Dieter Maria was that he looked exactly like Rudolf Hess.

There was no remark on the file to comment on this resemb-lance, but then it was not the sort of thing to interest an MI5 officer, whose job was to counter the enemy's efforts at spying. As long as a man was of no further use to the enemy, he was of no further interest to MI5. If he was to be of any use, he became our pigeon. In my job of trying to anticipate how a possible German resistance might operate I had set aside time for conversations – not more than that – with a cross section of internees and POWs. I thought it would be of use to gauge what you might call the spirit of the citizen in the Third Reich.

Perhaps I'm not very good at this sort of thing, but I spent a week travelling round the country not learning very much that was useful. There were some very dull conversations, one or two quite lively ones, but very few informative ones. I spent an interesting hour with a Jewish professor of philosophy whose internment on the grounds of his German citizenship was an embarrassment that

I'm glad he did not ask me to explain. The trip was keeping me away from London and away from Diana, and I almost cancelled the last day of it in favour of taking a convenient train back. I would have done, but for sharing a ministry car with a group captain who turned out to be a friend of Edward Buller's.

'Don't bother with the train, old chap. A very dodgy means of transport these days. Get yourself out to Wissington tomorrow ack emma. I'm flying back to Northolt. We'll keep you a seat.'

Getting myself out to Wissington the following morning turned out not to be easy or cheap. The group captain and several other officers had already left, having set off earlier than intended to keep ahead of weather. He had left no message concerning any late arrivals. Getting back into Leeds from Wissington meant hanging around for transport. It also meant missing the best train and eventually wasting a day and a night making a journey that the group captain had made in not much more than an hour. On the other hand, I was stuck for a while in Leeds, with time to do my duty, and so I met Dieter Maria Uhlsdorf.

There was a photograph on his file, of course, but as with all such photographs, the subject didn't look like anybody at all and certainly not himself. In the flesh the resemblance to Hess was instantly striking. After some pleasantries and enquiries as to his comfort, I commented on the resemblance.

'It has often been mentioned. We are exactly the same height also.'

'Really.'

'To the millimetre.' He said this with a grin of pride. 'Der Stellvertreter perhaps weighs a few kilos more than I. But I have been mistaken for him in Germany. It is very convenient if you want a good table.'

'You impersonated the Stellvertreter?' I laughed and widened my eyes. He laughed and shook his hands demurringly.

'Oh. Nothing of that kind. But I have found, you know, if I was going into a bar, some ordinary place, they would say to me, "You look just like Hess!" But . . . if I was going into some better kind of place, some place you would call very snob here, expensive, you understand, then the people would not be so sure that I was not really Hess. They would not dig me in the ribs, ja?' He was clearly pleased with his mastery of English idiom, because he leaned forward, patted my knee and repeated himself, laughing. 'They would not dare to dig me in the ribs. Just in case. The pity was, I could not so often afford these places.'

How often does it turn out like this? Quite by chance you come across a word, a man, an idea for the first time. The next day, in another place, going about other business, the same word or man or idea jostles you again, from another angle entirely. I got back to London and went straight to my club to bathe and eat. Diana had left a message with a telephone number. A male voice that made me think of polished amber answered my call. When its owner went to find Diana I was left listening to a distant chatter of other mellifluous voices. Music was playing.

'It's a wonderful party,' said Diana. 'Hop in a taxi.'

'It sounds like a very theatrical party. I hear evidence of tremendous elocution around you.'

'Come. You'll like them. They're great fun.'

I went of course, but I went with misgivings. I was tired and felt dull. Diana's theatrical friends were, I could hear, lively and sparkling. I should cut a rather poor figure and not be very entertaining when what I wanted to do was monopolise Diana's attention. But I was in love. I went.

The first few minutes after I arrived at the party didn't do much to put me at my ease. Diana was nowhere in sight and while there were many familiar faces, they belonged to people I didn't know. Meeting people whose appearance is famous – whose appearance may be the basis of their claim to fame – is something I still find a little embarrassing. The camera may not steal the soul, but it makes an odd bargain with believability. The first time I met Olivier, it was very much like being introduced to someone claiming to be Hector or Agamemnon. When he, in turn, introduced me to Vivien Leigh, he might as well have said, 'Do you know Helen? Helen's over here from Troy.'

I learned to enjoy the company of Diana's friends, but I wasn't enjoying it that night. I was out of it and what I overheard offered no way in. The anecdotes that made other people hoot meant nothing to me. The nicknames brought nobody to mind. I heard whole sentences – speeches – that were obviously English but might as well have been beautifully articulated Hittite for all they conveyed to me. Before long, their laughter was nothing but braying, and their obviously beautiful faces were just as obviously hideous. Somebody had been kind enough to give me a drink, a curious mixture with bourbon in it, and then had been heartless enough to find me uninteresting and move away.

A middle-aged woman in a Chanel dress passed me on her way into the room. Her face was entirely unknown to me, a circumstance that was, on this occasion, almost an invitation to converse.

'I wonder if you've seen Diana Fanshawe anywhere?'

'She's in one of the bedrooms with Dorian Lisle.'

I must have looked dismayed.

'They're getting ready.'

'Getting ready for what?'

'To perform. Go up.'

She was hailed from another quarter. Her face was transformed into a rapture of recognition in which, suddenly, there was something familiar after all, and she was gone across the room.

I went the other way, through the hall and up the stairs. On the first floor I could hear Diana's voice.

A bedroom door stood a few inches ajar and I tapped on it. I heard Diana laugh.

'Is that five minutes? We're almost there . . . '

I was reluctant to walk into a bedroom uninvited. On the other hand, I was not inclined to stand outside a bedroom door calling her name or announcing my own.

'Are you dressed?' was what I settled for and it felt foolish.

In a moment the door was opened by a stranger, but the stranger laughed, put her arms around my neck and kissed my cheek.

'You came, I was afraid you wouldn't. You sounded so tired, poor lamb.'

She was a stranger, of course, only for a moment. But it was a long moment. The woman who answered the door to me was Eva Braun. She took my hand and drew me into the room. A man was sitting before the mirrors of a dressing-table pencilling his eyebrows.

'Have you met Dorian Lisle?'

The man at the mirror turned. Everything about him was familiar. The dark hair parted on the right and falling diagonally down his brow, the absurd square of moustache. The small clenched mouth relaxed into a warm smile, however, and he stretched out his hand.

'You must be Verdon,' said Adolf Hitler. 'Diana talks of absolutely nobody else these days.'

I sat on the bed with my peculiar drink watching the actors add final touches to their own and each other's make-up.

'Now they've closed the West End theatres again, we have to keep ourselves amused, you see,' said Lisle, trimming gauze from the moustache.

Diana laughed.

'As long as we keep other people amused, darling, we shall be serving in our way!' She turned to me. 'Lisle has been told that he's a key actor and they don't want him in the forces. It's his duty to keep up morale.'

'I was deferred – we all were – until the end of the run. When the theatres went dark again, I thought I was off to the navy. Not likely! They won't have me at any price.'

'I'm sure it's a disappointment to you.'

He turned on his stool. Adolf Hitler addressed me in the voice of an English actor of the classical sort. His way of speaking was a kind of vocal topiary.

'As a matter of fact it is, old chum. Few things would please me better than the chance of being a hero. Or do you think I'm funking it?'

'I'm sorry if I've given you that impression. I didn't mean to.'

'Look, old man. Heaps of people have volunteered very cheerily, and they've never in their lives done anything or known anything that's made them sick with fear. They don't know how they're going to be when that moment comes. Well, I do know, because I've been sick with fear plenty of times. I mean sick. I mean vomiting sick. I mean standing in the wings smelling my own bile. On a first night in the West End, one does, you know. But one goes on. You don't really think there's an actor in town who couldn't manage the swagger to the recruiting office and a bit of flourish with his signature?'

'I have given you the wrong impression Mr Lisle, for which I apologise. Again.'

Dorian Lisle laughed uproariously then, and slapped my thigh. 'Oh, your face!' he said. 'Your face!'

The two of them were laughing and I began to see the joke.

'Oh Verdon,' said Diana, 'Dorian may be the most shocking coward in history, but he's not quite that pompous!'

They both roared with laughter again.

Dorian Lisle put away sticks of make-up in an Upmann's cigar box and turned to me again. 'I'm sorry, old man. I embarrassed you but one can't resist it. What do you think of Adolf?'

He struck an expression, quite suddenly, that was wholly Adolf Hitler and rose to his feet. His eyes burned, shooting their gleam towards some distant horizon. His lower lip worked with nervous energy, as if he were a man mentally rehearsing the first words of a speech to thousands. With his hands crossed flat in front of his fly buttons, he took a half-step forward and then raised his right hand, not in the full ceremonial version of the salute, but in the comfortable lower-case version that Hitler often used by way of return. The hairs stood on my neck. I wondered what the effect would have been on Dieter Maria.

The little sketch with which they entertained us was hilarious but the delight of the thing will not survive description after half a century. They entered as the newly wedded lovers from *The Merchant of Venice*, gazing into each other's eyes. 'In such a night as this . . . ' No, it is best not brought back. It was perfect at the time. Now, it could mean hardly anything. Much of it, anyway, was an extemporised dialogue with wits in the audience and impossible to recall. It was, at all events, hilarious and brought them tremendous applause. I was learning that next to being applauded the thing that actors like best is the opportunity to display how generously and beautifully they, too, can applaud. Afterwards, Diana rearranged her hair and make-up to look like Diana again, but Dorian Lisle stayed at the party as Adolf to the end. He removed the moustache finally because it interfered with the pleasure of drinking.

I walked with Diana back to her flat as there were no taxis to be had.

'Your Eva Braun is a great triumph, you know. You should tour it.'

'Oh, we are going to. Didn't you know?'

'I don't quite follow.'

'There's a rule now. For actors like Dorian. Their call-up is deferred but they are all going to do things for ENSA. It's Entertainments National Service. Going about with little fit-up companies to cheer up the troops.'

'I think I've heard of the idea.'

'Well, Dorian's worked up a little revue. Noel Coward has written something for him, too. He says he'll take it round the sort of places where you just can't, with the best will in the world, put on a serious play. Dorian would put on a play in a telephone box, so he must be thinking of some godforsaken places indeed.' She looked at me sidelong. 'Bullety sorts of places, too, you know.'

'Diana, I'm sure your thespian friends are quite as brave as anybody else. I honestly have the greatest admiration for people who'll stand up and entertain us and make us laugh when the bombs are falling. Now will you let me off?'

'You're sweet, Verdon. But then, you're an actor, too, aren't you?'

'Am I?'

'You played Colonel Ross to perfection.'

We talked of other things and arrived, too soon, at the steps to her apartment.

'Am I going to kiss you good-night?'

'I hope so,' she said, 'but not here. I don't sleep on the step.'

Waking up for the first time with someone you love is like waking up in a new life. If this observation is trite, I don't apologise. I remember looking at her hair on the pillow and watching the pulse beat in her startlingly naked neck, just beneath the translucent Meissen of her ear. I saw her shoulder turn in her drowsiness and the down on her cheek catch gold from the sunlight and gild her alabaster skin. I remember seeing all this even though I also remember that the blackout curtains were closely drawn and the room was entirely dark. Love, I suppose, is light.

The bombing raids were still frequent in London. We had not become inured to them because you never do, but we had become too accustomed to random destruction; to the arbitrary disappearance of the place we happened to be going to or past or through. The sight of people picking their way to work around and sometimes over rubble still hot from the flames was now too familiar to seem defiant and heroic, as it had at first. It was just an ordinary irritation. I remember hearing shop girls chatting, arms crossed on their breasts outside the shop they no longer worked at because it wasn't there any more. A hundred yards away, the street was blocked by the barriers that meant an unexploded bomb. They were waiting for the manager to tell them what they should do and while they waited, their heads were together as they talked in excited, hissing sentences about a girl who'd managed to get herself pregnant. The extraordinary had become ordinary; the ordinary was as interesting and exciting as ever. More so. One had to imagine that a lot of girls were getting themselves pregnant as a natural reaction to the possibility of having their young loves cut short. Ross speculated about how many babies were being conceived under mattresses rather than on top of them though I wasn't convinced that sheltering from the bombs was really quite as aphrodisiac as all that. I loathed the shelters and rarely went in them, or down into the tube stations, and couldn't under any circumstances have sheltered beneath mattresses or under the stairs. I didn't want to be caught in the street if the buildings were going to be blasted down about me but, for some reason, I felt safest up on a roof and so did Diana. We had sat out several raids behind the parapets of her apartment block in Kensington, arms about each other, with an eiderdown around us and a bottle of something cheerful to hand.

We went down to Hannington for the first weekend in April to stay with Maria and Sonny Trellick. Looking out of the window of the train going down to Hampshire at fields suddenly new and perfectly green, at hedges misty with the beginning of blossom, seeing horses running for no reason but the surge of spring, was to be ambushed by normality and caught entirely by surprise. I held Diana's hand like a boy as the train rattled along and we drank it in.

The Trellicks' house is a little landscape within a landscape, it has so many roofs and ridges of mossy tiles above its warm brick walls. Ivy grows around the mullions and as we arrived on that April afternoon, house martins were swooping up under the eaves, building their nests. It was so English that I laughed to see it.

In Ross's office the following Monday afternoon I tried to put together the bits and pieces and make an idea out of them.

'Up in Yorkshire I talked to an internee. He makes no bones about his sympathy with the Nazis, thinks they'll beat us in short order. Seems to think the only reason we haven't shot him in the neck and tossed him in a pit is because we know that, if we do, we'll be for the high jump when the swastika goes up the flagpole. The really interesting thing about him is he looks exactly like Rudolf Hess. By a sort of coincidence I went to a party with Diana Fanshawe the same night . . . '

'You went to a party with Diana Fanshawe, did you?'

'As it happens – don't look like that, Ross . . . '

'Have you been abusing your position, James?'

'I took her address and telephone number from government records, yes.'

'Well done. Carry on . . . '

'Diana and a friend, an actor fellow called Dorian Lisle, of whom you probably know, performed a satirical entertainment in which he played Hitler and she played Eva Braun. They really were very funny. More to the point, they were absolutely convincing. They were playing for laughs, of course, but some of the best laughs came when this chap Lisle played Adolf dead straight. The laughter was of a different kind, if you know what I mean. The way you'd laugh if someone were decapitated in front of you and you were hoping it was a trick and not the real thing. Quite eerie.'

'It sounds wonderful. I'm glad you get to such frightfully good parties. Quite envy you, but why do I need to know this?'

'Well, in between meeting the Hess fellow and being entertained by Adolf and Eva I was stuck in Leeds with time to kill waiting for a train. So I went to one of those little cinemas where they show nothing but newsreels and cartoons. Sat through Movietone a couple of times. I started thinking. The Germans are really much better at propaganda than we are. They've devoted themselves to the subject. We censor the press and the newsreels, we spoon feed them stuff, yes, but we don't fashion them into instruments of policy with the same ruthless science that Goebbels brings to bear.'

'Ruthless science isn't our long suit, laddie, no.'

'Goebbels has been using the newsreels for years. He controls them absolutely and the evidence is that he's done it with great success. The Germans love them, because the newsreels, probably more than anything else, told them that Germany was great again. The newsreels brought them the Führer's message and the Führer's soul. Certainly the Führer's image and the Führer's triumphs.'

'Don't waste any more time telling me how important the Hun thinks newsreels are. Get on.'

'After this I'm more or less busking, so bear with me. As I see it, the ordinary German citizen has been taught to place great faith in the newsreels. If the instrument is so powerful in Goebbels' hands it follows that the same instrument, in the hands of Goebbels' enemy, could be equally powerful.'

'I'm starting to get interested.'

'It would be a once and once only deception, probably, but if you could adulterate or corrupt the medium in some way, you might have a profound effect on public morale. Choosing your moment carefully, it could be a great advantage.'

'Adulterate or corrupt. Tell me how . . . '

'I imagine the distribution of films around the cinemas is

managed in much the same way in Germany as it is here. In each city or region there's a place where the reels are exchanged for passing round the circuit each week. Goebbels' central unit, or somebody, sends out so many copies, on such and such a day, to each of these exchanges. Imagine that a certain shipment is substituted, at the exchange or some other place down the line, for alternative newsreels . . . '

' . . . Adulterated or corrupted newsreels. Yes. But you haven't quite told me what that might mean.'

'I'm not entirely sure. There are a number of possibilities. These alternative newsreels must seem to be genuine, but imagine – just say what if – in the middle of one of Herr Hitler's tremendous harangues things went delirious agley.'

'Agley?'

'Like the best laid plans of mice and men . . . '

'In English we say awry.'

'What if the headline story were, I don't know . . . Hitler makes momentous speech to the Deutsche Volk. Martial musik. On comes Hitler, Eva Braun by his side, holding his hand perhaps. Hess is there, just a little behind him, looking glum. Imagine Hitler making the same sort of speech that our own dear once-and-former King Edward made on the radio not so long ago. "The game's up. I'm chucking it. Make your own arrangements. Thank you for your support. I'm going off now with the woman I love." Something like that.'

Ross looked at me. His expression was impossible to read. He toyed with his cigarette case, tossing it and catching it.

'Look, Ross, I'm not a scriptwriter but there must be plenty on the strength. They could come up with dozens of possibilities. It would depend on the effect you wanted to produce. If Hess suddenly started to talk like Donald Duck, it would go down well in the middle of one of Goebbels' Glory-of-the-Reich specials, don't you think? On the other hand, I'm sure we could be more subtle than that.'

'I get the drift. Doctored newsreels. Effect on civilian morale.'

'They could be used to stimulate an uprising. If it were to be done in Holland or France, timed right, it might be the starting pistol for civilian uprising and sabotage in the prelude to invasion. In the case of the Germans it might be just a matter of lowering morale. Then, it might just help to shake some of them out of their infatuation with the snake charmer. Call it the Fat Dutchman effect.'

'Enlighten me.'

'Goering once said, "If a single English bomber ever gets through to Berlin, you can call me a Fat Dutchman." I gather that our little air raid on Berlin didn't add up to much in terms of damage done, but there are Germans who now call Goering the Fat Dutchman. I think that means it was worth the effort.'

Ross went through the ritual of lighting a cigarette that always accompanied his process of reflection. When he was suitably obscured in smoke and had shaken his match vigorously and ground it into the ashtray, he looked at me again.

'You think it would be possible to substitute – what – hundreds of cans of film?'

'There is already a mechanism for shifting thousands of cans of film around. I should think it's a job done by fairly low-grade labour without any very elaborate security.'

'I dare say you're right.'

'It's exactly the sort of operation that resistance units are capable of tackling. Much easier than sabotaging trains, or blowing up bridges. It's the sort of thing that could be done by what you might call the man-in-the-street resistance worker. At the crudest, it's going to mean waylaying the deliveries, but it would surely be better if our friends were to get jobs in the business. Ideally we need some sympathetic entrepreneurs to go into the film-distribution business. I'm sure it can be done.'

'I'm going to put this up, old lad. I think it's barmy but that may be a recommendation. Give me a memo. Try to get some idea what it'll cost. Try to make it sound unbarmy and cheap. You never know.'

I was in films. Operation Dutchman was warmly approved in the highest circles and given the highest stamp of secrecy. My first act as producer was to have Dieter Maria moved from Yorkshire to a different place of internment. Wormwood Scrubs was more convenient for the studios at Ealing. I still wasn't sure whether Dieter Maria was to be a star or just a very convincing extra, but a man who looked just like Hess and spoke in the Munich dialect hardly needed to audition. My second act as producer was to bring both Diana and Dorian Lisle into my office and bind them formally with an oath under the Official Secrets Act. Diana swore the oath as if checking off a laundry list. Lisle, who was delighted by the ceremony, conferred upon it an unearthly solemnity. The thing was done in my linoleum-floored office, but Lisle achieved a sonority that made it seem as if he were swearing vows in a cathedral. My third act, under the powers granted to me, was to forbid Dorian to perform his Hitler impersonation at any time or place other than those authorised by me. This caused him a momentary dismay that was dispelled by Diana.

'You realise, Dorian, darling, that you've just become a secret weapon.'

The idea appealed to him very much.

I wanted Anthony Asquith to direct the filming, but Anthony was already working at full stretch on other kinds of filming for the war effort. Over a drink at Edward Buller's he recommended Percival Atwater and nobody could have been better for the job. Percival, it seemed, had studied every frame of Leni Riefenstahl's Nazi propaganda films. If anything, I thought him a little too much of an admirer.

'Remember, Atwater old chum, we want to make a newsreel, not *Triumph of the Will.*'

'Don't worry about that. All the German newsreel men are trying to remake *Triumph of the Will,* anyway.'

Atwater was a practical man and didn't confine himself to what you might call the dramatic and aesthetic problems. He had entered into the whole spirit of deception.

'When these things arrive in the projectionist's hands, they've got to be in the usual kind of film can.'

I must have looked dim.

'Film comes in light metal cans. They are reinforced by having a pattern stamped into the metal. A projectionist would immediately recognise an unusual kind of can. And the leader would have to be exactly the same kind that he's used to. That's the section of film spliced on to the head of the print for lacing up through the machine, with marks for focusing and synchronising sound and so on. No importance in itself, but a different kind of leader would just make him start noticing things. Really, you want the projectionist to grab the can, lace up the film, hit the button and go back to feeling up his girl or whatever the bastards normally do. Because mostly, I swear to you, they hardly notice what they're screening. You don't want them to notice, of course, so all those little details must be as normal as possible.'

'Then we need to get hold of some German film cans and so on.'

'And the labels and the paperwork and everything. All of that's important. You do all that sort of stuff and leave the film to me.'

It was not difficult to get hold of a current German newsreel in a standard-issue can. They were screened as a matter of course in neutral Switzerland and Spain. We made British Movietone News available, too, but we didn't get as many takers in those particular countries. The can the film goes out in is a detail that the film producer normally doesn't have to worry about. I was discovering that he already has enough to occupy him. Film-making involves many forms of activity and each of them, however trivial, has a name and is the unencroachable province of a specialist. However simple the duties of the specialist he must have at least one assistant whose function is not always apparent to the outsider. If the film industry set out to play a mouth organ, there would be somebody different to blow down each hole and they'd all have assistants. It would take a week to get through 'Three Blind Mice', and you wouldn't recognise the tune until a month later when their efforts had been edited together. After a while you begin, dimly, to see why some of this is necessary. At one frustrating moment I exclaimed about it all to Atwater.

'Oh, filming the evacuation of Dunkirk would be easy,' he said. 'You just have to be there with a camera. Faking the evacuation of

Dunkirk so as to film it would be vastly more complicated than the real thing. And then the light wouldn't be right. And when it was, half the boats would turn up and go away again before the soldiery arrived and you'd have to do the whole thing again ten times. But just think how many people it took to arrange the original cock-up. The film industry, cock up for cock up, is really much more efficient. You just deliver my Hess for the first day of shooting.'

We'd decided our first essay would be to prove the concept. Dieter Maria could hardly be asked to learn lines and act for the camera. He might not be willing and, anyway, he was a dye salesman, not an actor.

'Don't give him any idea what we want him to do. Just send him along, but dress him in a Party uniform like Hess's. That's all.'

A dressing-room was made secure with bars on the windows. A spy-hole was provided in the panel of the door. I thought all this was going a bit far but the Home Office, in the person of a pertinacious little whey-faced Scottish person, insisted on the precautions. Dieter Maria was brought to Ealing Studios in the company of two prison officers. As they had no idea why he was being taken from his cell, they were not communicative and Dieter Maria interpreted their silence in the most ominous way. When he was told to strip, and his clothes were taken away, he became nervous and agitated. I had wanted to explain at least something of our intentions to Dieter Maria, though it would have been difficult to judge quite what and how much to tell him. Atwater, though, was quite sure of what he wanted.

'Don't tell him a thing. If that makes him sweaty and anxious – and I'm sure it will – then that's all to the good. I want him keyed up.'

We left Dieter Maria in a state of doubt for an hour or so. This was not an intentional cruelty. It's just the way things happen when you're trying to make even the simplest piece of film. Other problems press themselves on your attention; nothing is ready when you need it to be ready; nothing works the first time you try it, not even an electric light. When they brought him the uniform that Berman's Theatrical Outfitters had supplied, Dieter Maria began to sweat even though he was wearing only his drawers, vest and socks. He refused to put it on and demanded to see the Red Cross. He got me.

The room stank. The vest clung to his belly, damp with fear.

'What's the trouble, old chap?'

'They are wanting me to wear this uniform. Why?'

'Do you not wish to wear it? It's a National Socialist Party uniform. Rather a good one.'

'I want my own clothes.'

'Your clothes have been taken away, I'm afraid.'

'Why?'

'They are very fine clothes made in Germany. We need them to give to our spies.'

'You will have a spy in Germany walking in my clothes?'

'I suppose that's the idea. Not my department.'

'Give me ordinary prison clothes, then.'

'I thought you were an admirer of the Party?'

'I know why you want to put me in these clothes. You will throw me to a mob.'

'That is not the sort of thing we do.'

'You are going to shoot me.'

'Only in a manner of speaking.'

His eyes widened and his lips went visibly dry.

'What are you going to do?'

'We are going to take some pictures of you. That is all. Please put on the clothes.'

He wrapped his arms around his ribs and rocked slowly back and forth against the wall with his head dipped to his chest. There was no looking into his eyes. They were pools of shadow under the bony ridge of his forehead and the thick brows.

He made no response at all when I leaned to touch his arm. When I spoke to him in German, he looked up so sharply that his head struck the wall behind him, though he seemed not to notice it. It was the first time I had used German to him.

'Please believe me, Dieter Maria, we do not intend you any harm. You are an internee. You are protected by international law. I am asking you to cooperate. Unfortunately, the Military Intelligence people are not entirely happy about you. They are inclined to believe that you were spying for the Reich. They do not believe that you should be treated as an internee, but as a suspected spy. Do you understand?'

His eyes glowed very white at the bottom of their dark pits. He understood.

'If you will cooperate with me, you remain the responsibility of my department, which is propaganda. Which would you rather be? An actor, or a spy?' I had used a word I had not meant to. Actor. Still, it was the other word that absorbed his attention. Spy.

'It is up to you. I will leave you for a few minutes to decide.'

When I came back to the dressing-room and looked through the judas hole, Dieter Maria was adjusting his tie. I watched for a little while as he stood taking in his own reflection. The sight absorbed him. An actor would have turned his head this way and that, catching his profile, working an expression. Dieter Maria stared dead straight at himself. His only movement was to stand suddenly taller to meet his own still gaze. I was looking at Hitler's deputy. So was Dieter Maria. Atwater wanted him to be on edge, so I omitted the courteous tap on the door and walked in impatiently, as if things were going wrong in some way. I gave him hardly a glance before holding the door wide.

'Good,' I said. 'Follow me.'

The moment of grand confidence he'd enjoyed looking in the mirror was gone. I hurried him down the corridors faster than there was any need for and took a roundabout route to the studio. When we finally passed through the double doors of the sound-proof entrance, Dieter Maria was sweating again.

In the middle of the sound stage was a rostrum, perhaps thirty feet long, swagged with German flags on either side of an enormous central swastika. Above the rostrum was a long speaker's dais, covered in scarlet cloth and bearing the outspread wings of the Nazi eagle in black and gold. Behind it and on either side, everything else was black. Tall flats that might have been scenery were covered with a dull black cloth. The scene was lit only by a bald working light, as comfortless as the light of a prison cell or, perhaps, some even more unpleasant corner of a prison. From somewhere distant in the gloom came Atwater's voice.

'Can you ask your chappie to sit at the dais, please? There's a chair for him.'

Leading Dieter Maria on to the sound stage and up behind the dais was like leading a baffled child. I almost took him by the hand. There was one chair behind the dais, not in the centre but a little way to the right. I tried to draw it back to usher Dieter Maria into it, but found that it was fixed rigidly to the floor.

'Just sit him down would you and tell him to wait. Oh, and tell him not to get up and walk around. Just wait there till we're ready.'

'He understands English, Atwater. I don't need to tell him.'

I smiled at Dieter Maria. He tried to smile back. It was just a little clench of his jaw that pressed his prominent top teeth into his bottom lip. He wiped his dense eyebrows with a thumb and then jerked upright as a powerful light came on, dazzling both of us. I patted him on the shoulder with a smile and left him.

I joined Atwater in the preview theatre to watch our first rushes. I was beginning to pick up this sort of jargon. It meant we were going to watch the first prints of unedited film straight from the camera in a room like a very select cinema.

'This may not be riveting stuff, but I'm rather pleased with it. I've just chopped some promising bits together that I wanted Tim to see. Sorry. Captain James, Tim Standish. Vice versa.'

Tim leaned across from a seat in the row in front of me and shook my hand. He had thick glasses and smelled of whisky and cigarettes. Dandruff crowded the slope of his shoulders.

'Tim's the writer.'

'Excellent,' I said, but perhaps I betrayed something that suggested I didn't immediately have faith.

'Tim has written some wonderfully funny stuff.'

'Has he? I haven't seen it yet.'

'For the cinema. Films. He hasn't written anything for us yet. What he's going to write depends on what we're about to see.'

He pushed a switch on the desk in front of him and murmured an instruction. The lights dimmed in our little cinema and images began to dance on the screen.

In a few moments, the image was of a long dais, swathed in Nazi flags. Seated behind it in what seemed a vast black space was Rudolf Hess. He looked sweaty and nervous. From time to time he looked up against the light with his eyes screwed up until they were just slits in the deep sockets. Sometimes he thought he heard noises and peered out into the gloom at the side of the dais. Once or twice he looked behind him. Gradually, it was clear, he got used to the idea that nothing much was about to happen and that he had been forgotten for a while. He yawned twice and managed to suppress another. Atwater tapped Standish on the shoulder and they nodded at each other, without taking their eyes from the screen. Dieter Maria's hands began to drum a little tattoo. Briefly he began to pick at something caught in his molars. Then he recollected that he was sitting under a bright light and was probably observed. There was an abrupt slash in the film where Atwater had cut out a lot of time, and then Hess began to pick at his teeth again. Boredom had clearly made him indifferent to observation. He looked about, glowering, and sat sharply back in his chair, folding his arms abruptly across his chest. In the gloom of the preview theatre, Atwater leaned forward to Standish, who cranked his head back and they muttered to each other, pointing at the screen from time to time. Standish scribbled notes continually.

On the screen, Dieter Maria – whom I now could only think of as Deputy Führer Hess – leaned abruptly forward over the dais and shouted. 'What is going on here? What is going on? I wish to cooperate. I will cooperate! But you should tell me what is going on.'

'Wonderful, wish he'd said it in German, mind,' said Standish.

'He does in a minute,' said Atwater. 'It gets better.'

More time had been slashed out of the film. Now the Deputy Führer hunched forward over the dais, clubbing the flat surface softly with his fists. Then in German he pleaded out into the world he could not see beyond the bright light.

'Please. I just wish to be told what is going on. Why am I here?'

He waited for an answer but no answer came. He called out again, louder and with hysteria beginning to show. 'Why am I here? Tell me what is going on!'

Standish clapped his hands in pleasure and turned quickly to Atwater, who sat back, nodding and smiling.

'Here it comes.'

Dieter Maria stood up suddenly, shouting in German. 'This is intolerable! I will not sit here! This light is killing me!'

Atwater's voice amplified very loud was heard on the film.

'Sit down or you will be shot immediately!'

You could see exactly where the voice had come from by the way Dieter Maria's head shot round, his eyes wide and white. He shrivelled back into his chair and stayed still and silent.

'He sits like that for twenty minutes. Doesn't move a muscle. A wonderful piece of film in its way but I can't think who'd want to watch it.' Atwater leaned forward to the button on his desk again. The lights came up and the screen was blank again.

'It's terrific,' said Standish. 'And the turn, when you tell him he'll be shot, that's spot on. They'll be eyeball to eyeball.'

'I had the speaker absolutely on the line, but just to make sure we put a little light on it that we could flash up. Bang. Looked straight at it.'

'Well, it's a piece of cake, old chum. Your Hess fellow is terrific though, isn't he? Absolutely, Hess to the life. Let's go and do some creative drinking.' Standish was already grabbing his coat and heading for the door. Atwater was getting ready to follow him.

'A moment if you will, gentlemen.'

Standish paused with the door held half open. He continued to stand with it held open, like a man in a hurry who might just give me half a moment of his time.

I waited until he reluctantly gave up his grip on the door and allowed it to close. The door made a little automatic sigh. Standish may have done the same.

'Gentlemen. Explain to me.'

'Oh right. I can shoot another film with the actors but without your Hess. Except that the actors will be working as if he's there and doing some of the thing we've just watched. Because the camera's fixed rigidly in the same position, I can combine the two into a little drama.' Standish pushed open the door again. 'Tell you in the pub.'

'Mr Standish, will you come here a moment.'

With a great display of weariness, Standish left the door and came a few paces back into the theatre.

'This is not something we will discuss in a pub . . . '

'Oh, for God's sake, don't take me so bloody literally, all I meant . . . '

'It's not important what you meant, Mr Standish. Just understand what I mean. I mean that if you talk, you will be dealt with. You will not be at liberty to talk thereafter.'

Standish got the idea and showed it by a shrug and a nod of his head. I began to realise why people in the sort of job I was doing tend to become megalomaniacs or thugs. It creeps up on you.

We had a final cut of our motion picture in less than a month and screened it for the W. Board. The critical reception was unanimously favourable. As to whether the thing might be in any way useful, opinion was divided. The print was sent down to Dytchley Park, one of the Prime Minister's safe rural retreats, for a private viewing. I was flattered by his request. Then, of course, Rudolf Hess knocked the bottom out of the whole idea by misappropriating a Messerschmitt, flying to Scotland and attempting to call on the Duke of Hamilton by parachute. Hess's behaviour was a surprise to everyone and to me a peculiarly irritating surprise. It led to an even greater surprise. I was called to Dytchley Park.

'Captain James. Sit down. If you care to help yourself to brandy, please do. I can't be quite so liberal with the cigars, I'm afraid. They are hard to get and they are something of an essential prop. National morale will sink if I am seen to go without one for too long.' I helped myself to brandy, though I knew it was stretching Winston's politeness, but the old man seemed to be in an hospitable and relaxed mood.

'I say that to you, James, because you obviously understand the significance of props and greasepaint. I have been impressed by your essay in motion pictures.'

'I think I'll count that as a good review, sir. Thank you. Even if it's so much wasted effort by now.'

'Deception, deception, deception, James.' He communed with his cigar for a while and during his silence I couldn't think of anything to say.

'Deception,' he said again, rising from his desk and then crossing the room to gaze out of the window. 'The worst of war isn't that good men have to kill. It is that they have to lie and deceive, and these are much harder habits to break. All the same, we must be the better killers and the better liars. Everything I hear about you tells me that you are one of the best and most accomplished liars we've got.'

'That is a rare compliment, sir.'

'It is, James, because there's a lot of runners in the stakes. And, frankly, I'm at the head of the them. You remember my saying, once upon a time, that we would fight them on the beaches and the landing grounds, in the hills and so on . . . That was a lie. We should hardly have been able to fight them at all. Once the Panzers were ashore, we simply had no weapons that would have stopped them.'

'But we would have fought them, all the same, sir. No lie there.'

He turned towards me and smiled. It was a short-lived rueful sort of smile that ended in a shrug. 'We didn't have the weapons to stop them. Not on the ground. But we had some rather good lies. And, if I may say so, some rather good liars. There's a kind of liar better even than you or me, James. Put your lie in the mouth of a fool who believes it, and you've got the best liar of all.'

When Winston summoned me to Dytchley Park I don't think it was especially in his mind to treat me to the discourse that followed. He was faced with a question I knew nothing of, and with making a decision whose consequences affected me only slightly, so why did he tell me so much? I can't say. Perhaps it was a necessary part of thinking out the problem.

'Hitler has a fool in the person of Rudolf Hess. He has flown here with a lie in which he believes: peace between Britain and Germany. We need not be detained by close scrutiny of the seven points of his proposal. They amount to a lunacy. It comes to this: we shall surrender, not shamefully, but with the honours of war; our people shall be spared further horrors; we shall then live in peace and contentment as allies of the Reich. Where the French have Pétain, a former field marshal and national hero, at their head, we shall have the Duke of Windsor, a leader of fashion and our former – now to be future – king. The warmonger Churchill will be sent packing.'

I laughed.

'Is the Duke of Windsor aware of the part he is to play?'

Winston did not laugh at all.

'Yes. Very well aware. He has been our fool. The fool through whose mouth this powerful lie has been . . . noised abroad.'

He looked at me with the gaze that everybody close to Winston knew and nobody who was not close ever saw. It was not the gaze of the favourite uncle or the teddy bear or the bulldog. In 1688, an earlier Churchill led the coup that threw a King of England off his throne. The fact came to mind as he gazed at me.

'The Duke of Windsor has engaged in conversations culminating in this proposal.'

'Discussions with the Germans? Direct discussions?'

He nodded. It was not easy to take in, but not impossible to believe. After his abdication, the Duke had visited Germany. He had met Hitler and Goebbels and been made welcome. He had enjoyed his welcome and paid compliments to his hosts. All that, though, was before the outbreak of war and, until very late in the day, Hitler had not been short of admirers in England. One might mention that the Bank of England had arranged loans for Germany after Hitler had come to power. Naturally, one does not mention it often. I mentioned it then, together with similar circumstances concerning other people in England who then – as now – drew a veil over company they had enjoyed or opinions they had held before the war. I thought the same veil might be large enough to screen the Duke.

'And, of course, he has a quite natural sympathy for things German, in normal times. His mother is German, after all. He has grown up speaking German as easily as English – '

Winston cut me off. 'That will certainly have been a help to him in these conversations.' The rebuke was in the tone. He gestured towards me with the cigar. 'Which took place after the fall of France.'

'Which would make it look at least a little like fraternising with the enemy.'

Winston made a sweep with his hand that may have been intended to dismiss my remark or disperse a cloud of smoke. The one mattered as much as the other.

'The Duke made his way, at that time, into Spain and then to Portugal. Countries where these contacts are by no means impossible to arrange.'

I began to understand.

'With perhaps one exception, sir, the Duke is the most conspicuously recognisable Englishman alive and not without some importance. It would be fair to assume constant vigilance on the part of our security services.'

Winston nodded, but it was as if his mind were really on something else. I believe he was making up his mind how much of the story it was useful to tell me. I carried on with my own thought.

'I assume, then, that he was – how can I put it? – allowed the freedom to embark on these negotiations.'

'We made use of his inclinations. We fostered his illusions. We sponsored his – I'll use your word – negotiations. We judged that it was in our interests for Hitler to believe that the English had no appetite for continuing a war against Germany and to let him conclude that an advantageous peace with England was in prospect. Windsor, it seems, really does believe these things, so we allowed the idea to ferment in his mind and in German minds together. We may have added more than a little yeast.' He laid down his cigar. 'We gave large scope to this delusive nonsense before we appointed him to his present duties in the – er – ' he groped in the air with his cigar, in an expressive pretence of forgetfulness, 'Bahamas. He sits impatiently, awaiting his country's call. You will understand why this deception was in our interests, hmm? Hitler's great aim is the destruction of Russia. He may call it a war against Bolshevism, but it wouldn't matter who or what ruled in Russia, this would be his purpose as it was the Kaiser's: a matter of necessity and, as Hitler sees it, destiny. But he knows that fighting on two fronts is folly.'

'He's seen at first hand what that did for the Kaiser, of course. Or, put another way, for the Duke of Windsor's Great-Uncle Willi.'

He nodded at me.

'But Hitler has done better than Great-Uncle Willi. He has taken the Kaiser's plan – the Schlieffen Plan – to second base: France is out of the game. If we would just lie down, he could start to travel east.'

'And the Duke has played his part in letting him believe that we would do just that.'

'Exactly. Herr Hitler has been making his preparations to travel east for three years. He has a timetable. He must commit his troops very soon. If he delays so much as a month after the snows melt, he runs the risk that his campaign will run into the Russian winter – a subject on which, you will remember, Napoleon has marked all our cards. If he delays another year, the Russians will have increased formidably in strength. The longer he goes on believing in this chimaera of peace with England, the closer he is pushed to the irrevocable first step of his war with Russia.'

'So you encouraged him with the most plausible voice that could possibly convey the lie. The voice of a man who happened to believe it – and happened to be born to the throne of England.'

He came back to the corner of his desk and looked down at me over his half-glasses, tapping the mahogany of the desk with his fingertips.

'Two fronts. Get him on two fronts. And then, young man, then . . . You understand?'

He clenched his square fist around the cigar and made quick short jabs with it.

'You have answered a question for me, sir. I am aware of the instruction that we are to make no propaganda use of Hess. It's an instruction people don't understand.'

'No. We have neither exulted over his defection nor put him

on display to the public gaze through newsreels and so on. A fine spectacle: Hitler's deputy, abject, mad and captive. It is what people expect. Should I do as people expect?'

'Clearly not, sir. Hitler must ask himself why we are making no public statements; why we are not using Hess for cheap propaganda. A perfectly good answer is that we are still listening to what Hess has to say. Perhaps we are arguing behind the scenes about our response. He knows that you, as the Arch Warmonger Churchill, would want to put Hess's head on a pole. As it isn't on a pole, he may well deduce that there are powerful voices arguing against you. He may deduce that the matter is not yet resolved but that you are not in the ascendant.'

It was very much the favourite uncle who smiled at me.

'That is an admirably lucid summary. It is my own thinking entirely. It leaves out only one other, and conclusive, reason for not putting Hess on display for the maximum possible propaganda advantage.'

He stayed silent for some moments.

'And that, sir, is . . . '

'The bugger's dead.'

There was a long silence. It was not my place to ask how he came to be dead. The cigar had finally lost its sweetness and Winston crushed it in a crystal ashtray. Outside in the park the shadows of the trees were growing long and the mist of new green among the branches glowed in the light of the low sun. Winston stood at the window.

'In public, Hitler says his deputy has had a brainstorm. But you have noticed that since Herr Hess's arrival the bombing offensive has ended? He has by no means abandoned the idea that Hess's embassy might bear fruit and he is ready either to play from the hand close to his chest or from the dummy. This makes it inconvenient to be without a Hess. We must be seen to have Hess among us. Can we, do you think, make use of your man? Can we pass him off as Hess for practical purposes? He seems to carry off his part very well in your amusing production.'

'He seems to, sir. He was filmed entirely alone. The rest of the action was fashioned to suit his behaviour and filmed later. The film you see is a clever blending of the two.'

'Extraordinary. You understand what I want? We must keep alive the idea that Hess is alive in England and in our hands. It has many advantages. Can your man be induced or trained or deceived into serving our turn?'

I thought about it over the glass of brandy. What came back to me was the picture of Uhlsdorf that I'd seen through the judas hole in the dressing-room door: Uhlsdorf, a few minutes away from being the nobody in the fear-damp vest and drawers, with his arms wrapped about himself and his cheeks white; Uhlsdorf in the uniform of high official in the Nazi Party and standing straight to meet his own reflection and, for the first time, recognising a man of some importance in it.

'I think he might.'

'Then, go away. Bring your ideas to me the day after tomorrow. Do not present them to, or discuss them with, anybody else. I need a Hess.'

As I was leaving he coughed to detain me a moment at the door.

'I didn't order his head for a pole. He died of a heart attack. Should there be any breach of security in this matter, however, I will most certainly have your head on a pole.'

I did not disbelieve my prime minister but, after all, in the course of our conversation Winston had told me that he was sometimes a liar. It didn't make much difference to my job, but I took some trouble to learn the truth. A medical memorandum found its way into my hands, as art dealers say, privately. It was a heart attack. Other things that I learned filled out the picture. Hess had been wounded twice in the Kaiser's War, once very gravely by a bullet passing right through his body, piercing a lung. For the rest of his life, continuous exertion left him breathless. He worried about his health. When he parachuted into Scotland, he carried patent medicines in his pockets. He had made a flight of nine hours into enemy territory, ending in a parachute drop, a broken ankle and interrogation. There followed a good deal of being bustled about the country and the shock and humiliation of receiving the treatment due to a criminal rather than the deputy head of state of the most powerful nation in Europe.

The interrogation was not severe, merely persistent. But as somebody who'd been there said to me, 'I think they may have kept him awake rather too long.'

We woke him in his cell at about one in the morning and sick dread scraped his face white. I looked down at him and his skin was screaming. He could find no other voice.

'Get your shoes on.'

The sergeant with me picked up his shoes from the floor and handed them to him. They were prison-issue shoes with soft felt soles, made to fall apart if they got wet. He took them as if they were objects of no meaning, put them on the bed beside him and reached for his clothes.

'You won't be needing them,' said the sergeant, 'just get your shoes on.'

He sat on the edge of the cot and looked up at me. He had found a voice but it was ragged and choked.

'Warum?'

'Ours not to reason. You must come with us.'

We took him from the cell along the silent landing and out of the prison block in his felt shoes and prison pyjamas and wrapped in a blanket.

The squaddie climbed behind the wheel, the sergeant beside him. I sat with Dieter Maria in the back of the Humber and as the prison gates opened to let us pass out I pulled the blanket up from around his shoulders and threw it over his head. Nobody in the car spoke until we had gone through Chobham. Then I told the driver to turn up a lane that took us through a wood. He turned off the lane on to a track and finally off the track and on to the leaves under the broad limbs of a stand of beech trees. I removed the blanket from Dieter Maria so that he caught sight of his surroundings in the second before the lights were doused.

We waited in silence. After a while I took out my cigarette case.

'Permission to smoke if you wish to, chaps.'

I offered my case to Dieter Maria. He stared at it as a man might stare at a noose.

'Why? I am nobody. I am nobody.' He spoke in German. Then he shook his hand impatiently at the cigarette case to wave it away. Like Hess, like me, he didn't smoke. I put the case away.

The sergeant lit a cigarette himself and in the flare of his match I saw Dieter Maria's face. There are men, plenty of them, who are better at doing the sort of thing that I was doing to Dieter Maria. They get better at it because they do it much more often and they enjoy the work. I feel sorry for them.

It was Dieter Maria who first heard the other car arriving. The rest of us paid no attention to it, even when it slid up alongside our own and came to a standstill. The man who got out of the second car was visible only as a slit of dimmed light from his hand torch. We heard the crunching of dry leaves as he crossed to the Humber. The sergeant wound down his window and the dimmed torch found it. The man behind the torch was still entirely invisible as he spoke.

'I hope you have a puncture outfit.'

'Only one for a bicycle I'm afraid,' said the sergeant. And they both laughed briefly.

The voice behind the light had no laughter in it a moment later, 'We've got him.'

The lamp went out and the sergeant turned to the back of the Humber and said, 'Well, Dieter Maria. It's time for you to make a decision.'

The fact that he said it in perfect Munich dialect was visibly what had the greatest effect on Dieter Maria.

'Dieter Maria,' I said, 'you know that the Stellvertreter made an heroic flight to England with the Führer's secret proposals for peace. The English refuse peace. They have treated the Führer's deputy like a criminal instead of a high representative of the greatest power in Europe. They have chosen war. This is regrettable and it is not what the Führer wanted or expected. He was, however, prepared for it. We cannot allow the British to hold the Deputy

Führer and it is our job to get him out of Britain. You do not need to know more about that. Do you find it easy to understand what I am saying to you?'

Dieter Maria nodded.

'We will take the Stellvertreter to safety. Your job is to take his place. If the British have their Hess in prison – actually, a very nice house – our task is easy. If the British are hunting for their Hess, not so. Do you understand?'

Dieter Maria nodded. I saw him look from me to the sergeant. We can have been no more than dense shadows to him.

'You are KommandoAbteilung?'

'That would be the simplest way of saying it. We carry out the Führer's work.'

'But there is now a problem, Dieter Maria,' said the sergeant. 'Now that you know the truth about Captain James, Captain James is at risk and so are we all.'

'No, no. No.'

'I'm afraid so. This means that you have a choice. You take the place of the Stellvertreter as we have said or you don't. We have no choice. If you choose not to take on this difficult and important task, then you already know too much. We would have to shoot you.'

The Sergeant drew on his cigarette. The glow reflected on the barrel of his revolver.'

'But do realise, Dieter Maria,' I said, 'that should you choose the option of being shot, you would still be helping to carry out the Führer's work and rescue the Stellvertreter. Your remains would be found by the British and it would be apparent to them that a KommandoAbteilung had, regrettably, penetrated British security and assassinated the Stellvertreter. It is obviously not good that the British should hold one who is so close to the mind of the Führer, to be interrogated at will. So you can choose how you wish to serve the Reich: as Rudolf Hess or as some . . . identifiable remains.'

The sergeant opened his door and slid out into the darkness. We listened to his footfall on the leafy floor and to the noise, like a distant waterfall, of wind in the leafy roof above us. The sergeant opened the boot and soon closed it again with a slam. Then the door beside Dieter Maria opened to admit, if not light, a less opaque darkness. The sergeant placed a parcel wrapped in brown paper on Dieter Maria's knees. It was just the sort of parcel in which your clothes might come back from a laundry. With quick movements he tore the paper and pulled away the string. These were not the clothes from Berman's Theatrical Costumiers that he had worn before. These were the original articles.

'Either way, you put these on.'

A few minutes later we led him, in his Luftwaffe uniform and high fur-lined flying boots, to the other car. I opened the back door for him and clicked my heels.

'Herr Hess.'

He climbed in and sat next to the other back-seat passenger, bulky in the shadow beside him. The sergeant opened the far door and switched on the internal light of the car.

Dieter Maria turned to see his companion and found that he was looking at himself in death. Rudolf Hess, in a Luftwaffe officer's uniform from Berman's, was slumped beside him, his head rolled back on the seat, his mouth open and the eyes under the dense brows so black and cavernous they might have been feasted on by crows.

Dieter Maria looked as if he was screaming but only slight gurgling noises came out of him.

'He is drugged,' said the sergeant. With the squaddie's help he folded Hess quickly out of the door and the two of them carried him to the Humber. The noise of his feet dragging through the dry leaves was what stuck in my mind. I've heard it in dreams many times. It had been my idea to show him Hess. It seemed to me that this glimpse of his *alter ego* made all the rest plausible. I had not quite imagined the moment of standing in the blackness listening to Dieter Maria, sitting in the little pool of pallid light that only made the darkness around him deeper and darker, breathing in the short jerks that come with fear or nausea, and hearing a dead man's feet dragging through the invisible leaf mould.

I have no superstitious fear of death or of things that surround death, but it took me a little while to collect myself and get in beside Dieter Maria.

'In your pocket you'll find some photographs. Breast pocket.'

He took them out. Pictures of a woman. A child. The woman with the child.

'This is your family. You remember them. On the way back, I'm going to give you all the news of them. News from home, Rudi.'

In the British Military Hospital, and through the course of his long imprisonment, the prisoner must have been examined by many doctors.

They found themselves treating a Rudolf Hess whose chest and back bore no sign of having been pierced and exited by a bullet that had passed through a lung. This is a trauma that leaves large scars and deformities. The prisoner in Spandau had no such scars. As far as I am aware, only one of the doctors who treated him has commented on this anomaly. Perhaps the others did not call up, or have available to them, the complete medical record of Rudolf Hess. Perhaps the medical record was falsified. That is, after all, quite likely. If so, it was not falsified by me. I did not expect the play to run that long.

Journey to Catalunya

It was a well-attended debate but nothing out of the ordinary. As always, the speakers stole a little wit and rather less wisdom from well-thumbed books of quotations. As always, history was ransacked for instances of something or the other, or for instances of the complete opposite with equal success. The Oxford Union is a playground version of the House of Commons. For some it is a rehearsal for the real thing, but for most it is another form of undergraduate fun. Some of us in Frewin Court that night – the ninth of February 1933 – hoped that the motion, 'That this House will in no circumstances fight for its King and Country', would come to the notice of a wider world. None of us foresaw that it would make us infamous.

Morton Drew-Page, pale-haired with a rower's frame and a strong-boned face, rising to speak from the floor of the house, waiting for the buzz that had greeted him to subside, was one who hoped that it would be noticed. He was a young man with serious and credible ambitions, but that was less newsworthy than the fact that he was the son of Sir Edwin Drew-Page, MP. Morton, as we all knew, was on his feet to speak for the motion. His father's politics, as most of the British Empire knew, were indivisible from what it would be polite to call muscular patriotism.

'Opponents of the motion, Mr Speaker, have pointed out circumstances in which the honourable members of this house could not, whatever their scruples, shun the fight. I agree with them. I go further. I say there may be principles for which honorable members might be obliged to fight.'

These remarks seemed dangerously un-pacifist from a man who was down to support the motion. The House listened.

'But "King and Country", Mr Speaker, is not a principle. It is a phrase. It may be stirring. It is certainly pompous. But it is no moral argument. "My country, right or wrong" is an infamous, immoral and intoxicated sentiment, Mr Speaker, and for once the original American scarcely needs translating . . . '

It got a few laughs but I regretted the line as too cheap. I was entitled to as I had written it.

'But permit me to offer the House, as even more germane to our own times, a more poetic expression of the same sentiment. These, Mr Speaker, are the words of perhaps the most famous of all battle hymns. The more alert members of the house will notice that the words are German.

Dir diesen Schwur, O Vaterland, mein hoechstes gut auf Erden,
In deinem Dienste ganz und rein soll meine Liebe werden.'

He carried it off well enough, considering that he did not know the language and had only my coaching and imperfect German to rely on. Still, he had the advantage of knowing exactly what the words meant. But then, so did every public schoolboy in his audience. A few began to realise as much as he went on.

'Kein zoegern und kein Zagen schwaech diese liebe Kraft,
Die immer schon die besten, als opfer dargebracht . . . '

We had planned that I would rise to catch the Speaker's eye but someone else was on his feet before me.

'Mr Speaker, sir, on a point of order, that the House might be favoured with a translation of this gibberish.'

'Certainly, Mr Speaker,' said Morton. ' "To thee, this I swear" – vow might be a better word – "O my country. Above anything else on earth, the devotion, whole and pure of my love . . . " '

Some people were already intoning the great melody from Holst to which the hymn is always set. Others were beginning to boo.

Morton let his voice ring. 'The grand old battle hymn translates quite perfectly into German. "I vow to thee my country – all earthly things above . . . " Indistinguishable, Mr Speaker. And I say that in *no circumstances* would I, or should anyone in this

House, go to war intoxicated by sentiments intended to addle our wits, that are – '

The noise rose to a babel. The Speaker hammered and called for order repeatedly.

' – that are indistinguishable, Mr Speaker, from those that may addle the wits of those we call enemies.'

Morton sat amid a most satisfactory uproar. He had played his part, I had played mine and a certain Leo Baumgartner, unwittingly, had played his. We had a victory for the motion of 275 to 153.

It was of interest to outsiders, after all. Someone in Frewin Court that night telephoned the German ambassador as soon as the vote was counted. Ribbentrop was as prompt to call Berlin. Mr Hitler was pleased by the evidence of decadence in the British ruling class. There are those who believe that our debate was a major cause of the Second World War. Fighting our various corners of it, less than ten years later, most of us – whichever way we'd voted – got the impression there was rather more to it.

' "Possibly the most distasteful part of last night's proceedings, amid much that was to be deplored, was the attempt to bring into disrepute the patriotic verses of 'I Vow to Thee, My Country'." '

Like actors after a first night, we had bought all the newspapers the following morning. We were in Morton's rooms and I was reading his notices to him.

' "This noblest of English hymns was mocked by comparing it with the battle hymn of the fascist Brownshirts." '

'What?'

'So it says here. "It is seldom that the debates of this once honourable society can have been sullied by a more contemptible blasphemy." '

'Blasphemy!' exclaimed Morton.

' "Contemptible blasphemy", it says.

'Where did they get the battle hymn of the SA stuff?'

'They are reporters. They either get it wrong or make it up.'

'Caused a certain amount of fuss among the chickens, anyway. I must get some champagne put on ice.'

Even Morton rarely said that at ten o'clock in the morning.

'He swallowed it whole, though. Rather good, that,' I said.

'The SA has a new anthem this morning,' said Morton, striking the pose and strutting, singing to the tune of the 'Ode to Joy'.

'Dir diesen Schwur, O Vaterland, mein hoechstes gut auf Erden,
In dumpty what was it ganz und rein soll meine Liebe werden . . .
Dum, der um dum, dum derra dum-dum, dum derra dum. '

Leo Baumgartner, in his German suit, was standing in the doorway. He, too, had a newspaper in his hand. 'You have seen this?'

Morton stood abashed. His hand descended.

'Don't you think it's extraordinary?' I said.

Leo's eyes were strangely calm. He closed the door carefully behind him.

'Do you understand why I have left Germany? I don't think you do. It will be hard for somebody who lives in a country like this, and who is not Jewish, to understand what is happening in Germany.'

'But, if I may explain . . . ' Morton began.

Leo cut him short. 'Allow me, if you will, to explain my own private interests. I do not wish to go back to a land which is now in the hands of gangsters who have my name already on their list. I am an intellectual, which always means an enemy of the demagogue, a socialist, which now means an enemy of the state, and I am a Jew. You know what that is? An enemy of the race.'

'But you are surely not going back to Germany?' said Morton.

'I am an alien. I have no position here.' He jabbed the newspaper with a finger. ' "Blasphemy" they call it. I thought some little college debating society. Not this . . . If they know that I have written this . . . blasphemy . . . a Jew and a German, I have come to this country and done this. Will there be some fellowship for Leo Baumgartner, do you think? This alien Jew? Who has mocked "I Vow to Thee My Country"? I will be deported.'

'I'm sorry,' said Morton. 'It was a point rather well made, I thought. And far from being a mockery, Verdon assures me your verse is much better than a mere translation. I'm only sorry you don't feel you can take the credit for it.'

'There will not be much credit in this, gentlemen.'

'The only people who know you wrote it are in this room, Leo,' I said. 'Nobody else is going to know.'

Doors are often flung open in fiction. In a long life I have seen the thing actually done on perhaps two occasions. It arrests the attention.

Where and when Sir Edwin Drew-Page had learned of last night's proceedings, I don't know. If it came to him over the breakfast table, he must have abandoned the plate in mid-egg to have reached Oxford so early. When he spoke, his voice came with all the icy menace of a whisper somehow incorporated into a bellow.

'You, sir, are a disgrace. A disgrace to your class, your country and your name!'

I am quite sure I have the entities betrayed in the correct order and I'm quite sure that I laughed, but that was shock. Morton's laugh was a much more calculated thing. The blow that silenced it was also a calculated thing. It was not a wild haymaker of any kind but a quick and scientific left jab followed by a straight right from the same book. Morton fell sprawling over an armchair. His father took a step forward, his fist still clenched and his shoulder lowered to throw another punch.

I seized the poker from the fireplace and shouted, 'Enough!'

Sir Edwin looked at me. I have a clear recollection of the cold ferocity in his eyes. After which my recollection drops a stitch or two as I collected the next straight right, if that's what it was.

Things became clear again only a few moments later, but in those moments the poker had transferred itself to Sir Edwin's fist and he was raising it above my head.

Morton hauled himself upright from the armchair. A referee would have pushed him back to his corner.

'Your fight's with me,' he said.

'Certainly it is. And you can send your second to my club, if you wish. But never show your face at Keryate again. Understand that.'

He flung the poker into the fireplace, cracking the tiles. He turned on his heel and for the first time saw Leo. He stopped with a snort filled with a curious satisfaction.

'And skulking in the background, the predictable Jew-boy.'

He did not fling or slam the door. He simply left.

I tested my jaw for cracks or missing pieces. It seemed to be intact. Morton's bleeding lip was now both visibly and, when he spoke, audibly swollen.

'Well, chaps,' he said, 'we've had more than our money's worth.' At the cost of some pain from his split lip he smiled. And there was no mistaking the gleam of triumph.

It was not the first violent encounter I had seen between these two men, father and son.

To tell Morton's story – and, less important but necessary in its way, my own – it would be best to go back a little, back to the precise moment when Morton, with his tennis racquets under his arm – real-tennis racquets, that is, this being late October – appeared alongside me to collect messages from his pigeonhole. I was already leafing through some of my own.

'I have freed some more hostages from the Da's dungeon, by the way. If you'd care to join me, we could interrogate one tonight.'

'You know, Morton, your father's kind of wine is probably the sort I ought not to be getting used to. Though I appreciate all you are doing for my education.'

'But that's what we're here for, Verdon.'

'Oh, dear,' I said. I was peering at a card written in a small but crisply legible hand.

'She declines the invitation to tea, does she?'

'Harding wants to see me in his rooms.'

I could already imagine Dr Harding laying out my latest essay like a prosecutor's exhibit, and making the suggestion that I do the gentlemanly thing, pack my traps, and make room at the University for somebody worth bothering with. I was conscious that I might have been slacking. Morton peered over my shoulder.

'If he's going to send you down, come up and drown your sorrows in claret. If he doesn't, we'll call it a celebration.' He laid his hand on my shoulder in mock sympathy. 'I'll go and draw the cork and let it breathe.'

Harding was not holding up my essay between finger and thumb. His hands were in his pockets and his deceptively youthful frame was propped indolently against the mullion of a window. When he turned it was as if he were not quite sure, for a moment or two, why I was there. Harding had what used to be called a fine head of hair and it was his paradoxical vanity to keep it unkempt. He ran his fingers through it, the way actors do to suggest the business of waking up, and then he began to take up books and replace them accurately on their shelves.

'I get the impression you're going to be a schoolmaster, Mr James.'

The accusation came as a surprise.

'I can only say I've never given any thought to becoming a schoolmaster, Dr Harding.'

'Which is just what leads so many people into becoming schoolmasters. You might be a textbook case. You'll take a degree, but not the degree you ought to take because you don't make the effort to do yourself justice. You have no family money to speak of. Have you?'

I laughed.

Harding knew that I depended on a bursary for which – to quote the statute – only 'the sons of indigent vicars of the Church of Ireland or the Church in Wales' were eligible. You might say that having a hard-up vicar for a father was my one academic trump. My father had lost most of his modest capital in the stock market crash and he was pleased, even surprised, that I managed so well on the slender allowance he could afford to give me. I never discussed my own investments with him, despite his great fondness for horses. Especially, I did not discuss the three big bets of my time at the University. Those were the double-or-quits bets. Double meant staying up at University with enough in my pocket for the occasional good dinner. Quits meant just what it said and going to look for a job. Each year I put pretty much all I had on a horse in the Gold Cup. Each year, as a matter of fact, I put it all on the same horse. Had that horse not been Golden Miller – may flowers never cease to grow on his grave – then schoolmastering, as Harding observed, was always going to be the first and likeliest job on offer.

'You will need to be respectably employed. You will find the school holidays convenient for travelling. Or writing, as you will tell yourself. It will seem a convenient stop-gap occupation until something else comes along. But nothing else will, dear fellow. And you'll find to your surprise, and possibly dismay, that you've become a schoolmaster.' He had climbed a pair of steps to replace a book on an upper shelf and now suddenly turned round and stared down at me in my chair. It was theatrical and deliberate, but it gave severe emphasis to his final sentence.

'Don't do it.'

'I really haven't – you're quite right – given much thought to what I'll do when I go down.'

'Well don't handicap yourself with a poor degree when you don't have to. Decide now that you are going to get a first.'

'I'm not being unnecessarily modest, but . . . '

There was a small note of affront in Harding's voice as he replied.

'I don't give that advice to anybody who might be incapable of taking it. Don't think there are people who get a first without breaking sweat. One or two may look like it, but they are just clever enough to pull down the blinds, and hide the amount of midnight oil they burn.'

Harding came down from his steps. For a while he was perfectly still, as if some sound inaudible to me had caught his attention. Then he uncoiled into movement, unhurried, a little abstracted, as if his mind had already moved on to other business. At his table he found paper and uncapped his pen.

'Dr Stoper's departure means I shall have to farm you out for next term and the remainder of this. Do you have any objections to taking modern-philosophy tutorials with a woman?'

'It's another thing to which I've never given any thought.'

'If you have, I can make some other arrangement. I realise that the idea is something of a shattering novelty in this university.'

'Novelty alone would seem to recommend the idea, then.'

He smiled at me. A rare thing for Harding.

'Good. She's in Norham Gardens.'

He scribbled the address and handed it to me.

'You will need to do some catching up.' He gave me a dry look. 'Dr Kennet is not a soft option.'

Dr Julia Kennet was the wife of Dr Alfred Kennet, the economist whose uncompelling lectures I had been skipping, so I imagined a matching kind of woman, heavily cardiganed and spreading into middle-age. The woman who opened the door to me in Norham Gardens came as a surprise. It was true that she wore a cardigan, but it only made her neat, small-boned body appear the more girlish.

The room she led me into had a broad bay window that might have made it cheerful, except that two great chestnut trees outside obscured most of the light. In the greenish gloom, she might almost have passed for a serious sixth-former. On the other hand, when she had been a sixth-former, with those dark serious eyes and incongruously sensuous mouth, she had probably been envied as one who could pass herself off as much older. It was a rare combination.

My partner at the first of these tutorials was a man called Dickinson or thereabouts in the directory. The only memorable thing about him was the magnificent monotone in which he delivered an essay on Utilitarianism.

I was ushering Dickinson out at the end of our second tutorial, when Dr Kennet said, 'Mr James, if you are not in a great hurry, I'd be glad if you could spare me a moment or two.'

She smiled a dry, formal smile. When the door had closed behind Dickinson, she opened a cabinet.

'Would you care for a drink?' she asked. 'Sherry or sherry is the choice, I'm afraid. Fino or amontillado. '

'Fino, thank you.'

A little puzzled, and wanting confidence to begin a conversation, I pretended an interest in the dying afternoon outside the window. Beneath the chestnuts was Dickinson, stooping to put cycling clips around his trousers. After peering skyward a moment or two, he took off his gown, wrapped his books in it and set off at a brisk walk along Norham Gardens towards the Banbury Road. There was no sign of a bicycle.

Dr Kennet joined me at the window and followed my glance.

'A solid second. Dr Harding thinks you might take a first but is afraid you could end up with a third. He doesn't see you as a solid second. Why is that?'

'I really don't know.'

'You were bored by Mr Dickinson's essay and I'm afraid you also allowed it to show. Do you think yourself Mr Dickinson's intellectual superior? Honesty is required.'

'Then, honestly, yes.'

She handed me the glass of fino.

'That being so – at least in your own opinion – shouldn't you entertain the ambition to do better than Mr Dickinson?'

'Perhaps I'm too vain to think that I'm competing with Mr Dickinson.'

'Then with whom?'

'I don't know, Dr Kennet. That's candid, too.'

'So you have no particular goal?'

'I haven't found one I think will do.'

'Do you believe in anything?'

'What kind of anything?'

'I leave that blank.'

'So do I, I'm afraid. Perhaps I wish I did believe in something.'

'God?'

'Well, not a god that could possibly care whether I do or not. That seems to be barking up far too small a tree.'

'Spinoza broadly agrees with you, I think, but he still has it among the principal aims of philosophy to establish a fit object of worship. Does he not?'

I came clean. 'I haven't read Spinoza.'

She smiled. 'And you don't go to church?'

'I sometimes do.'

'Isn't that hypocrisy?'

'I think it counts as loyalty. My father is a vicar.'

'So you do believe in loyalty?'

'That might be claiming a bit much. I happen to like my father. If I didn't, I might be a paid-up atheist.'

'I think it's still something like loyalty, then.'

'Well, at least he doesn't believe in theology, which is what people fall out about.'

'A vicar with no theology?'

'Oh, lots of it, but only as an intellectual game. He points out that the word religion just means "that which binds together". And as far as he's concerned, that's the point.'

'Etymology over theology.'

'More or less. And I say that's all very well, but then fascism is a word about binding people together, too. So I don't find the idea quite as automatically heart-warming as he does. The question is, what are they bound together for?'

'Many people think fascism has a lot to commend it. Especially if they are waiting for trains, apparently.'

'Dr Kennet, forgive me, but I'm still not sure why you asked me to stay.'

' Well, Mr James, none of us is quite sure what to make of you.' She laughed. 'But I'm sure we'll make something of you in the end.'

By now, darkness had settled in the corners of the room. She sat on the rug before the softly hissing gas-fire, tidying her legs away under her skirt in a way that made me think of her riding side-saddle.

'Why don't you sit down?'

She pointed at the other end of the rug. I had difficulty believing that it was what she meant until she actually patted the thing. With something of the care of a man lowering himself into slightly too hot a bath, I lowered myself to the rug, sherry and all, to sit opposite her in the firelight. I was so acutely self-conscious that I heard, but failed to take in for a while, what she was saying. When I caught up again, we were, it seemed, back to Bentham but I found I could still barely make sense of it. As she looked into the fire and absent-mindedly stroked her calf, she could have recited the rhyme about three blind mice and I'd quite likely have lost the thread. Walking back down St Giles, I realised that I was coming down with a common illness. The symptoms were altogether new to me but I was in no doubt about what they meant. Nobody ever is.

I was, therefore, pleased when for one reason or another it was arranged that Dickinson should take his tutorials at another time and I had Dr Kennet to myself once a week. It was hard to be well prepared. The formal topic I'd sweated over might not even get a look in, as she was a woman who liked to follow ideas wherever they led. It was not that much of a hopscotch from Hobbes, say, to the state of modern Europe, and so I found myself, on certain mornings, discussing Sir Edwin Drew-Page's politics with my tutor, while still slightly hungover from the business of looting his cellar – as an accessory after the fact – with his son the previous evening.

Most people now seem to think that Mosley and his fascists occupied the extreme right of British politics in those days. The truth is that a whole regiment of the ruling class comfortably outflanked Mosley, considering him and his proletarian party too lefty, too vulgar, too theatrical and far too feeble on the Jewish question. When A. K. Chesterton, cousin of the rather wittier writer, remarked at a public meeting in 1939 that 'the lamp-post was the best way to deal with a Jew', he was in no danger of being drummed out of any of his clubs. One of which was the House of Commons. In this company, Morton's old Da was thought of by some – certainly by himself – as leadership timber. Sir Edwin had a warning for our ancient universities. They should beware of the 'tide of crinkly-haired intellectuals' whose arrival, it seemed, had nothing to do with persecution. It was part of an international conspiracy to overthrow the British and Christian way of life and all that we held dear. The paper that carried this piece was popular and would have been thought eminently respectable.

Sir Edwin's opinion worked its way into discussion in the gloom of Norham Gardens. I offered the view that, as the Jewish population was small and the prejudice so widespread, it was likely that many people entertained a hostile idea about Jews without actually knowing any.

'Why might they?' she asked.

'I think part of it is just aping their betters.'

'Oh?'

'People suppose a duke will have nothing to do with a Jew. He certainly won't be a Jew. The prejudice must therefore be a sign of good breeding, so they take it up as an affectation.'

'Are they right about the prejudices of dukes, do you suppose?'

'I should think so. But that must be prejudice on my part. I don't know any dukes. In fact, I don't think I know any Jews, either.'

'Are you sure?'

'I don't think I do.'

'I think you know one.'

She tugged at the thin gold chain about her neck and slid out a shiny star from the collar of her blouse.

'How was I to know?' I laughed.

She smiled. 'If you'd had the breeding of a duke, you would surely have known immediately.'

Only Morton knew that I was smitten. Though even he did not know how smitten. I was almost too ashamed to admit that to myself.

'This might interest you,' I said to him, as we walked along the High, muffled against the January chill. 'Mrs Kennet – '

'The beautiful Mrs Kennet – '

'I beg your pardon. The beautiful Mrs Kennet – '

'The beautiful and brilliant Mrs Kennet – '

'Turns out to be Jewish.'

'Why would that be of particular interest to me?'

He swung on his heel and walked briskly away from me.

I found him later in his rooms experimenting with a curly-stemmed pipe.

'It's a mistake,' I said.

'What is?'

'The pipe. A curly job especially.'

'I'm smoking too many cigarettes,' he said. 'I thought it might be better. Not sure though.'

'I'm sorry about – I wasn't implying that . . . er . . . '

He waved his hand.

'Of course you were,' he said, and carried on inexpertly lighting his pipe. 'But if you want to know whether I share an opinion with the dear old Da, you can just bloody ask. I don't like being scraped at.'

He carried on sucking fire and making enough smoke to hide a destroyer.

'Navy Cut,' I said, reading the words on his tin of tobacco. 'At last the words make sense to me.'

'The Da has all sorts of opinions that might interest you.'

'Still,' I said, 'men are rarely so good or so bad as their opinions.'

He peered up at me, squinting through a heavy blue cloud. 'Who said that?'

'Can't remember. Somebody clever.'

'Somebody who hadn't met the dear old Da. Do you know, you might be right. This thing's a mistake. Be a good chap and open a window while I find some water to put on my bloody tongue. Of course, you haven't met the Da, have you? I suppose you'd better. Better come down to Keryate.'

'Of course there is a war coming, young man. The Bolsheviks want one and they are going to get one. No two ways about it. Be ready to get mud on your boots.'

'I'm sure you're right, sir. But my question is, will it settle anything? The last one doesn't seem to have done.'

Sir Edwin Drew-Page looked at me with the sort of withering distaste that a host is usually expected to disguise.

'The observation, if you don't mind my saying so, is fatuous.'

He returned to the business of sipping at his soup for a while. Lady Eveline Drew-Page at the opposite end of the table was untroubled. She smiled at me as if I had somehow charmed the old boy, eerily oblivious of the tone of his remark.

I occupied myself breaking bread, and was aware of the faint smell of mothballs from my evening dress. It did nothing for the flavour of the soup, though that hardly mattered as the soup was not good. Suddenly Sir Edwin Drew-Page let his spoon descend to his dish and leaned back with the air of a man interrupting me in full flow, as if I were prattling uncontrollably.

'Do you know why it's a fatuous remark?'

'No, sir, but I'm sure it is. I hardly ever say anything that isn't.'

A number of people smiled. Sir Edwin only rolled his eyeballs a little, showing them to be curiously yellowed, as if they were nicotine-stained.

'History is a continuous evolutionary struggle. War is part of that struggle. Not only inevitable, but necessary. Precisely because, in an evolutionary process – such as history – nothing is ever settled. It's not the three o'clock at Newmarket.'

There was a dull flash of yellow from his eye as he returned his attention to the soup. I returned to mine. Spoons dipped silently around the table.

The little commotion of the soup dishes being cleared away encouraged small talk and allowed me to strike up with the pleasant young woman on my left. All I knew of her was that her name was Alicia, and that she was in company with the Lucinda seated elsewhere at the table with Morton for a neighbour. Morton, usually a bright conversationalist was subdued on his home turf. It may not have been just the relationship with his father, for I saw that while he talked to Lucinda, his gaze drifted often across the table to Alicia. In those unlamented days of dressing for dinner and ladies 'withdrawing', to open a conversation with a stranger at dinner was a little like opening the bidding at contract bridge. I offered the duffer's bid, of 'What sports do you play?'

'Oh, the usual,' she said. 'Tennis and so on, but I have to partner somebody who doesn't mind losing, or they are inclined to get cross with me. Are you serious about games?'

'If I were good at any of them I would be terrifically serious. As it is, frivolity is thrust upon me.'

'Oh, then, perhaps we should be prepared to make a suicide pact here and now, and agree to be the losing double, should it ever arise.'

'We can be like Mr and Mrs Carlyle,' I said. ' Become a couple and so make only two people wretched instead of four. I should be honoured.'

It turned out that Alicia was studying art and was a painter, a claim she immediately deprecated by adding 'of sorts'. Our conversation was on the verge of flowering but Drew-Page leaned towards me on his elbow and began talking as if he had not ceased at any time to enjoy my undivided attention. But it was really Alicia he was addressing. He had lost the hectoring, contemptuous tone and had become more like a gruffly amiable uncle.

'The schoolbooks have a lot to answer for, of course. The War of this . . . The War of that . . . Spanish Succession, Jenkins' Ear. Tommy rot, all of it. Tommy rot.'

'Absolutely,' said Alicia.

'You take an interest in history, my dear?'

'Oh, certainly.'

'Well very few historians do. Not enough of an interest to understand it, anyway. One of the few who does is a woman. As it happens.'

'Really?'

'I will look out a copy of her work and put it in your hands.'

For the rest of the meal, Sir Edwin was genial in his own way. At last, ladies withdrew and the men smoked and drank according to custom. No disreputable stories were told. We talked, or rather Sir Edwin did, about history. His talk was richly illustrated from his own experience on the Western Front. He must be given credit for not even hinting that he had been twice decorated for gallantry in that conflict. Somehow or other, it was mentioned that my father was a vicar. The fact roused another of Sir Edwin's never-quite-sleeping dogs. In his opinion, the padres had mostly shirked the muck and bullets.

'The RCs showed our chaps up completely. You could find an RC padre with his little box of holy tricks crawling forward under the whizz-bangs to reach a dying man. I've no time for Popery, but I never saw one of our chaps do that.'

The discussion then followed a well-worn circuit that included the premise that there was no such thing as an atheist in a foxhole.

'It may be that a foxhole is not where people do their clearest thinking about these things,' I said.

I got the full yellow eyeball. 'You might be surprised how clearly a man can think in a foxhole. Let me know when you've been in one.'

The conversation was dead and buried. We joined the ladies. There was gramophone music and talk. Then there were cards at which, with some pleasure, I partnered Alicia. There was the offer – declined – of a late game of billiards, some significant yawning and then a walk into chillier parts of the house and bed. The evening's debit in Sir Edwin's cellar-book meant that I did not read for long before sleep overtook me.

In the first moment of being awake, I could not tell what kind of sound I had heard, only that there had been a sound and that it had come from somewhere inside my room. Electric light was still a novelty at Keryate, so there was no convenient lamp beside the bed. As I sat up I was aware of something beyond the foot of the bed. The sound came again. It was the sound of a knuckle tapping on the door but the knuckle was, distinctly, tapping on the inside and not the outside. Then I heard my name spoken quietly in a voice that was hesitant and urgent at the same time. I recognised the voice, even whispering, as that of my companion from dinner, Alicia.

'What is it?'

'I'd hoped you mightn't be asleep. I'm sorry.'

Dimly, in the pallor of moonlight that crept past the curtain's edge, I saw her make her way to the foot of my bed, where she sat taking slow deep breaths, a woman composing herself after something like an exertion. I sat up against my pillows, rather fuddled and waiting for a clue as to what might be expected of me. When out of my ground in this way, I usually manage to find something stupid to say. On this occasion it was: 'Are you ill?'

'No. But you probably think I'm mad.'

'Has something frightened you?'

She nodded. 'In a way.' Then something occurred to her. 'Oh. I hope I didn't frighten you.'

'Not at all.'

'I've just had the most embarrassing sort of time with Morton's father.'

'Oh.'

'He came to my room. Pretty much as I've come to yours. I woke up to find him tapping on the foot of my bed. Holding a nightlight.'

'How alarming.'

'It was, rather.'

And she began to giggle.

'Did he . . . do anything? Did he try to . . . ?'

She began to laugh, but suppressed it so as to make no sound. Then she composed herself and spoke in a mimicking kind of voice, like an actor in a school play.

'He told me that I had excited his deepest interest.'

She collapsed into the suppression of silent laughter again, her face in her hands, holding her elbows tight against her heaving ribs.

'He brought me a book.'

'He brought you a book?'

'Here. Look.'

I found myself holding the book in question. Looking at it, on the other hand, was problematic.

'Do you think you could find the light switch?' I asked.

A moment or two later I could see Alicia standing near the door in a fine silk dressing-gown of unmistakably masculine cut and vastly too big for her. I could also now see that I was holding a copy of something called *World Revolution: The Plot Against Civilisation* by Nesta Webster.

'It's by a woman, you see. Very important that I should read it. He had this tremendous look in his eye, saying that it would be very important to me. It seems my destiny was involved. He could absolutely tell, you see. And it's a frightfully important book and I would understand everything if I read it and so on. Do you think he's barmy?'

'Of course. But not so barmy he doesn't know exactly what he's doing creeping into your bedroom. You should have screamed. Very loudly.'

'Oh, one couldn't! It would be so shaming. Still, I can't quite understand why one is absurdly anxious to find a way out that is, more or less, polite. However frantic one might be. What is the etiquette, Verdon?'

'I'm afraid I really don't know.'

'Then – he'd been sitting on my bed for, oh, ages – he said he was beginning to freeze and did I mind if, just for a moment or two, he got in under the blankets. So I said, certainly he could, if he wished . . . '

'Really?'

'But I said would he mind taking his dressing-gown off first, because it was too chilly to bring under the blankets.'

'You did? That must have encouraged him, rather.'

'I thought, when he takes his dressing-gown off, I shall take to my heels, because he won't go chasing me about the stairs without a dressing-gown on. Nobody would do that surely?'

'I don't know. I don't know what rules of decorum apply to sex monsters.'

'My plan, you see – such as it was – was to scoot out of the other side of the bed while he was taking it off and make my dash for it. I did rather assume – and perhaps I was naïve – that there would be something under the dressing-gown. Not a stitch, Verdon. Not a stitch! Etiquette be damned.'

'You simply fled?'

'I was rather frozen for a moment, I'm afraid. And do you know, I think he was a tiny bit, well, abashed. He did rather scuttle for the blankets, if you know what I mean.'

'I can imagine. I think.'

'And then a sort of brilliant idea came to me. He just dropped the dressing-gown, you see. So I said, "You men are all the same: you will never hang anything up properly." Then I got out of bed, picked up his dressing-gown and went as if to hang it on a hook. Do you know, he waited in the bed as placidly as a lamb. Then I bolted, of course. With the dressing-gown. As you see. How he's going to get back to his own room in decency, I can't say.'

'And you kept hold of the book in all that?'

'Better than clutching a straw. Something to throw.'

We both laughed. Then we both stopped abruptly and listened to the silence for a few moments.

'Actually, I don't believe he was at all chilly,' she said, fingering the dressing-gown. 'It's a kind of quilted silk and frightfully cosy.'

'I suppose,' I said, 'if you go in for this night-stalking, you have to have the right sort of kit.'

'I knew all this was supposed to go on in country houses, but I thought it was restricted, rather, to married women only. You know what they say: an heir and a spare, then anything goes.'

'I'm not altogether up with the rules in these circles. But I must say, you are taking it with tremendous sang-froid.'

'Not so much that I shan't be leaving tomorrow.'

'What excuse will you make?'

She laughed.

'I will receive a telephone call tomorrow. I promise you. I always do the same thing for Celia Crammond when she's at house parties. We always pass on the telephone numbers to each other, and then, you see, we always call. And if the house party is fun, that's what you say. And that's all right. But if it isn't and somebody is trying to get you married off to some hopeless horror, you can now say, gosh, you've had a bit of bad news and really have to say thank you and dash.'

'Do you really? I mean, really have this arrangement?'

'Oh yes. You men don't understand. I promise you, a girl without a plan of escape is just dead meat these days.'

'I hadn't expected it all to be quite so educational.'

'And you won't tell anybody why? Why I'm off tomorrow, I mean.'

'No, of course not.'

'Especially not Morton.'

I thought for a moment. 'I'm sure you're right. Especially not Morton.'

We exchanged rooms for the rest of the night. There was no

trace of Sir Edwin's visit, or any clue as to how he had made his retreat in decency. Had he returned – never much of a probability – he would have found me wide awake and sitting up with Mrs Webster's important book. Despite the shortcomings of her style and a certain lack of rigour in her method, I could not put it down. Daylight came and she still had me hooked.

Here was the well from which Sir Edwin, and many others, drew deep draughts of their philosophy. The international conspiracy to which Sir Edwin so conversationally alluded was more complicated and more ancient than I could possibly have suspected. Mrs Webster explained that it began not with the Jews – and certainly not with anybody as recent as Marx – but with the Muslims, and in the Middle Ages. A fanatical band of warrior Muslims, calling themselves the Assassins, had subverted and converted a certain sect of the Crusader knights while they were in the Holy Land. Returning to Europe, while remaining outwardly Christians, these chaps became in reality a secret society, centred on the Knights Templar (if I've got that right: it's a long time since I read this), dedicated to the overthrow of Christian civilisation. In time and in turn, this conspiracy corrupted the Papacy, gave rise to Free-masonry, spawned the Humanism of the Renaissance, the atheistical 'Enlightenment' philosophy of the eighteenth century, the French Revolution and the later Russian Bolshevik edition. The most important point was that, thanks to the decadence of the modern age, this great conspiracy stood on the brink of final triumph. This summary of her work is, inevitably, unfair to Mrs Webster. Her analysis of the great conspiracy explains far more than I have hinted at.

There were, without question, more things in this philosophy than were dreamt of in heaven or earth. I read on. For a while I entertained the idea that a fatuous précis of all this, concocted into a kind of whodunnit, would be a certain bestseller.

At Keryate there was a wintertime tradition of playing badminton at a net rigged up in the hall. As the Drew-Pages claimed to have established this idea before it was ever thought of in the Duke of

Beaufort's house, the game should have been called Keryate. Alicia and I were paired to play Sir Edwin and Lucinda, when word came that there was a telephone call for Alicia. Soon after, she was making her apologies and saying her goodbyes and being driven to the station by Morton. As the chap now without a partner, I was happy to sit it out while the others played. It was a good time, I thought, to complete my reading. I went off to fetch Mrs Webster and sat on the staircase, reading her last few chapters.

'What's that you're buried in, my boy?' asked Sir Edwin, off the court between sets.

I held the book up so that he could read the title. 'I found this lying about,' I said.

'Did you really?' There was no embarrassment in his eye. 'And what do you think of it?'

'Interesting,' I said. 'It kept me up late into the night.'

He stared at me, gauging the probability of insolence.

'You have an enquiring mind, do you, Mr James?'

'I hope so.'

He took the book from my hands, as if judging its condition, and then handed it back to me snapped shut.

'The only work of history worth reading. You may keep it. With my compliments. We must always feed the enquiring mind.'

He walked away to the baseline.

As he prepared to serve, Morton returned. He strode into the hall and, without speaking, picked up a racquet and crossed the court trying it against the palm of his hand. Sir Edwin was not as much taken by surprise as I was, or Lucinda. He was alert enough to parry the blow, when it came, with his own racquet. What a fencer might have called a remise in tierce by Morton caught him what must have been a stinging blow on his left arm. Morton seemed icily possessed. It would have been a systematic thrashing, had it not been systematically parried for the most part by Sir Edwin, who stood his ground defiantly, without offering an offensive blow in return. The whole thing was conducted without a word until the racquet in Morton's hand splintered and broke. He threw it down and stood staring at his father, who now held his own racquet ready to strike. The two glared at each other. Morton was ready for the blow and was, clearly, not about to flinch.

The moment was broken by Sir Edwin.

'My service, I believe,' he said, stooping to pick up the dropped shuttlecock, and kicking the broken racquet off the court. 'If my son has finished his tantrum.'

But Lucinda, unfreezing, squealed and ran past me up the stairs, dropping her racquet .

'I think you owe her an apology,' said Sir Edwin, putting down his racquet. Morton had landed some cutting blows, and he must have been in some pain. It did not show. He walked away.

'She wasn't going to tell you,' I said, as we waited for the train.

'I know that telephone trick they do. I wanted to know why she was leaving. And she's an awful fibber. She'd never stand up in court.'

'It might have been more tactful to accept the fib.'

'Yes, it would have been the form. But, vanity, I suppose. And the opposite. Whatever that is. I had to get it out of her.'

'You were afraid it might have been something to do with you?'

'I was not especially charming last night. Rather a bear, I know.'

'And that mattered because, though you haven't altogether made it clear, you are inclined to be taken with her.'

'Give the chap a goldfish.'

'It's really not hard, Morton.'

'I think she's rather bright. She's got something about her.'

'I entirely agree.'

'She said you altogether played the white man, by the way. She apologises for your disturbed night.'

'Oh, let's not mention that.'

'And now, you see, I mean – I know it's not as if . . . I mean . . . Damn it.'

'You had thought . . . '

'Yes, I had thought . . . But it's out of the question. Now. It is, isn't it?'

'I believe it is.'

He fell into silence. The train was bang on time.

I realise that nowadays 'playing the white man' is a phrase loaded with offence. An idea that would have occurred to nobody in the 1930s. Well, no white man, anyway.

Dr Alfred & Dr Julia Kennet have pleasure in inviting . . . said the copperplate. The handwriting said it was *Drinks at 6.30*. Had we not come back early, the invitation would have lain in my pigeon-hole until well after all the drinks had been downed. I hurried to change.

The Kennets' house, behind the brooding defences of evergreen oaks in its bare and wintry garden, had an air of the convent about it, as many a North Oxford house did in those days. The gloomy entrance hall did nothing to dispel the impression. Several junior dons and a number of obvious undergraduates stood in the drawing-room. Already the cells were beginning to divide, so I had got the lateness just about right. Dr Kennet introduced me to the Dr Kennet who was her husband, a formality that was not allowed to occupy too much of his time before she led me to the drinks. Or rather, the drink, which was something new to me. It was a punch of warm red wine.

'What is this called?' I asked.

'It's *Glühwein*,' she said. 'Isn't it just the thing for a winter's day?'

'Calculated to produce a glow, then?'

'You speak German?'

'A little.'

'Oh, I didn't know. That is excellent.'

'Not especially excellent.'

'Oh it is. I must introduce you to Leo. He made the punch.'

She led me across the room and into a small group gathered about a man whose grey-flecked hair marked him for an elder. When we were introduced, I saw that the grey had arrived early. Leopold Baumgartner was no more than thirty.

His English was excellent – far better than my school German –

but now and then he would turn to me with a German phrase for which he needed an English prompt. Before an hour of this had passed, it seemed that we were friends.

'You and Leo seem to hit it off,' she said, when the time for leaving came. 'Perhaps you could make a point of . . . Oh, showing him the landmarks. He does need to get to know people.'

There seemed no obvious reason to suggest that I was one of the people Leo needed to know. In fact, over the next few days, it was he who introduced me to some rather august people who were trying to find him a niche in the University. In return, I could only introduce him to the obvious sights, some conspicuous old stones and, inevitably, the English pub and English beer. He was impressed by many of the old stones but not by the beer. For several centuries, he pointed out to me, Germany had lived under the protection of beer purity laws. The liquid put before him would, in Germany, have been not merely bad but illegally bad. I said it was an acquired taste. He said that he suspected that it was not a taste but merely a tolerance that the English acquired, for lack of an alternative. He had discovered by this time that drinkable wine – or any wine – was hard to come by in an English pub and coffee not even to be hoped for. No, it was not altogether a golden age but, despite these things, we were becoming firm friends.

'I'm going to speak from the floor. I've seen Hardie, so I think I'll get called.'

'Morton, if you get up on your hind legs, the Speaker will allow you to catch his eye.'

In a debate on the motion 'This House will in no circumstances fight for its King and Country', an intervention by the son of Sir Edwin Drew-Page, on either side, was not going to be overlooked. As Morton was to speak for and not against the motion, it would be welcomed with special glee. Whether Morton grasped this quite as fully as the rest of us, I've never been sure.

'What's the chance, do you suppose, that the newspapers will cover it?'

'There's usually an inch or so in *The Times*, isn't there?' I said.

'May be a bit more than an inch if we can win it. We need people to get the idea that we might, you know. Make damn sure there's a real reporter or two there. *Épater les bourgeois* and all that.'

'I think even the dimmest reporter might guess it will *épater* your dear old Da.'

'How he would hate to be identified with the bourgeoisie. But, if he chokes on his kedgeree, fair enough. Help me with the speech.'

'As long as we are not just carrying on the family quarrel.'

'The quarrel is between his view of civilisation and mine.'

'Isn't that something awfully like what it says on war memorials?'

'God! The hypocrisy! I truly hate that phrase: 'The Great War for Civilisation'. What does it say on German war memorials? If they'd won, you could bet your bottom Deutschmark it would say, 'In der grosse Krieg für Civilization' – or whatever it would be in German. You can probably tell me.'

'Do you know, Morton, I think I might be able to do better than that. Have you got a hymn book handy?'

He shook his head and looked at me sideways.

A low fire burned in the grate at the Lamb and Flag but it did not seem to make much difference to Leo. As I carried our beer back from the bar, he sat waiting and looking chilled. His German-cut suit and collar and overcoat also managed to make him look uncomfortably far from home.

'You know that Adolf Hitler is now Chancellor of Germany? That foolish old man von Hindenburg has bowed to this.'

'I saw the newspaper yesterday. But it's a minority government after all.'

'He will immediately call an election. That will be Hitler's idea.'

'You think so? His party might easily lose . . . '

'They have no intention of losing elections.'

'Well, politics is . . . '

'The National Socialists are not a political party. Adolf Hitler is not a politician. You will see no more politics in Germany.'

He took a draught of his beer and set down his glass, but the look of reproach and distaste now had nothing to do with German beer-purity laws.

'I need a favour, Leo,'

'From me? I am not in a very good position for the granting of favours,' he said.

'It's a bit of a tall order, but you are, really, just the chap.'

I put in front of him a copy of my college's hymnal, borrowed that very morning from the shelf in the chapel, and opened it at a page I had marked with an inserted sheet of paper.

'I've been trying to do a translation – well, a version in German – of this fellow here.'

He glanced at the hymnal and then took the piece of paper, on which he found my clumsy attempt. He read it through without laughing and then turned his attention to the English original.

'You know, this could almost be already a translation from German. It has a tone, you know, of the high late Romantic. Are you sure it is not?'

'I'm pretty sure it isn't, but you've more or less got the hole in one.'

'I have the whole in what?'

'Sorry. Hole in one. The golf thing.'

'Ah, golf.'

'I don't suppose you play.'

'You will find there are not many Jews in German golf clubs.'

'I'm afraid to say that most English golf clubs will not be different.'

He smiled and took another experimental sip of his beer. 'Of all the exclusions, this is one that I can bear.'

'Would you brush this up for me? Make it decent German. Better still, throw it away and do a more worthwhile translation. Do you think you might do something metrical, something with the right kind of dum-de-dum about it?'

'Oh, I'm sure I can do something . . . '

'The idea is to hold up the mirror, as it were. The sentiment should sound so perfectly right. In German, I mean.'

'Das ist fraglos. Where and when will you propose to hold up this mirror?'

'We have a debating society here. The Union.'

'And what are you debating?'

'Pacifism. For or against.'

'I see. A debating society. You know, they now sound like quite precious words.' He picked up the hymnal and put it in his pocket. 'I will do my best.'

Leo's remarkable piece of work was in my pigeonhole the following morning. I read it through to Morton.

'My God,' he said, 'it sounds like the absolute genuine article. Not that my German is good enough to be too critical.'

'It really does comes across as the goods, I assure you. I think it might go well to the Beethoven thing – "Ode to Joy".'

'Dum dum-dum da, da-da dum-dum . . . '

'That's the one. It fits pretty well . . . '

'No, I don't think I'll try singing it. For all I know there's a rule against singing and some twerp will pull me up on a point of order. The main thing is to get it into my head. Help me with the pronunciation. And pass my compliments to your German chum. I must send him a bottle of something good.'

The debate came and, for many of those who took part in it, never quite went.

On St Valentine's day, a box was delivered to the Union containing two hundred and seventy-five white feathers. Slightly dulling the humour of the thing, another box, with the same number of white feathers arrived shortly afterwards. These tokens – 'now available at a rate of two per person for all those who voted for the motion', as the Hon. Sec. put it – were taken as amusing. The attacks from parliamentarians, preachers and patriots became unamusing. In the reaction to the debate, as Morton complained, not one idea or argument mentioned in its course was referred to. Ideas and arguments did not enter into it. We had voted against King and Country. We were traitors and, obviously, cowards. It would, I'm sure, be possible to find in print the suggestion that we should have have been taken out and shot and buried in unmarked graves. Had this policy been adopted, similar unmarked graves would have been needed in the vicinity of the London School of Economics, the University of Aberystwyth, and many another institution where, about this same time, this or some similar motion was proposed and debated and carried just as it had been in Frewin Court.

At the next debate, a squad of patriotic undergraduates interrupted proceedings by ripping the recording page from the minute book and disappearing from the chamber with it.

An attempt was made to put everything right with a hastily arranged second debate, at which Mr Randolph Churchill proposed an exactly contrary motion. This debate, unlike the first, crammed the house to the rafters. The result was even more spectacular. Mr Churchill's party lost by 750 to 138. Not all of the English ruling class belonged to the Nordic League or the White Knights of Britain. Not by a long way.

The love that asks no question had learned that there are, after all, one or two to be asked. And so it should have done, with Passchendaele hardly the length of a childhood behind us. A box of white feathers was not likely to make us take another view of the practicality of pacifism. A week or two later, on the other hand, came something more instructive. Hitler had the German parliament building burned to the ground. The one and only act of the parliament that met after the Reichstag fire, in the Garrison Church at Potsdam, was to vote its own indefinite dissolution. I remembered Leo's prophesy: 'You will see no more politics in Germany.'

Nobody took the lesson more to heart than Morton, as it turned out.

'I don't think I can be bothered with the second act. How about you?'

'Not if it's very much like the first.'

'No reason to think otherwise. Let's find a pub and I'll make it up to you.'

I hadn't seen Morton more than two or three times since we had gone down from the University. I would still have called him my closest friend but our paths were drawing us in different ways. He had become more serious. I had become more frivolous. I had skipped the Civil Service exams altogether. Mrs Kennet had written me a reproving note and Harding had sent a longer and sterner letter. I had been surprised – and flattered – that they should have taken such notice of it. Had I not been enjoying a run of luck at the races, I might even have thought it over.

As we left the theatre that night, I had the idea that Morton was also going to voice his disapproval of the way I was spending my days. It was rather subtle of him, I thought, to have suggested going to see what he'd obviously known was a bad play, doomed to close.

We found ourselves in the kind of pub where you knew the real custom was some species of Citified day-labourer now at home and probably thinking of being abed. The landlord's best hope for custom after lighting-up time was a bad play. That night, business was beginning to pick up ominously, but there was still a snug, quiet corner for us and our pints.

'Do you remember an exchange you once had with my father,' he began, wiping froth from his newly grown moustache with a knuckle, 'about the educational value of spending time in a foxhole?'

'Vaguely.'

'And you said . . . ?'

'I don't remember.'

'You said that people probably didn't do their best thinking in foxholes.'

'Something like that, I dare say.'

'And he said you might be surprised.'

'Where is this leading, Morton?'

'What do you say we put it to the test?' He was staring down at his beer with a peculiar, still intensity.

'By doing what?'

He tilted his head and brought the same still intensity to looking me full in the face. I realised how infrequent that direct look is, even between friends.

'By going to Spain.'

I suppressed the urge to laugh. 'Why would a couple of chaps like us go to Spain?'

'I would have thought that needed no explanation.'

'Well, all right. I can see the motive. That's not the problem. I can't see what we might achieve.'

'Well, sometimes it may be an achievement just to stand up and be counted.'

'And if you happen to be lying dead in a ditch at the time of the counting?'

' "Go, tell the Spartans . . . " I mean, there are things you have to be ready to die for.'

'Speaking for myself, I think Spain may not be it.'

'It's not Spain. It's what you believe in or you don't.'

'I don't speak Spanish and I'm a rotten shot. It is, therefore, hard to see how I might make a decisive intervention, whatever my beliefs.'

'I'm being serious, Verdon.'

'So am I. We are not soldiers, Morton old man.'

'I happen to know you are not a rotten shot and, all right, the OTC doesn't make you a soldier but you and I can strip a rifle and use it. Anything else there is to learn, we can learn.'

'Or die in the attempt.'

'I'm astonished you can be so flippant.'

'I'm being perfectly serious.'

'Then face the serious question. Fascism – for or against?'

'You know my answer to that.'

'Then, right now, Spain is where the talking stops and doing something begins.'

'There is, of course, a Foreign Enlistment Act . . . '

'Phooey.' He waved his hand dismissively and narrowly missed sending his beer flying.

'And the practical business of actually getting there and signing on and . . . '

He leaned forward.

'Couldn't be simpler. You just get the Paris train at Victoria. Don't even need a passport. Then down to Perpignan, which is where you take the peseta or whatever. It's perfectly organised. Then over the mountains into Catalonia and Bob's your uncle.'

'Or, in this case, Joe might be.'

'Well, let's hope he is. Because Uncle Adolf is certainly stumping up for Franco and hay-rakes won't beat him. Adrian Ferney is coming back from China to go. A lot of people are going. And there ought to be a few more people of our sort.'

'Our sort?' I didn't want to mock him, but it could hardly sound like anything else. 'The officer class you mean? Subalterns at the Somme?'

He was silent for a while.

'I hope our sort,' he said at last, 'might have been the subalterns to shoot a few of their own generals.'

'I think you are loosely quoting the "Internationale".'

'Not too loosely.'

'Have you joined the Party?'

'No. But probably only because the papers would turn it into a Punch and Judy business. Because of the Da.'

'If you go to Spain, they'll make hay.'

'Doubt if there'll be too many gossip columnists in Spain to bother me with it, though. And anyway, they'll have to recognise that it's serious. It's about what kind of future there is going to be. It's not about me and the Da.'

'I hope not.'

'Well, I didn't really think you'd throw your hat in the air and shout, "Let's go!" '

'Whatever kind of future I might fight for, Morton, the dictatorship of the proletariat isn't it. As war cries go, it's even more pompous than "King and Country" and much more dishonest. Kings and countries can, at least, exist in the real world.'

'It is nevertheless an idea. It may not be a possible idea, but that doesn't necessarily make it a bad one.'

'That's not a belief I'd want to find myself clinging to in a Spanish foxhole.'

'Better to be in the company of people who have a belief worth fighting for.'

'I seem to hear your father's voice.'

He finished his beer and stood. I didn't.

'Morton, it is dangerous enough to join in the fighting. And we'll all get the chance to do that, I dare say. But it's much more dangerous to join in the believing.'

'Do you believe in nothing at all?'

'My right to be wrong.'

'Well, you'll have to fight for that soon enough.' He took an envelope from his inside pocket. 'I took the liberty, I hope you don't mind, of letting you in for this.'

I took the offered envelope from his hand. It bore only my name on the outside and was unsealed. Inside was the personal card of a partner in well-known firm of solicitors in Lincoln's Inn Fields.

'Would this be to do with your will?'

'I came into a certain amount at twenty-one. There's a trust and so on. Anyway he's the chap and I've named you as one of the executors. You can always say no, but it's utterly uncomplicated as these things go.'

'Then you were pretty sure I wouldn't take you up on Spain.'

He smiled

'You wouldn't think the wine was good enough.'

'Well, I'll pin this up somewhere.'

'Thank you. If you don't mind, I'll leave you here. Pity about the play.'

He put on his hat and strode to the door.

The following morning, far too early, the telephone rang. From the first syllable, I knew the voice. I managed to dismiss the feeling it produced that my brain had suddenly become spongy.

'Dr Harding,' I said. 'How good to hear from you.'

'Have you seen Morton Drew-Page?'

'As it happens, yes.'

'Has he told you his damn-fool plan?'

'About Spain? Yes. He has.'

'Did you manage to talk him out of it?'

'Failed, I'm afraid. He rather tried to talk me into it.'

'I take it he didn't?'

'He didn't.'

'You must try again.'

'If I get the chance.'

'You must make the chance.'

'But I don't think he's likely to listen. And . . . in the end, is it really up to us to . . . ?'

'Yes, it is. Now I don't like to think of you spending time at dismal race tracks in this raw November weather. Bad for you. Get to Paddington and come up. I'll give you lunch. Oh, and Mrs Kennet asked me to send you her regards if I were to speak to you.'

'That's kind of her.'

'I'll mention that you're coming. You never know, she might be free as well.'

He put the telephone down without further ceremony.

How did he know? How did he know of my peculiar weakness where Mrs Kennet was concerned? As far as I knew, I had never by word or deed betrayed myself to her or to anybody other than Drew-Page. But I knew my Harding. And it seemed he knew me. It didn't surprise me as much as it might have done.

When I arrived, the little table in Harding's room disappointed me by being set only for two, though Harding said it was possible that Dr Kennet might join us later. We were served in his uniquely unservile way by Victor, the most venerable of the college's scouts, who filled our glasses and then placed the decanter between us.

'I believe you'll enjoy that, Mr James. I certainly enjoyed decanting it.'

'Thank you, Victor,' said Harding, 'that will be all.'

Victor left us.

'The stewardship of the college cellar has been thrust upon me,' said Harding. 'Burdensome, of course, but it does allow the occasional privilege of cherry-picking. We are now drinking the sunshine of a vanished world. And what a vintage it was, the last summer of peace. Let me risk being even more florid. The business of educating men is much like making wine. Every year another crop, much of a muchness but, mysteriously, not the same. The makings are always that little bit different and the results can be very different. And very disappointing. But every so often, you know you've got the hope of something special. And then – especially then – you know the real result lies in the future. It seems to me that when you know that wine could mature into something exceptional, it is stupid to pour it away into the punch. It makes no sense to send talented men to take their chance of being annihilated. It would make more sense to insist on an amputation apiece before we bother educating them. Make them unfit to be wasted in bloody trenches.'

I sipped a little more of the wine.

'You may think that a slightly élitist view, I know. But the idea that Drew-Page is going to stick his fat head in the way of a sniper's bullet and spread a good brain on a corner of some foreign field is really unacceptable. Especially if he's doing it to outrage his father. You have to broaden his view.'

'How?'

'My first thought was that you should go with him.'

The wine, for a moment or two, tasted strange.

'My own brain is nearer fertiliser-grade, I take it?'

'That is not what I meant to suggest.'

'Anyway, I have already resisted the suggestion. From Morton.'

'Apart from simple self-preservation, what was your argument?'

'I don't think I gave him much of an argument. I just think it may be a somewhat intoxicated kind of decision.'

'Marching off to war often is. Let nobody say that Britain didn't want war in 1914. They were baying for it in the streets. Drunk out of their minds on martial spirit. But let's say I've decided to go. Talk me out of it. Tell me, as a principled chap, why not going to Spain is better than going.'

'Since I saw Morton I have given this some thought, as a matter of fact.'

'Always a good start. And?'

'Well, I think by going, the person you help most is Franco.'

'Ahh. Go on.'

'Franco's problem is that his actions are criminal. When he

brought his troops out, he embarked on an illegal coup against a legitimately elected government. When he got the Germans to fly those troops from North Africa to the Spanish mainland, he went a step further. The act of inviting a foreign power to take military action against one's own government, in this case an elected government, is the blackest possible treason.'

'Clearly.'

'Franco and his supporters have plenty of ammunition but they are short of legitimacy. Every foreigner, therefore, who goes to Spain to fight against him, in Franco's eyes, is a godsend. An International Brigade? A band of Marxists and Trotskyites? Foreign adventurers? Tools of a godless international conspiracy? Franco must be delighted to see them in the field. They are amateurs, they won't be united and they won't be decisive. But, as far as he is concerned, they are conclusive evidence that he is in the right and may present himself as the saviour of Spain.'

'I find that persuasive. Let me give you another argument. If Morton goes to Spain to fight alongside the Communists, then they will probably shoot him even if the Falangists don't. The anarchists and the different Communist factions hate each other much more than they hate Franco. It's no place for a naïf. Especially one who, in headline terms, is more use as a dead hero than a live volunteer.'

All at once he put down his wine. He seemed to be mastering a surge of anger that had caught him, as it caught me, by surprise. I had never seen emotion get the better of Harding.

'Fuck it!'

I was, frankly, shocked.

'There are more important things for him to do,' he went on more cooly.

He was silent for a moment or two. I could think of nothing to say. Then he looked back at me, perfectly composed. 'I hope you don't have to follow him to Spain but, if you do, I will see to it that you are not out of pocket. Whether you manage to bring him back or not. But you will do it?'

I sipped the wine. After a while, I nodded to Harding. Rather to my own surprise, it seemed that I would do it. Victor opened the door wide.

'Dr Kennet, sir.'

I realised I had never seen her outside her dim rooms in Norham Gardens. I had only ever seen her dressed for tutorials, which meant cardigans and sensible skirts and blouses that brushed her chin. On that day I was amazed by the disappearance of almost all trace of the North Oxford don. She wore a seemingly simple dress, though I realise now, with a little more experience of these things to guide me, that it had probably been made in Paris. It did not brush her chin. It had the quality of appearing to dance lightly about her slim frame as she moved. Her hair had been disciplined. Silver and red coral shone at the lobes of her ears and on a delicate chain around her neck. I think I could hear my own pulse as she walked in.

She had been to some more formal lunch, had slipped away early to join us and seemed to be in a spirited mood. She declined wine, having reached already what she said was her absolute limit of two glasses.

'It's so very good to see you, Dr Kennet,' I said.

'Julia,' she said.

Over the coffee, I found myself recounting the tale of Alicia's midnight adventure and my introduction to the picture of history as painted by Nesta Webster.

'It is the architecture that leads them into temptation,' she said. 'It's having back stairs and servants' passages to move about in and not be seen.'

'Would modernism in architecture make them moral?' I asked.

'It might, but they will never take to it,' said Harding. 'Isn't it part of the international Jewish conspiracy?'

'If Mrs Webster's thesis is barmy,' said Julia, 'it is not because she thinks that history is shaped by men conspiring. Any political party is an assortment of mutually hostile conspiracies temporarily huddled together to gain advantage over other conspiracies even more hostile.'

'An equally good definition of the senior common room,' said

Harding. 'And an especially good definition of left-wing parties in Spain.'

We left Harding's rooms and walked to the High.

'Where are you going now,' she asked.

'Chasing Morton to Spain, it seems.'

'I meant right now.'

'I thought I had time for a stroll before I catch my train.'

There had been no plan for a stroll before I found myself in her company.

'You might stroll with me up to Norham Gardens,' she said with a laugh. 'Will that afford enough nostalgia?'

'More than,' I said.

We arrived at the familiar house, skulking behind its two chestnuts.

'Would you care for, oh, I don't know . . . ' she looked at her watch. 'Tea, I suppose.'

The room basked in its usual gloom. In fact, more than usual, as the reading light was not on.

'There's a little kitchen through there.' She pointed to a door that I had always assumed belonged to a cupboard rather than a room. 'See what you can find in there. And give me a moment or two.' Left alone, I discovered that the kitchen was, indeed, little more than a cupboard equipped with a sink, a gas ring and a few shelves. The shelves were almost entirely bare. Three cups hung on hooks. There was a teapot and a tin caddy that turned out to contain a small quantity of Earl Grey tea. I heard her come back into the room behind me. I stepped out of the little cupboard-kitchen. She was removing her earrings with small, exquisitely feminine movements of her fingers on the little silver screws. She put them down beside the pen on her table and shook out her hair.

'There's a little Earl Grey,' I said. 'That's about all.'

'Then what would you prefer?' I must have looked puzzled. She smiled and touched my cheek. 'To make tea for me or to make love to me?'

I was as startled and immobile as she knew I would be.

'The first kiss is interestingly difficult, isn't it? But I think you would like to. And I should like it. If I am wrong there is always tea.'

She took my hand, placed it on her breast and drew me backwards with her, until she was half-sitting amid the books on her reading desk. You'd have to be suspicious of any man who could have managed eloquence. Still, I might have done better than, 'Oh God, Dr Kennet . . . '

She laughed and kissed me. It was a kiss different from any other in my, admittedly – and by modern standards, laughably – limited experience. It was a declaration of intent and consent and it didn't take any expertise at all to recognise it. Finally she drew her lips away.

'Oh, I think there is also a bottle of wine. Not very good, I'm afraid. Somebody brought it . . . '

'Julia, Julia. You don't know how . . . How long I have wanted just to touch you.'

'You think not?'

'Did you? Did you know?'

'You must think me very stupid.' She traced my face from chin to brow with the tip of her finger. 'But it would never have been right when you were *in statu pupilarii*. It is all right now, though. I hope you agree.'

'Except, of course, that you have a husband. Who might, I dare say, arrive at any time. And, quite rightly, set about me with a horse-whip.'

'Oh, he never comes here. I only use these rooms for teaching.'

'Does that make it all right?'

'Yes, bless him. We get on perfectly well. But we don't do . . . this.'

She underlined her meaning.

'Why are you married?'

'Because we are compatible and companionable and we respect each other. What more is required?'

'This?'

She removed my tie and then began to undo all my shirt buttons, starting at the top.

'Oh, but imagine. It would come down to every Sunday and Wednesday. Endless repetition. Dreadful idea. We are happily married because we accommodate each other's whims.'

'And your husband's whim is . . . '

'Chastity.'

'How unusual.'

'Not as unusual as you might think. In fact, his corner of the common room is quite close to being an atheist monastery.'

It was not unusual in those days for a heterosexual recent graduate to be unsure as to whether he still counted as a virgin or not. If there had been some confusion, then very soon – just as soon, in one sense, as you might expect – the question was settled leaving no room for doubt.

Afterwards we once again sat – only this time naked – in the glow of the softly hissing gas-fire and sipped wine. It was an uninspiring Côtes du Rhône, but there are circumstances that make almost any wine taste well.

'This had better not be just the once,' I said, 'or I am going to be the saddest man in the world.'

'Do you think you can cope with a secret affair?' she laughed. 'It must be very demanding. And I would have to insist on a high order of secrecy.'

'You mustn't mock me. I am hopelessly in love with you.'

'I'm not mocking,' she said. 'But it would have to be like that. That's just a given.'

'I don't know whether I'd be any good at a secret affair. I've not really had any practice.'

'It usually comes quite naturally to people.'

'Is that a shockingly cynical thing to say? I'm not sure. It makes you sound cynical.'

'Oh, the dreariest people are leading secret lives. Almost everybody, I dare say. If they weren't, what they have would be hardly bearable.'

'What a bleak idea.'

'How many people would admit to their daydreams without embarassment?'

'Oh, if one counts daydreams as life . . . '

'It is the life of the imagination. What is more important? Ask any genius.'

I leaned to kiss her breast.

'I don't know any to ask. I do know that – in certain respects – I will no longer be content with the life of the imagination.'

'You are showing signs of not being content at all.'

'Should I apologise?'

'Certainly not.'

It was a long and wine-stained kiss, a languidly urgent declaration of intent, until suddenly she broke off and her lips were brushing my ear.

'I wonder if we can find something new for your unconfessable daydreams. I wonder.'

She was right about daydreams.

The vine-stitched hillsides of the Rhône went speeding by under the rolling plume of smoke and steam. As I looked out, drowsing, at what were presumably the low hills of the Côte d'Or, I was seeing the hollow of Julia's astonishingly white throat, the whiteness of her blue-veined breasts. It wasn't the rhythm of the train I was hearing, but other, rhythmic, ecstatic sounds that had been new to me and at least as alarming as they had been stimulating. Julia had been right. I could not have owned up to this daydream. Not to Alicia, anyway, sitting opposite me at the time, sipping coffee from her slightly swaying cup. I wondered, briefly, what it was she was thinking about as she, too, stared out at France.

We had kept up an acquaintance and I knew that she was then living in Paris, with hopes of becoming an art-dealer, earning a little besides with sketches of the latest fashions for the English press. Her real plan, I think, was simply to enjoy living in Paris. As I was going to have to cross the city to change trains, it seemed a good idea to meet.

In fact, it was pretty much the only idea I had. After all, I could do no more than repeat myself to Morton, even if I could find him. On the other hand, Alicia, unusual and – as I well knew – resourceful

Alicia, the girl with 'something about her', might connect with Morton in a way that was open to nobody else in the world.

We lunched at her favourite fish-restaurant where aproned waiters set before us a not-so-miniature glacier covered in fruits de mer.

'You know that he went out and got stone-drunk the day he saw the announcement of your engagement?'

She shook her head.

'He did. He treated me to champagne the day you broke it off, too.'

'He wrote me a sweet little note on the first of those occasions. He didn't write on the second.'

'He wouldn't, would he?'

'I suppose not.'

'Not a thing a gent could possibly do, my dear. But you could write to him, now. And tell him he's being a chump.'

'That's not fair,' she said sharply. 'And it's not right.'

'No, but perhaps it's what you ought to tell him.'

'That wouldn't do anything.'

'It might, coming from you.'

'No. It's what heroes are supposed to do. Leave weeping women behind them. It's part of the test.'

'Yes, but you could at least make him pass it.'

'Why bother? He is the stuff that heroes are made of. Everybody's always known that. And he's not a chump. I think he's profoundly moral.'

'Yes, so do I. But you can be profoundly moral and still do the wrong thing.'

'Why is it the wrong thing?'

'It's the wrong thing the way rushing into a blazing house is usually the wrong thing. There comes a time when the right thing is to think about saving the houses next door. And that time has come, since the fire brigade was not bold enough to turn out.'

'You mean Baldwin and the government?'

'They stood back. They will live to regret it but what can a few volunteers do?'

'Are they so few?'

'A few hundred? A few thousand? Heroes, yes. Will they alter the outcome? No. If the Republic can't save itself without them, it won't save itself with them. However bravely they spill their blood.'

There was a momentary void in our conversation, as if she had suddenly lost interest.

'Did he really drink himself silly?'

'Right into the scuppers.'

'Then why has he never . . . ?'

'The night of Nesta. He has never recovered from the embarrassment.'

'Embarrassment, phooey. It was all a hoot, looking back.'

'Not when Morton looks back. It's still an outrage. It just somehow tore all the rest of the pages from your book.'

'Well it's stupid of him.' There was a hint of angry emphasis in her voice. 'As if it mattered. As if it had anything to do with . . . Anything. Anything about us, anyway. Not that we had even, as it were, got as far as being an 'us'. But always, after that, whenever we met, it was as if he were trying to go by on the other side of the street. Did he really get drunk?' I didn't think it was necessary to repeat the information. 'Oh, let him go and get his head blown off, if he must. Let him. Serve him right.'

There was a silence. She set about a crustacean's limb with the surgical tools provided.

'What are you going to do?' she asked at last.

'Go down to Perpignan. Then Spain, if I have to. Try to catch up with him.'

'And?'

'Well, if I find him before he's signed up, try to talk him out of it. If he already has, then, try even harder, I suppose. What else can I do?'

'But if you couldn't talk him out of it in London . . . '

'Maybe following him to Spain adds a level of conviction that sitting in a pub in London doesn't.'

'What time is your train?'

'Eight-thirty, Gare de Lyon.'

'Well that gives me time to pack. I'm coming with you.'

Unusual and resourceful, as I say. And I had thought it might take me the whole afternoon to persuade her.

In Perpignan we booked into a hotel, where I left Alicia to take a leisurely soak. After two days on trains it might have been top of my list, too, but not for as long as the cafés and bars were open. You are supposed to know the politics of the clientele from the name of a French bar but the code did not mean much to me as I went around peering into one after another – Cafés of the Republic, of the Sport, Cafés of the owner's name, even a Café of the Universe that was possibly the smallest of the lot. Then I found the Café de la Paix. I am told that Cafés of the Peace usually date from the peace that concluded the Franco-Prussian War, so I may or may not have been cracking the code in thinking there was a left-wing ring to it. All the same, I wasn't wrong about the clientele. The elbows on the zinc bar were all wrapped in the universal blue of French working men, while the table-tops were inlaid with chequered squares. Two games of chess were in progress, the players seemingly oblivious of the noise. The Café de la Paix united the proletarian and the intellectual. It was probably what I was looking for. The chess players may have been oblivious of the noise but they noticed the silence that fell, as if by a stage direction, the moment I entered.

There are times when a stranger's best course is to follow the profession of strangeness. I tipped my hat to the company.

'Bonsoir, madame. Bonsoir, messieurs,' I said cheerfully, in a language bearing almost no resemblance to that spoken by the French. The silence walked with me to the bar.

Madame turned an eye towards me without adjusting its expression in any way.

'A vin rouge, s'il vous plait,' was my order, still in the confident tones of the Home Counties.

The little balloon of red wine was put wordlessly before me.

'Cheers,' I said. The wine was meagre and sour but I smiled as I looked about the company at the tables. 'Any English?'

The silence was finally punctured. 'We shot all the bloody

English,' came a voice from the Valleys. There was amusement at several tables. 'So why don't you just pipe down?'

I walked to his table and held up my glass.

'Hello, Taffy. Iechyd da.'

I drank to his health. He lifted his own glass and sipped. I drew a chair to his table and held out my hand.

It turned out that there were two Englishmen there, after all, and they had not been shot. Not up to then, anyway, whatever might have become of them in time. To make it seem more like a music-hall joke somehow come to life, you could take your pick from my Taffy, a miner, the Scot beside him – a laid-off shipyard man – and an Irishman whose former occupation I never learned, as he communicated nothing but a morose hostility to what he obviously regarded as my extravagant Englishness.

None of these men could credibly have said they were in Perpignan for anything other than their real reason. On the other hand, they had to keep up a fiction, even if, in some cases, they were unsure what fiction they might offer if it were called for.

Most had begun their journeys with supposed weekend trips to Paris, trips that then could be made without a passport. By travelling on they had become legally dubious immigrants. Few will now remember the famous *fiches*, the little bits of paper bearing the details of every guest under the roof of every hotel and pension, that used to be collected nightly by policemen and absorbed, nightly, into the enormous intestines of French bureaucracy. These men without passports could not have stayed in hotels, even if they had had the money. They stayed in the houses of French trade unionists, Communists or expatriate Catalonians. An evening in the Café de la Paix did not seem especially clandestine and you might have deduced that the gendarmerie of Perpignan was turning a blind eye but, all the same, the volunteers did not announce their business with banners and bugles. All the likely candidates in the Café de la Paix had already volunteered and were waiting to begin the onward trip into Spain. It seems there is no kind of soldiering that does not involve kicking your heels and waiting for an order to move. They were not free with information, even when I had overcome their reluctance to talk at all.

'You can find out all you want by signing up,' said Taffy.

I decided on a little fiction.

'If I go into Spain, it will be with a pen, not a gun,' I said, 'and free to come and go as best I can. You need people to get the story out.'

'You a reporter?'

'A writer.'

It helped. But it didn't get me closer to finding Morton. It was clear that these men had not run into him. Nor had anyone at the other bars to which they directed me.

Back at the hotel, I reported the results, or lack of them, to Alicia.

'It seems the recruits stay here until there's something of a blob of them. Then they are taken up to the Pyrenees in lorries. These chaps are vague about the arrangements up there, but they do know that it's a back way in and a stiffish walk up and over. On the other side, it seems they go down to Figueras, probably, but it may be somewhere else, and start training. If you think all that's a bit hazy, ask would they be any better informed as raw recruits in a regular army. I think not.'

'And we don't know whether Morton has passed this way or not?'

'No.'

'So we may even be in the wrong town.'

'Perpignan was certainly in his mind.'

'You only spoke to the volunteers?'

'Yes.'

'Maybe it's the people behind the bar we should speak to?'

'I had enough trouble coaxing anything out of the chaps. And I doubt my French is good enough to get much out of the locals. But yours is.'

'Perhaps,' she said.

I thought of Madame's blank, sceptical, all-seeing gaze.

'We should speak with Madame de la Paix.'

The hotel's evening meal had not represented the splendours of French cuisine. The odds and ends of fromages blancs offered for its epilogue lay jaundiced and withered on the board. We waved them away. The waiter removed them with undiminished reverence like an imbecile altar-boy. A *digestif* at the Café de la Paix was in order.

Early-to-bed-and-early-to-rise is still a way of life in provincial France. In pre-war days, when electric light was just another thing, if a new thing, to be thrifty with, it was even earlier to bed.

When we reached the door of the café it was barred. A single light bulb still burned and we could see Madame behind her bar, swabbing and battening down for the night. I rattled a door which might have been made, aged and allowed to fall into its unpainted decay precisely for the purpose of being rattled. But Madame ignored the sound. I rattled again, she looked up, shook her head briefly and returned to her washing-up.

Alicia took it up. She pressed her face close to the glass and tapped, softly but insistently. Madame stared. Alicia kept up the soft tapping. At last, Madame put down the swab and came to the door, noisily exaggerating the trouble she had in undoing bolts and bars to open it.

The Parisian accent of Alicia's rapid and perfect French would probably have counted against her had it been entirely native, but there was another note in her voice that persuaded Madame to draw back the door and allow us in. It was a note meaningful among women, alarming to men, that announces confidences of the heart. Evolution might account for it but, all the same, I was impressed by Alicia's ability to summon it up at will.

We entered. Madame locked and barred the door again behind us. Alicia's French was much better than mine and much of what she had to say was spoken in low tones and unfinished sentences, or rather, sentences finished in the mind of Madame. Still, I can give a summary. It seems that Alicia and her lover had parted in circumstances that were unfortunate. A quarrel, such as lovers have. And now he had gone off marching to war. A Quixotic thing to do, terrible. She was afraid that he had made up his mind to this because of what had passed between them. She was even more afraid that he would be killed, that she would never see him alive again. It was imperative that she find him and see him before he crossed the mountains, to set things right before, perhaps, they were set for ever. Because she loved him so terribly and his last letter was tearing her heart. I believe there may have been the shadow, no more, of a hint that he might go to his death knowing nothing of the child she had conceived. Perhaps Madame, who must see so much, had seen him? Heard of him? He was a man one would not forget if one had seen him but once.

Madame shook her head, more in sorrow than denial. An Englishman? There had been no shortage of Englishmen. Madame was astonished that the English should be so Republican. It was contrary to everything that one was told. Tall and blond? Was that not as much as to say English? No, she did not remember names well. She remembered people by their habits, their preferences. Faces she remembered.

'Draw him,' I said to Alicia. 'Do one of your sketches.'

'I wonder if I can,' she said. 'Give me a pen, a pencil. Anything.'

I still have the sketch, the ink now brown and sere-looking, on the back of a little card that mentions that the *plat du jour* was lapin aux prunes. The deft caricature in a few bold lines astonishes me still. It was Morton.

Alicia turned the card round and slid it over the table. Madame adjusted her wire-rimmed glasses. She pursed her lips. A certain questioning light sprang into her eyes.

'Ah,' I said, 'since you last saw him, Morton has grown a moustache.'

'Pardon, madame,' said Alicia, taking back the picture. 'What kind of moustache?'

'Try Ronald Colman.'

She added a gesture of a moustache and returned the picture to Madame.

She looked at it and gave a short laugh. 'You have a talent, madame. It is Mr Palmer.' Parmeurre was the sound, with a throaty trill for an extra syllable. 'But he is not one of these volunteers. He is far from that. He is not going to war.' She laughed. 'I do not believe it.'

'You don't believe he is a *brigadista*,' I said, 'this Mr Palmer?'

'There are not many of his age, m'sieu.'

'His age? About?'

'Certainly he has passed the fifty mark.' With that she gave a quizzical look at Alicia. It was obvious that she did not rule out the idea of an older lover. In fact, something in her look suggested that she was not surprised.

Alicia gave a rueful smile. 'That is not my man, madame,' she said, pulling the little caricature back across the table.

Madame shrugged.

I turned the card and looked again at the features. 'You said you had a poor memory for names, madame. But you remember this man's name?'

'Of course. It is the name of a fine wine of Margaux, m'sieu. Chateau Palmer. Perhaps you know it?'

'Certainly, madame.'

'A famous wine,' Madame smiled, 'is an an aide to the memory, certainly.'

'Does he come to your café?'

She laughed. 'No, no. That would never happen. He stays at the *seigneurie* at Vissac. He is a guest of Monsieur le Comte. I believe he is here for the hunting.'

'You are acquainted with Monsieur le Comte, perhaps?'

'When I am not tied to this café, m'sieu, I go to my family house, in Vissac. It is a small house. The *seigneurie* is a great house. But the whole of Vissac knows who comes and goes. I have two brothers who are also great hunters.'

'Is it far, Vissac?'

'Not so far. An hour on the road.'

'Why do we want to know?' asked Alicia.

'The dear old Da – I have reason to know – is highly partial to a bottle of Château Palmer. Who can blame him? Often quite as good as Château Margaux, but classed a third growth, so . . . '

'Let's not discuss the wine now.'

'No. I think we should find out whether the family likeness is . . . '
I turned the little sketch on the table, ' . . . entirely coincidental.'

'Of course, it's him,' she said.

'Well, if Monsieur Palmer is the Da by any other name, he's not here by coincidence.'

We apologised to Madame for our intrusion, learned the where-abouts of Vissac, and left.

'Voilà, m'sieu, le château.' The *garagiste* had been obliging. A tall and stately Renault with a short and amiable driver were ours for the day, by the day, at a modest rate. Léon made a little conjuror's gesture as the Renault rounded the bend and the Château de Vissac was suddenly no longer hidden by the trees.

Château can be a misleading word. When it doesn't mean a castle, or a vineyard, it may signify a palace to rival Chatsworth or Blenheim, or simply an old house with a good few windows. Vissac was a *gentilhommière* nearer the latter class than the first, but it had some grandeur. It stood behind its iron gates and stone piers with the air of calm but ghostly self-satisfaction that marks the real thing among châteaux. I had Léon slow down. Almost all the shutters were closed and yet the house was occupied. A pair of motor cars stood almost out of sight on one flank. Faintly, I could hear the barking of a dog. A little farther on I had Léon stop.

'I'll admit to wishing,' I said to Alicia, 'that I had something more like a plan, right now.'

'If Mr Palmer turns out to be just that, and no more, we are wasting time we can't afford. We probably ought to be in Spain by now.'

'I know, but I've got it in my bones about Mr Palmer. Your sketch is too convincing.' I looked at the house. 'He's the Da, and he's here.'

'And his plan?'

'The last time I saw the Da and Morton in the same room, it went to the Da by a technical knockout. I caught a bit of a sucker punch myself, as it happens. The last but one time I saw them together, Morton was wrecking a badminton racquet on him. I'm just wondering whether it turns out to be best of three.'

'Why the Mr Palmer business? Why an alias?'

'That's the bit I like least. Do you want to go through with this?' I asked.

She twisted the wedding ring, bought that morning in Perpignan. 'In for a pound,' she said.

I squeezed her hand.

'Then let us pay a call on M'sieu le Comte.'

'Good-day, madame. I wonder if M'sieu le Comte is at home?'

'He is not at home to visitors, m'sieu.'

'I understand, madame. Then perhaps you would be so kind as to tell Mr Palmer that I am here to see him.'

There was a pause.

'Who shall I say has called?'

'Tell him it is Mr Léoville-Barton.'

'Kindly wait, m'sieu.'

She closed the door and left me with the terrace to call my own. It seemed to me that when a second-growth St Julien called on a third-growth Margaux, somebody would be pretty well obliged to come to the door, if only out of curiosity. But it was only the house-keeper, if that's what she was, who returned.

'Please enter, m'sieu.'

So it seemed that someone had been at least curious enough. The entrance hall of the Château de Vissac had been painted all over in a pale green very like, in tone and dullness, the green of mouldy cheese. At least a century had passed since the paint had left the brush. A tracery of dark lines that had once been gilded still gleamed a recollection of their former brightness here and there. There were portraits on the walls, and on the floor an enormous pile of firewood and a felling axe.

The housekeeper led the way through one room and into another where the furniture looked comfortable, old and well used. The only object suggestive of the twentieth century was a gramophone. Madame made a gesture that seemed to offer me the room on a take-it-or-leave-it basis and then retreated. There was nothing especially disconcerting in her behaviour. It was the sound of the key turning in the lock that was unsettling.

When the inner door of the room was opened, there was no mistaking the man who entered for anybody but the Comte de Vissac. An English toff spends much of his life dressed for mucking out the stables, even though other people actually do it, and Etonians used to cultivate a slovenliness all their own, but these ideas have never crossed the channel. The bearing of a French aristocrat will always remind you that there is such a thing in life as best handwriting.

From his expression, it seemed that I had reminded Monsieur le Comte that there was such a thing as illegible scrawl.

'And you are Monsieur Léoville-Barton?' he said, with more than a hint of scepticism.

I laughed with as much innocent good cheer as I could manage.

'Of course not, monsieur. Forgive my sense of humour.' I gave him my name. 'My wife and Monsieur Palmer are old acquaintances. As a matter of fact, it was at Keryate that we met, you know.'

The Comte de Vissac looked at me as he might have looked at an imbecile.

'It is kind of you to honour me by calling, but might I ask why?'

'Of course. It occurred to me, when I learned that Mr Palmer was your guest here, that his son might not be so very far away. All things considered. He's a good friend of mine, you see, and, as a matter of fact, I am his executor. And do you know . . . it is a responsibility that has begun to weigh on my mind.'

There was a change in the temperature of his gaze. I was perhaps no longer quite the idiot I had been.

The inner door, that Monsieur le Comte had not quite closed behind him, was pushed open and Mr Palmer revealed himself. That is to say, Sir Edwin Drew-Page entered. A few years had passed since he had flung the poker aside and left my college rooms. I could not help a glance at his hands to make sure that he had not just recently picked up another.

'It's James, isn't it? One of the White Feather Johnnies.'

'I believe they were in the air the last time we met, Sir Edwin.'

'I'm not sure why you're here, or how you came to be, Mr James, but I think you're making a fool of yourself.'

'I'm here on a very simple errand, Sir Edwin. I imagine it is much like yours. To stop Morton from going to Spain.'

The two men looked at me in a silence that admitted their surprise.

'And how were you going to go about it?' asked Sir Edwin, at last.

'By persuasion, I hoped.'

'Fat chance.'

'And you?'

'By more positive methods.'

Sir Edwin seemed pleased by what must have been the visible response on my face.

'And did you succeed?'

The comte held up a finger and moved it from side to side like the finger of a metronome.

Sir Edwin smiled. 'It would be a discourtesy to our host to carry on this discussion of ours, Mr James.'

'But now that you are here,' said the comte, 'you must certainly stay.'

'Kind of you, but my wife is waiting in the car. And the driver is engaged to . . . '

'Your driver is on the way back to Perpignan, monsieur. With his account settled.'

For a moment, I felt as if I weren't breathing the right kind of air. Then I heard steps in the adjoining room and the sound of the lock turning. The housekeeper opened the door behind me and ushered in Alicia, who had no reason to do other than keep up the pretence of a social call. So I did as much and introduced her to le Comte de Vissac.

'Bonjour, m'sieu. Sir Edwin, hello! It's been rather a long time.'

It was a strangely cheerful note to strike in the circumstances. Nothing had prepared Sir Edwin for meeting a woman he had not seen since the night she had made off with his dressing-gown and a copy of Nesta Webster. It showed. But his recovery, to give him his due, was magnificent.

'Good God. And how do you do, my dear. I hadn't heard you had married.'

'We are still on honeymoon really. It's more or less the same thing when you elope.'

The comte declared himself charmed by this news and turned to the housekeeper. 'Agathe, a room for Mr and Mrs James. And we are two more at table.'

'A room will not be necessary, m'sieu. We did not plan to stay.'

The comte smiled.

'Nor had I foreseen it, m'sieu. But, until certain affairs are resolved, I insist. You must be my guests.'

'Better, then, that we get down to business. You might begin by telling me where Morton is.'

The comte looked at Sir Edwin.

'You say you came here to talk him out of it. Why?'

'I'm one of the White Feather Johnnies, remember? Why should I find somebody else's republic more of a persuader than king and country?'

'Then it's something of a distasteful irony to find scum like you in my corner, Mr James.'

'Your distaste is no greater than my own, Sir Edwin.'

'But then,' said Alicia, 'history has a way of making strange bed-fellows. Don't you agree?'

There was a moment of catalepsy for Sir Edwin. And then he decided to laugh. A little too much, a little too genially.

'Or not, as the case may be, my dear.'

'Quite.'

'So where,' I asked, 'is he?'

Sir Edwin turned back to me. 'You seem to have been clever enough to work it out. He's here, of course.'

He and the comte looked at each other. There was a barely imperceptible nod of agreement between them.

'Come with me,' said the comte.

He led us through the house to a staircase that spiralled broadly up a tower. From the staircase he led us along corridors that owed their gloom to the fact that every window was shuttered. He tapped at a door, received no reply, opened it and paused.

'I hope he will be pleased to see you. And I very much hope that he will return to England with you.'

We stepped into a small but comfortably appointed sitting-room with modern furniture. The comte crossed the room and tapped at an inner door.

'You have visitors, m'sieu. Mr and Mrs James are here to see you.'

The comte smiled at us and left. The sound of his footsteps had receded completely along the corridor and, distinctly, down the stone steps of the broad tower, before the inner door opened. Morton stood astonished.

'Alicia and I were just passing, old chap,' I said.

'Do you mean to tell me you two are married?'

It was clear that this idea was at least as dismaying as anything else that had happened to him lately.

'Only for the day, Morton. A married couple paying a visit is so much harder to brush off.'

'And much less likely to get coshed,' added Alicia.

Morton was still too dumbfounded to smile, but soon enough he told us his tale.

'We walked into it like innocents, Verdon. I suppose it's just what we were. It was on the train down from Paris, I fell in with a couple of chaps. A Danish fellow and an Englishman. It got to be pretty obvious that we were all three heading for Spain the same way for the same reason. We got on rather well, I'm glad to say. Would have been a bad sign if we hadn't, after all. Then, about Nîmes, a French chap joined us. Seemed just sociable at first. Then he said he knew perfectly well where we were bound and asked if we were *au fait* with the arrangements in Perpignan and onwards from there. Which, of course, we weren't. None of us knew the first thing. So he said, righty ho, he'd put us right, because it wasn't quite as straightforward as we might have thought. He was part of the organisation, you see. And he'd been up in Paris and knew that the French government was going to move against recruitment on

French soil and, oh, all sorts of things. We swallowed the lot, I'm afraid. And when we got off the train we were simply led by the nose. We were taken to separate houses. And I didn't see the other two again. I was brought up here. I honestly thought it was all part of the . . . part of the business. And then my father walked in. Which was a bit of a curious turn for things to take. I should think you can work it out from there.'

'Are they holding the other two as hostages?'

'It was their misfortune to bump into me on the train. That's all they did wrong.'

'Spell out the threat for me.'

'Well, I'm perfectly free to carry on to Spain. Just that, if I do, the other two are as good as dead.'

'Your father isn't really saying he'll shoot them, or something, is he?'

'He doesn't have to be that crude. He and Monsieur le Comte and a lot more like them have contacts with the Falange and the Condor lot. They'll be taken over the Pyrenees. Probably thinking they're on the way to a Republican brigade. The other side, they'll just be picked up. Maybe they'll be called prisoners. Maybe spies. They may or may not end up dead in a ditch the same day. What chance would you give them?'

'Wouldn't be attractive odds.'

'I can't go forward. I can't go back. If I do agree to chuck it I certainly can't be sure – whatever they say – that these fellows won't just be taken over the hills and slung into the bag anyway. In fact I believe that's just what will happen.'

'It is strange,' said Alicia, suddenly. 'It is so strange.'

We both looked at her.

'You can march off to a war, which is to say that you are ready to go and kill as many as it takes. But when it's a matter of one or two particular people you met on a train, you just stop in your tracks.'

There was pain, impatience and surprise in Morton's voice. 'It's an entirely different thing.'

'How different?' she said.

'I would be sending them in cold blood . . . '

'As you would if you were ordering them to attack a machine gun or something.'

' . . . in cold blood, to their deaths, when nothing could possibly be gained by it.'

'Something would be gained by it.'

'What?'

'You would get to Spain to fight for the Republic. Which was your objective, surely? Those two chaps would be unfortunate casualties in your first skirmish. You were ambushed, after all.'

'I can't believe that you are talking like this.'

'Really, Morton? I'm only mentioning what is obvious. War involves arranging for people to die. I imagine that the people who do it best are the ones who can best stomach that simple truth. There is even a chance they'd be treated as prisoners. In your shoes, Napoleon would not have paused for breath.'

'I'm not under any delusions about being Napoleon. I set out to be a volunteer, that's all.'

'For reasons that may have been more to do with you than with Spain.'

'There is no shortage of reasons. And enough of them are good ones.'

'But not good enough to send two chaps you don't know to their deaths in cold blood?'

There was a silence before Morton spoke.

'Of course I can't do that.'

'Lives go in the balance in war, Morton. If you think you are allowed to weigh just your own, you're asking for quite a privilege, it seems to me.'

After a while, Morton smiled a small, resigned, rueful smile. He closed his eyes.

'If you're going to make a soldier, Morton, go back and make yourself the best soldier you know how to be. Don't go into this war or any war as an amateur.'

'And looking at the business in hand,' I said, 'if amateurs are to go to Spain, two would be better than one.'

There was a long silence. Then Morton opened his eyes. 'The other two, you mean?'

'Unless Alicia can lecture them out of it, too. But I shouldn't think that's on the cards.'

'I turn back, the other two go on?'

'Via the correct pass, that is.'

'And why are they . . . ' Morton tossed his head towards the door, 'going to keep their word?'

'Because we can now send an observer,' I said. Though I can't say I was wholly enthusiastic about what I meant.

The Da had, after all, got what he wanted, but then, so had I. So had Harding. There wasn't going to be a Drew-Page hero fighting under the Red Flag in Spain. Morton was already, perhaps, on the north-bound train out of Perpignan with Alicia, who had also got what she wanted. But then, I had pretty well put my whole stake on the idea that it is more or less impossible to argue with a clever woman who knows what she wants.

I had staked something else, too. Morton's feelings for Alicia were no mystery to me and I was now even more sure of hers for him. It was short odds, then, on their entering into the holy estate that Alicia and I had just spent a little time mimicking, if incompletely. I remembered Morton's face, and his voice, when we walked in on him as Mr and Mrs. How often, in the years to come, would he want to be reminded of that cheap but golden ring on her finger? Perhaps these things would mean less now than then, but I knew that for the sake of friendship I had thrown something from the heart of that friendship into the kitty. And would lose it.

Opposite me in the back of the corrugated van, as we bounced and swung southward up into the mountains, sat the blond Danish volunteer and a dark thin fellow in his twenties from the north of England. They had spent two days in a farmhouse and were altogether ignorant of what had passed concerning them. They had taken all that waiting and knowing nothing as, more or less, what they had expected. One was older, one younger than me, and each believed he was on the way to playing a man's part in history. Yet, as I looked at them, both seemed boys and I felt inexplicably old.

The driver of the van was a man I thought I recognised from among the blue overalled clientele at the Café de la Paix. The man beside him, who was to guide us up the mountain was a complete, and completely silent, stranger. Had Monsieur le Comte double-crossed us, it was still possible that somebody was up there in the pass, waiting to make sure that we were to play no further part in history, boys or not. Dealing with M'sieu le Comte and the Da, it had seemed unlikely that they would have a hand in my murder. We had struck a bargain after all. And I had left too many markers. It had all seemed good and sufficient in the drawing-room at Vissac. In the back of the truck as the rain began to rattle on the roof, it seemed less convincing. The possibility of fascist *chasseurs* behind Pyrenean rocks seemed convincingly stronger with every climbing turn of the road.

I was glad, therefore, that there had been time to sit in M'sieu le Comte's charming little library and write a letter to another clever woman, hard to argue with. Doing my best to write as much between the lines as possible, and erring too much on the side of flippancy for obvious reasons, I let her know that, for me at least, love and secrecy did not make bedfellows. I was just despairing of the first attempt, when Morton came in and sat down on a chair near the writing-desk. He didn't speak immediately. I laid down the pen and waited.

'She's one hell of a girl.'

'She is.'

'I'd better marry her quick. Before you capitalise on being the first to have slipped a ring on her finger.' He gave me half of a laugh and half of an odd sort of look.

'A *ruse de guerre*, old man. Nothing more. Absolutely nothing more.'

He gave me the second half of the laugh. 'Yes, I know. But it was rather a moment for me, you understand. When you walked in as the blissful newlyweds. You of all people.'

'Get each other back to England and tie the knot, Morton.'

'Yes,' he said and then nodded for a while, as if he were taking in a debating point.

'People are going to say I funked it, I suppose.'

'What people?'

'People.'

'Did you put an announcement in the papers about where you were going?'

'Not exactly. But . . . '

'Who knew?'

'You.'

'And . . . ?'

'I wrote to my mother, of course.'

'Who obviously gossiped with your father. And . . . ?'

'Actually, that's about it, apart from Archie Griffith, of course.'

'Archie is . . . ?'

'The editor – well, the entire staff really – of a somewhat recherché journal called *Manifesto*. That may have an exclamation mark.'

'But not an enormous number of readers.'

'Well no. Not even in the CP. A lot of the comrades won't forget that he is a one-time anarcho-syndicalist. But then, as no two anarcho-syndicalists agree on what the words actually mean, what is there to object to?'

'Depends how many proletarian angels you think you can fit on a pinhead.'

'All the same, he's a bright chap. Well, bright for a Cambridge man. We have some good conversations.'

'And you talked about going to Spain . . . '

'Yes.'

'Who else, then?'

'Nobody. That's it. I didn't want to make a song and dance for reasons you understand.'

'Then who . . . ?'

'Who . . . ?'

I decided to shelve the thought. 'Then who's going to say you funked it, apart from Archie?'

Morton made a wry face.

'And he probably won't. Just before I left, he suddenly suggested I should stay and write for *Manifesto* instead.'

'I shouldn't do that. Avoid the stain of Anarcho-Syndicalism at all costs.'

'Quite.' He almost laughed. 'What about you? Quite sure about this going up the mountain business?'

'Wouldn't be doing it otherwise.'

'You trust them?'

'No. But I trust the fact that they have to honour the bargain. I'm going to give you a couple of letters to take back, in case it takes a day or two.'

'Then I should leave you to write them.'

He stood and offered me his hand.

'Thanks.'

After Morton left, I did not immediately pick up the pen but sat back and turned over the question I had shelved. I realised that Harding had never mentioned to me how he'd heard of Morton's decision. Lady Drew-Page seemed an unlikely source. Which left only the former anarcho-syndicalist editor of *Manifesto* – or possibly *Manifesto!*

The exclamation mark seemed to fit. It seemed an improbable connection.

And yet I felt sure that the connection existed. Word had come to Harding, from somebody, after all. If it was not directly from the apostle of world revolution, with or without an exclamation mark, then that implied an intermediary of whom I knew nothing. Was Harding's eagerness to dissuade Morton – to have me dissuade Morton, that is – entirely his own idea? Or somebody else's? The red editor, too, had change his tune at some point and joined the campaign of dissuasion. I had the sense, all at once, of having been caught up in rather more machinery than I had been aware of. It came to me with a sudden, displeasing, certainty that Julia's appearance at the end of my lunch with Harding – and all that followed – was connected with the same machinery. Perhaps Nesta Webster had infected my mind with notions of conspiracy and wheels within wheels. Or perhaps I was just waking up, a little late, to something about the way of the world and how people are used in it. I had woken up, too, to the difference between what I felt for Julia and the thing that drew Morton and Alicia so inevitably together. This, you understand, was not the detached observation of the psychological observer. It was only the private admission of how much I envied Morton, how much I admired Alicia. I threw the unfinished draft of my letter into the fire and wrote another. It was much shorter. There was no trace in this version of the infatuated lover or of any meanings between lines. I simply asked her to save me the trouble of writing to Harding by letting him know that I had done his bidding. It seemed the most economical way of letting them know that I assumed a complicity. It spared me the trouble of writing anything as clumsy as an accusation. In fact, it was a long time before I would have known quite what to accuse them of. That moment lay many years in the future. You will have understood it already. The expression 'Cambridge spies' being now a part of the language, it will have occurred to you that it would be surprising if there had been no Oxford spies and no machinery for recruiting them. Whether it reflects any credit on the older university that, in achieving rather less publicity, the Oxford spies were obviously rather better at the job is open to debate.

The road became a track. When that ran out, we walked. The man who led us spoke not a word. It was a long, lung-bursting climb at an unvaried, unrelenting pace through the rain. At last, we sat waiting for new guides in a pen of gathered stones on a shepherds' track looking down into Catalunya.

When they came, they were speaking Catalan, they shook hands and they didn't shoot us. The two lads shouldered their packs again and turned to me. They weren't sure what my role in the operation was, and at no time had they asked. As they stretched out their hands to me, the fact struck me as poignant.

'Thanks,' they said, one after the other, without quite knowing what it was they were thanking me for, as it must have been clear that I was no guide to the mountain tracks.

They turned and left the shelter, in the footsteps of the Catalunyans. I watched them go down the stony track and thought of what I'd said to Taffy in the Café de la Paix.

I had a pen with me after all. I thought about London and my pleasant but pointless existence. I thought about Julia, saw her propped up on an elbow, her dark hair falling on the pillow, her pale skin glowing against the crumpled sheets, looking at me obliquely with dark intelligent eyes. Even the smell of her came back to me, just as it had in the little library of the château when I sat watching my discarded letter to her burn in the grate. The memory became a sensation in my skin, of lying supine and soft-limbed, wanting only to be there. Wanting the passage of time to be cancelled. It wouldn't be love, but how would I resist? As my father would have said, 'If you can't be strong, you had better be somewhere else.'

The little party going down into Spain was not yet out of sight.

'Au revoir,' I said to the *montagnard* who had brought us up. 'Je descends par là.'

I followed them down into Catalunya.

The Resurrection of the Lord

It was one of those malicious November days in London when the rain blows right in your face, no matter which way you walk down the street, no matter what way the street faces. Having failed to engage a taxi, I arrived at my club, wet and chilled, to the sympathetic welcome of the porter easing me out of my coat. In discarding the dripping umbrella and curling hat, I discarded also the plans I had made for the day. Two new ones took their place: to put myself outside some hot steak and kidney and a pint of champagne and, later, to make myself comfortable in the library and write some long overdue letters.

The eating and drinking part of the scheme went through without any problem. Hugo Mainstone joined me, which was enjoyable because he is such a marvellous gossip, but I was glad that he had to go back to Whitehall because I wanted the rest of the afternoon to myself. There was an excellent fire in the library, which made it almost enjoyable to hear the rain lashing at the window. I settled myself with a sheaf of paper and uncapped my pen. Then the steward came in. Mr Hugh Vaughan had telephoned in the course of the morning. He had asked me to call him back at my earliest convenience. The steward hoped I had seen the message that he had left for me on the board.

I hadn't even looked. I didn't want messages. The steward apologised for drawing my attention to the matter but conveyed that when Mr Vaughan had telephoned he had laid stress on the anxiety with which he awaited my reply. I hope I am getting across something of the manner of address of the club's senior steward of those days. All the same, I thought about not replying. Hugh sought and consumed advice the way some men seek and consume strong drink or other gratifications. Giving him advice, which was what his friends did all the time, would have been a more satisfying pastime had he been more inclined to the taking of it. Hugh always found himself in a quandary over any matter large or small. Whenever opportunity knocked, as it did often because he was a lucky and likeable man, Hugh would consult everybody but himself. He would take great pains to get straight in his mind the various arguments for this or that course of action. Then he would do nothing. It was a good thing that he did not depend for his fortune on replying to opportunity when it knocked.

It was not an afternoon for giving advice. Now that I think to mention it, no afternoon is good for giving advice or for taking it. Four o'clock seems to be the sticky patch for the human brain. It's a good time for dozing or taking tea. The message told me that he was at Gwynant. I should have known better, but I called Hugh on the telephone.

'Verdon, it's extremely good of you to call.'

'Not at all, Hugh. It occurred to me that you might be looking for a word of guidance on some matter.'

The banter was lost on him.

'Could you possibly come down here. Now, I mean. Could you get on a train and come. Please.'

'You want me to come to Gwynant? Tonight? But Hugh, it takes for ever to get to Gwynant.'

'Please, Verdon. I know I'm imposing and I wouldn't ask you, but it is important. I simply do not know what to do. Please, Verdon. I'm sure you're the only man who can help . . . if not, I'm afraid I'm finished.'

'Good God, Hugh, what's happened?'

'I can't tell you. Not on the telephone, but it's rather serious, I'm afraid. It's about as serious as a thing can be. Please, Verdon. You're the only man I can turn to.'

'Hugh, the weather is appalling, I'm rather tired and Plas Gwynant is not at its most seductive in November. It really is out of the question.' Rain scourged the window with a sudden rattle of extra viciousness. I said nothing for a while. Hugh didn't, either. I could sense the echoing hall of Plas Gwynant.

'If you could give me some idea . . . '

'If you can't come to Gwynant, then I quite understand. I don't know yet what jail they'll put me in, but I'll let you know and you could perhaps come to see me there.'

I didn't say anything. Nor did Hugh. He didn't laugh. He didn't explain the joke.

'Hugh . . . Are you being serious? I believe you are.'

'Never more so, Verdon.'

'If you'll have somebody meet the next Holyhead boat train, Hugh, I'll be on it.'

'Thank you, Verdon. I'll meet you myself.' He laughed faintly and briefly. 'There's nobody else. There are no servants at the Plas any more. I'm the only living soul in the place.'

The porter's *Bradshaw* told me there was just time to finish the letter I was writing, pack a bag and take a cab to Euston. Within the hour I was watching the rain streak along darkening windows as the Holyhead train rattled me to Wales.

The estate of Gwynant lies between the mountains and the sea, inexhaustibly watered by a thousand streams coming down from the wilderness. Looking back from the slopes of Mynydd Goch on a summer's day, its woods and pastures and its hay meadows, billowy with flowers, fill your eye with a prospect of Eden. In the blue distance lie the salt marshes and the wide sands of a great estuary. The picture in my mind is now, perhaps, sepia-tinged, but I doubt if things have changed very much. I'm told that Gwynant is now one of the few places where you can still see a hay meadow with wildflowers. The house, Plas Gwynant, stands on a slight elevation. It might once have been an island, but the sea has long since been called away on other business.

On the Gwynant estate, in its great days, everything was of the estate. If a cottage was built, it was built of bricks fired on the estate, laid with lime that had been burned on the estate. It was roofed with slate from quarries that were the fount of the Gwynant fortune. The produce of the estate was once carried under sail to Liverpool and Bristol from the quays of Porth Gwynant, where today you will find pleasure yachts bobbing on the tide, or beam ended in the mud. Until not very long ago, whole families lived out their lives without ever travelling beyond his lordship's bounds and without ever eating a mouthful that had not been grown, raised, shot or hooked, netted or snared on his lordship's acres. Gwynant was a world apart, and the heir apparent to that world was my friend Hugh Vaughan.

I first got to know Gwynant when Hugh and I were undergraduates and I was sometimes a guest in the vacations. Plas Gwynant is an enormous jumble of grey stone. Many of the best or worst bits, according to your taste or sense of humour, were tricked up in Gothic by Humphrey Vaughan, the first Baron Gwynant of Gwynant. The second baron was Hugh's uncle, and the house had been Hugh's home since the age of eight. The entrance hall somewhat resembles the Great Hall of Westminster, on a not very much reduced scale. The first baron's object, apart from overawing his visitors, was to provide space for the display of his trophies, the pursuit of game being the consuming passion of his life. The inclination of the wealthy at that time was to travel the world with a gun, shipping back severed heads. An earlier generation, answering an urge that was not so very different, would have travelled to the Mediterranean with a tutor and sent back pictures and busts. Humphrey Vaughan, being a new aristocrat, followed the fashion of his day with the utmost enthusiasm. He studded his walls with the heads of every kind of animal a gentleman might shoot, each with the date and place of death recorded on a little tablet with the initials of the marksman. Considerable herds of okapi and gazelle from Africa occupied the lower regions. Lions and tigers ranged above them. Higher still were the antlered stags' heads, a colossal moose at the centre. From the hall, high passages led to other chambers and every step of the way you had the company of bestial heads, the trophies, mostly, of more recent Vaughans. At a turn in the westerly passage, the visitor was apt to be startled by the first victim of all this carnage to be preserved in his entirety. A brown bear stood in the corner, hugging a portion of tree trunk and staring with a blistering eye at the door of the billiard room. In that room, as in most rooms of the house, there were smaller and less terrifying examples of the taxidermist's skill. Walls bristled with the masks of foxes and badgers and otters. Somewhere about the house, under glass, in some imposture of its wild surroundings, you'd have found an example of every kind of bird and small mammal to be met with in these islands. Most of these preservations were convincingly morbid but certain of them were vivid and persuasive. In the library was a tableau presenting a hen harrier descending on a stuffed brown hen alarmed for her stuffed little amber chicks, all watched by a quick little stoat. It was in bizarre taste, perhaps, but remarkable work. Among the taxidermists who had served the hall, at least one had ranked as something of an artist.

Tanat Evans of Coed y Bwlch was the man with the special gift and he and I were acquainted. The day I met him, Hugh was engaged with some family business or other in Chester and I had gone up to the Llyn to shoot, with Tanat's son Emyr for a guide and companion. A sudden turn in the weather had driven us down the mountain through mist and sleet. Emyr was impervious to rain as to cold. His pace was never hurried but his foot never slipped or took a wrong step and so our descent was rapid. Left to myself, I might have died of exposure. As it was, I was very glad to see the smoke curling from his father's chimney.

Old Tanat evicted his cat from the fireside chair in my favour and set the black kettle on its hook over the coals and poked up a little blaze. His son stretched his hands towards the fire and called it cheerful, which was as close to an admission of human frailty as I ever knew him to come. Gamekeepers are obliged to be suspicious of their fellow men and on pretty bad terms with nature. They set traps and lay poisons. They display by their gates the strange gibbets of dead crows and hawks that are the sign of their trade. As a result, both neighbours and nature are inclined to be suspicious of gamekeepers and so they are not the most talkative of breeds. Having two generations of them together does not make them any more garrulous. The best way to get to know men like Tanat is to spend a long time not saying very much to them. Emyr left us after our pot of tea to make his rounds. Tanat and I stayed on either side of the fire.

When the kettle burbled again he made another pot of tea, and I remembered that in the pocket of my coat, that hung dripping in the kitchen, was a flask of whisky. We fortified our cups and as the afternoon settled to an early gloom, so we settled finally into easy talk. The outlines of Tanat's life were simple and clear. He had been born on the estate at Sarn y Bryn. He had been schooled on the estate at Ysgol Gwynant. He had been a gamekeeper on the estate all his life thereafter, starting in the time of the Old Lord Gwynant, by which, of course, he meant the first baron who had covered so much wall with trophies. So far as his age and accumulation of small infirmities would allow, he still helped his son in his old line of work. He was at pains to tell me that his cottage and the comforts he enjoyed were everything a man of his age could wish for. All in all, he seemed as perfectly contented as the cat curled up by the fender. While we were talking of the past he got up and went to his scullery, promising to show me something. He came back with an earthenware bottle, taking dust off it with his sleeve.

'I wonder if this will interest you, Mr James.'

He laid the bottle in my hand, without any suggestion of opening it. I turned it in the firelight and made out the words embossed in a disc on the rough surface. 'Gwynant' was spelled out in an arc, and curved underneath, 'Gaudeamus'. In the centre of the label was the date 1891.

'Brewed for some special occasion?' I asked.

'Indeed, it was. For the arrival of a son and heir to Gwynant, Mr James. Celebration ale, it was. Enough was brewed for every man, woman and child on the estate to drink a health. To wet the baby's head as they say. It was a great holiday. Lord Gwynant, you see, had a first wife that could not conceive. He was above the age of fifty before his second wife gave him a son.'

'This would have been Hugh's father's cousin, David?'

'A boy of marvellous promise, Mr James. I took him up by the Llyn many times, where Emyr has been taking you today. I would say I taught him to shoot, but in truth it was little teaching he needed. If I said he was a man when he was still a boy, would you understand me?'

I looked at the top of the bottle. The stopper was still wired, grimy and stained with rust.

'Did you not . . . wet the baby's head?'

'Very well, indeed. But my sisters and brothers-in-law were tee-total and what was their share, well, I had it. I don't know why, but I had a sentiment to keep a few bottles and not to open them.'

In the glow of the fire, the cat stretched himself, licked a paw to draw across his ear, licked it a second time but seemed to forget what he was about and curled up again to sleep the luxurious sleep of fireside cats for centuries past.

I looked at the old bottle. 'Do you suppose it would be drinkable, after more than forty years?'

'I do not suppose so. But it was drinkable after twenty-one years. I opened a bottle then. Miraculous, it seemed. That was in 1912 at the coming of age, Mr James. There was a celebration. A holiday if you like! The school was closed and all the children brought to the house to sing for the family. And sat down after to the biggest feast they ever had seen. Sweet wine, as well, they had, which was not approved of by everybody, but that was his lordship's whim and I don't see there was harm done. There were races and sports and prizes of money – all the sportsmen of the country were up for competing. A man would run very hard for a chance of ten shillings in those days. Great sports, indeed. A fat ox was roasted at Ty Newydd for David Vaughan at his coming of age and it was not three years before we saw him buried. They brought him back from France and it was said at first his wounds were not too bad, but he died in London in a grand house, I believe, that was turned into a hospital for officers. He had been at a ball, once, in the same house and died in the room where the dancing had been. The body was brought here on a day that was like today and buried at St Mary's on another that was the same. Wicked wet. I opened one of those bottles after the funeral. A sip of it was all I had but it was as good as any beer I ever tasted. A sip was all I took. The rest I poured on the ground, up by the Llyn, where you have been today with Emyr. The year after, the younger brother, Philip, was killed also, but there was no body brought home to bury. And no bottle from his christening to open, of course, but there you are, the first born-must have that privilege.'

He picked the bottle back out of my hand and returned it to his scullery.

The rain had stopped, and as Emyr had sent word to the house, a trap was sent to take me back. As we drew up the road to Plas Gwynant on its little promontory, the house was no more than a bulky shadow against the last effort of light in the western sky.

At dinner, Lord Gwynant turned to me. 'You went up to the Llyn? Not the day for it.'

'It wasn't,' I said. 'I had a good soaking and no sport at all.'

'Surprised Emyr took you up at all. He sniffs the weather pretty well, usually.'

'I may have been difficult to dissuade. We came down pretty smartly, all the same, and dried out at his father's cottage.'

'Old Tanat. How is he keeping?'

'Pretty well as far as I could see. But I doubt if he's given to complaining much.'

'No. The old sort, Tanat Evans. No complaining.' He raised his glass to his lips. 'Good health to him.'

Lord Gwynant's own health, cruelly enough, was about to collapse. He had two years left to live and those two years were pitiful.

Had it lain in his power, the title and the estate would have been willed to Hugh but that did not lie in his power. They passed to Hugh's father but whatever his uncle could exclude from the inheritance, he did. As much as possible of the cash, with unchallengeable control of the quarries, was left in Hugh's hands and not his father's. Anyone to whom the name of Humphrey Vaughan was familiar would have known why.

Humphrey Vaughan was not among the mourners at the funeral, a lapse that was more or less excusable, for in those days it took the better part of three weeks to get home from his part of Africa. The day before his liner was due to dock, Hugh called on me. 'I have to go down to meet him, Verdon, I know. But I'd like to have company. Your company if you could spare the time.'

'You've seen him, what, twice in twenty years, Hugh? Things have surely changed.'

'Yes. I'm not afraid of him any more. I shouldn't think I'll like him any better.'

'He may have changed. He may be more pitiable now.'

'He may be more contemptible, Verdon. He lives off some unsavoury speculations out there – his women among them. They're not a very agreeable crowd he mixes with.'

'He's not the worst of them, Hugh.'

'No, he doesn't run to the superlative, not even in that.'

'Don't bother with hating him.'

'He killed my mother, Verdon.'

'Her death was an accident, Hugh.'

'Her death was his fault.'

'But an accident.'

'And he was glad to be rid of her.'

'Well . . . when he went to Africa and you went to your uncle, Hugh, you were also glad to be rid of him.'

'Yes, I was. I hate to think what a wretched bloody specimen I'd have been, otherwise. Come with me. Get us both through it, Verdon.'

We met him at Southampton. Nowadays, the aeroplane conveniently annihilates distance. Ocean liners did not. They used to bring it with them. Humphrey Vaughan peered at the drizzling sky with the eyes of a man who had come a long way.

'Bloody country. Always bloody raining.'

I saw Hugh suppress a retort, as if the remark offended him, though it seemed only banter to me.

'I thought you African chaps were always tickled pink to see drizzle and green grass again, Lord Gwynant.'

He smiled, more or less.

'Suppose we'd better be. Going to see plenty in Wales.'

He and Hugh shook hands. It would have been a brief greeting, but Humphrey Vaughan clamped his son's hand for an extra second or two while he looked over his features.

'Your mother's son, no mistake,' he said, letting Hugh's hand drop. Hugh drove and kept up his silence. I kept up a kind of conversation. The new Lord Gwynant sat in the back of the car occasionally taking a silver flask from the pocket of his coat and drawing privately on its contents. People who'd disembarked from an ocean voyage had a certain smell about them. Part of it was the distinctive bouquet of shipboard laundry mixed with the camphor of long-stored clothes and the leathery musk of suitcases and cabin trunks, all mixed with the one smell made up of a hundred smells, starting with paint and ending with rust, that attaches itself to everything aboard a ship. Part of it was more primal. People who have not lived among us smell different. Neither a woman's scent nor a man's bay rum, with or without other alcohol, can disguise it. The different Lines disembarked passengers bearing subtly different smells. A blind man would have had no difficulty distinguishing between a P & O man just back from India and a passenger of the Cunard Line just ashore from New York. Lord Gwynant smelled of Union Castle, brandy and Africa. I thought it might take more than a few score head of okapi and gazelle on his walls to make him feel at home.

The scene of his arrival at Gwynant a few days later was described to me in a letter from Hugh.

You know that we had a blazing row in London the evening after we fetched him from S'hampton. We had another on the train. Not quite as spectacular but embarrassing all the same, and either great fun or a great inconvenience to fellow diners *en route* to Holyhead. He was fairly drunk by the time we arrived but I'll be fair and say he was not incapable. I realise that since he arrived on these shores I've not seen him when he wasn't drunk but have never seen him incapable. He had drunk enough when we had the business meeting with the trustees, etc., in London, but he didn't miss much. He certainly didn't miss the fact that Uncle David had put something of a ditch between him and most of the cash that didn't go in death duties. Hence blazing row. Row on train rather more of a personal thing, at least on the surface, but by the time we arrived you will be in no doubt as to the state of relations. Imagine, then. A beautiful day and Porth Gwynant *en fête*. Bunting and flags in the street. All the jubilee stuff out again and children from Ysgol Gwynant waiting to present flowers and sing songs. I'm only glad that Jarman fetched us from the station by car and not – as I believe he'd planned – in the landau. I swear the tenantry would have unshafted the horses and pulled the pair of us the last mile to the house. He was better than boorish, to be fair once again, but not much better. The whole thing embarrassed me no end and I was glad when it was over. Not that it was over before Stephens presented the household people. He had them lined up in the hall, starched and scrubbed and dropping curtsies. Lord G. simply turns to me and says, 'Where does the money come from to pay these buggers?' This was not a good start. He is extremely agitated about the money. The trouble is that you can't come to a reasonable agreement with the man. He knows that the estate will need money. He knows that I have it and that I am willing to come to an arrangement, but the very idea of an arrangement sticks in his throat. So he seems to have decided he'd rather slit his throat than learn to swallow. I tell him that the money will be there for anything that is a proper expenditure on the estate. He explodes at this and says I will only spend money that's going to come back to me. That I'm only waiting for him to die. That sort of thing. The worst of it is that there has to be some truth in the charge, but I swear to you, Verdon, it's not just self-interest. If he could get his hands on the money, I believe he'd be off to Africa where it would buy him the life of Reilly. Mind you, I think by now he's pretty much *non grata* even in the Dark Continent. He has, of course, gone through all of his own and all of my mother's money and, obviously, he has debts, but he refuses to be candid about them. If we could come to an agreement, I might be able to pay them off. Would this be wise? He complains that Gwynant does not offer the sort of company he likes to keep. I think this has something to do with fornication, and Gwynant, as you may imagine, is not quite Africa in this regard, so he wants the use of the Chelsea flat. I explained that you have a five-year lease that's absolutely unbreakable, so he doesn't care for you, either. I'll find a flat somewhere, but don't worry, you shan't have him for a neighbour. Better this than have him run up hotel bills that I'm bound to have to pay in the end. It is reasonable that he should have some kind of *pied-à-terre* and some kind of social life, I suppose, though it's bound to be awkward. I'm preparing for another tussle. Best thing would be if he'd only go back to Africa and some sort of allowance could be made. Would I be the first son to send his father out a remittance man? You probably know the answer to that. Never mind, though, because I don't think he'll go. He'd rather be back there, all things being equal, but from what I gather they aren't as equal as all that. There's a husband who's promised to shoot him and one or two others ready to take more orthodox (and legal) steps should he show his face. I will see you before the thirteenth. Will you be at Tommy S's? I hope so.

I wrote back and offered to terminate the lease. The reply was a telegram. 'Your generous offer gratefully declined.'

Hugh met me from the Holyhead train that November night, striding along the platform with his face turned away from the stinging rain. He grasped my arm and clasped my hand with an urgent strength that said more than any words could have done. 'Foul night,' was as much as he said. We faced an hour's drive by night through the mountains. The roads were running torrents in places and quantities of rock sluiced down by the water were a frequent obstacle. Though I knew him to be a skilful driver, I thought that Hugh was driving rather too fast in the circumstances and wasn't inclined to distract him with conversation. For his part, he said nothing until we pulled up on the gravel at Plas Gwynant. He switched off the engine and sat back in his seat, turning to me. 'Thank you for coming, Verdon. I really do need your advice. The problem is, you see, I've killed my father.'

The passage led to the billiard-room that I had associated, until that evening anyway, with the hum of after-dinner chat and laughter and fine Havana smoke. Now, the room Hugh led me into was dark and shuttered and the tapping of our footsteps rang a little in the emptiness. Hugh turned on the light and it was starkly clear why he was in need of advice.

Humphrey Vaughan, the third Baron Gwynant, was stretched out dead on his own billiard-table. You might have said that he was lying in state except that he was wearing pyjamas with a Norfolk jacket. The waxy pallor rather suited his features and it occurred to me that we should arrange for someone to make a death mask. He had been dead long enough for the rigor to have passed and when I turned his head under the light it moved easily, but the weight of it caught the hand by surprise.

'How long?' I asked.

'This morning. About nine o'clock.'

The skin was broken and bloody on the left temple. No degree of medical expertise was required to see that his neck was broken.

'And how?'

'He fell from the turn in the stairs.'

'That's not quite a whole tale, Hugh.'

'We fought and I hit him. He was lashing me with a poker at the time.'

'What did you hit him with?'

'Nothing. My hand. But I caught him when he was off his balance – swiping out with the poker, you see – and he went over. Over the banister. On to the stairs. Went to the bottom and he was . . . ' Hugh gestured hopelessly at the corpse.

To a reasonably tidy mind it was clear that the events of the day fell into one of three categories: murder, manslaughter or accident. Any decision between the three was the business of the police and the coroner.

'Hugh, why have you called me? You should have called a doctor, the police and a solicitor in that order.'

I know. Yes. But it's the estate, you see. It's the estate.'

Leaving Lord Gwynant to silence and darkness on his billiard-table, I took Hugh to a small study, lit a fire and descended to the cellar. At most times of anxiety, my advice is to indulge in some small pleasure. On the present occasion I found a bottle of Dow's 1920, decanted it and fetched it up to the study. 'I think the principle is pretty much the same as hot sweet tea, Hugh, but it's a good deal more agreeable.'

The first glass we sipped and drained in silence. With the second we returned to the only possible subject.

'Was it another row about money?'

'Of course.'

'Forgive me, Hugh, but was there a fault on both sides, here? Was it really quite impossible to come to an understanding and make an accommodation with him?'

'Yes. Impossible.'

We sipped port. I arranged another log on the fire.

'I said it was about money, Verdon, but it was about much more than money. It was about Gwynant. I think it was his fixed idea to destroy as much of it as he could before he died. My uncle was always a wealthy man; the great man in Gwynant, of course, but a man of some consequence beyond that. The trouble was my father thought he was the more gifted of the two – in some ways, he was – and he resented being the lesser man in the world. But damn it, Verdon, he could have been whatever he wanted to be and he chose to be what he was – and that was a lesser kind of man. In the end he thought life had short-changed him by giving him – far too late – an inheritance that he couldn't quite squander as he pleased. When he started selling things off he claimed he had to, because of the money business. But it wasn't that. It was the lesser man's revenge, Verdon. Undoing what better men have done.'

'Perhaps if your uncle had not taken so much trouble to keep things out of his hands, Hugh, it would have turned out differently. He might have risen in his own eyes.'

'It would have been a long shot, Verdon. Too much spite in him. You remember when he stepped off the gangway in Southampton, what he said to me? "Your mother's son, all right," or something on those lines.'

'I remember.'

'You know what he meant, I assume? He meant I was my

mother's son but not his. After so many years, Verdon, and that's the first thing he chose to say.'

'Is it true?'

'You must have heard it mentioned. It's not an especially dark secret.'

'I have, Hugh, but in my experience common knowledge often turns out to be a special form of widespread ignorance.'

'Well, it's true in this case. My mother loved him quite madly, I think. It made her wretched that she couldn't provide him with a child. He certainly made her wretched about it. In fact, he was a bastard to her about it. So much so that she ended up in somebody else's arms and was somewhat surprised by the result. Me.'

'Something of a surprise to him, too, one assumes.'

'It had simply not occurred to either of them that the problem might have been his.'

'They contemplated divorce?'

'I'm sure they did. The family talked them out of it. Just unthinkable. They were reconciled, more or less. Except that he never was. He couldn't reconcile himself to anything.'

Hugh looked at the spot of carmine left in the bottom of his glass and glowing in the firelight. I heard him laugh. It was the sort of laugh you hear from a chess player forced to recognise that he's been check-mated.

'Of course he has his way better dead than alive. Dying is his trump card, really.'

'I don't follow you, Hugh.'

'Death duties, Verdon. If he wanted to do as much damage as he could to the Gwynant estate then he's doing exactly the right thing by lying there dead. If the estate faces the levy again that's twice in two years. It will mean a lot of breaking up and selling. I inherit, of course, but if I'm about to be hanged – ' I waved the idea aside. 'No, listen, Verdon. If that were to happen, it would be three lots of death duties in as many years. The estate would be finished. Must I explain why I can't bear that idea?'

'No,' I said.

'Some of the tenants would be pleased to buy their farms, of course, but they would be a minority of the people who depend on this estate, Verdon. And it's not just that. It's something you either believe in or you don't. An estate like Gwynant, for good or ill, is a tiny nation. It has its habits and its customs and its loyalties. Dear God, Verdon, it has its dues and its obligations, its myths and legends and its own bloody laws. I found that he'd given notice to a whole raft of tenants. I was appalled. Two days ago, I arrived to find he'd had a blazing fit and sacked everybody in the house.'

'All at once?'

'He heard someone, the groom, I think, talking in Welsh to one of the other servants and sacked them. He can accept Swahili in Africa but not Welsh in Wales, it seems. Stephens interceded so he sacked Stephens. Mrs Bowen gave her notice in protest. He told her to get out of the house that instant. The rest of the servants went with her.'

'I wonder how long he would have lasted without servants?'

'He couldn't draw water for himself, Verdon. But he insisted he wouldn't take them back. Servants are ten a penny, he said. But he'd been living on what he could scrape out of the larder for two days because he didn't know how to hire somebody. He didn't know who to call and he was too arrogant to ask.'

'Do you think he was going mad, Hugh?'

'No. Just perverse. A madman doesn't see what's really going on. He did. The worse it was, the more he liked it. He wouldn't spend money on putting things right about the house and he wouldn't let me spend the money. There are places were the roof is pretty far gone. For want of a hundred pounds now, it'll be thousands in a few years. But he refused to have any work done. I told him the money was there. He refused it. He said I was waiting for him to die. I said he was absolutely right. There was a short discussion of the way I came into the world and he started laying into me with the poker. Does this sort of thing happen in a lot of families?'

'Just as many as you'd think. If the results aren't always fatal, it's mainly luck.'

Tears began to flow down Hugh's cheeks. After a while, he sighed and wiped his face with a hand.

'I'm not sure what you think I can do, Hugh.'

He looked up at me and though his cheeks were still damp with tears, there was no sign of weeping in his look.

'Oh, I've worked that out, Verdon. I have to die before him.'

I looked at him, and I suppose my expression was as blank as my mind.

'If I die before him, I won't inherit, so there'll be no duty to pay on my death, do you see? The title and the estate will go to my cousin Audley. He's only thirteen. There would be time, you see . . . time to recoup . . . And time for me to arrange things so that Gwynant can, with a bit of luck, go on being Gwynant.'

'Forgive me, Hugh, but the baron is already dead and you aren't. The order has rather been determined.'

'No, Verdon. Look. I killed him. If I were tried, they'd find me guilty . . . '

'That's not a foregone conclusion, Hugh . . . '

'I killed him. They would hang me. Now, what's the point of going through all that business. There's no need for the hangman, I'll do that part myself . . . '

'Hugh – '

'No, Verdon. Please listen. I will kill myself. I simply want you to arrange things with certificates and so on so that my death will come first.'

'Simply . . . ?'

'I'm sure you can do this sort of thing, Verdon. You know all sorts of people. I know you've arranged some . . . some tricky sorts of things for other people. I know you can do it. So much depends on it, and it seems such a small detail to arrange, really. Not that I'm making light of it, Verdon. I know that I'm asking rather a lot.'

I sat in silence for some time. When a man has gone a little out of his mind, you save yourself the trouble of reasoning with him. Not that Hugh had lost his reason entirely. His scheme may have been mad and a little fraudulent, but – seen strictly as a method of minimising the tax liabilities – it was quite logical. While logic is not everything, one had to think the thing out to its conclusion, all the same.

'Hugh, it would hardly be possible to get a doctor to fiddle the certificates. I really wouldn't know how to go about suggesting the idea.'

'Can't we keep doctors and all that sort of thing out of it?'

'Not easily. And not at all if you're thinking of doing away with yourself in the very near future. Having two corpses in the same house would certainly give rise to a stewards' inquiry. Who died before whom is a question that would invite the most attentive scrutiny. So I suggest you drop that plan.'

'Just . . . just tell me how we can do it, Verdon.'

'It needs a little thinking about, Hugh.'

The unheated billiard-room of a Welsh house in November provides pretty nearly the same conditions as a mortuary, so we had a little time for thinking. Hugh eventually fell asleep in the deep armchair. I covered him with a coat, took the port and a glass and went back to the billiard-room to commune with the man at what you might call the still centre of things.

Some may think it odd or unnatural or even, perhaps, perverted in some way to spend a few hours drinking port in the company of a corpse. I'm not going to recommend that you should do so whenever the opportunity might present itself but, all the same, I think you would find it not as disagreeable a way of passing the time as all that. It is not without its rewards. Mere squeamishness over the presence of a corpse is easily overcome. It is no more than a hardly defined superstitious *frisson* which thousands of very useful citizens have long since forgotten, or they would not be able to do their jobs. Beyond that, you will find that the company of the dead is extremely peaceful. For one thing they do not often interrupt the flow of your thoughts. They are not as entirely free from movement and sound as people are inclined to think, but generally they do not interrupt. Then, too, their presence puts everything into a clear perspective. That of course is not the presence of the dead but of death itself. The light of death is very like the light of the desert, which chisels things to a fine clarity and brings the far mountains very close, without diminishing the sense of space and distance. I have spent a little time in the desert and know why prophets retire into these places. At Gwynant I learned why St Jerome is always depicted with a skull on the desk of his study.

I think I mentioned that death rather suited Lord Gwynant's features. The skin had always been close to his bones, his eyes always deeply set. If anything, he was handsomer dead than alive by the addition of a certain grave authority that he had never had in life. The lines that an irascible temperament had etched seemed, now they were immobile, to have acquired the air of cold command. More than faintly, he reminded me of Bellini's doge, Leonardo Loredan. Ever since that night, in fact, that ruler of Venice has seemed to me to be unmistakably a Welshman. I walked around the table where he lay brightly illumined amid the encircling gloom and imagined him, not in pyjamas and Norfolk jacket, but in the damasked cope and silks of the doge. Then it occurred to me that the canopied lights of the billiard-table were probably rather warm, so I switched them off and left the room in darkness.

Returning to the study where I had left Hugh, I passed once again along the passage where the walls were studded with the heads of game. Electric lighting was still considered experimental at Plas Gwynant and had not been installed in all rooms, so these heads cast bizarre shadows that swung on the wall as I passed with the lamp in my hand. The shadows on the wall showed a gap where, by the regular pattern, there should have been the head of some quite large beast, its place still marked by the little wooden tablet that belonged to it. The inscription had been painted not long before and so was clear enough to read when I held up the lamp. A buffalo, shot in India ten years or so before, was missing from the herd. Something came back to me.

When I rejoined Hugh in the study, he had woken from his uncomfortable sleep and was pouring the last of the port.

'Hugh, where is the buffalo?'

'Where is what?'

'The buffalo. Out there in the passage there's a head missing. A buffalo. 'Where is it?'

'There was something wrong with it.'

'What was wrong with it?'

'They hadn't done a very good job or something. The people who stuffed it I mean. What the hell do you want to know for?'

'Bear with me. Where has it gone?'

'It's been sent to Tanat Evans to see if he can do anything with it.'

Tanat Evans. I was pleased to hear that he was still alive.

'Oh, he's still alive,' said Hugh. 'Still in the cottage at Coed y Bwlch.'

'And from what you say, he's still capable of work?'

'Hardly. He wasn't sure he could still manage to do anything. He's fit for his age but he's well over eighty. My uncle asked him to try what he could with the buffalo. I suppose he couldn't do much or he'd have brought it back by now. But never mind the buffalo, Verdon. Have you thought . . . ?'

'Yes, I've thought, Hugh. And I shall carry on thinking. Get some sleep. I will see you in the morning. But if you slit your throat in the night, I assure you I'll do nothing at all to alter the clock. So don't even consider it.'

The following morning we breakfasted on omelettes and tea. At last I thought it right to give Hugh an answer.

'I've thought over your idea, Hugh. I think something of the kind would be best and it ought to be arranged.'

He reached across the table and gripped my arm in gratitude. In return, I gripped his with force enough to carry my meaning.

'Understand, Hugh, that if we once begin we must go through to the end. If it can be done at all, it can't be done just by the two of us. Other people will have to play a part. I don't know who and I don't know how many, but they will put themselves at some risk. You are the man who must keep his nerve. If you start you must go through with it, whatever it takes.'

'Yes.'

'And you must be guided by me.'

'Yes.'

'Then there is no immediate hurry. We are going to have to prepare your father for his eventual disappearance.'

'Eventual?'

'I thought about this last night in a quiet moment or two with

146

him. It is obvious that he will have to disappear leaving no body to be found.'

'I suppose that is obvious, yes.'

'He won't be the first Welshman to disappear without trace from his country seat. Arthur Humphreys Owen of Glansevern walked out through the drawing-room window one night for a smoke and was never seen again.'

'Extraordinary things you know, Verdon. The name is familiar . . . '

'It might well be. Another chap from the same family disappeared just as abruptly – if rather more conclusively – a few years ago. He may also have decided to go outside for a smoke. He was over the English Channel in an airliner at the time. Whatever was in his mind, he opened the door and stepped outside.'

Hugh became very still for a moment then looked up at me with perfect calm. 'And you think that's what I should do?'

'No, Hugh, no. I mentioned that simply because it is of interest, that's all.'

He laid down his fork on his plate, wiped his lip with the napkin and put it beside his plate. The condemned man completed a fastidious breakfast, I thought.

'It strikes me as rather a good way to do it,' he said.

'But a waste, Hugh. Good God, we'll be at war in a year. There'll be no shortage of the means to die. Lots of people are going to be doing it. It would be much more fitting for you to wait for an occasion when it might do some good. It would better suit the interests of justice, surely.'

'Thank you for pointing that out, Verdon. Thank you.' It was a moment or two before he came to the implication. 'Can we wait that long? What do we do with Lord Gwynant?'

I walked down to the cottage at Coed y Bwlch after breakfast and found Tanat Evans in the little yard beside his cottage feeding his hens. He threw down the food with a trembling movement of his hand but I was glad to see that when he stopped to look at me, as I leaned over his gate, the hand that hovered over the meal in the bowl was calm and still.

'Good-morning, Mr Tanat Evans.'

He made no answer for a few moments, then walked cautiously towards the gate.

'My eyes are not so very good, sir. I'll have to look at you with my spectacles on, if you don't mind?'

'Not at all,' I said, 'though you're not missing very much if you don't.'

As he fetched the spectacles from his waistcoat pocket with one hand, the bowl of meal almost slipped from the other. The shower of corn caused a flutter of excitement among the hens. I hoped that Tanat was still up to playing his more than crucial role in my plan.

'If I'm not mistaken, it is Mr James. You are not seeking shelter this morning?'

'No, Evans, I am not. But I may be about to ask you a much greater favour than that. Do you know of a John Price of Newtown?'

'I know a John Price of Fechain and a John Price, Maengwyn, but I have never been to Newtown, Mr James.'

'This particular John Price has been dead a hundred and fifty years or so, Evans. A man that had three wives.'

'Oh! Price of Newtown that mummified the wives, the first and then the second, and had them in his house till he married the third. And she would not have them by her and had them buried like Christians.'

'You see, I thought with your interests you might know of him.'

He leaned on his gate and so did I and we talked a little more about John Price of Newtown who kept his mummified wives beside his bed.

The Welsh gentry, it must be said, had provided ample precedent for most parts of my plan.

While I was in conversation with Tanat, Hugh motored into Porth Gwynant where Stephens was in lodgings, waiting a reply from the agency that would find him another place. It was Hugh's job to tell him that he would not need to look for another place and that things had changed at the Plas. If Stephens was willing to return, his first job would be to find or send word to the other dismissed servants of the house and gather those of them willing to return. That, as things turned out, was not all of them. It was enough. On my walk back from Tanat Evans's cottage, I called into the little general store in Coed y Bwlch, where my eye was caught by a jar of marbles in the window. I bought a dozen, which I thought would be more than enough for my purpose.

It is not how things are done in murder cases. The murderer had declared himself at the outset. The little cast of dramatis personae called together in the drawing-room had, as yet, no notion that a murder had even taken place.

'You will have realised that a serious matter has arisen or you wouldn't be here. It is something that concerns the future of Gwynant. Before we talk about the future, Mr Hugh has something to say to you.'

Hugh stood before the fire. The words he needed were very simple ones, but he could not find them.

'Shall I . . . ?' I asked him.

After a moment he moved briskly to the door and opened it wide. 'Best, I think, to let everybody see for themselves.'

He led the way across the antlered hall and down the passage and past the study to the billiard room. I ushered the company out after him and brought up the rear. I thought someone might have gasped or cried out. No one did. They walked slowly around the table looking at the baron lying in the colourless wintry gloom. They seemed like tourists at a monumental tomb.

'You can see that my father is dead. I want you to know that I killed him,' said Hugh, standing at the cue rack.

I held the door open and the little band of sightseers completed its tour of the table and filed out again back to the drawing-room. It was my turn to speak.

'You are now all aware that Lord Gwynant is dead. The only people in the world so far aware of that fact are in this room. At some time or other, the world must be told but there are few or none whose happiness will be profoundly affected by the news. And none outside Gwynant whose prospects in life will be altered in any way.'

One of the most surprising things about people is how difficult it can be to surprise them. I might have been reading out the minutes of the last meeting of the local history society.

'On the other hand, the interests and the expectations of people in and near to this room are very closely touched by this development. My friend Hugh has put to me a certain proposal which he hopes is in the interests of the estate and everybody on it.'

I briefly summarised the liability – the cumulative liabilities – falling on the family under the ordinary provisions of estate tax. Clearly the implications were understood. I looked carefully at each face in turn and saw no note of doubt or incomprehension. What I saw was passive but intense anticipation.

'Mr Hugh points out to me that it will be greatly to the advantage of the estate if the date of registration of his own death precedes that of his father.'

At this a flicker of what Keats might have recognised as wild surmise was visible in the eyes of my listeners.

'Lord Gwynant died in the course of a struggle. A coroner's verdict would probably lead to a trial. A court might find Mr Hugh guilty of murder. I think that outcome not probable but it is certainly possible. Hugh knows that he ought to place his fate in the hands of twelve good men. He should stand trial and face the chance of being hanged. Were it not for the implications such an outcome would have for the estate, I'm sure you know that Mr Hugh would not hesitate to hand himself over to the authorities straight away. He has asked me to make it clear to you that he is not asking you to choose between your loyalty to those authorities and your loyalty to him. The choice is between the ordinary course of justice and the course of history. The history of Gwynant.

If you choose the ordinary course of justice, that may well entail the end of the history of Gwynant. That may not mean catastrophe. Who can tell? It may bring improvements we cannot imagine. We do not know who will buy what part of the estate, who will buy what farm, or wood, or moor, or who may buy this house should it be auctioned. You may take the view – I would be wrong to try to persuade you otherwise – that no law of nature says that it is right for a Vaughan and only a Vaughan of Gwynant to have the stewardship of these things. The fact that it has been so for a long time is not, of itself, much of an argument. To many minds that might be an argument for change. Mr Hugh's conduct and his uncle's conduct before him are the only persuasive arguments known to me that I can put before you. You know better – much better – than I do what those arguments are worth. You don't need me to turn them into words. What can I say to you? You will not find the reason for your choice in my words but in your own hearts when you consider the future of Gwynant. Remember, no one is asking you to choose whether Mr Hugh will die or not die. The choice is rather, shall he die now and, perhaps, Gwynant with him; or shall he die later and bequeath whatever he can of Gwynant to posterity? We shall be leaving it to Mr Hugh to find, as he feels he must, the occasion to atone with his own life for the life of his father.'

I looked about the room in silence, and all of them looked back at me, in silence. I saw Jarman, standing below a lamp, his hollow cheeks in deep shadow; Mrs Bowen seated on the Louis-Quatorze she had been almost superstitiously afraid to take her place on, and of which she was now entirely oblivious; Owen, the general man, whose nearly crimson features had paled almost to pink and whose habit of nervously clearing his throat had, for once, fallen into complete abeyance. Stephens, short, plump and composed, stood with his hands one upon the other on the back of a chair. He might have been waiting for a sign to bring in the soup. Sometimes they looked at me and sometimes at Hugh, but no one spoke.

'It would hardly be right to ask you to argue this matter out aloud with me or each other and certainly not with Mr Hugh. And yet, either we all agree on the one course, or it must be the other. If even one of us believes that it would be wrong to postpone justice, then Mr Hugh will call the police tonight. A public show of hands can hardly be the way to decide, but we must know whether we are unanimous, or not.'

I picked up a bag that I had put on the table in front of me. Under it on the inlaid pattern stood seven black chessmen. The bag was the sort of thing we used in those days to put shoes in when travelling. Nowadays, I use the plastic things one gets from supermarkets but in those days a shoe-bag was made of stout cotton with a drawstring. From my pocket I took a handful of marbles.

'There is a way for us all to state our decision in a secret ballot. I am putting in this bag a marble for each one of us in this room.' The seven marbles clicked into the bottom of the bag. From the table I took the seven black pawns. 'And with them, a pawn for each of us. I'm going to ask each of you to take from the bag one or the other, a pawn or a marble. If you feel that you can square it with your conscience to postpone justice, take out a pawn. You will feel the shape. Don't look at it and don't allow any of the rest of us to see what your choice is.'

I went round them one by one with the bag. One by one they took whichever they chose. I went back to the table where I had placed a large ashtray and with no ceremony at all emptied the bag. The glass marbles chattered and bounced on the crystal. Six of them. And one pawn.

When the sound of the marbles in the ashtray ceased the silence was profound. It was broken by the scraping of Hugh's chair.

'Thank you, all of you. It's good to have a decision. I have a telephone call to make.'

Hugh walked from the room and crossed to the study.

In the drawing-room no one moved. They seemed transfixed and it was hard to know how to bring their part in things to a close. Rather oddly, I heard myself saying, 'There is no further business to attend to, thank you all very much.'

Then Emyr walked forward from the back of the room to the table in front of me. He picked out the pawn and clenched it in his hand. Then he took the marble from his pocket and dropped it among the others.

'Don't tell him it was me, Mr James. But I wanted to know if he would.'

'No, Emyr, you've changed your mind, that's all. But the ballot was final.'

He hesitated, staring at the marbles.

'Emyr, he'll be very grateful to you. You have taken an enormous burden off his shoulders. It is by far the easier way for him.'

Emyr ran from the room. Through the open door of the study he could see Hugh at the telephone. I saw Emyr cross the hall in very few strides and put himself in front of Hugh. He opened his clenched fist to show him the pawn. I saw Hugh's face. Though it was turned only a little towards me, I could read it easily and I read dismay. A man who thought he had been excused a terrible duty had found himself in Gethsemane after all.

There were two objects, as I saw it, in preserving Lord Gwynant. The first was to avoid the dangers that attended immediate disposal of the corpse. A body buried may be dug up, a body discharged overboard from a small boat may be brought up in a trawl or washed ashore. Burning a body requires, as anyone who has been down to the Ganges at Benares will know, a good deal of fuel and a conspicuous blaze. The process makes itself conspicuous in other ways as well. This sort of thing is best not done in haste or while in a state of distress. The friends who arranged the cremation of the poet Shelley on an Italian beach thought the idea fitting and romantic before they put the torch to the kindling. Their accounts tell us that they regretted the notion shortly afterwards.

While we could hardly give Lord Gwynant a funeral with plumed horses, I had a deep objection, as did Hugh, to the idea of mere disposal. It would not have been right to abbreviate the obsequies to a secret indecency. In time, and after the reflection that time would allow, it would be for me to arrange the matter in some fit way. Until then he could have been kept as an embalmed corpse in his own cellar, awaiting a very private funeral at the right time. That, however, would not quite have met our needs.

The corollary of the fact that Lord Gwynant had to disappear was that it was necessary for him to appear, or be capable of appearing, until shortly before the date of his disappearance. Then the seven years would begin to run until the legal presumption of his death. This was the second object of his preservation. To remove all trace of Lord Gwynant immediately would entail a risk that the clock would begin to run too soon, should somebody begin to make enquiries about him. Lord Gwynant should be seen occasionally about the place. An unsociable man like Humphrey Vaughan was not necessarily seen about very frequently, but even a recluse or an invalid would be seen from time to time. His passing through the town in a motor car would be remarked now and again, at the very least. So, in addition to the simple business of preservation by embalming, a degree of taxidermy was also required so that the world might, occasionally, catch a glimpse of him, and see some lifelike flash of his old self.

I had explained what was necessary to Tanat Evans and suggested that I might help him as an extra pair of hands. To my vast relief, he declined my offer. Emyr would be his only assistant. It was a good thing that Plas Gwynant had been brought thoroughly up to date in respect of plumbing and running water, which was not always the case in country houses in the 1930s. I supplied them with formaldehyde and a number of scalpels. Horsehair, iron wire and other small necessities Tanat supplied from his own stock. They worked in the principal bathroom while Hugh and I waited, mostly in silence, in the drawing-room. It was the earliest in the day that I have ever pulled the stopper from the Scotch indoors, though I've enjoyed the stuff for breakfast when stalking deer. I had no idea at the start of the day how long the business might take and I hadn't asked. I imagined that, for all his experience with beasts and birds, even Tanat had no way of knowing.

When they came down to the drawing-room after their third day of work, it was long after dark and the lamps were lit. Each of them accepted a glass of whisky with a hand that was, I confess, steadier than mine.

'It is done,' said Tanat.

'I had no notion that it would take so long, Evans.'

'It would have been quicker but for the neck being broken, Mr James. That had to be put right, of course, and the wire I had thought to use, well, it wasn't strong enough. It is very heavy, the head, and the wire I was using was bending, but we got it right in the end.'

Hugh was looking pale and I took the trouble to refill his glass. 'We doubled and trebled the wire on itself, you see, and the advantage is the head is able to be adjusted a little. If you are ready, sir, to take a look? I hope you will think it all you were expecting.'

It was very much more.

They had adjusted the head with a pensive inclination, slightly sideways and drooping towards the collar bone. Tanat had been right about the glass eyes. Even with formaldehyde, he had insisted, the originals would seem unnatural. The pupils were the problem. They either open up entirely or close tight, I can't remember which. Getting hold of the glass eyes had presented a slight difficulty. A singleton is the usual order. The customer requiring a matching pair will be the subject of curiosity. I was obliged to impersonate the proprietor of a seaside waxworks when making out the order and there was some delay in filling it. Lord Gwynant had been obliged to wait several days in his wine cellar, wrapped in oil cloth and packed in ice.

Tanat had done well with the eyes. At one moment, while Hugh and I were pacing about the drawing-room, it had occurred to me to go up to the scene of the operation and say that he must on no account give Lord Gwynant the sort of glare that made such an impression on everyone who saw the brown bear opposite the billiard-room door. It was not difficult to resist the impulse to interrupt the two men but the possibility had troubled me again as we made our way to the bathroom. My fears had been groundless. I should not have forgotten that Tanat Evans was the Cellini of taxidermists. Lord Gwynant's expression turned out to be not at all like the bear's. Tanat had arranged him in the wheelchair that Hugh's uncle had used before him. His head was supported by his left hand, all but the index finger folded under his cheek bone. His gaze was deflected downwards, as if he were reading something on his knee, or perhaps reflecting on something he had just read there. There seemed a pregnant possibility that he would look up the moment he became aware that you were in the room.

I commented on the very natural composure of the muscles of the face and the convincing and recognisable expression they created. 'It was the setting of the expression that took the time, Mr James. Anybody could do the job and have him look half mad or stark terrified but it's not what you want.'

'No,' I said.

Both men stood back in silence to gaze at his lordship.

'It's the best you've ever done, Da. I'll say that,' said Emyr.

It was no special prescience of mine that saw war was around the corner. Anyone with common sense knew that and by 1938 there was enough common sense about for the government to start printing the ration-books. The ration-book business comes to mind because, of course, Lord Gwynant was issued with his ration-book in the course of time. If I remember rightly, some kind of emergency census was conducted soon after war broke out and Stephens quite naturally included Lord Gwynant among the inhabitants of Plas Gwynant. In due course, the ration-book arrived.

A meeting of the household, whom I now thought of as The Trustees, decided that the extra should be given from time to time to local families whose fathers were on active service or in the merchant marine. When even a smallholding, let alone an estate like Gwynant, could feed its people perfectly well, rationing or no, this could hardly have involved a very great sacrifice, not even had Lord Gwynant been blessed with a heartier appetite. All the same, in the harbour cottages of Porth Gwynant, it was a token very well received. Indeed, I believe it may have caused the first flicker of public affection for the new Lord Gwynant.

At the time, Hugh was in France with the Expeditionary Force.

Chapelle D'ou. May ?

VERDON, MY OLD FRIEND – Something of a brief lull here, not that I understand why. As far as I can see, there's no reason Jerry shouldn't just keep coming, roll us up and spit us out. I hope it doesn't mean that somebody, somewhere is talking about surrender. I'm giving this to someone who may get back sooner than I, though how this shambles can hope to be embarked, I can't see. Anyway, I hope this gets to you. Some of us are going to have to stay here, dig in and hold them up as long as we can. Ils ne passeront pas. Except that ils passeront, of course. No two ways about it. But we'll have done our bit. I very much hope that

I'll have done mine, and that you will think I've discharged my obligations.

This letter was written in the first hours of daylight and reached me on the evening of the same day. It was the day we pulled back two squadrons of fighters from the lost cause. The men they left on the ground had long days of a slogging match to bear. Many of them were at last embarked only to be blown out of the water. The Hurricanes were back at Biggin Hill in less than twenty minutes. The pilot of one of them had Hugh's letter tucked under his MaeWest. As we sat in the smoking-room at my club, the flight lieutenant was not in an especially ebullient mood. Not many people were, so there was no need to excuse the long silence into which the letter threw me. After a while my messenger drained the last of his whisky and looked around him.

'Dead-and-alive sort of hole. Why don't we go to a pub and get drunk?'

'You should get drunk, by all means,' I said, 'but I don't think you should get drunk with me.'

'Why not?'

'You should get drunk with people of your own sort.'

'What the hell does that mean, Verdon?'

'You should drink with heroes, I should drink with clerks.'

'Oh, come on, Verdon. You've pestered everybody to get into some kind of show. Everybody knows that.'

'And some of them say you can afford to be importunate when you know perfectly well you'll be turned down. Thanks for your trouble, Paddy, but I won't join you. And you'll have a better time if I don't.' I said goodbye to him on the steps of the club. When he was four months older, Paddy Synge was to be widely known as a member of that band of heroes with the shortest collective title in the history of human conflict. He would never be five months older. If I felt some foreshadowing of that as I watched him walk towards Piccadilly, it wasn't clairvoyance. It was how things were. I put Hugh's letter in an inside pocket and did what Paddy was going to do. I went to a pub and set myself steadily to the task of getting drunk, but I did it alone. Until the time came when I couldn't think straight at all, I thought about Hugh and about what I had to do at Gwynant. Except that I didn't have to do it. In front of me today is a copy of the citation for the award of the MC to Lieutenant Hugh Vaughan.

> Realising the imperative need for immediate action, and unable to communicate with his men or his commanding officer, Lieutenant Vaughan, with entire disregard for his own chances of survival, attacked the Panzer whose fire was preventing their withdrawal. Without any covering fire, Lieutenant Vaughan crossed fifty yards of open ground and killed the driver of the tank who was operating with his clear vision panel open. This was an exceptional feat of marksmanship. Climbing aboard the tank, Lieutenant Vaughan disabled it further with a grenade attack via a damaged engine ventilator. During this attack, Lieutenant Jones came under fire from a German position fifty yards away. His commanding officer, now relieved by Lieutenant Vaughan's action, was able to bring a machine gun to bear and suppress the enemy fire.
>
> The crew of the Panzer surrendered to Lieutenant Vaughan, but the prisoners were abandoned as Lieutenant Vaughan's company continued its withdrawal.

There were plenty of people who thought the award should have been the VC. Some observed that it probably would have been had Lieutenant Vaughan – now Captain Vaughan, of course – been available to be ballyhooed a bit in the cause of public morale. He was not available, of course. He had been taken prisoner later the same day, having stayed behind to cover the withdrawal of his company to an embarkation point. The Red Cross report said that he had received excellent treatment for his wounds and that he was recovering well. A footnote to the report said that Lieutenant Vaughan was much admired by his captors and was embarrassed to be the object of privileged treatment on this account.

When this report reached England, I was obliged to send a telegram to Stephens cancelling certain preparatory arrangements that

we had made that would have led, in their turn, to the cancelling of
Lord Gwynant's ration-book. It began to look as if Lord Gwynant
would be distributing his points and coupons to the needy for some
time. It was a long time before I received a letter from Hugh
through the Red Cross.

DEAR VERDON – I want to say how grateful I am that you agreed
to help me. Glad in a particular way that I didn't foresee. I hope
and believe that it justifies everything that we did. It's true, as you
said, that if we'd gone about it another way, there would have
been one less chap available to do his bit. But I don't make the
mistake of thinking my bit has been all that important. Hard to
have any such illusion in these times. The important thing that
I want you to understand is that, the other way, I'd never have
come to forgive the old man. Never have had a chance to,
perhaps. To understand all is to forgive all. You will recall which
particular Frenchman said that. I'm afraid I don't have any works
of reference to hand. Did he observe that you can also start by
forgiving and find that you then begin to understand? It's a more
practical way round, too. Not such a tall order. If you have to
start off understanding all, not much forgiving will get done. I'm
glad I was given the chance. Glad he was, too. I am acutely aware
that you are left in a potentially embarrassing position and it must
be time to unburden yourself of any obligation towards me.

Again, many thanks. Your friend,

HUGH VAUGHAN

I wrote back to him, via the Red Cross.

DEAR HUGH – It is good to hear that you are well and especially
good to know that you are on much better terms with your
father. It pleases me very much to hear that. I have had a
meeting with The Trustees and they have resolved – *nem. con.* –
to maintain the status quo. There are no developments that need
concern you. Your father's health continues much as ever, but he
was recently well enough to attend a concert in Porth Gwynant
in aid of the Spitfire Fund. Unfortunately he had to leave early

and was not able to address the company, but he gave every indication of enjoying the music. I have spoken to Stephens about this, wondering if these outings were altogether wise, but he assures me that they are not hazardous to his lordship and the community is always glad to see his lordship out and about. He is really quite a popular man down there now, as he gives his rations to people who might otherwise go very short. The needs of everybody at the Plas, of course, are met abundantly by the garden and the game alone. Not to mention the cellar. All is well. Try to keep your spirits up.

Ever yours,

VERDON

It was in 1943 that they made their escape from the camp. Out of a dozen, two were shot and seven recaptured inside twelve hours. Hugh and the two Australians, Robertson and McIntyre, reached Spain after weeks of extraordinary dangers and privations and with the help of many brave men and women. I could not do justice to that story. An account of it is to be found in Alan McIntyre's book, *Thorn in Their Side*. Robertson, of course, was lost when the ship bringing him from Portugal was torpedoed in the Western Approaches. McIntyre and Hugh reached England, collected their back pay and returned to soldiering.

He walked into the club in a captain's uniform so new it looked as if it might have stood up on its own.

'Fits me like a pair of curtains, I know,' he said, 'but by the time I get used to the pips, I intend to have put a bit of weight back on.'

'I'll buy you the best dinner in town just to get the ball rolling. What are you drinking?'

'Nothing. Just water. Had a touch of hepatitis some time back.'

He did not look remotely jaundiced. He was thin and his face was quite different. It was Hugh's face but pared and heavily engraved. I had expected him to be pale, because one thinks of prisoners as pale, but he was as weatherworn as a shepherd.

'You must get up to Gwynant if you want to fatten up. How much leave have they given you?'

'Nobody wants to see me for two weeks. And yes, I must get up to Gwynant.' His tone was negligent. It suggested that getting up to Gwynant might be a social duty he was in danger of overlooking.

There was about him an enveloping air of not belonging. Just as his body did not belong inside the crisp uniform, so the worn face was out of place among the sleek and comfortable furnishings and sleekly comfortable clubmen. The steady blue eyes that turned to me did not belong to the Hugh that I had known.

Here was the gaze of a man you might catch sight of through the window of a train, a man who has stopped at some place that happens not to be his destination.

'Sorry,' he said at last. 'I know we ought to talk about Gwynant.'

'Oh, you'll find things pretty much as they were. You got my letters?'

'Allowing for the censor's habit of taking out sentences at random, yes, I got them. Thank you. I didn't quite understand. My father seems to have recovered enough to go out to concerts. Is that right?'

'Not often, Hugh. On occasions when his position really demands it. *Noblesse oblige.* You understand.'

'No,' he said. 'Not sure I do.'

'Well, like you I was surprised and . . . alarmed to hear that he'd been out and about. But Stephens tells me his outings have been very carefully supervised. They try to spare him the trouble of having to be sociable and that sort of thing.'

'I hope they succeed.'

In my wallet I had a clipping from the *Cambrian Post and Echo.* 'Stephens sent me this. You might care to see it.'

MUSICAL FEAST AT PORTH GWYNANT

Music by Handel was among the splendid offerings at a Noson Lawen given at Porth Gwynant Grammar School by the Gwynant Choral Society last Saturday. The Society's patron, Lord Gwynant, who is confined to a wheelchair by ill-health resulting from his many years in Africa, attended the concert. Although his lordship was obliged to leave before the national anthem was played, he made it known that he was delighted by the proceedings and paid the Society the compliment of saying that their performance was 'up to the highest professional standards'. Commenting on the fact that the composer Handel was a German by birth, Mr Rhodri Evans pointed out that he had lived and worked in London and would surely have been pleased that his music was helping to raise money for the Spitfire Fund to defend the city he loved. George Handel is not the only German the Society has plans to enlist. Mozart, Bach and Beethoven will all be contributing to their concerts in the coming season, said Mr Evans.

'I gather from Stephens that Lord Gwynant not only left early, he also arrived a little late, but our reporter is too polite to mention it.'

'Why? I mean why did he go at all?'

'Because, Hugh, in these times it seems there's a limit to the number of patriotic events you can decline to attend.'

'But he's . . . extremely ill. Surely people understand?'

'Not too ill, some local people have said, to go taking motor trips using up precious rationed petrol. I'm afraid it was my idea that he should occasionally be seen abroad in the Daimler.'

'I still don't see . . . '

'I think they were right, Hugh. There are rumours, you know, that certain people in Wales are disaffected. It is said that German bombers have been guided in to their raids on Liverpool by radio transmissions from Wales.'

'Good God! There can't be any truth in it.'

'I dare say not, Hugh, but rumours are one part of our diet that isn't rationed. As I say, I suggested the motor outings, and it was also my idea that he should usually take these trips in the evening as darkness was beginning to fall. When the rumours about the radio signals began to circulate, somebody added to them by wondering where it was that his lordship went. They'd worked out that he didn't call on anybody. Somebody seems to have thought a Daimler would be big enough to conceal a radio as powerful as you like. A few people seem to have remembered that before he went to Africa, he had more than a little regard for the Nazis. It seems he once said that 'this country needs either Mosley or Mussolini in charge and I don't much mind which'.

'He certainly didn't say it at Gwynant. He was hardly ever there.'

'He was quoted in a national paper. They remember these things up in your misty hills.'

'You seem very well up on the gossip at Gwynant.'

'Stephens keeps me abreast. He also told me that his lordship decided to make it clear that he was right behind the war.'

'Stephens should do as you tell him, Verdon.'

'I can't always be available, Hugh. We should be very grateful to Stephens. He has a cool head. We should be very glad that he also has fallen arches and the services won't take him. Anyway, I don't think your father will be making too many trips in the future.'

He didn't say anything. For some time he looked at the far wall of the smoking-room with his man-on-a-train eyes, then suddenly he looked back at me and I saw for a moment the old Hugh. 'It wasn't supposed to go on this long.'

'Nobody ever said how long, Hugh.'

'It should have been a matter of hours. Minutes, even. That's all. A little adjustment. How did we get here? How did we come so far on this road?'

'By taking the first step along it, Hugh.'

'I can't remember why, any more. Well, I can remember, I just can't remember why it was important.'

'It was to preserve something, Hugh. And the reason for preserving things is just that: that the best of us will sometimes forget that they are worth preserving.'

He was silent for a while again, and the man-on-a-train look returned to his eyes.

'I can't go up to Gwynant, Verdon. I'm sorry, but I can't.'

'It will be expected, Hugh.'

'That's why I can't go. For one thing they'd treat me as a hero which is a degree of deception I can't altogether stoop to.'

'It wouldn't be a deception.'

'It would, Verdon. I'm not a hero and if you want proof I'm

giving it to you: I'm not going to Gwynant. I'm not going because I haven't got the stomach for it. I'm funking it. I wake up in the night with the sweats, screaming. I'm not going there. I know that I never will go there again.'

'Then let's not discuss it further. I'll tell you what, why don't we go to a play? Then we could meet some people for a little supper and go on.'

'Will we get tickets for anything good?'

'Oh yes. I can get tickets.'

'I suppose you know somebody?'

'As it happens.'

'I should have remembered. You know everybody.'

'I wouldn't say that. I seem to have bumped into some actors lately, that's all. Would you care for it? A play, I mean.'

'Well, a man who can't drink during the evening needs something to take his mind off it. A play sounds splendid.'

The play was entirely forgettable but we had a thoroughly good time clapping at the end of it. It had been enjoyable and Diana, especially, had been bright and winning, rather outshining the leads, I thought. As we made our way out of the theatre the conversation around us had the pleasant fizz that you hear when people feel they've had a jolly good night of it.

'What did you think of Diana Fanshawe?'

'Which one was she?'

'She played the younger sister. The one with the shocking secret.'

'Oh, I thought she was marvellous.'

'Good, because you're going to meet her. If you can't drink, you'd better be introduced to some other intoxicants.'

There was a crush backstage and I almost regretted bringing Hugh along. With his weather-beaten face and uniform, he seemed more out of place than ever. Perhaps, even worse, not out of place at all but very much an extra. A spear-carrier. In a welter of people taking an extraordinary amount of notice of each other, no one took much notice of Hugh, but of that I'm sure he was glad.

It wasn't until we had arranged ourselves at a pair of tables at the Lapin that any of the theatrical crowd really noticed him.

'I've got your rank, old chap, but I don't think anyone's given me your name and number. I'm Dorian Lisle.'

'Dear me,' said Hugh. 'So you are. I didn't realise the moustache wasn't real. Hugh Vaughan. I enjoyed the play very much.'

'As long as you were completely taken in by the moustache, dear boy, then my life and training have not been in vain. God bless you for your kind words.'

Dorian turned to the rest of the company while breaking a bread roll in an entirely absentminded way that had all the gravity of priestly ritual about it and spoke effortlessly above the chatter. 'Captain Vaughan is kind enough to tell me that he thinks my moustache is an absolute triumph. I shall certainly keep it.'

'The play may close but the moustache will run and run,' said somebody.

Dorian turned back to Hugh.

'Well, you know what we've been doing. What have you been up to Hugh, my dear?'

In his present state I was unsure how receptive Hugh might be to Dorian's bravura style of conversation. I need not have worried. I saw him smile for the first time in the day.

'Nothing nearly so entertaining, I'm afraid. In fact I've been doing remarkably little for the last two years.'

'I thought to look at you you might have been out in the desert.'

' 'Fraid not.'

'You've been doing something admirable or you wouldn't have that ribbon for me to admire. That's something rather gallant, isn't it?'

'Rather a long time ago and it's not nearly as convincing as your moustache. Let's not talk about it.'

I knew that Hugh would rather not have spoken about himself at all, and that he would certainly not want me to tell the company why he had been decorated. On the other hand, as the object of Dorian's interest he had become the object of everybody's interest.

'When Hugh says he hasn't done much for a couple of years, Dorian, he may be right. It depends whether you think escaping from a prisoner-of-war camp counts as much.'

It brought the attention of the pair of tables.

'Oh, well done,' said somebody.

'I know you. You're the chap I've read about. You were all over the papers,' said Hermione Street.

'Were they kind to you, darling? They've been beastly to me,' put in somebody, earning a modest bouquet of laughter.

'We are in the company of an authentic hero,' said Dorian Lisle. 'Now, as you know, I am shortly to play an authentic hero myself, so talk among yourselves while I hog Captain Vaughan and get some tips.'

I would not have believed that egocentricity could have been put to such tactful use, but I knew that Dorian had seen Hugh's discomfort and had eased him off the hook of attention. The actor turned to him and offered the bottle of wine.

'I've been told not to for a couple of years,' said Hugh.

'Wartime years count double,' said Dorian. 'When did they tell you that?'

'About a year ago.'

'Well there you are.'

'It was something of a joke at the time. Not much Chablis about.'

'This really is very good.'

Hugh smiled and pushed his glass forward.

It's not that actors are like children: actors are children. They are children who have that best of all costumes in the dressing-up box, a real grown-up body to play in. But the fact is, of course, that most of the grown-ups are really involved in make-believe all the time without recognising what they are doing. At least the actors know. It makes their company agreeable to me. That evening at the Lapin, I could see that it was agreeable to Hugh as well, and the more pleasurable because it was a novelty. He felt himself to be a bogus hero, so perhaps it was therapeutic to be in the company of men and women who were bogus heroes and heroines by profession. The food was better by far, but really we were at a children's party.

Except that the children had proper grown-up bodies to play in.

'What was it you dreamed of most frequently? When you were in your prisoner-of-war camp?'

We were drinking brandy by this time and people had got up and moved about the tables. Other people had joined us and one or two had left. There was an empty chair now between Hermione Street and Hugh, and she leaned with one arm along the back of it to ask him her question.

Hugh smiled back a little blankly, as if surprised to be spoken to. One glass of wine has its effect on a man who has drunk nothing for a year.

'What did you see in your dreams? Hearth and home? Family? Old friends? Green fields?'

'All of those.'

'What blameless dreams you heroes have.'

'No. All my dreams are nightmares.'

Hermione Street laughed and then inclined her head, widening her eyes. 'Do you mean that?'

He looked at her without saying anything.

'Did you not dream of lovers?'

'None to dream of.'

'I find that hard to believe.'

'Well it's true,' said Hugh.

'You must have loved somebody once. At least once.' She looked at him with disconcertingly open eyes. 'Was it a boy or a girl?' Hugh laughed a delighted laugh. From some – many – people the question might have been malicious. In that company and from Hermione Street it was entirely without sting. It was as if he were being asked whether he would prefer a blue party hat or a red one. Yet at the same time, it was a serious question. Finally he looked back straight into her direct blue gaze.

'I don't know. Perhaps I am a very late developer.'

'Perhaps nobody has completed your education,' she said.

With a little movement of her outstretched fingertips she touched the two pips on his shoulder. Her arm on the chairback between them was pale and shapely. It was the arm of an odalisque, or a Venus or a Bathsheba or some other woman whose business it was to be naked, and beckoning.

We went on to wherever – I really can't remember – and we

danced. I danced with Diana and Hugh danced with Diana for form's sake and with Hermione.

When, for form's sake, Hermione danced with somebody else, Hugh found me in a corner by the bar.

'What do I do, Verdon?'

'Ah. You are yourself again, Hugh.'

'I'm afraid I'm not, Verdon. Look, Hermione has – er . . . she's made it quite unequivocally clear that she – er . . . she wants to go to bed with me.'

'It may have taken her slightly longer to make it clear to you, Hugh, than to the rest of us. You are not mistaken.'

'For God's sake, Verdon!'

'Don't you like her? She is rather vain, but very good fun. And extremely beautiful. Oh, and she doesn't offer this privilege to just anybody. She must have taken to you very strongly.'

'But her husband, for God's sake.'

'Dorian, you mean?'

'He can't be . . . entirely unaware of . . . '

' . . . her inclinations? Of course not. But I doubt if there'll be any question of jealousy arising. Unless of course, you think he's fallen for you as well? That has happened. In that case they have a pact and neither of them would go for you. They do think the world of each other, you see.'

'Do I? Let's assume I do.'

'It's not such an unusual arrangement as all that, Hugh.'

'No. I suppose not.'

'Don't you want to go to bed with her?'

'Yes, I do. Very much. But then any man who'd just danced with her the way I have would give you the same answer to the same question. The question is, should I? What does it mean? Why does she want to go to bed with me?'

'I suppose her reasons are just as arbitrary as yours. Dance with her again and discuss it to music.'

'I don't want those things, Verdon.'

'What things?'

'Whatever people mean by falling in love.'

'I'm not sure that's necessarily involved, is it?'

'She said as much.'

'Well you probably mean something different by it from what Hermione means. She enjoys falling in love and is said to have a quite magical talent for it. I gather that it's one of the most exciting and bewildering things that can happen to a man. Being chosen as an object of adoration by Hermione, I mean. I've certainly seen one or two excited and bewildered men in her company.'

'Well, you're not about to see another. Make my apologies. Put it down to the hepatitis.'

'Shall I call you tomorrow?'

'Please. There are things we have to arrange, after all.'

He picked up my glass, drained what little was left in it and in a moment, quietly, had gone.

My job meant having to travel about the country with no obligation to disclose my business and I was, by now, a frequent traveller aboard cadge-as-cadge-can airlines. It made getting to Gwynant easier than it had been before the war, as long as the Anson didn't crash into the side of Snowdon. Several had, and they'd done it in the sort of weather we were flying through. I had felt sick and sad before we took off. I was now sick, sad and frightened. The machine was sometimes thrown upwards or downwards so abruptly, and so far, that I could hear and feel the air being sucked in or out of the cabin in noisy, wrenching gasps. Through the window I could see – just – one engine churning its way through the opaque world of black cloud.

I called up to the pilot. 'Do you know where we are?'

She pointed casually to an instrument on the panel in front of her. 'Piece of cake,' she said.

They really did say things like that. I sat back in my seat and tightened the strap. It passed through my mind that the non-chalance that all aircrew seemed to affect in those days was probably quite genuine. When the odds on dying sooner rather than later had come down as short as they had, the real worry was whether you were going to do it quickly or slowly. Flying into a mountain was probably as quick as you could get, so we were quids in.

The Anson broke cloud over the Menai Straits low enough to rattle the Marquess of Anglesey's windows at Plas Newydd. The prospect of religious conversion receded as I heard the undercarriage cranking down. I recognised in the distance, pewter bright under a fragment of clear sky between the storms, the wide sands of the estuary by Porth Gwynant. As I watched, and as the Anson's wing swung away, the light moved and the gleam that I knew to be Gwynant vanished again into darkness and distance and black rain.

I scrounged an Austin, but I scrounged one with windscreen wipers that didn't work and it was a long time before I found myself opening the gate at Plas Gwynant.

There was no longer anyone living in the lodge, but there was a pretence of habitation. Curtains had been left at the windows but the dilemma of whether they looked more convincing drawn or open had been resolved by compromise. They were half-drawn.

Stephens heard the Austin on the drive and had opened the door to me before I reached the steps. He was in shirtsleeves, but had not omitted the black band of mourning about his right arm.

'I've put you in Mr Hugh's room, sir, because it was the one room that was always kept aired and ready, but if you'd rather another . . . '

'No, that will suit me very well,' I said.

We met in the drawing-room again. Nothing had changed about the room, and not much among the people, save that Hugh was not there. We had known that we would meet again in this way. It was implicit in everything that we had said and done at that first meeting in that same room, but that fact did not make the heart any lighter. When everyone had taken a seat and Stephens had closed the door, I stood and looked around their faces. They were not expectant, curious or uncertain as they had been on the first occasion. They were composed and resigned, but not, despite the black bands, funereal. They were something more detached than that. It was as if they were waiting in court for some grave sentence to be pronounced on somebody or other.

I am not religious, but I recognise the need for these things.

'It will be right, I think, for us to begin with a prayer.'

I could feel that this was approved and together we called upon God, our help in ages past.

After the 'Amen' came a hush so deep it was as if the world had fallen mute, which in a way it had. The rain had stopped.

'I'm sure you'll want to know something about Hugh and how he met his end.'

'We have no doubt how he will have met his end,' said Emyr. 'With very great courage, I am sure.'

'That is quite certain,' I said. 'I meant that I thought you would like to know the circumstances.'

Heads nodded and eyes were turned towards me.

'I cannot speak directly about the operation in which Hugh lost his life, or tell you where it took place. I can tell you that we are going to win this war and before we do we are going to have to put armies ashore on the mainland of Europe. Doing that will be the most hazardous, the most difficult and the most important single effort of the struggle we are in. Knowing what we are going to meet when we reach those beaches will be crucial. Finding out what we shall meet, in the sort of detail that we need, can only be done by going there. It can only be done by men getting on to those beaches at night, in small boats or landed from submarines, to survey the nature and strength of the defences. Sometimes, intentionally or not, to test them. That is the sort of operation for which Hugh volunteered and in which he lost his life.'

Emyr was sitting with his gnarled hands clenched on the handle of his stick. He pushed his face hard against his knuckles and nodded slightly back and forth.

A little weak sunlight filtered through the tall windows and showed me something brighter in the eyes around the room: the gleam of tears held back. I did not tell them that the operation had been a rehearsal and that Hugh had been drowned when his boat was run down by a submarine. It was a period of confusion in darkness and a bad sea and just the sort of flaw in the plan that rehearsals are meant to uncover. The cost was four men dead in a boat capsized and pulled under the water. Four men for whom no immediate search was made. It was thought they were on their way to make a landing on the coast of Dorset. What if it was a rehearsal? What if it was Dorset? A month later it might have been Dieppe or Deauville.

'There is one great part of our business remaining. The matter of a final resting place for Lord Gwynant. This was left in my hands, as you know, and all the remaining parties with any interest in the matter are now in this room. All the parties with one exception, of course.'

They looked at me.

'That is Lord Gwynant. I assume he is still in the house?'

Stephens nodded a butler's assent.

'And his condition has not changed?'

'Changed?' asked Emyr.

'Changed in any way for the worse?' I asked. 'I know he could hardly change for the better, but has there been any change for the worse? Has his condition altered in any way that might make for difficulties in moving him?'

'His condition is entirely unaltered,' said Emyr. 'He has been very well looked after by Mr Stephens.'

There was a very slight note of indignation in Emyr's voice. I nodded apologetically to acknowledge that the question had been superfluous.

'It will be necessary for Lord Gwynant to make an appearance at least once more. After that, if I may sketch out his itinerary to you, he will leave Gwynant for London. His plan will be to stay in Mr Hugh's flat in Westminster where it is expected he will regain his health sufficiently to take occasional walks, especially when his chronic insomnia makes the nights tedious for him. Stephens and Mrs Bowen will be able to report the frequency of these bouts of insomnia, which developed during the latter years at Gwynant. From one of his nocturnal walks he will not return. His disappearance will be reported to the police and added to the list of similar unsolved mysteries on their files.'

There was no need for them to know any of the circumstantial details that I had in mind for Lord Gwynant's residence in Westminster. Hugh's flat was in a corner of London where the policy of the residents was to be as little aware of their neighbours as possible. Those neighbours included Church House and a Catholic convent, inward-looking institutions even before the days of the blackout. It was a convenient place in other ways, too. On Lord Gwynant's final walk he might easily reach the bank of the Thames in a minute or two, or reach the other side of Westminster Bridge in another five. Or, of course, he might not reach the other side, according to the depth of his depression at the time.

'Are you really going to take his lordship all the way to London?'

'No, Mrs Bowen. It is of great importance that there should be no trace of his lordship to be found in London. This will be easiest to achieve if he is never there.'

The next part of my explanation to them was the most difficult. I lived and worked in a world in which it was of vital importance that as many people as possible knew as little as was necessary of the affairs in which they were caught up. I wondered if they realised that they now lived in the same sort of world. They had, after all, played their parts faithfully and with unfailing discretion. I hoped that they would understand that what was required of them now was ignorance. I had to withhold from them any knowledge of the final arrangements for Lord Gwynant's interment.

There is some reason that I should hold it back even now, as the British government continues to regard certain arrangements of this kind, made during the war years, as matters best kept secret. You see, the accident that had befallen Hugh was not an unusual occurrence. Training and rehearsal was a great part of our war effort in England in 1943. The training was often – it had to be – as realistic as possible. That inevitably led to accidents, misfortunes and casualties. Thousands of men died as Hugh had died. Several entire platoons of American infantry were lost attempting to land on the coast of Pembrokeshire. Canadians, Australians, New Zealanders, as well as our own troops, were killed by accident or incompetence in dismayingly large numbers. There were obvious reasons for not publicising these failures. There was an argument for saying that they were not failures but lessons learned that would lead to eventual successes, the saving of thousands of other lives and the shortening of the war.

Still, if they were not failures, they were at least embarrassments. No one wanted to tell the folks back in America that they had sent their boys to be drowned or butchered or blown up by mines in the wrong place while trying to liberate Milford Haven. Bodies nowadays are flown home from the farthest zones of war. In those days that was impossible. If they fell somewhere embarrassingly short of the battlefield itself, they were buried with some honour but little ceremony in plots not conspicuously marked. Somebody was given the job of arranging these discreet funerals. Proper channels were set up for the conduct of the business. My own department sometimes had need to use these channels. If you wonder why so much land requisitioned during the war has been retained, even now, by the Ministry of Defence you may reflect that there are in England war graves with no crosses or memorials to mark them. Their location is reverently marked on maps in the possession of the relevant department. It is thought best that they should lie undisturbed and unknown. It has been decided that it would not best serve the memory of these gallant but, unfortunately, squandered men that their remains should be turned up by farmers digging drainage ditches or contractors misled into thinking they were building on virgin ground.

I had made the necessary arrangements for Lord Gwynant to lie in one of these noble plots. I remember that there was a form to be completed. I think I entered Humphrey Vaughan under the category of Irregular Civilian Casualty. It was, I'm afraid, a heading that covered a multitude of misdemeanours in the treatment of aliens and suspected spies. I think I may also have described him as a British Empire citizen. I hope so.

It was now necessary to offer the world a last glimpse of Humphrey Vaughan. The advantage of the Daimler was that it was high and capacious and its doors were large. It had required very little contrivance to make it accommodate a passenger in a wheelchair. Two ramps, stowed on the running boards, could be inclined from little brackets so that embarking and disembarking was quite an easy job. A passenger seated in a wheelchair rode somewhat higher than he would have done on the ordinary seat and the chauffeur was obliged to drive with special care so that the chair did not move dangerously about the compartment. All this conferred a certain majesty on the progress of car and passenger as Jarman drove down the narrow lane from the Plas to Porth Gwynant as the glow of daylight was fading over the sea. Light still gleamed on the peaks of mountains in the east, but night was climbing on the slopes.

The Daimler was not frugal with petrol but, as Lord Gwynant's journeys in it were infrequent, it had not been difficult to hoard up enough coupons to enable him to motor to Crewe to catch a London train.

The road to Crewe passes by Coed y Bwlch, where Tanat and Emyr waited with the garment I had provided and which had been in my kit aboard the Anson. I call it a garment, though to call it a bag would be more honest. Irregular Casualties were not often buried in wooden coffins. They were sent off in stout naval canvas. It was Tanat and Emyr's task to prepare his lordship for his final journey in this bag – an undertaking that required a certain re-arrangement of his posture – and despatch him in the Daimler on the road to Crewe. Except that Crewe was not the Daimler's destination. Some miles down the road from Coed y Bwlch I had arranged a rendezvous, where I waited by a field gate in a Bedford with a sergeant of the Pioneer Corps at the wheel. The Pioneer Corps's prime function, as the sergeant put it to me, was shifting muck, and Pioneers were not expected to provide intellectually stimulating company. On that score, by reputation, the Pioneers came about equal with a cavalry regiment, as long as you cheated up the intellectual credentials of the cavalry by including the horses. All the same, we wiled away the time playing cribbage in the Bedford's cab and the sergeant gave me his opinions on the conduct of the war. It was as sound a commentary as I have heard, then or since. 'It's one fucking fuck-up after another. And when they've done, they'll only go and fuck it up again.' Succinct and hard to argue with, I thought.

The sergeant had just laid down a hand that put him in a winning position and was moving the half-burned match along the board when I saw what I hoped were the Daimler's shrouded lights moving over the shoulder of the hill.

'Your game.'

I gave him the half-crown that rode on it. He spun it expertly into the air with a flick of his thumb, caught it and made it disappear into his pocket with a magician's flourish.

'Ta very much. Give you another game whenever you like.' I climbed down from the cab, taking a red-shaded torch with me. Pinning back the gate with a stone, I picked my way around the mud patch and into the road.

A few moments later I was in no doubt. It was the Daimler. Nothing else could have been so bulky against the sky and making so lazy a noise. I flicked the red shade off the torch and signalled the turn through the gate into the field.

It seemed I was mistaken. The car came on steadily down the lane with no sign of stopping. I stepped out and held the torch straight up in front of me where there was no possibility of the driver's failing to see it.

And then I knew that it was the Daimler. The light of my torch fell on Jarman at the wheel. Apart from pulling over the road to miss me, he did not acknowledge me at all. As the car passed, the light of my torch brushed the figure in the back. Lord Gwynant, quite unbagged, was sitting upright and leaning a little forward. He jolted in his seat as he went by. The Daimler passed me and was gone into the darkness. Perhaps it was the movement and the shadow. Or perhaps since Tanat had first done his work a certain desiccation had changed the set of his features. Lord Gwynant's expression impressed itself on me in that brief glimpse by a pallid light. The little sharp glint of his teeth put it somewhere between a laugh and a sneer. It just might have been the frozen beginnings of a scream. I switched off the torch and stood in the darkness.

'Wrong lot?' asked the sergeant.

'No. Right lot,' I said.

' 'Nother fuck-up.'

'Yes. It seems so.'

'Drive after 'em?'

I thought for a few moments. But not many.

'No.'

I had the sergeant drop me off at Tanat's cottage. There was nobody at home but the door was unlocked as such doors always were in those days. I let myself in, lit a lamp and took a seat beside a fire whose coals were not quite dead.

I had not much more than an hour to wait before I heard their boots on the lane and heard them pause as they saw the lamplight. I imagine that in the pause they had a certain hesitation about who was to enter and face me first. It was Emyr. All he did was to nod to me before hanging his coat and hat behind the door. He walked over to the fire and poked at it. The last of the ashy coals fell through the bars with a few drooping sparks but he continued to stare into the hearth, as if expecting a blaze to flare up.

Tanat hung his hat.

'Would you care for a bottle of beer, Mr James?' he said, and stepped out into the scullery.

'We just come back from the house,' said Emyr. 'Mr Stephens was going to tell you all about it.'

'As I'm here, perhaps you'd be kind enough to tell me now.'

I let my eye fall on the stout naval canvas that lay rolled on the floor beneath the table. The cat was just then moving in a circle on the top of it, making a depression into which it settled. Emyr glanced at it and then back at the poker in his hand.

'Dad best, I think.'

Tanat came back in from the scullery with two bottles of beer. The bottles were old and dusty and their tops were clenched with rusty wire. He wiped each with his shirt sleeve and stood them on the table.

'Emyr, fetch a mug, boy. A glass for Mr James. Be sure it is clean.'

'Where did Jarman go with Lord Gwynant?'

'A quiet place, Mr James.'

'Why? Why did you not do as we agreed?'

'There was a meeting after.'

'It was agreed by everybody,' said Emyr, coming back from the scullery with two mugs and a glass. The glass had the name of a public house etched on it. When he gave it to me I took out my handkerchief and began to wipe it.

'I'm sorry if it is not clean,' said Emyr.

'I'm just giving it a polish, Emyr. I think this is somewhat special beer.'

'We will see if it has been keeping,' said Tanat, but his old hands were defeated by the rusty wire. He handed the job to Emyr who took out his knife and prised the wire from the neck of each bottle. The beer had been keeping remarkably well. As it was more than fifty years old, it was miraculous that it was drinkable at all, but it was, indeed, better than merely drinkable. It was dark and still. Rich and dense to the taste.

We looked at each other and that was enough. There was no need for comment.

'What does that mean, Mr James? I'm sure that you will know.' Tanat pointed to the embossed medallion on the bottle.

'Gaudeamus? It means, "Let us rejoice", Tanat.'

He turned the bottle round to study the writing again.

'Perhaps it is not appropriate. We will not rejoice, no. But we prefer things as they have been, Mr James.'

Emyr nodded. 'Everybody is agreed. We prefer things as they have been.'

I took a sip of the strange beer. It was hard to know where to begin to explain to them the impossibility of their position.

'Now that Mr Hugh is no longer here, who is to conduct the affairs of the estate? Every year there are a hundred things to do. Matters of business to be attended to. Hugh's cousin must inherit. Lord Gwynant must be properly and decently buried.'

'Mr Hugh's cousin is a boy of military age.'

'He's in the navy, I think. Yes.'

They looked at me as if a look said all they wished.

'The problem of death duties is somewhat different now,' I said.

'Mr Hugh left much of his interest in the estate in the form of a trust.'

'And you are a trustee, Mr James,' said Emyr.

'Surely there is the answer to the question you ask,' said Tanat.

'I would naturally step aside when Hugh's cousin David inherits. It is essential that should happen.'

'He will inherit if he survives.'

'Tanat. Lord Gwynant must be laid to rest and the duty paid. And that is all there is to it.'

Tanat drank his beer very slowly from the mug. He drank it with great attention.

'We prefer things as they have been.'

I got back to London in need of distraction. Diana was out of town but Hermione was usually 'at home' on certain afternoons, if she were not in rehearsal. It was one of those afternoons and I called, slightly earlier than was entirely polite.

She called a greeting from the drawing-room as I climbed the stairs. I remembered the words of a famous theatre critic. 'Her voice always tinkles,' he had written, 'but sometimes it tinkles like a silver spoon on china, and sometimes like an entire crystal chandelier crashing to the floor.' This afternoon, it was a strangely muffled tinkling.

She was sitting on a straight-backed chair close to the window as if she were sitting for a portrait. A view over the tops of trees to the park beyond was the background. Or would have been. A young woman in overalls, whom I took at first to be a hairdresser, was bending attentively over her.

'You mayn't kiss me, I'm afraid. Not just yet. Find yourself something to drink. This will not quite take for ever.' She rolled her eyes at the young woman. 'Will it?'

The young woman made no answer but walked round to the other side of Hermione and opened up an instrument like a pair of forceps and then closed its tips gently on her head. One tip went on her occiput and one on the tip of her nose.

The young woman made a note on the pad that lay beside her,

then took up another position and closed the callipers again on Hermione's head.

'It's nothing to do with phrenology, darling, I promise. I'm being measured for Madame Tussaud's. Are you impressed?'

The Glittering Prize

It used to take about an hour, not much more, to reach Steerham Park from Piccadilly in a Bentley. I should make it clear that it would have been someone else's Bentley. It would take much longer today. The house is now open to the public and is worth a visit. The portraits are more rewarding than they sometimes are in country houses, especially the Zoffany of Lady Caroline Bullen and the two Vandykes. The Zoffany is – or was – in the passageway between the library and the pretty blue room called, for some reason, the parlour. The Vandykes are on the stair to the gallery. The family trees of eighteenth-century England must have been all branch and no stem, to judge by most of the portraits. Nobody looks remotely related either to their forefathers or anybody alive today, but everyone appears close kin to everybody else painted around 1750, the women especially. Zoffany's Lady Caroline is an exception. She is very much a descendant of the Edward Bullen seen by Van Dyck. She has the sombre, regretful eyes and the distinctive set of the lips. You might think she'd been on the point of speaking but had decided . . . what? To bite her tongue? Save her breath? Savour a private joke? Van Dyck has been entirely frank with the Bullen nose where Zoffany may have exercised discretion, but these two faces from two different centuries are, unmistakably, family. You could never go up to the gallery in the company of my friend Edward Bullen without looking sideways and being a little disconcerted to see those same features bobbing up the stair beside you. He claimed he could never see the likeness.

I hadn't seen Edward for months on end. I hadn't even bumped into him at parties or the theatre. He was taking his political career seriously and politics, in the remapped world after the Second World War, was getting back into its stride as a competitive business. Edward was parliamentary secretary to someone whose name now escapes me, just as it now seems to have escaped the historians, but who was then thought quite the coming man. There had been late sittings and great issues and so on, but I wasn't keeping abreast of it all. I'd been in Deauville with Donald Crozier aboard the extravagantly impractical yacht he was then in love with. We sailed back in balmy weather, nearly becalmed most of the time.

A message had been left for me at the club and I picked it up with one or two others after I'd had a good soak – a pleasure that Donald's yacht, though beautiful and well appointed, did not afford – and started on a long pink gin. The message said, 'Come this weekend. Telephone if you can't.' It came not from Edward but from Fanny, his mother.

I had to turn to the steward for help.

'Harrison, what day is it?'

'It is Saturday, sir.'

I called Fanny Bullen to make my belated apologies, and began to explain about being becalmed and the rest of it but she was not inclined to listen.

'Verdon. I'm so pleased you called. When could you be here?'

'I don't know when I could be there, Lady Bullen. I'm in Cowes now; I'll get a ferry to Southampton and then it's a matter of trains. Goodness knows . . . '

'Don't do any of that, Verdon. Somebody can take you across to Chichester and we'll have a car waiting for you.'

'Lady Bullen, I'm not sure that there is anyone who can take me across to Chichester.'

'Stay where you are.'

She had hung up. Before I'd reached the end of the gin there was a voice at my shoulder. Fifteen minutes later my kit had been slung aboard a twin-screwed motor launch and I was struggling to keep my feet as it leapt from wave-top to wave-top. My helmsman was a rear admiral, only slightly acquainted with Lady Bullen but pleased to perform this small favour for her. A chauffeur – not Lady

Bullen's chauffeur, but somebody else's – was waiting at the landing stage at Chichester. I dwell on these details to make it clear that Fanny Bullen, charming when she wanted to be and imperious without even trying to be, was a woman who could get things done. It was clear that I was being summoned to make myself useful, but it was hard to imagine in what way. If there was anything in the world that Verdon James could do for her, she surely knew ten people who could do it better.

Making your way down the drive to Steerham, you might at first be driving deeper into woodland and not to a house at all, were you not allowed that famous far-off glimpse of chimneys and gable tops. This promising spectacle is lost as your way curves below a green slope often grazed by deer. You find it again, doubled by its own reflection – if the lilies are not too thick on the lake – as the drive leads you beside the waters and ushers you to the great door. Repton was responsible for some adjustments to the landscape, but not for Steerham's famous oddity, the Baron's Bridge. Like the bridge at Avignon, it fails to reach the other side. It is half a bridge thrown out across an ornamental water fashioned to resemble some ambling stretch of the Thames or Severn. The first Baron Bullen began the bridge in anticipation of his elevation to an earldom. The celebration was premature. The king went mad, patronage passed to another faction and the baron ran out of money. There was no further advancement for man or bridge. He ordered the work stopped and declared himself more pleased with half a bridge than he would have been with a whole one. Ornamental ruins were, if anything, more fashionable than ornamental bridges. By the middle of the twentieth century it wasn't a matter of running out of money for bridges. Most families had run out of the money to keep up such houses at all. Even those who hadn't run out of money in an age of supertax, like the Bullens, had run out of reasons for spending it all on the maintenance of a glory they no longer had reasons for living in. For all practical purposes, the Bullens were already living in the apartment that would remain to them when the house went to the National Trust.

I had not expected to be the only guest at dinner. Lady Bullen and Sir William came down. A place was waiting for Edward but he did not appear.

'I'm afraid he's working at his papers,' said Sir William. He said very little more for the length of the meal. Conversation was, famously, not among his interests. One talked with Fanny Bullen. Whenever I brought Edward's name into the conversation, though, she deftly changed the subject. Clearly, whatever had to be said was not to be said in front of the servants. The burgundy was deeply pleasing, so I fell into enjoying that and letting the time pass. The wine, if anything, was rather too good for the occasion, and Lady Bullen noticed my appreciatively raised eyebrow.

'When I told Edward you were coming he gave instructions to decant a couple of bottles of that.'

'It was extremely good of him.'

We carried on eating in silence. It was good of Edward, but also odd. Odd, I mean, for a chap to leave his chair empty next to you, but order up a worthwhile wine in this way. There was something else that should have alerted the hairs on my neck. I knew the vintage, you see. Years before on a sunny day, while lying in Port Meadow with a few friends, still an undergraduate, it had entered Edward's head to lay down wine against his wedding day.

'Have you someone in mind?' I asked him.

'Not at all. But I suppose I will marry.'

'I suppose you will. Edward. Do you want me to choose a bride for you?'

'No. You can choose the wine, Verdon. What should I lay down? The best wine for the greatest number from my not bottomless purse.'

Most of what I knew about wine had come to me courtesy of my friend Morton Drew-Page, and his energetic looting of his father's famous cellar. By mere association, I had by this time gained perhaps more of a reputation than I deserved.

'Greater love hath no man than he shall lay down his wine for his friends and you will need rather a lot of it. A good Aloxe Corton Premier Cru can give you every bit as good a wine as a Grand Cru

Corton and rather more of it for your money. The right one would give you plenty of time to think about it. Probably for ever.'

He had laughed.

'Oh, I may not be able to wait that long.'

The meal was a simple one and soon over. Coffee was brought to the drawing-room and only then, with the door firmly closed, was the subject broached.

'Edward is not working on his papers, Verdon. He has drafted his resignation. Did you know?'

'No. Why?'

'He won't talk about it, Verdon.'

'You say he's drafted it. He hasn't submitted it?'

'He said that he had to wait for a moment when it would be . . . When it would not embarrass the party.'

'I can see that this would not be the ideal time. Any resignations now might easily be misunderstood. But is he out of sympathy with the party? Out of favour? It's not the impression I had.'

'His reasons aren't political. They are personal. It is worse than that. Yesterday he tried . . . Pratchett found him in the lake. We thought he'd fallen from the bridge. It wasn't that. He had, the truth was, he had . . . '

She turned her face from the fire and looked at me. There was nothing imperious in her eye now: just pain and bewilderment. And love. She was such an entirely unsentimental woman that it usually wouldn't enter your head that she loved her children as much as any mother. She couldn't say the words.

Sir William spoke them instead.

'Tried to do away with himself.'

I found it impossible to say anything. We looked at each other for a while until eventually Sir William found the composure to carry on.

'We thought it was an accident. Pratchett was very good. He's an ambulance man, you see. St John's. Volunteer. It's a thing we've always encouraged. Luckily. Luckily. He had all the – er . . . artificial respiration . . . knew how to do it. The fact is, that Edward was not . . . glad to have been pulled out of the water.'

'And it's clear from what you say that you don't know why?'

Lady Bullen shook her head.

'He has not said. He has always had dark moods, but that you know. You always seemed to have the knack of pulling him out of them.'

'I think those moods are part of the price, aren't they?' I said. 'For burning himself up the way he does when he's . . . the other Edward. The one who leaves us all rather breathless in his wake. Didn't Sir Winston call it the "Black Dog"?'

'The dog seems to have been getting bigger and blacker in the years since the war, I'd say. And lately, much blacker.' She looked briefly at Sir William, who nodded.

'He had a good war. But a hard one, you know.'

'The north Atlantic was nobody's idea of a rest cure,' I said. 'I know that.'

'For a while we thought, oh, just adjusting again, you know. Had its problems for a lot of people,' said Lady Bullen. 'But . . . '

She looked back into the fire. It was William Bullen who spoke.

'I don't know whether you know about my family. Every now and again one of them goes completely barmy. There isn't a word that doesn't make it sound comical, you know, Verdon. Barmy, loony, insane. It isn't very comical. They rot in the brain somehow.'

'Does it have a name, this congenital affliction?'

'Bullens' disease will do. But no, not strictly speaking. Only the symptoms have names. And one of the first – the first mental symptoms – is a marked suppression of the vital spirits. My father suffered acutely and a great-uncle, for instance, spent the last fifteen years of his life constantly under vigilance because of his suicidal tendencies. So naturally, one wonders.'

'It would be extraordinary to appear at his age, of course,' said Lady Bullen, 'but these things are never altogether predictable, are they?'

'Had you ever noticed the beginnings of any symptoms in him?'

'No.'

'Do you think he has, perhaps, noticed something himself? Whatever it might be?'

'We have never talked about it. It's not a thing one does.'

I wanted to be clear. 'You have never discussed this disease with Edward?'

Sir William stared a long time at the border of a Persian rug.

'It's something we talk about in the family when the time comes. When there's any talk of marrying. We talk about it then and, well, people make up their own minds what they must do.'

He walked across to the sofa and stood beside his wife. They glanced at each other without speaking, as fellow mourners might, arriving at a funeral.

'And that question has not so far arisen.'

Good wine leaves its flavour in your mouth a long time. I was still tasting the wine put aside for Edward's wedding.

The morning brought a cloudless sky and a colourless wintry light to Steerham; the sort of day that confirms the autumn and says that hard frosts are not so far behind. Some of the oaks were green and some had begun to turn. The smoke of cottage hearths rose in straight transparent columns of blue above their chimneys and crows sat motionless on the boughs or walked on the turf. I sat with Edward, who had taken a little to eat in his room, and looked out from his high window on a scene as tranquil and English as could be imagined.

'Do you wish you'd been left in the lake?'

He didn't answer for a long time.

'No.'

'I'm glad about that.'

'If only because it seems a rather timid thing to do.'

'Killing yourself you mean?'

'Yes,' he said after another silence.

'I don't know. Hamlet seemed to think it took rather a lot of courage.'

'Hamlet's wrong. It just turns out to be more difficult than you think.'

'Sir William thinks . . . I'm just going to rush at this, Edward – I can't think of another way – he thinks you're afraid that you are going the way of your grandfather.'

'Syphilis, you mean?' He nearly laughed. 'No. I haven't got syphilis. Tell him.'

I watched the pedestrian crows on the lawn for a while.

'Your father tells me that it wasn't syphilis . . . '

I prepared to explain to Edward what William Bullen had told me, but he turned on his pillow and laughed a weary dismissive laugh.

'No, no. Well, I know all about that. Do they really think I don't?'

'Clearly you do.'

'Verdon, the only inherited madness in this family is that each generation waits for the announcement of nuptials before they mention the inherited madness of the Bullen's. But each generation already knows. They used to call it the Black Bile of the Bullens. And I'll tell you something else. It doesn't exist. It's a figment. You know what it is? It's exactly what they say it isn't. It's syphilis. The hereditary affliction of the Bullens is fornication, Verdon. My grandfather ended up in a sanatorium in Pau because he'd spent too much time in the brothels in Paris. But someone back then seems to have decided they'd rather believe that it's a defect in the blood. That's what's barmy.'

'If I'm to ignore the possibility of hereditary madness, or syphilis, do I also ignore the possibility that you've contracted some more commonplace disease in the usual way?'

'Do you really think I'd kill myself because I'd caught a disease?'

'I was thinking of something banal like a broken heart. People do become very dejected about these things.'

'Well, not in this case. I wanted to kill myself, Verdon. It really is as simple as that. I wanted to kill myself because I didn't want the bother of living the rest of my life. That's all.'

His head fell back on the pillow and his eyes closed.

'Did you leave a note? It's the custom, you know.'

'I left my resignation.'

'Doesn't quite explain anything, Edward, does it?'

'It explains that I am disenchanted with politics and can't see a future for myself.'

'Very well. Give up politics and devote yourself to the bar. Take silk and . . . '

'Oh, Verdon. Can't you just accept that I can't see any future for myself that I happen to want. And the fact is, I don't have a future in politics, which is what I care about.'

'Edward, you have a reason – and it must be a very forceful one – for believing that. I wish I knew what the reason is.'

'Verdon, it's possible that you are being obtuse, which isn't like you. But it doesn't matter. There wouldn't be anything you could do about it.'

Perhaps I was being obtuse. I could see that the effort of talking and even of eating the scrap that he'd had for breakfast had left him lethargic, so I prepared to leave him. As I touched his shoulder, he let his cheek fall on to the pillow and looked away from me at the wall.

'Perhaps it is a disease. I don't know. Maybe it becomes a disease. I'm rambling, Verdon. Ignore it. Just leave me, will you.'

I walked slowly down the stair, and passed my friend, as painted by Van Dyck in doublet and piccadills, looking dark and saturnine and full of importance. I felt glad that there are no ancient portraits in my family. Neither I nor anyone else expects, or ever expected, much of Verdon James. As I turned into the hall from the bottom stair, Benbow, having arranged the day's newly arrived post on the table, was opening the box where we all put our letters for sending. I'd put two or three there myself the night before, explaining my sudden change of plans to a number of people. For as long as I had been coming to Steerham the box had been there, a tall affair of darkly figured mahogany with a handsome baroque curve to it. A slot had been cut in its top for envelopes. It was the first time that it had occurred to me that the thing was, in fact, a Georgian knife box.

'How appropriate that is, Benbow. The box.'

'Is it, sir?'

'Many more have been stabbed to the heart by letters than ever were by knives.'

'Oh, sir, I will vouch for that.'

He took the letters away to the waiting postman. I looked at the box for a few moments, empty as it was of everything except for one idea. I went back up the stairs and tapped on Edward's door.

He carried on looking at the wall as I said it. The complete immobility of his head was itself a complete answer. I said the words again, a mere statement, not a question.

'You are being blackmailed.'

In a little while he'd told me a great deal. Of course, I knew so much of his story to begin with that there were things he did not have to explain. Rather than try to tell it in his words, it will be better to tell you in mine. I will be able, perhaps, to give you rather more of the picture that way. You know that Edward Bullen was a handsome man. He would never have been less than handsome though now, in his thirties, the chiselling of his dark features was becoming more heavy handed than it had been when I first knew him. What had once been an occasional shade of melancholy in his expression had become more often a touch of the morose. At twenty, though, there was a blameless perfection about him that had filled the eye. Bear in mind when this was. A few years before, Europe had drenched its earth in the blood of millions of young men. The world ached with their terrible absence. At crossroads and market squares, in college cloisters and on chapel walls you could read, freshly cut in stone or cast in bronze, the terrible list of their names. The swathe was broadest in proportion among the subalterns and the captains, the barely shaven young officers, schooled to lead. You could read their names and ranks in any church in any county, on bright brass plates beneath the newly dedicated windows. They had all of them one rank, one title, one name in place of all those names. Beloved son. They were also brothers and cousins and friends, and would have been lovers and husbands and fathers. Each name was not one gap in the ranks but many. There were so many hearts to be pierced that I believe not many were immune to such beauty as Edward's in his youth, not young or old, not man or woman.

In some people, rich or poor, youth is a kind of splendour; in others, a kind of embarrassment. Richard St Just d'Oliphant Butler-Boyle should have been among the splendid, if only to live up to the magnificence of his initials. If he'd had the seed of splendour in him, he'd have pretended that his stammer was an affectation that it pleased him to keep rather than abandon, but when he stammered his body was racked by apology and humiliation. If he stammered for an unusually long time, it was as if all his clothes had fallen off. Yet he was a fencer of unusual ability. Perhaps the mask was the important thing. Fencing is combat face to face, yet faceless; intimate but impersonal. Whatever the reason, something was released in him that was otherwise inhibited. He was quick and sure with the special quality of repose, even at speed, that only the best have. I was not much of a swordsman, always finishing somewhere near the bottom of the pool. I joined in so that others could have the pleasure of occasional victories without having to be very good. Really, my pleasure was to watch. It's a paradoxical sport, disciplined and elegant to the point of being ascetic, yet sensual in the extreme. A point scored is, after all, a breast pierced.

Edward was a good fencer, and easily had the beating of most of us, but not Butler-Boyle. Men who win at one sport do not generally like to lose at another, and boxers like Edward certainly do not. Boxers have an emotional foible, all the same: when a good boxer loses to a better, you'll see him throw his arms around his conqueror's neck. The etiquette of fencing forbids that sort of thing, but perhaps something like it happened between them.

They fenced and went in for a lot of foil practice together, meeting earlier than the rest of us at the drill-hall where we fenced, and often staying later. Apart from that, for a long time they hardly mixed socially, so it surprised me when Edward mentioned that he'd invited Richard Butler-Boyle to Steerham during the long vacation. I should not have said it surprised me. It would be more honest to say that I was slightly put out. I wasn't the only one to feel a little resentment, now and then, at the way Butler-Boyle some-times absorbed Edward's attention and admiration. We were a jolly crowd, and like all undergraduate crowds, very pleased with ourselves. Our great affectation was to believe that we knew every-thing about serious things but took nothing seriously. Our great business was talk and we believed our talk to be wonderfully bright and amusing. Butler-Boyle was not shaped for these sportive tricks. Apart from the fencing, he wasn't really a member of our crowd at all and it was hard to see how he could be. All the same, Edward invited him down to Steerham for a reading party in one of those endless Elysian summers in which I seem to remember growing up.

The idea of a reading party must seem quaint and probably risible to undergraduates nowadays. Reading itself is probably thought old-fashioned, but in those more primitive days education meant doing rather a lot of it. The reading party was a pleasant way of finding time, in the vacation, for one or two educational things that so easily get jostled out of the way in the social life of the term. The first essential was a congenial crowd and the second a large house for them to infest. Even then, the stands of large country houses were being severely thinned. People started to think it was better to sell up and spend while they were alive rather than be forced, when they were dead, to sell up and be taxed. Everyone who hadn't sold up had cousins who had and those who clung on mostly believed they would be the last, or nearly. The world, it seemed, had changed utterly and was still changing. The old were relieved or dismayed in different degrees. For the young it was a reason for throwing what Mr Coward called a marvellous party, like first-class passengers on the last crossing of one of those grand Atlantic liners, too costly to keep or run or repair, still magnificent but about to become scrap. Even reading could be turned into an elegant way of passing the time. A party.

The mornings were for reading. You could choose not to, of course, but the rule was not to disturb those who chose to. You could read wherever you chose to read. At Steerham, hardly any-one chose the library, whose gloom was intended to preserve the books. The orangery was a favourite. The little temple at the end of the alley of yews was sought by the more confident sort of women. It may not have been ideal for reading, but if one wore white or cream it set one off very well. It had been built, for no very good reason, as a temple of Triton, but was called the Temple of Diana, because Lady Diana Manners was supposed to have retreated there to read letters from her admirers. That summer Butler-Boyle established himself in it, not for any coquettish reason, but probably because it was a place in which you could not be surprised and were unlikely to suffer casual intrusion. Anyone who wished to intrude had fifty yards to walk in your full view, so people could hardly come up and then affect to be surprised to find you there. Butler-Boyle was, as always, *en garde*.

In the afternoon you read or you talked. And then there was tea. Unless it rained, tea was always brought out to the lawn and was the signal for the bookworms to come out and join the talkers. There was no rule, but it would have been unthinkable to miss tea. I've grown old, but toast and honey at four o'clock will do now what it did then and what it has done for me since I was a child. It will make me feel that somewhere in the world there is safety. The rule was – I don't know who made these rules – that there should be no serious talk at teatime. Books were dropped. Gossip and teasing was taken up instead. The evening was dinner and talk, and gramophone records and silliness and seriousness in more or less equal proportions. Every day was the same, yet every day was different because it had been shaped by the day before, and always, the day before, you had learned something new; about books, about ideas, about each other, about yourself.

There came a teatime when I learned about jealousy. Edward and Butler-Boyle walked on to the lawn, Edward stooping slightly and inclining his head to listen. I could not hear a word of what Butler-Boyle was saying, but I could hear and see that he was not stammering in the least. They would not give tea a miss, of course, but they walked in that slowly engrossed way that people have when they are walking nowhere in particular. When they reached the rest of us, I knew, they would break off talking and be cheerful and social. At least Edward would be cheerful. He'd ask had anyone heard the test-match score and debate the value of putting on a spinner or start up some conversation of that sort. But watching them walk towards the little encampment of rattan table and chairs, it was clear that they had no particular thought of tea, or of joining the rest of us. Their only thought was to stretch out the last few moments they had to themselves. I knew with complete certainty that Edward loved him, just by their pace across the lawn.

It is strange that jealousy should be the most potent and consuming of emotions. Anyone who has felt its sudden onset knows that what nature has bequeathed to us in jealousy is quite simply a strong disposition to kill the rival. In our kind of society this is no longer a useful emotion and I wonder that we haven't evolved out of it.

I had, of course, never breathed a word of this terrible moment of jealousy to Edward, not until that day, years later, when he lay pale and weak in his bed telling me how it came about that he was being blackmailed.

He looked at me. 'Is that why you went back to town?'

I laughed. 'I'm surprised you even noticed at the time.'

'I think you left rather than stay and risk being spiteful. Because you're better than that.'

'I hope you're right. I'll pretend you are. You were head over heels, weren't you, that summer?'

'I could cure his stammer, you know. It was like the laying on of hands. I could touch him and he'd be able to speak. It makes you feel that you have something special. He was a very good talker, too, you know. When the impediment was gone, he talked the way he fenced. He genuinely had a mind that shed light on things. The odd thing – I don't know that it is odd, really – was that by the next term, I couldn't make his stammer go away. That part of it didn't work any more, but we used to write. We met only very occasionally but we kept up the letters, long after that summer.'

'I assume, the business in hand being what it is, that these were what you'd call love letters?'

He gave a little acknowledging shrug. 'Partly.'

'But enough?'

'Oh yes. It wasn't really a physical relationship, you know. Hardly at all. But we did write to each other for a while in those terms. Longing . . . aching . . . adapting freely from the Song of Songs – I'm sure you know the sort of thing.'

'Yes, I do. Surely you could call it all an undergraduate exercise in the genre? I suppose to a large extent that's what it was. Are they really so damaging, these letters?'

He smiled and nodded. 'They're enough. He kept every letter I ever wrote to him over something like ten years.'

I was surprised and it showed.

'Oh yes. We were in touch for that long.'

'I'm amazed. I don't believe I set eyes on him after we went down from the University. Where did you hide him?'

'I didn't hide him.'

'Unfortunate choice of word, old chum, forgive me. Where was he all this time?'

'He started a school. He had some very interesting, and not necessarily unsound, ideas about education. I tried to talk him out of it, of course. For one thing there was the stammer.'

'Not an advantage.'

'He said that's what assistant masters were for. It was for him to lay down the principles and inspire the troops; for others to carry out the orders in the trenches, or in this case, classrooms.'

'Pretty much the same thing, I always thought. Did it work out?'

'Better than you might have thought. The other trouble – after the stammer, I mean – was that your customers tend to be conservative in their tastes. There aren't many who want even tepidly radical ideas. Still, there were almost enough to keep a school going. Especially through the war. Richard was fairly well off, anyway, so it wasn't a disaster, but after the war he couldn't keep it going. It didn't pay and it wasn't going to. It took him too long to stop fooling himself about it, because he genuinely loved the idea of education. He really believed, I think, that he could build an important school that would play a part in changing things. He had that kind of faith in his ideas. It was a very grand ambition. Hopeless but grand. We used to discuss it in our letters over the years. After a time I tried to restore his sense of proportion, but it was no good. When you start a school in Shropshire, you more or less make up your own world. I could never get him to see the truth.'

I will not have been the first to laugh, and to apologise for laughing, at the thought of Richard St Just d'Oliphant Butler-Boyle, with his fine mind and dreadful stammer, lost in Shropshire, nurturing an élite to change the world – the day after tomorrow.

'Oh, it was laughable,' said Edward, 'but peculiarly noble in its way. He wasn't out for himself and actually running a school, the real business rather than the idea, was a kind of hair shirt for him, I think.'

'He closed the school down, presumably?'

'He died.'

The one subject Richard Butler-Boyle, headmaster of Weston School, Shropshire, taught the boys himself was fencing. The boy was not to blame, as Richard made clear. He himself had been careless. He let himself be distracted – so many calamities on his mind, I suppose – turning to a sudden disturbance as his pupil had lunged. It would have been of no importance, except that the buttoned point had broken from the foil as it struck his hip. The unprotected blade, deflected inwards by the bone, entered the peritoneum. The wound was not deep, but it led to septicaemia. He was dead in a week.

'I remember your going down to Shropshire for a funeral. You didn't tell me it was Richard's.'

'Didn't I? Perhaps not. Anyway, I went down and for one reason or another it was convenient to travel the night before and stay at the Something-or-other-Arms. And that's where I met him. Do you know, I thought the fellow was just being courteous. I thought he'd come down to the hotel to keep me company for a while, as I was on my own and knew nobody. You don't look at a man and say, "Hello. This fellow's a blackmailer." You've no idea what a blackmailer might look like. Especially when it has not occurred to you that you might be blackmailed.'

'What does a blackmailer look like?' I asked. 'In this case?'

'This one looked exactly like an assistant master at a failed private school. Do you know, I put up with his company because I thought he was trying to be kind. He insisted on buying me a beer and he talked about the accident and about the school and what a shame it all was. He was rather gloomy about his prospects as a suddenly unemployed Latin and geography teacher and I encouraged him to cheer up, the way one always does in a situation like that. "Plenty of jobs for chaps like you", that sort of thing. You can imagine the conversation. I think I really did feel sorry for him. He kept saying what a beautiful man Richard was and how much he had valued my advice and support over the years. I just didn't connect.'

'I suppose when you go into blackmailing for the first time, you probably have to grope your way a little. I doubt if there's a good book on the subject you could turn to.'

'He left me in the bar at about ten. Said he'd see me at the funeral and so on and then he asked me, actually asked me, if I'd mind if he wrote to me. It seemed odd. It was odd, but it still didn't seem odd enough to make me think very much the worse of him. I said, certainly, if he wished. Well, of course, he did write.'

DEAR MR BULLEN – It was a pleasure to make your acquaintance, even in the distressing circumstance of Richard's funeral. I hope I was not too full of my own troubles during the evening we spent in the lounge bar. If the prospects seemed gloomy then, they are, unfortunately, no brighter now. These are very hard times for the private schools and as Weston has closed down halfway through the academic year the chances of finding a new post are exceedingly slim. Gabbitas-Thring have so far come up with nothing that I could possibly consider. On the other hand, an opportunity has presented itself in a quite different field. I could set myself up, in a modest way, in the philatelic business, could I but raise five hundred pounds. My savings unfortunately amount to only a trifle more than two hundred and fifty, so I must raise the remainder where I can. There is no point in approaching a bank, of course.

On the strength of our very brief acquaintance, I would hardly turn in your direction, but I am emboldened by the knowledge that we have common bonds of affection for our late friend. He was a very good and close friend, in different ways, to both of us,

I believe. In view of this connection I am hopeful that you will look at the investment of two hundred and fifty pounds in a favourable light.

It has fallen to me, as deputy head, to put the school's business in order and to sort out Richard's papers, correspondence, etc. Anything that relates to you, which is a good deal, I will separate from the chaff and send on to you the moment I have the opportunity.

Yours very sincerely,

JEREMIAH SEYMOUR

'You might not have noticed that you were being blackmailed, it is so blandly done.'

'It almost escaped me. Do you know, I think if I'd written back to him and said no, I think he might not have gone on with it at all.'

'It didn't stop at two hundred and fifty, I don't suppose. How much has he had from you?'

'More than a thousand. Quite a bit more. And he gets greedier.'

Edward put another letter into my hand. The date was much more recent.

DEAR MR BULLEN – I must congratulate you on the upward step you have recently taken in your career, of which I read details in *The Times*. I entertain no doubts that you are destined, deservedly, for the highest office. Our dear and lamented friend Richard expected no less. This much was clear from the affectionate regard in which I know he always held you and I am sure that this upward step in your career would have given him no less pleasure than it gives me.

It occurs to me that this may be an opportune moment for you to refresh your investment in philately. A thousand pounds invested now will, I'm sure, prove very worthwhile over the years to come. Once again, my heartiest congratulations and Godspeed.

Yours most sincerely . . .

'Have you paid it?'

'No.'

'And is this enough to make you despair? Are you so afraid that these letters might come out?'

'Verdon, I'm afraid of the truth. And you know what the truth is? That I will pay, and go on paying. There's the despair. The more I do, the harder I work, the more I achieve, the greedier he'll get. And the more I pay him the harder it will be ever to stop paying him. I saw it all very clearly, like posts along the road stretching away. So I resigned. At least, I decided I would and I wrote the letter. I thought that would do it, you see. It was only when I read over my own letter of resignation that it came to doing away with myself. It seemed to me that everything in life, including life itself, was pointless and polluted. Do you see it? Morally speaking, if that's not a ridiculous word to use, he has my life in checkmate. There was nothing wrong, nothing I can feel was wrong, in my affection for Richard, apart from a few excessively flowery letters. I wouldn't write letters like that today, not to anybody, but that's on the grounds of literary taste rather than anything else. Grieving is a special kind of love, isn't it? It ought to be an especially pure kind of love. And instead, it turned into this. I could see no way to go on that meant anything to me. I'm not sure I do now.'

I took him by the hand. There was a long silence between us.

'Is there a way?' he said, finally.

'Of course,' I said. 'There always is. It's up to us to find it.'

'Verdon, if there was a way out of blackmail I should think everyone would know of it and that would be an end of blackmail. But while the law is what it is, and emotions are what they are, there will be blackmail. Don't offer me any false comfort. Be a friend and don't do that.'

I found it hard to deny Edward's point. If there were an easy way to slip the bonds of blackmail, plenty of people would know of it. In those days, plenty of people were being blackmailed, after all. It seems odd, looking back on it, that people then were less inquisitive, less censorious and more accommodating about the sexual foibles of public figures. What they got up to between the sheets was not considered so very important as long as the relations enjoyed were enjoyed by at least one member of each sex. The blackmailer's rich seam lay in this one oddity: for a man to sleep with his friend's wife was commonplace and unimportant; to sleep with his friend was a crime of terrible consequence attracting a jail sentence, public abomination and disgrace. The hypocrisy which is now delivered broadside was then concentrated upon a very small target, with correspondingly terrible effect. What do blackmailers go in for now? What trifles do the Jeremiah Seymours of the world snaffle up and turn to account? Nowadays, I suppose, they work for newspapers, draw a regular salary and are far too proud to put their silence up for sale.

I advised Edward to pay Seymour but to pay the man less than he asked.

'You are not in such a weak position as all that, you know. He has a gun to your head but he can only shoot once. He can't shoot you a little bit. If you don't pay him he has the spiteful satisfaction of discharging the one shot he's got. As long as you pay him some-thing, he has the hope of more and he won't want to spend that one round. Write to him pleasantly and say that you can't justify quite that sort of investment in philately. Send him another two-fifty. It won't satisfy him, but it will be too good to resist, I'm sure. He'll want to stay in the game. Make a point of referring to it as an investment, the way he does.'

'Why do you say that? I've always just put money in an envelope. I don't feel like writing to him.'

'No. Send a cheque. Write a covering letter. Begin it "My Dear Seymour . . . " and refer to your interest in philately. You don't have to be too chummy . . . '

'I'm glad about that . . . But why should I?'

'This man probably has no relationship in the world that is quite as close, and none, I daresay, as precious to him, as this one with you. Enter into his little conceit of the investment and so on. It is a fancy of his. It tells us something important about him, that he goes about it this way. I just don't know yet why it's important. A different man would take pleasure in crudely threatening. Mr

Seymour does not. He takes pleasure – I think that is obvious – in this rather gentlemanly charade. Now when one man holds another by a chain, the chain may be pulled two ways. Already we know something of the way he inclines. So we will nudge him in the direction he already leans. When you consider it, you are more powerful than you think. The relationship between blackmailer and blackmailed is one of peculiar intimacy and there is always power in intimacy. It is a matter of waiting out the game until you recognise your power and see the opportunity to use it.'

The Bullens were in a more cheerful frame of mind when I left Steerham than they had been when I'd arrived. All the same, I felt slightly fraudulent. True, I had bucked them up a little and conveyed a certain optimism. In truth, though, it was hard to see very good grounds for that optimism. I was in the same position as the rest of the world: I knew no way out of blackmail. I was due to spend a weekend in Yorkshire, and needed a day or two in London to equip myself for country pursuits. It seemed a good idea to find a little extra time to make the acquaintance of Mr Seymour, the first blackmailer in my circle. The philately business was not just a fiction, after all. Seymour had bought a small but established business in that line at an address in Holloway. At Paddington, I found two journals on the newsagent's shelves devoted to the interests of the stamp collector. By the time I'd read them through, I had learned a little about the enthusiasm and picked up something of its jargon, but the essential lure of the pastime continued to escape me, as it does to this day. Mr Seymour had a small advertisement in both. His advertisement carried a line in italics – *Personal callers welcome.*

A bell rang as you entered Mr Seymour's shop. It continued to dance on its spring for some time after you had entered and closed the door. It made a merry noise, very much at odds with the gloom and silence of the place. After a while the bell fell silent but continued to fidget on its spring, as if it shared your embarrassment. There was something of a wait before Mr Seymour came into the shop from the sombre passageway that led to the rear quarters.

He'd a well-scrubbed sort of face and thin, sandy, receding hair that exposed a great deal of pink scalp. He was carrying a napkin and wiping his lips and it was clear that I had interrupted him at a meal, but his manner was courteous.

'Good-afternoon. What can I do for you?'

'I don't yet know enough to answer you,' I said, 'but I'm attracted to the idea of starting a stamp collection. Where do I begin?'

'You've begun very well,' he answered. 'You've begun here, and that could hardly be improved on.'

'I saw your advertisement in *The Philatelist*.'

'What gave you the idea of starting a collection? I ask because there are lots of different reasons people have for collecting stamps, you know. Some people take an interest in history and some in geography and some just like them the way other people like pictures – they are little pictures, after all, aren't they – and other people like . . . oh, all sorts of other things. If I had an idea of what attracts you, then I'm sure we could start off along the right sort of lines.'

I had browsed the entry under Philately in the encyclopaedia at Steerham. It had not, unfortunately, excited my interest, and my eyes had become heavy after the first few paragraphs of section one: History of the Posts.

'It's the history of the thing more than anything else,' I said.

His eyes glowed in his already glowing face. 'Do you know, I really do think – it's a personal thing of course – but I do think that is the best basis of all for an interest in philately.'

'And geography, too, I suppose,' I said. 'Can't avoid it, really. Wasn't Brazil the second country to adopt the postage stamp?'

'Indeed, indeed,' he enthused.

'Not that I know very much about all that, but I think I'd care to build a collection that tells the story, if you see what I mean. Rather than just an assembly of stamps.'

Seymour was now beaming. Partly, no doubt, because his own interests lay in this direction – he was after all a former teacher of geography and Latin – but more likely because an historical collection of stamps would involve rather more of an outlay of cash. He immediately probed to discover how sound the prospect of free spending might be, like a man biting a coin that might be gold, or might not.

'You realise, of course, that a collection of a definitive historical nature would not be the cheapest sort of collection to acquire – though a surprising amount can be done without too daunting an expenditure.'

'Oh, I'm not especially rich,' I said in the perfectly sincere way that especially rich people have when they use the same words, 'but if I'm going to start a collection, I'd like it to be worth something. I shouldn't mind if it proved to be a bit of an investment, either.'

'That is perfectly possible. Perfectly possible, Mr – er . . . ?'

We introduced ourselves. I allowed myself the slight dishonesty of inverting my name, the way a German would, to become James Verdon. Then with great patience, and some pleasure, at least on his part, Mr Seymour initiated me into the first rites of stamp collecting. In the course of our talk he let me know, with some gravity, that he had a number of titled clients and that the king himself was a devoted philatelist. I allowed myself to be impressed by this fact, which seemed to me bizarre. I had a mental picture of His Majesty sitting at his albums, by a shaded lamp, inspecting row upon row of small pictures of his own profile.

There were, as Mr Seymour said, many reasons for collecting stamps. By the time I left him, I had made a number of purchases including several books on the subject and a handsome album bound in morocco leather, together with a number of stamps and covers which were to form the nucleus of my collection. I had also formed a good picture of the man I had come to think of as a sort of opponent.

While I was making the beginnings of a stamp collection, Edward recovered his common sense. I had torn up his letter of resignation and he did not draft another. Within a month or two, his friends had the satisfaction of reading reports of his performance in the House. Inner circles had always thought him marked for the top. The press was beginning to make the opinion public property. A leading article in one of the more sonorous newspapers struck the note.

Edward Bullen is still a young man. In a man of ability, it is hard to see how this can be a great disadvantage, and Mr Bullen is, unquestionably, a man of ability. In the present leadership of his party may be found a number of men of whom it might be said, as it was said of Lord North, that they 'fill a chair'. It is perhaps time that some of them got up and emptied their chairs in favour of younger talents more attuned to the times. Some may think it early in the day for Turks quite as young as Mr Bullen and his like – for there are others – to stand at the despatch box. No one should think it too early for the way to be prepared for them. That way should not be too long or winding.

I had written leading articles myself, and knew that these things were not the mere musings of the man at the typewriter. Here was the not-so-distant sound of political knives being sharpened.

The weekend it was published, this leader caused some lively and cheerful discussion at the Hampshire house of Sir Kenneth Evenlode. I happened to be staying there and Edward drove over from Steerham, having been put down to bat at five for Sir Kenneth's XI in the match played every year by long custom against the village team. It should be admitted that the writer of the leading article was a useful left-arm slow-bowler batting at nine in the same team. It might also be mentioned that the Bullens had a family connection through cousins with the proprietor of the newspaper. If things are done altogether differently nowadays, I should be very surprised.

The leading article was not, for me, quite the most interesting development in Edward's career to come to light that weekend. We made our way from the house and along the lane to the pitch, debating the unpromising look of the weather. The path led us through the churchyard where Evenlodes long since bowled out lay peacefully in what Morton Drew-Page once, walking the same path with me, called 'that other *Wisden*'. You know how it is with a good remark. One likes to revive it from time to time, especially, for some reason, with people who already know it. I turned to find Edward. He was some way behind, walking with Hugo Truewitt's sister Marina. They were walking in that slowly engrossed way that people have when they are walking nowhere in particular. He was stooping slightly and inclining his head to listen. From time to time he swung the bat he carried, or tapped it against his toe as they paused as if it were a stick that he might at another moment toss away into the brambles without a thought. He was the only cricketer on that walk who had paid no attention to the sky. It made me wonderfully happy to see it. I may have felt a little envy. But certainly no jealousy.

I was twelfth man and was to be called on only to take on the drinks, unless the batting went as low as eight, in which case I'd do the running for Tommy Whitworth, who had a false foot but was the best fielder at silly point you'd ever hope to see. In fact, I was not called on at all, as the skies turned to ink and the day was lost to steady rain. The weather gave me the opportunity to exchange a few words with our opening bat as he took off the pads. His name, without omission of any part of the title that adorned it, had been mentioned to me with some reverence by Mr Seymour. Our opener was a philatelist whose collection stood in the first rank. I mentioned that I had taken up the fancy and, as true enthusiasts do, he opened his heart to me. His warm words of advice and warnings of pitfall and snare would have been invaluable to anybody seriously beginning a collection. He thought Seymour was 'less of a charlatan' than many a dealer.

On my next visit to Mr Seymour, I mentioned the judgement of my fellow guest, adding a little embroidery to the hem of the thing to turn it into rather more of a compliment. I always hope that I am not a snob, not because I try to be virtuous, but because I try not to be muddle-headed. Seymour's head was hopelessly muddled by snobbery, just as I had expected it would be. The effect on him of this aristocratic notice was worth watching. We usually talk about people swelling with pride. Seymour almost shrivelled with pleasure and obsequiousness. He wrapped himself around the compliment like the late grape that wrinkles on the vine to concentrate its sugars.

I looked about his shop. It had been attended to diligently with wax polish, and his wares were arranged neatly and without imagination in bright glass cases. Despite the polish, the room was a dingy one in a dingy building in a dispiriting street.

'Do you never think of moving to more convenient premises?' I asked him. 'You are rather out of the way here.'

'If I could,' he answered, 'I'd move to the Burlington Arcade or somewhere of the kind tomorrow. If I could.'

'That would certainly be more convenient. Surely the increase in business would make it worth your while? Chaps like me would certainly be able to call much more often.'

He talked of the difficulty, the cost, the risk – and he talked with undisguised longing. I took what opportunity I could to excite his imagination with the lustre of a Mayfair address without appearing to take too close an interest in his affairs.

The next letter was not long in coming.

'He wants two hundred and seventy-five, Verdon.'

'He has ambitions to move his business to the West End. Perhaps he's found a lease. I have to say that I have been encouraging him rather.'

'Verdon, why?'

'I think it's what we want.'

He got up out of his chair and paced the length of the fireside rug two or three times.

'He wants enough when he's a little nobody in Holloway, Verdon. What's he going to want when he's strolling down Piccadilly? What are you up to?'

'Edward, I want him to make a success of this business of his and so should you. The difference between a blackmailer and his victim is that the victim has a reputation and a future to lose, the black-mailer nothing of the kind. The most dangerous blackmailer is the nobody. I want Mr Seymour to feel that he is somebody. Might I make a suggestion? It would enormously increase Mr Seymour's standing in the world if he were to be invited to write, oh, a hundred or so words a month in a respectable newspaper. Philatelist's Corner. You know the sort of thing I mean.'

Edward looked at me with extreme disapproval. I persisted.

'He would begin to think he really was somebody, then.'

'I wish I could follow your thought processes, Verdon.'

'We will build him up until he has something he is terrified of losing. Mr Seymour would be a thoroughly sound choice as a philatelic correspondent. He'd give excellent value, I'm sure.'

The English class system could not be kept up by the simple self-interest of the people at the top. It depends even more on the voluntary subscriptions of those who come lower down. Seymour was clearly a willing subscriber. When he moved his shop to the West End he moved, and not only in his own eyes I'm sure, higher by a good bound. It was not in one of the fashionable arcades but Piccadilly was not too many steps away. He had brought some of his glass cabinets with him from Holloway. There they had looked finer than their circumstances. Now they looked like shabby inter-lopers, but Mr Seymour stood among them, glowingly pink, his fleshy neck pinched by a cruelly starched collar, and with the air of a man who had begun to be somebody. One morning, shortly after he had opened for business at his new address, I was walking down Curzon Street and saw him stop opposite Trumpers. After a moment, he walked on but then turned abruptly and crossed the street. The next time I saw him, his thinning hair was freshly cut and gleaming. It is not that he had entirely acquired the confident demeanour of other men who called from time to time at Trumpers on their way to and from their clubs but he approached as close as was likely for a failed schoolmaster. I called at his premises later in the week. To my surprise, Mr Seymour offered me a glass of sherry.

'To be honest, Mr Verdon, I should be glad of your advice.'

'It's not usually worth very much,' I said, 'but I'll certainly take a glass of sherry for it.'

He poured two glasses of amontillado and leaned back against one of his cabinets as if composing a sentence whose precise phraseology carried some legal or perhaps philosophical import. He pursed his lips once or twice as if about to begin but regressed to the phase of inward gestation with a sip or two of sherry. Finally he pulled at the bottom of his waistcoat and began.

'I am considering writing what I believe they call a column in one of the more serious papers. I have been asked to do so, anyway.'

He managed to convey that the request might almost constitute a nuisance.

'To write about stamps, you mean?' I was impressed.

'On the subject of philately, of course.' He smiled self-deprecatingly. 'I would not venture my opinion on any other subject, but this is the one area in which I know whereof I speak. So to speak. You might read such a column, I take it?'

'I dare say I would. Especially if it were informative.'

'Now that is just the point. What sort of information does the general reader want? I should be very glad to hear your views. They would be most helpful to me.'

I gave him my views. He wished to refill my glass, but unfortunately I was late for an engagement. It seems my views were most helpful to him. I was flattered that he accepted my suggestion for his pseudonym. The little monthly corner by 'Denarius' became required reading among stamp collectors.

Edward and I were walking in St James's after lunching at his club. The moment he told me his news, I knew that he had raised the curtain on what I thought of as Act Three of the drama. I hoped that there were to be only three acts and that, in the end, the play would not turn out to be a tragedy.

While it was news, it was nobody's idea of a scoop to learn that Marina Truewitt had accepted his proposal of marriage and that their engagement was shortly to be announced. You will have guessed that I had encouraged the friendship between Edward and Marina and was delighted to hear what he said. She was a woman of intelligence, humour and forceful character and exactly what Edward needed in a wife. Fortunately, she had decided this herself and before long Edward had had little choice but to propose to her.

He stopped and leaned against the balustrade of the bridge. 'I'm not sure I know what I'm doing, Verdon. I find that I've promised to marry Marina. How can I do it? She is so marvellous and she makes me feel so extraordinarily strong that I lose sight of things. But I can't . . . I can't marry her. Can I?'

'Why not? She is exactly right for you. You know it. She has judgement, Edward, and nothing could possibly overawe her. Exactly the woman for Downing Street.'

'Verdon. I wasn't putting her forward for a professional vacancy. I asked her to marry me because I love her.'

'I know that, Edward. It's just not the sort of thing a chap mentions, except when he's in love. Which I'm not. Which is lucky for you because if I were it would be with Marina.'

'But I can't marry her.'

'You must.'

'But you know why I can't. The worst that can happen is I'll have to resign, and I'll have no future. Well, nowadays I can look on it with a certain amount of equanimity. I'll take what comes. But I've no right to let . . . to take Marina on board to suffer, if it comes to it, exactly the same fate. It's obvious, Verdon. One can't do that and I shouldn't have put myself or her in this position. I did, because . . . ' He peered over into the water for a long time. It wasn't a sentence he had to finish. Not to someone who knew Marina.

'Edward, Marina's happiness is important to me, too. As is yours. I think it's very important, not just for the two of you, but for lots of people. For the country, even, if that doesn't sound too silly. So we will now sort this business out for good.'

He looked at me and shrugged wearily.

'But we can't.'

'I will. I think I can do it; it will cost a bit of money, but I think it will come back to us. And it will be settled once and for all.'

There was a slight alarm that he was anxious to convert to amusement on his face as he turned to me.

'Whatever you're suggesting, I hope it is entirely legal, Verdon.'

'Legal as Letters Patent, old chum. It occurs to me that you should settle a date for the wedding somewhat after the King's Birthday, Edward.'

He looked at me with a sort of amused resignation.

'If you say so, Verdon.'

'Let's go to Bond Street and I'll help you choose something for Marina. You can not entirely trust your own taste in these things.'

*

Lady Bullen fingered the single row of pearls and let them fall back upon her bosom. I always want to touch perfect pearls but contented myself with enjoying their soft glow while waiting for her to turn over what I had said. At length she spoke, ticking off her points on the fingers of her left hand.

'There are three things, aren't there? How it is done – the practical side, I mean; to whom does one go these days? Then there's the money. What will it cost? How much would be sensible? And then there's the problem of . . . overcoming one's revulsion.'

She turned in her chair and looked at me. The play of the light on the orient of the pearls was lovely to see. The lucidity of her mind was no less pleasing. I was glad not to be dealing with her husband, who would, I knew, have been far too much prey to his emotions. The revulsion was the problem. We were discussing certain aspects of the English appetite for class distinction. The English are no longer entirely agreed that their class system is a good thing but at least it has a kind of honesty. Nobody pretends that it isn't there, or that it is anything other than what it is. As long as you have the right money, there is no difficulty about buying yourself a title in England. Once upon a time, you gave the cash directly to the king, who was glad of it because he was always hard up. Nowadays you hand it to the political parties because they are hard up. Now and again, the trade in honours gets to be so brisk and careless that people pretend to regard it with distaste. One such fit of indignation, long ago, persuaded Parliament to pass an act to abolish the trade. They might as well have passed an act to abolish the North Pole, but at least it had the effect of restoring the air of hush and circumspection.

'I understand that fully, Lady Bullen. Your revulsion is quite natural and I share it. But in the present case, I look at it like this: while we're sitting here, someone not very far away is necking a chicken for our soup. Mrs Parry is in her kitchen dressing a hare. There's a natural revulsion to be overcome in doing these things but it is worth it for the excellence of the result.'

'One might feel badly about the other people on the list, all the same.'

'There'll be quite a lot of third-rate politicians and doubtful bankers in the list. A blackmailer will surely find people to feel at home with.'

'I don't always appreciate your humour, Verdon. Think of all those ambassadors and diplomats. All waiting for their K. Men of the best sort.'

'There can be few subjects in which senior diplomats are better versed than blackmail, Lady Bullen.'

'You might have done frightfully well in the Foreign Service, Verdon. Did you never think of it?'

'No, Lady Bullen.'

'Why not?'

'I shouldn't have known anybody. I wasn't at Eton.'

'And there's your humour, of course. You would probably have ended up in Ulan Bator. Let's talk about the money. How much would one have to think of?' Her face betrayed no emotion. The pearls continued to glow contentedly on her bosom.

'I don't really know. But it will cost something.'

'And the other thing? With whom does one do business?' And then she shook her hand, dropping the pearls again. 'I suppose I do not need to know. But let us not try to raise him too high.'

'Just high enough for him not to want to lose his footing. At any price.'

The view from the window was not grand, though it offered a glimpse of the Victoria Tower down a cleft between the unimposing rearquarters of other buildings with even worse views. To make up for it, the office itself was charming. Only the filing cabinet made any suggestion of being businesslike. The carpet was a supple and delicate Tabriz and in place of a desk was a round table, exquisitely inlaid, on which books and papers lay in neat, overlapping piles, as if divided into suits. Over the mantel, where one might have expected a portrait, or an impressionist landscape, was a Tibetan prayer banner in a plain frame. Apart from these things the room was almost ascetic. The man sitting at the table was apologetic.

'I'm sorry I can't offer you tea, but I really can't bear the mess. If it came up in a tin mug, one wouldn't mind so much, but it seems to involve more vessels and machinery than the Spithead Review and I really can't bear to see it all over the place. You don't mind?'

Alastair McLaren's peculiar fastidiousness was well known. He had been known at Cambridge for having banned every kind of food and drink and, for a while, anything made of leather from his rooms at Cambridge. He had been known for other things, too. Brief intense friendships, brief intense poetry published in a review, edited by himself, whose life in print was brief but intense and succeeded in bringing his reputation even as far as Oxford. His views, as expressed in some of his verse and a great deal of entertaining conversation, amounted to a conviction that the remainder of history was going to be brief but intense. At least, it would be intense for those with the intelligence to realise that it was going to be brief. He was an intellectual and aesthetic equivalent of the sandwich-board man who claims the end of the world is nigh. Unlike the sandwich-board man, he did not disguise that he was delighted by the idea. Alastair McLaren had become more sober in appearance and his hair was vanishing prematurely, but it was clear that he had not, like so many men, changed out of recognition as he began to approach middle age. We passed the usual pleasantries back and forth, invoking the names of mutual acquaintances and other items of common recall, and then glided into business. I explained all the details of Edward's case and laid my plan, such as it was, fully before him, only keeping back Edward's name or anything that might have suggested it. McLaren steepled his fingers under his chin and absorbed all of it with the impassivity of a cat in a window. Then he looked at me with an intense sparkle in his eye.

'It is elegant. I am drawn to the idea. Yes, we must put this into effect.'

'I am pleased you approve.'

'Once you've drawn the outlines of the thing, Verdon, it's rather like being given a pretty clock. One couldn't do other than wind it up and wait for it to strike. I should think, in principle, from what you say, any degree of distinction, however small, will do it. There probably isn't an order of distinction low enough to miss the mark.'

'I'm sure you're right, but one feels . . . '

'I know what you're going to say,' said McLaren. 'The nature of the drama demands worthier props than, say, a British Empire Medal.'

'I think so. While it would be interesting to discover how small a gong a man like this will sell his soul for, that isn't the object of this exercise. The object is to free one's friend, not to conduct an experiment.'

McLaren stretched himself a little. The resemblance to a cat in a window was sometimes extraordinary .

'I had thought of a CBE, perhaps,' I said. 'What sort of money would that take?'

'I've no idea. Does anyone make a market in them? People with the money to buy dignities want more than that, don't they? They want something they will hear on people's lips every day. They don't want to have to peer at envelopes, and suffer pangs if it's not there. Not how vanity works at all.'

'But I suppose it could be arranged . . . A CBE, I mean. The shop must be open.'

'No. I won't do it. People who get those things may be quite decent, diligent souls, who have done sterling things in their way. I feel they shouldn't have to rub shoulders with a blackmailer.'

'Yes, I understand your feelings . . . '

'A knighthood then?'

'I think it will have to be. Services to philately.'

'That would be most appropriate. The King will very likely approve.'

He raised his slightly feline eyebrow. 'Do you think?'

'Oh, yes. He collects stamps.'

'Really. What a wonderful thing to know. So beautifully symmetrical. I must take a look at your stamp dealer and then we should find a day when we can have lunch.'

I suggested my club. He dismissed the notion with a glance. 'Oh no. Dingy hole. Not at any of mine, either. Let's go somewhere jazzy.'

This was heartening. Alastair McLaren was a member of a number of clubs far grander than mine, all of them necessary in a line of work that might be called political arbitrage. If we were to lunch at one of his clubs, then my business would have been only one of the things on his mind. If we went somewhere to enjoy ourselves, it meant that my scheme had caught his fancy.

As it turned out, neither of us had to play the host as we bumped into each other a few weeks later as fellow guests down in Buckinghamshire. I had been invited, as usual, because otherwise they would have been thirteen. Alastair had been invited because, I suppose, the business of the weekend could not have gone ahead without him.

By the middle of the afternoon, most of the party had taken to the river in small boats with the idea of picnicking on an island. If you've done this sort of thing, you'll know that while the platonic idea of the thing is very fine, the experience in the real world is usually vexatious. I stayed behind to enjoy the afternoon dozing over the view of the gardens from the high terrace of the house, which seemed a more agreeable pastime than getting wet elbows. Alastair was of the same mind.

'We shall be the dry-bobs this afternoon,' he said.

We settled ourselves in a pair of armchairs and a bottle of hock was made to appear. The earlier conversation had been exclusively political, as you might expect. It led me to wonder aloud to Alastair why, with his advantages, he remained a staff officer rather than a commander in the line. Why did he not stand for Parliament?

'No, no, Verdon. While I think I'm a very appealing sort of person, of course, I'm not everybody's cup of tea. Every so often, a politician has to make himself appealing to as many people as possible, most of them rather ugly and unimportant. Whatever that takes, I don't have it. Some people have it without trying, of course. Edward Bullen, for instance.'

I sipped a little of the hock, not knowing whether this was a guess, a probe or a coincidence.

'I saw Bullen the other day in Sanctuary Yard talking to some kind of deputation from Liverpool. Probably Communists. Certainly incomprehensible. It's not their anger that's incomprehensible, of course, merely what they say. But there they were, talking to Bullen, and Bullen talking to them, on terms of perfect amicability. You could see it in their faces: they thought him a fine chap. I don't believe he understands their lives any better than I – indeed, not nearly as well as I – but these same Liverpudlians would probably have been ready to tear a chap like me limb from limb.'

'You'd put money on Bullen, then?'

'Oh, dear, I'm not a betting man, Verdon. I would never bet on a race unless I was absolutely sure that I had rigged it from start to finish, from the stable lads to the Jockey Club. I don't like doubtful things. I like to turn them into certainties. But I like Bullen, if that's what you mean. I shouldn't mind seeing him do well. You two were at Oxford together, weren't you?'

'Yes, but he was the serious scholar.'

'Didn't get his fellowship at All Souls, though.'

I realised that McLaren had not brought Edward into the conversation because he had begun to nose out his involvement in our business. It was simply the ordinary watchfulness that clever men maintain towards each other. I wanted to take the conversation away from Edward and the surest way to do that was to turn it to Alastair himself.

'Why does it satisfy you, Alastair? Working to rig the races, I mean. You are much cleverer than the people you serve.'

'Did you never build a sandcastle, Verdon?'

I had to confess that I never had.

'Then perhaps you don't realise that the whole point of building a sandcastle is the returning of the tide, Verdon. The tide. That's the most thrilling part. You know for the first time, and never more clearly, that you may be tiny but you work in a realm of enormous forces. The more elaborate the sandcastle, the more painstaking and devoted the labour, the more delicious is the moment when that first little scurry of water licks away the first few grains. You never see a child cry to see it, do you? When he sees a turret topple, his only regret is that it wasn't higher. By the way, I think I may be able to do rather well by your philatelist. What would you say to Denarius Seymour brackets Bart. Hmmm?'

I was shocked to silence for a while.

'A baronetcy?'

'A Bart.'

'Surely that is hardly possible?' I was feeling a strong flush of the revulsion that Fanny Bullen had commented on. I was also feeling a degree of alarm. I had perhaps not made things perfectly clear with McLaren. Perhaps he had an exaggerated – a hugely exaggerated – idea of the fund available. A Bart was surely a very expensive thing. It was probably the only time in my life that I came close to saying, 'Steady on, old man.'

'I'm amazed that it would be possible, even for you, to arrange that,' I said, 'but even if it were, the funds wouldn't go to it.'

A slight impatience flickered across his face.

'Never mind the money. Let's just see if we can do it.'

I was as awed as any child watching the tide eat at the ramparts of his sandcastle. In this case, however, the tide or some other powerful force appeared to be building the sandcastle, which was even more impressive.

'I'm almost alarmed at what we might have set in train here, Alastair. It is becoming a bigger thing than I imagined. Certainly a more conspicuous thing and that's what worries me. Won't people be rather inclined to ask, 'Who is this chap?' I'm not quite sure that's what we want.'

'Certainly they will ask. And we'll tell them that he is the descendant of a second cousin of the Earl of Oswestry whose title was extinguished by attainder at the time of James II. His Majesty may be inclined to forgive and forget and restore the family to dignity.'

'Is any of this true?'

'Of course it isn't. But something like it is probably true of anybody you stop in the street. If breeding is what you're looking for, the English aristocracy have been pretty spectacular breeders through history. The thing is, you were absolutely right: the King is frightfully keen on philately. I believe that he may think it fitting to elevate the fancy in this way.' He raised his glass and smiled. 'Let's see if it can be done.'

There is nothing new in the mania for celebrity and glamour and ballyhoo. In the world of post-war austerity, when all we had plenty of was whatever you needed for fighting a war, the lives of the rich, the titled and the beautiful were parcelled up in daily portions, just as they are today. The press was more polite and the pictures were not in colour, but the pleasure of gawping was no different.

The engagement of Edward and Marina was just the sort of story that the gossip editors wanted to print and readers wanted to read. News of Edward's engagement to Marina Truewitt was given quite a splash in several newspapers. The couple were photogenic and clearly in love and so had their season in the spotlight.

Congratulations came in from all quarters. Edward put a letter in front of me, having found me at my flat on the Embankment.

DEAR MR BULLEN – The announcement of your engagement to Miss Truewitt is very pleasing to hear about. Please allow me to join the hundreds who must now be urging their congratulations upon you. All the pictures and stories in the newspapers are, I hope, very gratifying to you, even though you are so much used to being in the public eye. They show that you and your bride-to-be are held in great and widespread affection by the public.

Clearly, you are beginning a new chapter of your life, a chapter that I'm sure will be a very happy one. In the new state of affairs, you may no longer wish to continue with your investments in philately. If that is so, I would quite understand, and perhaps it is time to bring our affairs to a conclusion. Let me know when it would be convenient for us to meet. I'm sure we can tie up any outstanding matters in a way that will be perfectly, and finally, satisfactory all round. Awaiting your reply, I am, as ever,

Your humble and obedient servant,

JEREMIAH SEYMOUR

'What's your opinion, Verdon?'

'Until you pick up a snake, Edward, you're inclined to think his skin must be very slimy. You are surprised to find that it is pleasantly smooth and perfectly dry. Mr Seymour's manner, on the other hand, is so pleasantly smooth it is a shock to remember what extraordinarily slimy stuff you are handling. I rather wish he'd cut words out of a newspaper.'

'But what does he mean? Does he mean what I take him to mean? Do you suppose?'

'You take him to mean that he's offering to return your correspondence for one last, large consideration?'

'I suppose that's it.'

'Well, he may mean it. But he began by suggesting that he'd return these things to your keeping after one first, small consideration. What has he done that should make you believe him now?'

'Nothing. You're right.'

He leaned against my mantelpiece and prodded the coals with a poker in moody absorption.

'One can't help thinking there could be an end to it, though. By way of a simple piece of business, I mean. Pay him enough.'

'There is no such thing as enough. You're about to be married. You would prefer a clean, blank page. He knows how your thoughts run. His letter suggests that he understands perfectly how you are placed and that he's prepared to accommodate you, like a decent chap. Well, of course. Like most blackmailers, Seymour is a decent chap who'll do the decent thing. Is this beginning to sound ridiculous? It should.'

'Of course. He'll play me for all it's worth. What do you suggest?'

'I think it's time to try Mr Seymour's steel.'

He looked at me, his elbow on the mantel and his eyes flickering with reflected firelight and, also, with a certain doubtfulness.

'How?'

'Write to him and tell him that your interest in philately has waned. Tell him . . . tell him that you have learned of certain developments relating to philately – and especially to his position in the trade – and it all leads you to review the importance of the portfolio he holds. Tell him you've found out one or two interesting things about him. It'll rattle him a bit. He'll think it's bluff, probably, but he won't be entirely sure. He won't quite know what to make of it and he certainly won't do anything too precipitate. Now's the time to rattle him a bit, because, oddly enough, he thinks he's in a rather better position now that you're marrying Marina. And, as it happens, he isn't.'

'I don't follow.'

'That's because you haven't spent the time I have thinking about your affairs, Edward. You're too busy. Look, he thinks he's rather well placed, right now. Before this, he only had one bullet to fire. Now he thinks he has two. If you don't pay up, he can send some incriminating billets-doux to Marina. Now, while she might break off the engagement, she probably won't tell the world. So your career isn't ended and Seymour still has the big bullet and you're properly cowed.'

'I can follow his thinking all right, Verdon. And to be honest it seems sound. It's yours I don't follow. You say his position is weaker than he thinks.'

'And it is. He has two bullets, but they have to be fired in order. There's no point firing the big one first. That gives us the advantage of knowing exactly what his next move will be if we push him into making it. That is the greatest of all advantages. It is the winning advantage in any game you mention.'

'It might be a winning advantage if one had a weapon with which to riposte.'

'We will have. For now, it's enough to make him circumspect and keep him a little rattled. If you play chess, and unexpectedly offer a piece for the taking, your man will look about the board a long time, rubbing his nose, before he takes it. He won't fire the bullet that would cause Marina to break the engagement, not until the last possible moment before the wedding. Of course he won't, because what he really wants is the money. Then of course, if he does pull the first trigger, he'll find the shot was a dud. That will give us even more time.'

'What do you mean by a dud?'

'I mean it won't work. If he sends her one or all of the letters you ever wrote to Richard, she won't break off the engagement.'

'Please, Verdon, don't gamble with things like that. Marina means . . . You know what she means to me.'

'I'm not gambling, Edward.' I did my best to look feline and composed. 'I'm not gambling because I have been very careful to fix the race. From stable lads to Jockey Club as Alastair McLaren would say.'

'How have you fixed it?'

'Marina already knows that you were in love with Richard, a long time ago when you were hardly more than boys, and that you wrote some exquisite but embarrassing letters.'

'She does not.'

'She does, Edward, because I told her. I told her before you were engaged. She's a very intelligent woman.'

'You bastard.'

He turned from the fireside and picked up his hat and coat on the way out. I heard the slam of the front door.

There was no need to explain my actions to Edward. His emotions, with which I could not argue, would subside, then his brain would take over and he would see the argument for himself. He would be able to reason it out just as I had. Probably, there would be no need for either of us to mention that particular matter again. In the meantime, I wished to hear from McLaren. Our plans were, by their nature, forced to adopt a certain timetable. Honours are published at particular times of the year. Once it was apparent that a bargain could be struck, Bullen money would go into a special coffer kept by McLaren's party. Then Seymour's name would appear on the list that went forward to Number Ten. The list had next to be formally submitted to the King. The King was not expected to find fault with the list. Letters would then be sent to those whom it would now please His Majesty to recognise or elevate. These letters were – are – to their recipients uniquely thrilling. They inform you that His Majesty is minded to confer upon you such or such an honour. The writer asks you to confirm that you would be minded to accept it . . .

The recipients are not expected to find fault with this letter.

There is only one thing that has ever given me much more than a moment's regret about not being rich. Of course, for the greater part of my life I've been lucky enough to enjoy most of the things that come from being rich. Sometimes I've been hard up, and there has been no one at hand to open a bottle of something good. No matter, I've been content to drink water, treating it with respect and serving it to myself in the best available vessel. Plain water has given me great pleasure. There are all sorts of things money can't buy, and all sorts of things you don't need money for, but neither list includes bespoke shoes. The thing to envy most about the rich is the shoes on their feet. I am told that everybody's feet are of a slightly different size, right from left. If you're rich, so are your shoes.

Once, in a momentary flush of good fortune, I had been to Lobb's and had my lasts made. By the time the shoes were made, the tide had turned and I'd been obliged to borrow the money to settle for them. Since then, my lasts had not often come out of store.

It was a few weeks after my conversation on the terrace with McLaren, as I was walking up St James's Street one dusty afternoon, that I saw him coming out of the shoemakers. I thought of my beautiful lasts, cellared somewhere deep within, and felt a pang for them.

McLaren was hurrying but, seeing me, he caught me by the elbow to make me walk a few paces with him.

'Can't do the Bart for your chap. PM's office is full of dead straight bats, these days. Lloyd-George would not be amused.'

'I'm sorry to hear it,' I said.

'Would have been a rather good trick if we could have picked it up, but never mind.'

'Ah, but Alastair . . . For you, this might be just part of the rubber. For me it was rather an important trick. I'm left with no game to play at all.'

'Not at all, old chap, we'll think of something. Come round the corner to Fortnum's with me and we'll mull it a bit more.'

We walked briskly into Piccadilly. There are times when answers stare you in the face. It is only a matter of looking up and seeing them. I stopped on the pavement and touched Alastair's sleeve. He stopped and followed my gaze. He understood instantly and both of us laughed.

'Oh, the very thing,' he said. 'Won't cost you a penny.'

*

There was now an assistant at Seymour's shop and it was a little time before the proprietor could be fetched to attend to me. When he came into the shop he gave the impression, by the abrupt way he put on his glasses, that it was an annoyance to have been called out. When he recognised me his manner changed in a moment.

'Mr Verdon, I am delighted that you have called. Would you care to step into my office?'

He had, lately, been putting on weight. His jowls were sleek and pink and shiny and his manner was inclining ever further towards pomp. The whole principle of my plan had been that he should start to think himself somebody, and he was responding splendidly. He installed me in the more comfortable of the chairs and offered me sherry, which I declined with an explanatory glance at his clock.

'May I press you again by saying that I'd like you to drink to my good fortune?'

'Have you done some lucrative business with stamps or are you getting married, Mr Seymour?'

We laughed a little.

'You might say the former. And the latter may not be altogether out of the question. Please join me. Because, let me be frank, I also wish to ask a favour of you.'

I let him pour me a glass.

'I'll have to fill you in on certain things. You know that I write on matters philatelic for a certain newspaper?' He seemed to have forgotten that I had suggested his nom de plume. I nodded and murmured. 'Well, I can only put it down to that, really. But some time ago I received a call from an address not so very far from here. One might say *the* address not so very far from here.' His eyes twinkled with pleasure. His lips glowed moist as he relished his sherry and something more besides. 'I was asked to make a certain part of my stock available for the perusal of His Majesty.' He looked at me with satisfaction, waiting to see the impress his words would make. I did not disappoint him.

'That is surely very flattering, Mr Seymour.'

'I will admit that I was indeed flattered, Mr James. I put together the items mentioned and some other things, treated myself to a taxicab and went, as and when I'd been told, to the Palace. Do you know . . . ' He laughed. It was a boyish, self-deprecating laugh, meant to convey that he had not in any way become vain or lofty, despite the distinction conferred upon him. 'When the taxicab drew up at the gates, I really didn't believe the policeman would let me in. My main thought was how I would be able to face paying the driver when he brought me home again. But the policeman did let me in. I couldn't resist giving him a little wave. Felt foolish the moment I did it, of course, but the fellow actually gave me a salute. I can't tell you, Mr James, how grand one can feel being saluted by a policeman. Perhaps you know, of course . . . ' He looked at me. I shrugged a sad denial. He carried on. 'I was met by a secretary – or possibly he was an equerry, I wouldn't really know – and led what must have been half a mile. I didn't have to carry my wares, you'll be glad to know. A couple of footmen did that. Then the equerry explained to me that what I had brought would be taken to His Majesty, who would give it his attention as soon as he was able. I was to be at hand, in case His Majesty wished to raise a query. And I was just left there. No tea. No sherry. Just left. The fellow said I needn't worry about being kept too long because His Majesty was a stickler about punctuality and that sort of thing and didn't allow people to take up more than their allotted time. So I waited and looked at the furniture and the pictures – all very good, I'm sure, but I'm no expert. After half an hour the chap came back, the footmen fetched my bits of stock and I was ushered back the same half-mile or so and out of the door. I had to walk back past the policeman and a lot of guardsmen and look for a cab. Altogether, the strangest afternoon of my life.'

'Did His Majesty not buy anything?'

'Oh yes. A list had been made out. I sent everything round the following morning. Got the cheque a week later. I'm rather sorry to say the King does not sign the cheques. He ought to, oughtn't he? Quite a lot of people wouldn't cash them, I dare say. Signed by a fellow called Parker. The thing is that I've been called a few times since then, and the King has favoured me with one or two other little orders by post.'

'I'm extremely pleased for you, old chap. Didn't I urge you to get out of that dingy little place in Holloway? Can you imagine you'd have been saluted through the Palace gates if you hadn't taken my advice?'

'I've always been glad that you urged me as you did, Mr Verdon. It was exactly what was in my own mind, of course, but a word at the right time is so often the spur to action, don't you find? It was very much the right word at the right time. And I thank you for it.'

He raised his glass in my direction. 'And now I'd like to ask you for another word or two of advice, if I may?'

'Please do,' I said.

'His Majesty has favoured me with his custom. What do you know of the possibility, the likelihood . . . What does one do, I mean, to get the Royal Warrant?'

I had expected that it would be my part to dangle this bait before him. My expression of surprise and pleasure was, therefore, entirely honest.

'I believe,' I said, 'that the first requirement is to serve His Majesty for at least five years.' His shiny face crumpled. 'But there are bound to be exceptions . . . ' He looked at me as a dog might, thinking that you have a biscuit hidden somewhere. 'I'll see whom I can talk to for you.' His tongue almost lolled.

A lion and a unicorn. These were enough, and more than enough, of an elevation for my purpose. A lion and a unicorn gilded over the shop or in a tracery of gold leaf on the pane of the door. This was the prize. Enough to let Seymour feel it come within his grasp and then to let him see the fabulous beasts pale and recede in his imagination.

I made a call to McLaren.

'He wants to know how to apply for the Royal Warrant, Alastair. It seems he's sold some twopenny blues – and a rather beautiful album and a special sort of magnifying glass and I don't know what else – to the King.'

McLaren laughed.

'He has to bend the knee and ask.'

'How about the jockey and the stewards and so forth?'

'Will he get it? Oh, I'd take a punt on it.'

It turned out, as McLaren had said, that one simply applied for the warrant. One wrote to the Comptroller of the Household, or some such, applying for the warrant to use the royal coat of arms with the words 'By Appointment'. There was a short answer if the King was not disposed in your favour and a much longer one if he was. It was longer because it laid down exact terms and conditions and caveats concerning the use of the royal coat of arms, all of which you'd expect. In sum all this amounted to the condition that the recipient must in no way besmirch the royal arms or bring them or their associations into disrepute. Whatever word was laid in the ear of the Comptroller of the Household, a man who was probably a member of one of McLaren's many clubs, Seymour had his answer and it was the long one.

To mark his new grandeur he had the whole of his shopfront rebuilt. The expense was great but the result was splendid. Above the shop where his name had formerly been painted, it could now be seen in gilded relief. When first done it looked as if the shopfitters had made a mistake. They had failed to get the thing properly in the centre. The space left over, of course, was to receive the Royal Warrant. This was an elaborate piece of construction and painting, as Seymour was sparing no expense, and it all had to be made by craftsman in the City. The splendid crest was still in their workshop when the rest of the shop was finished and the paint drying. So, for a while, the shopfront looked a touch asymmetrical and awkward.

This was the time that I paid my last visit to J. Seymour (Philatelic) Ltd. He received me with more than his usual good cheer. It made it even more of a pleasure for me to produce the morocco-bound album that I had bought from him.

'My collection,' I said. 'I think I'd like you to buy it from me.'

'Oh,' he said, quite taken off balance. 'I'll be glad to look at it, and maybe give you a price.'

'No, Mr Seymour, I will tell you the price. In fact, I have made out the invoice.'

I drew his attention to the single sheet from an invoice book that I had slipped inside the cover of the album. There was only one entry on it, under the heading Total. It was exactly what Edward had paid him as a victim.

It took him a little while. He stared at it, saying nothing. His breathing altered audibly. He continued to look at the invoice, the way a chess player looks at the position on the board.

'Oh, and I'll want something for the stamps as well,' I said.

He did not look up as the bell above the door rang out and a strikingly handsome young woman entered.

'Ah, Miss Truewitt,' I said, 'may I introduce you to Mr Seymour. Mr Seymour, this is Miss Truewitt. Perhaps you know of her?'

From then on, Seymour's composure wasn't up to it. He said nothing, nodded slightly and lost much of his sheen. I suggested that we should withdraw into his office. He stood aside and ushered us with a gesture but still without a word. It was clear that simply, physically, he could not speak. Marina sat. Seymour and I remained standing.

'You will be wondering, Mr Seymour, what you can possibly do for Miss Truewitt?'

He made no answer of any kind, so I continued.

'Just as you and I collect stamps, Miss Truewitt collects letters. She would like to collect some letters from you.'

Seymour's cheeks had become peculiarly mottled and he was trembling the way one does after a close brush with a nasty accident.

I admit that what happened next owed something to a taste for theatricals that I've never quite been able to outgrow. There weren't so very many workshops that were accustomed to the specialist sort of work, so it had not been hard to find the one doing the job for Seymour. I had taken it on myself to make arrangements for delivery of the work. The thing had been waiting in a van round the corner when I was introducing Marina to Seymour. Seymour's assistant tapped on the office door.

'The men have come with the coat of arms, Mr Seymour. It really does look very grand, sir, I must say.'

'Very good. A moment.' Seymour had found his voice, but not the note of pleasure that surely should have been his at this moment.

'Oh, Seymour, old man. Let us go and see your splendid Warrant. It will cheer you up.'

We went out into his shop. The craftsmen were showing a little impatience.

'If it's all the same to you, sir, if you can tell us exactly how you want it, we'll get it up there straight away. We've to be back in Holborn by four.'

I held up a hand.

'A moment. Mr Seymour may not be wanting the goods.'

I turned to Seymour.

'It would be a pity to put it up and then have to take it down again. Don't you think so, Seymour, old chap? It may have to go back yet.'

Seymour led me back into his office. With hands that were still trembling he opened his safe. It was a large, capacious safe, adapted for the fireproof storage of documents and, in this case, the more valuable parts of Seymour's stock. From it he took a bundle of letters tied with tape and handed them to me. I restrained him as he was about to close the safe and pulled the door wide. He made no effort to prevent me. He had lost his tautness, somehow, like a balloon that had started to deflate. There were other bundles of letters. I looked from him to them.

'Really, Mr Seymour.'

'Please,' he said. 'As to the money. I will have to make an arrangement with my bank. If you will allow me a few days.'

I opened the door and spoke to the men who were due in Holborn by four.

'You had better leave that for now. Mr Seymour will let you know when he's ready for it to go up.'

Mr Seymour nodded. He had the air of a man afraid that he might throw up. I had a sense, not altogether welcome but educational, of the particular malign pleasure that a blackmailer can take in his work.

I was in the happy position of being able to remove a cloud from the minds of several other men besides Edward Bullen by arranging an anonymous return of the letters. I suppose the recipients put it down to a sudden urge of decency on the part of J. Seymour, By Appointment . . .

The Murder of Crows

The road from Moscow to Smolensk is a good, straight road that goes directly about its business. In nearly four hundred kilometres it finds hardly a hill to impede it or a town to distract it. The punctuations are mainly monuments and memorials, and villages are conspicuous by their absence, because this is the invaders' road. The French and the Germans, and even the Poles before them, burned Smolensk and swept eastwards along this road with irresistible armies and big ideas. In each case they made the return journey without those advantages. Marching to Moscow, the conquering armies marched, as conquerors do, towards the sunrise. In retreat, they stumbled into the sunset that mocked them as they died. Every road is two roads. Especially this road.

My driver was the friend of a man I had met only the day before in Moscow. He was going to Smolensk and I was happy to pay for the petrol and a little on top. The place I wanted to get to was some way outside Smolensk, away from the road and on the banks of the Dnieper. He set me down at a minor junction where the poorly made road had been milled into deep, dusty pits by turning trucks and tractors. As my new and brief acquaintance pulled away again heading for Smolensk, I began to walk towards the forest and the village of Klamovo. The road to Klamovo is really just a stony, orange scar of track between now neglected fields. It decays into dust and then to no more than beaten turf long before the traveller sees any of Klamovo's dozen or so rooftops among the trees.

I had been told that a driver with a car or a cart would be waiting for me at the main road but I was not especially surprised or dismayed to find no such welcome. Having always avoided sports, I can still manage to walk for a pastime, though my pace is easy and I carry little. The few things I need fit comfortably in a little canvas bag on my back. I walked along the track knowing that the driver, should he come, would know me at once for the expected Englishman. Failing all else he would know me by my shoes. Few strangers walked this track and fewer still would be found walking it in a stout pair of brogues.

The walk had its pleasures. Between the islands of grass, much of the countryside was a sort of archipelago of marshy hollows and margins, green with alders and rush and flag, and quick with the glittering flight of dragonflies. The rest was a forest that formed the entire horizon, near or far. Very soon, I was walking where the trees came close to hand. The eye might take in thousands at a glance and every tree a birch. If you are accustomed to English oaks and limes and chestnuts, they are rather trivial trees, the canopy of their little leaves as delicate as agitated lace held up against the sky, their noise a sort of childish whisper among the slender silver trunks. The trees may be slight, but the forest is not. You imagine, whether it is strictly true or not, that the whisper of leaves may be one continuous message passed without interruption to the borders of Mongolia.

I had been walking for half an hour before I saw the Lada. It was rust-stained and not many of its visible parts had started out in the same car. In a cloud of dust, it bucked its way towards me and came to a stop, its driver leaning out and wafting at the air with a forage cap.

His name was Alexei and he greeted me with a handclasp and the kind of wide grin that an Englishman might save for a friend he had cherished from his schooldays. His welcome was encouraging. We had both lived long lives, worlds apart. We had both, I guessed, played small parts in the machinery of mutual suspicion. Much history was dismissed in that single handshake. I climbed in and Alexei made a brusque and dusty three-point turn.

'Timofei is very happy that you come.'

I smiled and nodded between grimaces. The Lada's springs had long since collapsed under the combined violence of the potholed track and Alexei's driving.

The way came down at last to a mere stripe of wheel-worn grass across a green meadow. Meadow is an English translation that does not suggest anything like that vast level lake of grass in the vaster continent of forest. The trees on its farther side were blue with distance. In the hem of the forest closer at hand, a herd of cows, much the same colour as the pale dust on my shoes, had sought the shade. Some of the cows were hobbled, their forelegs linked by short, fraying ropes, and small, unprofitable looking sheep grazed with them, even between their hooves. The scene would have seemed familiar to a subject of the Czar. If there had been a collective farm, and of course there had been, it had come and gone.

An old woman and a girl attended the cows and Alexei called a greeting, so I waved and smiled also. The old woman replied with a swing of the stick and a smile that was not without its grace even reduced to three teeth. The girl did not smile but stepped behind the old woman, lifting a corner of her elder's shawl to cover herself to the eyes. She could have hidden herself as completely by deploying the metre or so of blonde hair that tumbled out from beneath her headscarf and fell behind her shoulders, but it would not quite have served her purpose. I have no doubt that her grand-mother had warned her never to let a stranger see that she was young, pretty and well shaped. Desirable and exploitable.

There was no sense of plan to the hamlet of Klamovo, no street or square or green. No two houses faced quite the same way. Doors and windows and eaves were painted here and there, in defiance of dereliction, in patterns of bold primary colours. Each house had a garden in which flowers and vegetables grew indiscriminately. Each garden had a fence into which had been adapted, just as indis-criminately, anything that served to make good a gap: rusting implements, parts of old machinery, shards of broken furniture.

Alexei turned the Lada in between two wooden houses, up a small bank, past another pair of houses and stopped with a rasp of the handbrake outside another that stood without a companion on a slight brow. A number of geese, grazing the muddy slope between a disorderly fence and the river's bank, hissed their usual noisy challenge as we got out of the car.

As I looked at the house, the door was opened and an old man, leaning heavily on a stick, stepped out into the sunlight at the top of the skewed wooden steps. He steadied himself against the handrail and moved the stick to his left hand. He could barely grip it and it seemed to give him no support, but he had his right hand free to extend towards me as I climbed the steps.

'Timothy,' I said.

As I grasped his hand he smiled. It was the wreck of a smile and only half his face was still completely up to it. He spoke with the special deliberation of a man who had been deprived of speech by a stroke and had laboured to recover the power.

'My dear chap, it's very good of you to come.'

Despite everything, it was still his voice. Had we met in complete darkness I would have known that this was Timothy Gray, former fellow of All Souls College, Oxford. Stick, stroke, slur and all; pink-headed, slack-cheeked and shuffling, this was still Timothy. He still had the air of a man just managing to suppress his impatience. It was a characteristic that had always made him enemies, especially among those who saw in it his estimate of their intelligence or the superiority of his own. It had survived forty years of exile and a stroke.

His name once meant something but is not remembered now, so I should tell you what was once well known about Timothy Gray. The queue of Englishmen applying to take up residence in the Soviet Union was never long. Anyone in the queue was likely to be thought a crackpot by their countrymen, even on the left. For the most part, they were thought of as crackpots by the Russians and were accordingly refused entry in almost every case. Gray was one of the exceptions whose application was accepted.

Until 1956 he was just another of the left-wing intellectuals who combined an academic life with forays into the public arena through journalism and the occasional thin book explaining knotty political things in intelligent everyday language. 'Long-Vacation Lefties' they were called by more sweat-stained socialists. Men like Tim Gray marched to Aldermaston once a year, voted Labour, and admitted to having flirted with the CP in the ardent idealism of their pre-war youth. But they lived in Hampstead or North Oxford, holidayed by walking in the Alps and wintered in the cosy gloom of college cloisters sustained by the steady circulation of vintage port.

Despite his fellowship, Gray had a vigorous and readable style and for a while had a *carte-blanche* column in one of the popular newspapers. In a later age, we would have called Gray a media don. He would have been well known on television. In those days, an academic could excite the same kind of envy in the common room by being heard on radio discussion programmes.

Tim was a natural panellist, as was the back-bench war-horse Marcus Cunningham QC. The two became regular opponents. Both had wit and could turn a phrase, both knew that to lose the appearance of civility was to lose the argument. Still, there was no mistaking the mutual loathing. Their contests became compulsory listening. The final match came when Colonel Nasser nationalised the Suez Canal, and the British government so far lost its place in the handbook of history as to invade Egypt. Cunningham declared that the invasion was 'imperative for the salvation of the Empire'. Tim's answer was outright mockery. Cunningham came back with the charge that Tim, as a left-winger, had strangely little to say about the Soviet tanks arriving in Budapest. Tim affected to be surprised that Cunningham had even noticed these events, when not so long before he had looked with equanimity on Hitler's invasion of Czechoslovakia. Cunningham, well known to have been numbered among the appeasers, now began to lose the art of concealing his anger. He wondered whether the conduct of men who sought to avoid a war, successfully or not, was open to criticism by one of 'the two hundred and seventy-five cowards and traitors who had so infamously voted to turn their backs on King and Country'. Tim Gray had not, in fact, been among that number because he simply had not been present, but he was far too pleased by the anger of the accusation to deny it. He did not struggle to deny, either, that he was a friend to the Soviet Union. At least, he said, it was a country where they were trying to walk towards the future with their eyes open. Cunningham's wit altogether deserted him. 'If the Soviet Union is your idea of the future,' he said, 'why don't you go and live there.'

The only remarkable thing about this unremarkable taunt was that within a month or so Tim had done exactly that. The bitter aftermath of Suez was still hogging the news. Tim's arrival in Moscow merited no more than a small paragraph in most of the English papers, after which he was forgotten entirely.

'What happened to the apartment, Tim? You had an apartment surely, in Moscow?'

The side of his mouth that he could still work, worked heavily. I wasn't sure whether he was thinking of spitting.

'The crooks,' he said. 'The crooks. All crooks, now.'

I'd heard other stories like it. From his arrival in Moscow, Timothy had been, at least nominally, employed by a literary institute. At first, as I knew, his intelligence and knowledge of men and affairs had been useful in the analysis of British policy. As his exile wore on, his usefulness declined. Then, for many years, he was employed to translate, into ideologically careful English, a catalogue of approved Soviet literature and drama, with critical notes supplied by himself. He was never allowed to teach in any Soviet institute or university. On the collapse – temporary as it may prove to be – of the Soviet Union, ownership of the apartment block passed into a realm of uncertainty. Old inhabitants were replaced, after whatever inducements, by Muscovites better adapted to the new economy. It was a desirable block, well placed, after all. At first, no one seemed altogether sure of what to do with Timothy or how to persuade him to leave. He was entitled to his tenure though the influence of the institute that employed him. Men had come to him with a suitcase full of dollars and a polite offer. As the institute withered, and became a mere name with no meaning, the men had become less polite, the inducements smaller.

'But I had to stick to my guns. Where could I go? Then suddenly, they stopped bothering me at all. Frightened off the turf, you see. Much bigger fish came swimming in. Much bigger fish.'

The bigger fish took the form of a company owned by Arkady Veslikov, a man with close relations in the political families that contested the government of Moscow. To understand the broad outlines of Timothy's tale you need grasp just two things. The first is that in any city where people are making money, it may be an attractive proposition to demolish a building such as an old apartment block and put up offices. Moscow is no different from any other city in this regard. The second thing you need to know is how different it is in one crucial respect. Under a Soviet-era law, property which becomes the subject of permission for a change of use reverts to the ownership of the state. It was a page of the statute book that had been very little thumbed in a state that owned everything anyway, and Veslikov was not alone in his ignorance of it. His political enemies allowed him to buy the apartment block, waited for his application for a change of use, granted it and then sequestrated the entire parcel in the name of the people. The people then, oddly enough, chose to sell it off. The identity of the buyers would come as no surprise to you. Nor to Arkady Veslikov.

'Veslikov made a lot of fuss about it,' said Timothy. 'Until his car was blown up. Quieter now.'

Timothy, too, was quiet for a long time. Then he shook his head slowly.

'They'd have left me to die in a ditch. Would have done, if it hadn't been for Alexei.'

'He found you this place?'

'All relatives, practically. Whole village. They always used to send him potatoes. Anyway I'm here now. Here for good. Here for all eternity.'

'Here in this village, you mean?'

He looked at me with an expression that was perfectly blank.

'Good as anywhere, better than most of the alternatives. They can bury me in the forest. Alexei, have we some more of this?'

Timothy waved his good hand in the direction of the bottle.

'We have very much, yes.'

'Would you be a good chap . . . ?'

Alexei left the room and I heard his boots on the steps outside.

'The refrigerator. Next door, you understand. What do you think of the Crimean Widow? Russian champagne? A couple of dollars a bottle. The trick is to have the couple of dollars.'

'How do you manage? You have a pension?'

He laughed. 'Oh yes. The Institute pension. Thousands of roubles, old chap. Thousands and thousands of roubles. Except, of course, thousands of roubles aren't worth a dollar any more. Worth nothing.'

'Then . . . ?'

'Subsistence, more or less. Up till this . . . ' he glanced at his idle left arm, 'I could grow vegetables and generally fend, you know. But they're extremely good in the village. Don't know why. Extremely good. But the pension is hardly tobacco money, now. Which at least means the fact that it doesn't usually come isn't as much of a bugger as it might have been.'

I swirled the last inch of the Russian champagne in the glass, to allay a moment of embarrassment.

'If there's anything I can . . . '

'God, man! I didn't ask you all this bloody way to touch you for money.'

Anger comes readily to old men, especially old men whose lives have long since withered on the vine, but really he was covering embarrassment. If it wasn't money he wanted then it could only be something more and not less. In the silence I emptied my glass.

'Alexei seems to take no end of trouble.'

'Alexei is an Anglophile. He reads Jane Austen.'

In a little while Alexei returned with another bottle of gassy Crimean wine. He pushed out the plastic stopper with elaborate joviality and refilled the glasses from the gush.

'Who do you see? Who is still there to be seen? I used to get *The Times* in Moscow. Kept up with the obituaries. No good here.'

'I'm surprised at how many of us are still soldiering on, Tim, but I don't see so many people now.'

'Midgeley. Still going?'

'South of France. Third wife. Can't bear widowerhood.'

'Should start to seem normal at his age, for God's sake. What about Stanhope?'

'Died, oh, two years ago.'

'What sort of obituary did he get?'

'Quarter page.'

'Up or down?'

'Down.'

'Picture?'

'I believe there was.'

'Hmm. What did they give Kingsley?'

'Not dead yet.'

'Bloody ought to be.'

'Lost all his money. Lloyds.'

'Here's to ruin.'

'This stuff likes you, Tim. I notice you talk more easily after a few glasses.'

'It's true. You'd think the other way, wouldn't you? Odd thing is, before the stroke I spoke Russian for preference. Easier. After, when I had to work at it, I could only get back the English. Odd. Russian comes if I'm not thinking about it, but I can't seem to get it out when I do want to think about it. And this is a country where you do want to think about what you say. A bugger. Still, doesn't matter here. Klamovo. What matters here is getting your potatoes up.'

In the evening Alexei led us across a little path to what he called the dacha, the sixty-odd-year-old Russian half ushering, half supporting the unsteady eighty-odd-year-old Englishman as if he were himself only a boy. The dacha was something between a large shed and a small chalet set at the end of a little empaled allotment. Its wooden walls sloped inwards. You might have thought, as I did, that this feature had something to do with resisting the weight of snow on the flat roof. I learned that it was nothing of the sort. The great meadow we had crossed had, once, been used as an airfield. Aeroplanes had been delivered to it disassembled, the detached wings lying alongside each fuselage in a single great timber packing case, whose load determined its sloping shape. The discarded timber cases, fine stout structures, had been put on skids and hitched to horse teams or tractors and pulled away by villagers. And had become dachas.

Below the roof was a single chamber with a bed, a table, some chairs. There were shelves and hooks for gardening implements and, among these, a few books. There was even electric light, supplied by a wire slung between trees.

'Bit of a retreat,' said Gray. 'This is where I write.'

On this night it was prepared as a place to eat, sitting out on the little platform that extended the single chamber into the world. It was a good place to choose because it faced west towards the wide horizon and a calm, unhectic sunset. Hours before, Alexei had lit a fire of logs. Now he brought a spade from a corner of the dacha and heaped some of the hot ash into a kind of metal basket. Over these embers he laid skewers of lamb. As the meat slowly broiled he poured spiced oil and wine over it. If ever the embers blazed up he took pains to douse the flames, so the lamb cooked slowly.

As the sun settled, bold specks of gold began to gleam, far away, above the dark band of trees.

'Cathedral in Smolensk,' said Alexei. 'You are religious man?'

I shook my head.

'It is no matter, you should go to Mass and hear choir. Very good.'

The tiny golden flares were suddenly extinguished and night marched beyond Smolensk. Alexei threw logs on the fire and sparks rose in urgent swirls.

'You said this is where you write . . . '

'Ah. Yes. I have been writing.'

There was a little discomfort in the following silence. I had made an assumption as to why, when he had heard I was in Moscow, Timothy Gray had asked me to come all this way. I was about to be offered his memoirs. He would ask me whether I thought any publishers in England would be interested. He would wonder what I thought the market might be, pointing out with feigned diffidence that his manuscript dealt with events of some historical interest. He would tell me that the truth about certain matters had never come out, but the real tale was told in his pages. That there were people who would want certain things suppressed. Almost everybody believes these things about their own memoirs. You will understand that Tim was not the first of my acquaintance with whom I had gone through this conversation. All the same, I waited in silence.

'A sort of account, you know. One's life and times.'

In the growing gloom, the smell of the shashlik seemed to become even more seductive.

'What do you think? Would anyone be interested?'

'I honestly don't know very much about that sort of thing, Tim. Sebastian Helliger, you remember, came out with his memoirs a couple of years ago. Didn't sell at all.'

He had that look of barely suppressed impatience.

'Your book would be a different proposition altogether, of course. You'd have observations to make of real historical interest, I'm sure . . . '

'One or two, just possibly,' he murmured.

'But are people interested, just now, in that bit of history that happened to be our lives. Publishers ask what's "now". A love affair with the Soviet Union may not be what excites them. I could be wrong.'

His face was immobile, his expression impossible to read.

The savour of the shashlik filled the air. We ate it mostly in silence and rarely have I eaten meat more perfectly cooked.

The last breeze had settled with the setting of the sun and the fire had settled into nothing more than a somnolent glow. As I put my teeth to a last nugget of lamb, Tim tipped his head towards me and the red glow of the embers settled in his eye. I knew we were about to return to the subject of his memoirs. I was ready with the promise that I would read the manuscript, that I would pass it to my agent if I thought it ready . . . and so on. But I was not ready for the question that came.

'Did you know that you were rejected by the KGB?'

After a while, I laughed.

'I wasn't aware that I'd applied.'

'You were considered.'

'Was I? When was this?'

'A long time ago, of course.'

'And by whom? '

'By Alfred Kennet.'

The frozen muscles on one side of his face made his smile

almost theatrically enigmatic in the glow of the fire as he turned to me. But I could see that he was not trying to shock me, or tease up my interest in his memoirs. There was nothing distorted or enigmatic in his eyes. They were simply the eyes of a man with not much time left who was anxious to know that I believed him.

'Alfred? Alfred Kennet? The profoundly grey economics don?'

'Kennet had the job of picking out likely people and then, if he was given the instruction to do so, to woo them to the cause. Or have them wooed.'

Tim slowly leafed through the bundle of papers between cardboard covers on his knee, his own clumsiness irritating him. At last, he handed me a piece of paper. It was a photocopy of some smaller document, the poor Russian paper already yellowing with age.

The moment I unfolded the brittle sheet in the light of the lantern that Alexei held above my shoulder, I knew. It was the handwriting of commentaries on my undergraduate essays; it was the writing from occasional notes that turned up among the invitations landing in my pigeonhole, long ago. It was the writing of two or three letters that Dr Kennet had written to me in the years after leaving Oxford. I was surprised at how familiar the writing still was. Small, quick, unmistakable. Tim was right. It was Kennet's. But he had hold of the wrong bit of the stick. It was not Alfred Kennet's writing, but Julia's.

J. A prospect. Has good mind. Suspect intellectual stamina but compensating flashes of originality. He may not wish to sit for the Civil Service. Not easy to see what prizes he aims for. Could and should be encouraged to sit. Money important to him? Aware of his lack of it and his apparent lack of ambition the harder to understand therefore, but too little ambition a better starting point than too much.

I looked up at Gray. His eyes had been on me while I was reading and didn't flicker now.

'And this is a memorandum to whom?'

'Who the first reader might have been is lost to me, I'm afraid. But to the KGB, at any rate. It is from their files.'

'It could be from one academic to another about practically any-body. Tutor to dean, say.'

'Just so.'

I might not have been convinced, had not the memorandum been put in my hand in a village beside the Dnieper in the depths of the Russian forest by a man who had left London for Moscow in the 1950s and had never been back.

'And J is?' I asked, though it was a damn-fool question.

'You, of course.'

I stayed silent for some time. Then I picked up the yellowing paper and turned it to him.

'This, by the way, is not Alfred Kennet's writing. It's his wife's. Julia's.'

He reached out a shaking hand. I gave him back the paper and he stared at it.

'Good God, so it is. A bit of misfiling by some bugger. Julia. So it is.'

'Did you know her?'

'Yes. Like you. In every sense of the word.' His mouth twitched. I thought it was a little laugh at first, but it was only the effort of speaking. 'That was her task.'

'Her task?'

'They mainly wanted heteros out of Oxford. Homos out of Cambridge, heteros Oxford. Idea was . . . '

' . . . it helped to keep the two networks separate.'

'Exactly. Less likely to penetrate each other.' This time he did laugh.

I didn't join him.

'So you were – er – put in for the examination.' He chewed on his lip a moment. 'Passed with flying colours. You'll be glad to know.'

I wasn't. Not especially.

'How did you get hold of this stuff?'

'Yeltsin time, there was a fire-sale in the country. You could buy anything.' He picked at the corners of the papers on his knee. 'I thought these might be a little pension policy, you know. If I could have got home.'

'You mean you might have blackmailed me?'

'Well, not you. You didn't sign up.'

'The others?'

'Call it what you like. They owed me something.'

'And now?'

'I know I won't leave here. So it's historical interest, I suppose. Couldn't get away with this stuff now. When it all started going to hell a few years ago, you could buy anything.'

'And what kind of work would have fallen to me, had I been recruited?'

'Alexei's department. I told you. He's an Anglophile. He reads Jane Austen.'

Alexei smiled.

'You, you would now be retired from highest level Civil Service. With also excellent pension and your K. Sir Alexander Verdon James, KCB.'

I was slightly taken aback. Not many people knew or ever used the first name on my birth certificate.

'I appreciate your confidence in me.'

Alexei sketched out what I might have achieved in my alternative career in one of the Soviet Union's most successful teams. It was the one, he claimed, that had helped to manage British defence policy for almost half a century. My part might perhaps have lain in the preparation of briefings for what are called, often over the sound of gnashing teeth, wide-ranging policy reviews. The first part of this intellectual exercise is to establish that the way you have been wasting effort and money to date is no longer appropriate or effective. The second part is to formulate a new way of wasting effort and money that will last until the next wide-ranging policy review.

Alexei ticked off projects into which money and science had been poured. There were names I knew. Blue Streak. Blue Steel. Chevaline. TSR2. He pronounced the repeated word 'cancelled' with a kind of relish, though with the stress on the second syllable. It sounded very Russian. There were American weapons, such as Skybolt and the F111, the cheaper alternatives for which we British expensively abandoned our own devices. Except that it turned out that they weren't cheaper after all, or did not work, and so were cancelled in their turn after further policy reviews. A sorry history of waste and compromised capacity, no doubt, but whether it could all be chalked up as a series of battle honours for Soviet intelligence, as Alexei claimed, I don't know.

'You may be claiming for conspiracy some of the achievements of mere incompetence,' I said.

Tim sneered.

'If there was no Russian ventriloquist, then the performance of the dummies is all the more remarkable. Do you remember who was Minister for Defence Procurement when they cancelled TSR2?'

'No.'

'Stonehouse mean anything?'

'Good God, so he was.'

Alexei laughed. 'Later fake his own suicide. Leave clothes on beach. False passport. Disappear. This is highly suggestible man, mmm? Putty in your hands.'

'But I was not recruited. And you, Tim . . . '

'Oh, no. I was not recruited, either. I became far too public a figure far too early.' The vanity had survived, impressively in its way, through a half-century of obscurity. 'But I'd worked it all out, you see. I knew who had been.'

'A dangerous thing.'

'Oh, it was. That is why I, er . . . I, er . . . defected, as they say.'

'Or were instructed to defect?'

He nodded.

'I could have named half a dozen of them by '56. And they knew it. Once we'd invaded Suez, of course, there was a green light for them to go into Hungary. Question was, would I stay loyal to the cause when the tanks were rolling around Budapest? Some, I gather, were for arranging an accident for me, others for making me the offer. Which in the end, I accepted.'

He looked about him. It was now dark outside the ring of fire glow. Here and there the light of a small, dim bulb leaked from a window. Beyond the house lay the audible silence of the forest.

'They promised me something better than this.'

'I'll try, Tim. To find a publisher for the memoirs.'

He sat silent for a long moment.

'I need the money, should there be any. But . . . ' and he laughed a little desiccated laugh, ' . . . probably not for very long. Still, if you'd be kind enough to take care of the manuscript.'

I nodded.

'Something else might interest you.'

He reached into his pocket and pulled out a further, single, sheet of paper. It was folded into two. Carefully and with some difficulty he unfolded it and passed it to me. On it was a list but the fire did not throw enough light to read it by and Alexei had gone off about some housekeeping business of his own taking the lantern.

'I can't read it, I'm afraid. Is it a list of names?'

He lay back and nodded and then began to intone those names. 'Stanley Hogarth, Oliver Pilkington, Reece Meredith, Katherine Lambert, David Dennison.'

'These would all be Oxonians, I take it?'

'They are the ones I'm interested in.'

'Why them especially?'

'Because I think one of them – maybe more than one of them – killed Julia Kennet.'

'Julia Kennet died in the Blitz.'

'Maybe she did.'

'What do you know about it?'

'Not enough to hang anybody. I don't have it on a piece of paper with a rubber stamp. I just put things together. Scraps.'

The snapshot vision. Unbidden. Julia, naked, motionless, her eyes closed. White breasts. White even beside the sheet. That I remembered lifting gently and drawing over her head. For a little lover's joke. As if she were a corpse. La petite mort.

'Why?'

'She was disillusioned.'

'The Hitler–Stalin pact?'

'Even before that, I think.'

'Deeply disillusioned, then.'

'I think they were told to get rid of her.'

'This may be somewhere I don't want to go, Tim.'

He peered for a long time into the embers. Then nodded slowly with deep fatigue. 'Well. Long time ago.'

'Long way to go back.'

He nodded again.

'I'm done for, old man.' He almost smiled. 'For tonight I mean. Weary.'

'I'll take the manuscript, Tim. See what I can do.'

A bed had been made for me inside the hut that Gray and Alexei called the dacha and I was provided with a crude table and an electric light. If it surprises you that a hamlet that has no road should have electricity, it may surprise you even more to learn that this electricity came without meters or bills. The electricity was the proof that there had been a revolution. With the manuscript, I had picked up the folder of photocopied documents. It would not have been intelligent to think of exporting them in my baggage. Apart from anything else, and much as I liked Alexei, I was well aware that the ex-KGB man is a creature that does not exist. So I spent some of the night transcribing what I thought of interest into my notebook in the highly corrupt form of shorthand that my Pitman had become over the years.

There was another memorandum in Julia's writing concerning 'J' in which, oddly for someone who learned early that I had no religion, she discussed that very thing.

J. His religious persuasion? C. of E., probably, though he may be nonconformist. Should I invite him to evensong? Is he ready for this? Clubs?

Assuming C. of E. to mean orthodox in sexual matters, then non-conformist was self-explanatory. Evensong was equally decipherable. 'Clubs' was a momentary puzzle. I thought at first she was using the ranking of suits in bridge, in which case she had not rated me highly. But I realise it was an open question about my acceptability in certain realms. It was important to be clubbable and right-kind-of-clubbable at that. There are people who tell me things have changed.

Breakfast was a kind of sausage, mostly composed of fat, accompanied by tomatoes, pickled garlic and warm milk, all brought to the dacha by Alexei.

'How is Timothy this morning?'

Alexei rocked his head in the Russian equivalent of the Gallic shrug. 'I think he has too much champagne. He is in not good temper.' He laughed, or tried to, and then dropped the pretence. 'He is not good in morning because of paralysis. He needs to be like engine . . . ' Alexei made a revolving gesture with his hand.

'He needs to warm up.'

'Yes. Warm up.'

'How will he manage when the winter comes?' I asked.

Alexei looked up at the clear morning sky as if gauging the turning of the season. Although it was barely the end of August, there had been something close to frost in the air when I had woken at dawn. Mist had lain on the ground, belly-high to the herd of pale, immobile cows, turning them into a shadowy fleet of galleons hove to on a grey sea.

'Winter comes soon. Yes. We make . . . ' he sought the word, 'provision.'

I had a short list of questions to ask Timothy. They were obvious questions and not the sort to slip one's mind. All the same, at my age one writes things down because one may forget anything. I had no intention of staying another night in Klamovo and it is not the sort of place you drop in on when you happen to be passing.

I folded the piece of paper and put it into my shirt pocket then strolled the fifty yards or so to the earth closet where I spent five minutes or so. I then went back to the hut to put the roll of lavatory paper back into my bag. You don't make a gift of your lavatory paper in Klamovo, not even to an old friend with a stroke. Then, with the manuscript and the folder under my arm, I walked down the path to the house, hoping that Tim had warmed up. I was about to tap on the door when Alexei opened it.

'I was coming for you,' he said.

He was alive, after a fashion. Every so often he'd breathe with a sloppy, flabby sort of sound, but looking into his eyes was looking into a void and it was clear he had no power of movement. In most places, one would have telephoned for an ambulance, rushed to bring a doctor. Even though one knew death was already a fact, if not quite an accomplished fact, one might have felt some urgency, even panic. One might have felt anger that useless things were not done quickly. Being in Klamovo, one was relieved of all the necessity to stir up excitement. He was nearly dead. There was nothing meaningful that could be done and nobody to go through compulsory futile motions. I did the things one does instead. I spoke to him in a loud clear voice, repeating his name, asking him whether he could hear me and hoping to God he couldn't, for he certainly could make no reply. I took his pulse, information of no possible use, except as an indication that this hideously suspended state was not to last long. It was weak but surprised me by being steady, almost untroubled. I lowered his hand gently and that is when I saw the shred of paper clutched in his paralysed hand. There was a feeling of taking something against his will that came with prising his fingers from around the paper, but I knew that was a mere muscular accident. Though I'm not usually given to this sort of sentiment, I had a strong feeling that if there was anything on that paper it was meant for my eyes.

There was nothing on it. So much for strong sentiment. It was less than half a sheet of coarse paper from a lined notebook, jaggedly ripped and crumpled. I smoothed it, turned it, found both sides blank and put it aside. As I did so, Tim suddenly jerked and said, 'Oops.'

Or at least, odd as it was, that is what he seemed to say. With a tremendous internal spasm, he made the same sound again.

'Oops.'

For a moment his eyes stared at me and with another spasm he made a version of the same sound.

'Loops.'

The spasm stopped.

'Sweet.' It was a low, exhausted sound and the last he made, or was ever going to, even though the last wretched ebb of life was still in him.

I had run out of things to do and, straightening up, turned to Alexei. Whatever was next, it was for him to do it. He was running his broad right hand through his iron-grey hair and his eyes were moist with tears.

'There is no doctor,' he said.

'No,' I said.

He stepped across the room and slipped his big hand gently across Tim's shoulder and round his neck, feeling under his jawbone. The carotid artery runs here. It is the conduit of blood to the brain and so it is not surprising that pressure on the carotid, cutting off the flow of blood, should send a message to the brain. It is somewhat surprising, though, that such a message causes the brain to send out one of its own. It sends a message to the heart, commanding it to cease beating. This is an odd quirk of the nervous system, but an even odder one, when you know about these things, is how little pressure it takes to cause the brain to send out its final command. I don't know where Alexei had been trained or what form his training had taken but I could see that his hands were precise and his movements informed. I stepped outside on to the top of the rickety steps.

The morning was becoming warmer and a bird of prey was making the first exploratory circle of the day above the trees. An old man and a fat woman were advancing on the grass of the vast meadow with scythes, making two swathes of late hay by slow steps. Though the weather would soon turn, the rhythm of each scythe was steady and without urgency, as little daunted by the extent of its task as the pendulum of a clock. Behind me an Englishman died in a corner of a foreign field that is for ever Russia and my hands tensed with a little passage of anguish, because, after all, I'd known him when he was young and clever and full of promise. I knew that what was ending in this alien place was a story of waste and a life of irrelevance. We were exactly of an age, too, and in those circumstances the little indignities of death are discouraging. It was feeling my hands clench that snapped my mind to something else. I felt in my fingers why the paper Tim had held was blank. He had torn the sheet, perhaps the moment before the stroke had hit his brain. He had been writing something in a notebook, or on a page taken from a notebook. Then he had thought better of it and torn the sheet in two. I mimed the action to myself. It fitted exactly. What he had written happened to be on the other part of the page.

I went back in.

Alexei was sitting with him on the floor, cradling his head. We managed with some difficulty to get him from the floor to the bed and into the conventional attitude of peaceful departure.

'There is telephone at office of farm. I will report. Then I take you to Smolensk for train.' He paused as if waiting for an answer to a question he hadn't asked. 'What do you think you will do?'

'I will go to London. I'm flying tomorrow.'

'About these memoirs. And things that he spoke to you?'

'I don't know.'

'They are interesting things to you?'

'Yes.'

'That is pity. Better it is all forgotten.' He smiled.

The Lada started at the third or fourth attempt and Alexei drove off to make his telephone call. I looked for the piece of paper. There was nothing so orderly and convenient as a waste-paper basket, but then he would not have had time to be orderly anyway. I looked about the floor and under the bed and table. It was not clean and examination showed that Tim's was only one, though by far the largest, of the corpses in the room. The others, ignoring the insects that a good Buddhist would certainly count, included a sparrow-sized bird whose feathers and bones lay in disorganised association with a substance like dried glue in the space behind his washstand. There were other remains, too, and the small debris of meals, but nowhere could I find the remains of a note or letter, of the last thing that Tim Gray had written. There was no paper, but there was a notebook, thrown up on top of books on a shelf. If I was right, of course, Tim could not have put it there himself. The state of the room told me that Tim had hardly been so fastidious that he would use his last gasp to tidy away his notebook. I took it down, all the same, and thumbed through it. Only the first few pages were written on in a heavy, jagged writing. It was a record of planting in a vegetable patch, with notes of crops taken. Tomatoes had done well, I could see, because the weights were accompanied by an exclamation mark. What was of interest to me, though, was that the page after the last entry had been ripped out, leaving little tufts of its paper at the staples. If my assumption was correct, and Tim had been hit by the fatal stroke so soon after ripping the page that some of the paper was still clenched in his hand, then he had not put the notebook up on the shelf. It followed that Alexei had done that. It then followed that Alexei had some reason for having done it. When you enter a room to find a man dying on the floor, tidying up isn't what you do first. But Alexei had tidied away this notebook before I had arrived. I felt sure that Alexei had also tidied away the rest of the page, and with it whatever Tim had written. I went to the stove and opened the little iron door. On the grey ashes was a small, black immolation of paper. The crisp remains had been broken into small flakes. I closed the door of the stove. As a minder, Alexei had looked after Tim well. I glanced along the shelves at Tim's books. Some of them, evidently, his own translations of Russian works. A complete Arden Shakespeare seemed a bit of a prize to find in Klamovo. On the next shelf was a collection of the famous old green and orange Penguins, mixed with an odd assortment of books that looked as if they might have been bought at airports by Russian diplomats and passed on in a friendly way. And then, the surprise of Tim's library. A London *A to Z*. As an oddity in Klamovo, this perhaps ranked even higher than the Arden Shake-speare. It was old, but looked even older, it was so well thumbed. I picked it up, feeling a pang, a deep pang, of pity for the exile. I imagined Tim taking his imaginary strolls around town with its help. Sometimes taking trips out to suburbs that he had known, where friends lived perhaps, reminding himself of the lie of the streets, sometimes finding that his memory had played him false. Had he really brought it with him? Would anyone have thought of that? In some ways, even, it might have been an inspired idea. Somebody's perfect Desert Island book, you might think. Or did the Alexeis supply him with it as a useful reference text, along with the Russian-English dictionary? I thumbed it and, in the usual way, it fell open, broken-backed, at the places you'd expect. A folded sheet of paper fell out of it. Opened up, it turned out to be a photocopy of an enlarged section of an *A to Z* page, with little round blobs marked in various places on the original, evidently with a slightly scratchy fountain pen. The page covered Pimlico and Victoria. There, in fact, was Vincent Square, where Ross and I had our little office during the war. I took the sort of walk around familiar territory that I had imagined Tim making. Down through a cluster of the black spots and round the corner into Lupus Street. It is surely a strange old foreign and ancient word for a London Street. *Lupus*, the wolf. *Homo homini lupus.* Man, the wolf to man. Oops. Loops. Sweet. His last effort to make any sense in the world. Lupus Street.

The Lada gave loud advance notice of its return. I folded the sheet back carefully into the *A to Z*, slipped the book into my pocket and went out to meet Alexei.

The following day, Alexei did not drive me to the railway station in Smolensk. Instead, he drove me to Moscow, all the way to Shere-metevo, but not in the Lada. It was not a brand new Mercedes that he brought out from some barn or other about the village, but it was neither old nor shabby. There is no such thing as an ex-KGB man.

'For these journeys is better car.'

My little bag went on to the back seat. I had Tim's manuscript and the cardboard folder in my hand. I put those on the back seat as well.

'You might as well have these,' I said. 'I dare say they'd take them from me at the airport, anyway.'

'I think that is possible.' He smiled. 'Do you like Elgar?'

'I do,' I said.

'I like very much Cello Concerto. Is almost Russian music. Jacqueline du Pré. You know Rostropovich hear Jacqueline du Pré and he never after play this music.' He touched a button and as we drove the dusty strip across the meadow, the dark familiar melody swelled around us.

I had been in two minds about it. A lot of me did not want to rake over ashes so long cold. I had kept up with Julia for a while. She had written an appreciative letter to me about the odd pieces I'd sent back and managed to get published from my six months in Spain. We exchanged more letters and enjoyed the occasional dinner. We had even spent an agreeable night in a London hotel and the bed was as enjoyable as the breakfast, just as necessary but not much more meaningful. We were not who we had been a year or so before. Spain had made me much less confident about *Homo sapiens* in general but a little more confident about myself. I could still be overawed by her intellectual rigour but now I could begin to see that it was, in its way, her handicap. By the time the war started we'd fallen out of the habit of writing. I heard, some while after the event, that she'd been killed in a raid in April 1941. It was a raid in which several other people I knew also died and so, all in all, it was a time I did not especially want to go back to. But I did. It was a loose tooth and I couldn't leave it alone.

So I found myself in the Public Records Office looking out her death certificate. She died in St Thomas's Hospital. Cause of death, head injuries due to enemy action. I had misremembered or, perhaps, had never quite had it straight. She had been killed in October 1940.

It did not take much browsing to discover that Alfred Kennet had lived on until 1963. A contemporary *Who's Who* told me that he had married again and that number two (1949) was Katherine Pilkington, née Lambert, widow of Captain Oliver Pilkington, DSO.

This single entry in *Who's Who*, then, ticked off two of the names on Tim's list and tied them both to Alfred Kennet. No children were mentioned.

In turn, it took little effort to discover that Katherine had been a good bit younger than Alfred and even a little younger than me.

Arithmetic and female longevity suggested that she might still be alive. A woman in her early forties when her second husband dies, on the other hand, is always likely to have changed her name again.

I knew that the companionship of the Distinguished Service Order usually bottomed out at the rank of major. It was clear that Katherine Lambert's first husband had done something exceptional to get it. Oliver Pilkington's DSO had been gazetted in 1944, for action in the Italian Campaign. As the award was a posthumous one, the citation had the character of an obituary, otherwise it might not have told me that Captain Pilkington had forcefully requested permission – a permission reluctantly granted – to resign from the Ministry of Aircraft Production in 1941, in order to volunteer for active service.

The others on Tim's list presented no difficulty. I may have given a rueful smile to see that Stanley Hogarth had spent a blameless career in the Civil Service, notably with the post-war Ministry of Supply and what is now called the Ministry of Defence. Retired with his K and I'd only just missed him. Died in Lymington, according to an obituary less than a year old.

David Dennison, also now knighted, had led a similarly unspectacular life of service to his country, mostly in the Foreign Office. Finding no obituary or other evidence of Sir Dennis's death, it seemed reasonable to think that he was still a member of the two predictable clubs listed in *Who's Who*.

Reece Meredith was a trickier subject. He was not in *Who's Who* or any other directory that sprang to mind. Still, he was an Oxford man and, to judge by the name, emphatically Welsh. In Oxford, Welsh went with Jesus. It was not odds-on as bets went, but worth trying. I called my old friend, Iolo Anthony.

'Reece Meredith, how odd you should mention him.'

'He was a Jesus man, then?'

'Yes. A chap's name doesn't turn up for donkey's years and then he's all over the place.'

'Is he?'

'I exaggerate. He was mentioned in the *Jesus College Record* that dropped on the mat yesterday.'

'Why does that sound ominous?'

Iolo laughed. 'Quite right. Down among the dead men.'

'Big obituary?'

'Well no. Not the usual signed-by-old-pal number. It was more, "The College has learned with regret . . . " and so on. Seems it wasn't as recent as all that.'

'And what did they say about him?'

'Oh, brilliant chemist. First to make something or the other go fizz, or whatever. Good war for a backroom boy. Carried out chemical analyses for the Manhattan Project.'

'Did he? And after?'

'Bit of professing. Numerous consultancies, I think was the phrase. Ill health was mentioned. As well it might be.'

'Why do you say that?'

'Ah, because Johnny Owen says he turned up at a gaudy once, and Johnny got out of him that he worked at Porton Down.'

'Well, dearie me. Did you know him?'

'Sort of. Not well. Typical boffin type. Good golfer though. I played with him in university tournaments a couple of times. Got his half-blue, I think. Trialled for it certainly. What brings him up?'

'Oh, I bumped into someone who thinks he was probably a spy.'

Iolo laughed. 'There was no mention in the *College Record*.'

I didn't mention the possibility that he might also have been a murderer.

I sat in the little cubby hole with the sloping ceiling that I dignify by calling it my study and poured myself a glass of an excellent Tempranillo. The wines with illustrious names that once I could afford are now only occasional treats. Unfortunately, I have become rather poorer while they have become vastly – indeed, absurdly – more expensive. A great compensating change has come over the world. Huge quantities of good wine now come behind labels with no snob value to cash and from countries that, perhaps, you used to think made only vinegar. This Tempranillo was beginning to show the orange glow of age in a most satisfactory way. Not everyone agrees with me, but I believe that most red wines improve for a quarter of an hour or so standing in the glass. I put the Tempranillo on my desk and left it to its own devices while I reviewed my findings. They did not add up to a great deal. An eccentric Englishman, out of touch for many decades, now out of touch for all eternity, had said that Julia had been murdered. Without any corroborating evidence, he had given me the names of five people who were, possibly, implicated. I could join the dots linking two of those names to Julia's husband, which proved nothing at all. It did not even suggest anything, other than that these people moved in the same world, which amounted only to the information we began with.

On the other hand, I had two lifelong civil servants who had earned their Ks, a civil servant who'd resigned and was now in the ranks of the distinguished war dead, and a scientist, lately deceased, from one of the less-well-illuminated corners of government service. It was a kind of pattern. It was clear that any of these men could have been useful to the KGB. If Tim was right, then they had been in the spying business and, it would seem, pretty good at it, as that information had not travelled. I knew nothing of any work Katherine Lambert had done. In the pattern, she served only to connect the world of the dons with the world of government service. Hardly exceptional or exceptionable.

Except. Except that of all the widowers in the world, Captain Pilkington's widow married Julia's.

I had written the names on a piece of paper and drawn in lines connecting them and circles grouping them. Naturally there was a line connecting Julia with Alfred but that was her only direct connection. Otherwise, she was out on her own. I drew in dotted connections between Julia and the other men. Without the dotted lines, she was hardly a member of the group at all. With the dotted lines she might have been intimately connected. Of all the males, only Dennison was, as far as I knew, still alive. I went back to his *Who's Who* entry and read it again, reminding myself which college he had been up at. As it happens, it was the college of which Kennet had been a fellow. It was a fair bet that he had been a direct contemporary of mine at the University. It wasn't a great effort to confirm that that was, indeed, the case. We had gone up in the same year. But, then, so had a thousand or two other chaps I had not met. Kennet's, anyway, was a college at which I had known hardly anybody.

Once upon a time *Who's Who* listed a private address for pretty well every entry. These are more security-conscious times, but if you know a man's clubs, and provided that you are a clubbable sort, then finding his address will not tax your ingenuity. Dennison, it turned out, had kept up his memberships at the reduced rate for members living abroad, and his mail was redirected to an address in France, down in the Languedoc. It was farther than I wished to go.

Katherine née Lambert had been a trickier proposition. Having no starting point, and happening to be in the British Library one day on other business, I had decided to look her up under any and all of her possible names in the general catalogue. She must have been an intelligent woman. She had been a don's wife. She might have become a don herself. It was certainly not wholly unlikely that she had written something and had it published. A longish shot, but very little trouble to check on and it came in handsomely.

Katherine Lambert had published three novels in the 1970s. *A Criminal Element, Acid Test* and *A Radical Solution.* I formed the idea that Katherine Lambert had studied chemistry. It didn't seem at all a long shot to bet that these were detective novels, in which the detective would use his – or, a better bet, her – special knowledge of chemistry to solve the mysteries. These bets came in, too. Katherine Kennet had published, also in the 1970s, a plain woman's guide to the chemistry of everyday life, called *How Mayonnaise Works.* More usefully to me, Katherine Kennet had also published, in 1987, *The Tomb Monuments of Shakespeare's England.* The dust jackets of the detective books had mentioned that the author had learned her chemistry at Oxford. *How Mayonnaise Works* had told me that she was an MA and a D.Phil. and a member of an august chemical society. A skim through the detective adventures led to nothing that made me slow down. The plots were clearly the important things and, I supposed, as well worked as chemical formulae. The chemistry might have been convincing but the characters were not. The little book about tomb monuments, illustrated with the author's own photographs, told me, in her introduction, exactly which Warwickshire village Katherine Kennet lived in. The vignette photograph on the dust jacket of the mayonnaise book gave me an idea of what she looked like. Or had looked like, anyway, at least twenty years ago. I say 'at least', because the woman in the vignette seemed younger than the fifty-odd I calculated she must have been on publication day. You would never have called her any kind of orthodox beauty, but there was something about her face that pressed itself on your attention the way beauty does. It was an imposing face that I could still bring easily to mind as I turned in my chair and reached for the wine. It had deep, lasting flavour of the kind that unfolds slowly. It almost purred as it woke up.

I set it down again and spread out the photocopied page from the *A to Z* that I'd brought from Tim's dacha. There, at the Westminster end of Lupus Street, was the collection of dots, some overlapping. The brainwork had taken me a little longer than it ought to have done, especially considering that I'd had an office in the middle of all this at just the time the dots became relevant. I pulled another photocopy, one that I'd had sent by a man at the War Museum. Same dots. It had been somebody's task, in those grim days, to mark a map with the sites of all the bomb strikes, and this in front of me was the pattern that had fallen in Pimlico in a certain week in October 1940. The week that Julia died.

I wondered who had requested Tim's copy, and who had sent it to him in Moscow. On my more recent copy were a couple of extra marks, fresh in red ink and made by me. A short browse in the old electoral rolls had let me fill them in. An R. D. I. Meredith had lived under one dot. A certain D. C. Dennison had lived under the other. Their addresses were convenient ones for young men who worked in various government offices. But if they'd been at home during the raid, they would have had a noisy and nervous time of it. I pushed the maps aside. The picture that was forming in my mind made them unpleasant to look at. I pulled towards me a small softbound book, privately published, with photographs by the author, that had been sent to me by a helpful friend in Warwickshire.

*

She was not just an imposing face but an altogether imposing woman. The photograph on the mayonnaise book had not lied. Certainly, the woman with the trowel in her hand laying bricks on a garden wall looked a good deal younger than what must have been her mid-seventies. Yet, despite the greyed hair, there was no mistaking the face as she stood back and looked sternly at the work in progress. Here, in a large and workworn boiler suit, was the writer of *How Mayonnaise Works*. A small electric cement mixer stood nearby, beside a pile of sand and a stack of bricks. While my cab driver went through the usual lengthy charade of finding change, I watched her as she buttered a brick with stiff mortar, trimmed it with deft flicks of the trowel blade, and then laid it in place with a few adjusting taps of the handle. The driver's transaction was at last settled, not too much to his dissatisfaction, as I would need him for the return, and I stepped out and looked about the village. There are many like it within an hour or so's drive of Oxford. This one had the advantage of the railway station not too far away, from which I had come. Katherine, I guessed, would have plenty of neighbours of her own sort of age in a place like this. It was the kind of place that people retire to. I'd looked at a few myself, years before, but had come to the conclusion that you can have too much of those good things, peace and quiet. And, perhaps, too many neighbours of your own sort of age. I am a London creature.

I took the few steps to her garden gate, opened it and raised my hat to her. She straightened up, a brick in one rubber-gloved hand, trowel in the other.

'Good-afternoon, Mrs Kennet. I'm the chap who wants to trouble you about the tomb.'

'Oh. Mr . . . Mr . . . ?'

'James.'

'I remember perfectly now. Mr Verdon James?'

'At your service.'

'I shall be at yours, Mr James, but I must finish this mix and then clean the mixer.'

'You seem to be a most accomplished bricklayer.'

'I used to be better. It's really very simple, very satisfying and it keeps you fit.'

'I imagine.'

'Most of the women here bake cakes and make jam. I build walls. Why don't you go down to the church and take a look at the Corbetts? And then I'll join you.'

'Will it be open?'

'No, but you look respectable. I'll give you the key.'

I walked in through the lych-gate and between the yews. The churchyard had suffered somewhat from the tidying-up process that allowed the grass to be mowed by machinery. Old tombstones were ranged along the south wall. I glanced at the usual selection of notices and appeals on the noticeboard inside the porch. Some of them were signed by 'David', whom I took to be the Reverend David Ingoldby, as named beside the lych-gate above the times of services, and whom I had first called to say that I would like to take some photographs of the Corbetts' tomb. The bet, of course, was that he would say, 'Ah, you must have read Mrs Kennet's book.' Another bet that came in. To which I replied that I had been unable to obtain a copy of Mrs Kennet's book. 'But, my dear fellow, I'm sure she'll sell you one. She lives a hundred yards away. Why don't you give her a call? She has a key to the church, anyway, and she can certainly tell you more about the Corbetts and their monument than I ever could. I'll give you her number.'

I was lying, of course. I had read Mrs Kennet's book on tomb monuments quite thoroughly.

The churchyard had been sanitised in the twentieth century but the interior had at least escaped the improvers of the nineteenth. There was even a rood-screen. It was the sort of church my father would have approved of.

The Corbetts, Sir Digby and Lady Elinor, lay on their backs staring at the same spot on the roof of the north aisle that they had stared at for four centuries and more. A faithful hound lay curled and sleeping at their four feet. The effigies had once been brightly painted. Some of the colours had darkened, others still glowed. Much was chipped. Sir Digby had lost a lot of his nose. Lady Elinor had lost some herself but the vandalism was obviously of ancient date.

When Mrs Kennet arrived, now in tweed skirt and cardigan, I was taking photographs.

'Sorry to keep you waiting so long.'

'Quite all right. I've been getting acquainted. You didn't by any chance bring a copy of your book?'

'I should have done, shouldn't I? I'll give you one later. Don't ask me to sign it. The unsigned ones are the rarities.'

I smiled.

'A long time ago, I used to know somebody else of the name of Kennet. Alfred. An economist at Oxford.'

She smiled.

'That was my husband.'

I looked amazed. It wasn't difficult.

'Surely not. He would have been much older than you.'

'I am seventy-five.'

She said it with the smile of one who knew how the statement was usually greeted.

'I would never have believed it.'

'Well, I am. Wish I weren't.'

'Even so . . . He would have been, oh . . . '

'He was somewhat older. I was his second wife.'

'Ah . . . Because, you see, I had a few tutorials with his wife. First wife, that would be. Julia.'

'Ah. Julia. Yes.'

The slight hesitation might have been just an ordinary response to the naming and raising of first wives. You could have put the slight suggestion of a drop in temperature down to the same thing.

'What an extraordinary thing,' I said. 'Extraordinary.'

'Not really,' she said. 'It's a very small world. The older I get the smaller it gets. I don't think I ever meet anybody now who doesn't already fit in somewhere.'

'It's true, isn't it? And I suppose if you start off with two people who have an interest in tomb monuments, the odds probably go up. The vicar tells me your book is indispensable on the subject.'

'To tell you the truth, I wrote it so that I could give talks. It gives me something to do and it pays rather well, for an old widow. But the secret is, you have to have a book, and then people think you must be a terrific expert.' She laughed. 'I hope you are not thinking of muscling in on my patch.'

'I wouldn't dare. I am reminded, though, that Lady Elinor here, with her poor little chipped nose, was a second wife too.'

'Yes, she was.'

'Something a bit murky, if I remember, in the history of the first wife. Didn't he denounce her or something?'

'He denounced her for corresponding with Catholics in the uprising. 1569. Denounced his own wife. Lady Mary.'

'I suppose the name didn't help.'

'Oh, he wanted to get rid of her. It's obvious. It was all very stagey. He had her apartments searched, conveniently found a missal and a letter from one of the Northern knights. Nothing blameable in the letter or we'd know what it was, and it was probably years old. Still. enough at the time to get her nicely out of the way.'

'Yes, I had the idea it was something like that. Was she hanged or burned or what? I can't remember.'

'No. She was imprisoned. It was really a form of house arrest, in – er . . . Oh, dear, I'm supposed to know. Seventy-five, that's the trouble. All in the notes when I do the talk.'

'I'm afraid I'm older and worse.'

'Anyway, somebody's house. And she died. Poisoned I'm quite sure.'

'Enter Lady Elinor into the marital chamber.'

'I should think she already knew the way.'

'Isn't there some suggestion that he denounced her to get in first? Before she denounced him?'

'Are you sure you haven't read my book?'

'I'd be very pleased to. I think I got that from a history of Catholic families.'

'Well, you're right. After the rising was put down, the Pope ex-communicated Elizabeth – which supposedly meant she was de-throned, as well – and that's when it all began to get nasty. Much ill-feeling and general faggot-lighting. The theory goes that he was the real Catholic, planted the missal on the unwanted wife and got his retaliation in first, as they say. And put himself well in with the authorities. It is quite possible that these two permanent members of our little Anglican congregation,' she waved a hand over the supine figures, 'were always Catholics on the quiet and, therefore, officially traitors. But here they are.'

'Eminently respectable traitors. And murderers?'

'Quite possibly.'

'Plus ça change . . . '

'How do you mean?'

'You know, I wondered if that's what had attracted you, first off, to the whole subject.'

She looked at me steadily.

'I don't follow you.'

You wouldn't usually think a seventy-five-year-old widow could manage to be physically intimidating. Not even to an eighty-odd-year-old man, given reasonable health. Mrs Kennet, on the other hand, was a seventy-five-year-old widow who laid bricks for a pastime. A deft hand with a shiny steel trowel. She was intimidating.

'I knew Julia a little better than I suggested. I slept with her. As a very young man. Or, more to the point – and I think you will follow me here – she made a point of sleeping with me.'

She was still intimidating. Fortunately, she seemed also to be completely immobilised.

'You were very young when you married Oliver Pilkington. Just before the war. I looked it up. Of course, a lot of people can say they don't know what they are getting into when they marry. But perhaps you did. I think you probably shared his ideals. Didn't you?'

I stroked the head of Sir Digby down to the broken nose.

'And I do understand. They were ideals.'

I saw the first sign in her eye of something beginning to give. But she said nothing.

'Tell me why Oliver resigned from the Ministry and joined the infantry. I just want to know if I'm right.'

There was a long silence. I did not break it.

'Who are you?'

'Just who I say I am.'

'Who are you acting for?' Even under stress, she corrected herself. Or maybe it was a symptom of the stress. 'For whom?'

'For Julia.'

It was a little shudder. A jerk. As if she had been lightly punched in the stomach. But it was enough. I knew I wasn't flying a kite any more.

'Was he sickened by it?'

For a while she did and said nothing. Then very slowly she nodded. Then she stopped and was immobile again. I realised that she was showing the symptoms of shock. I gestured in what I hoped was a kindly way towards the nearest pew. She sat, obediently and gratefully.

Collioure, out of season, has the tinge of desolation that comes of seeming to have more restaurants than diners. It is the common fate of towns on the coast of the Mediterranean, but Collioure bears it with a little more style than some of its neighbours. It is a spruced-up town. There is a touch of the miniature Mediterranean Eastbourne about it, but with the Pyrenees and Cap Béar in place of Beachy Head. The marriage of mountains and sea makes for windy weather, but many people might think it an excellent place to retire to. Sir David Dennison, KCB, had evidently been one of those people. His address – Villa Bonconseil, 17 Rue Bellver de St Cyprien – was easily found in the local telephone directory. A little mimicry of telephone marketing confirmed that Sir David was in residence. Before strolling up there, it seemed agreeable to take another cup of coffee and watch the waves go about their work of tidying up the beach. My journey to this part of the world, while far from sentimental, was in its way a repeat of a much earlier journey in my life, to Perpignan, just up the road. That journey had eaten up a good part of three days. This time it had taken hardly more than an afternoon, and most of that had been checking in and waiting to pass security.

Yet here I was, after a long night's not very good sleep, wishing yet again that the French might one day grasp the idea of breakfast, and ordering more coffee. There was good reason for not hurrying. It seemed a good bet that the café one geriatric Englishman of a certain background chooses for his coffee and croissants is likely to be the *relais* chosen by another geriatric Englishman, of a similar background, out for his morning stroll. If Sir David were to turn up, he would save me the trouble of finding an excuse to call on him. It wasn't odds on, but it came in. Except that Sir David's morning outing could not be called a stroll.

Among the many deplorable things about growing old is the deplorable pleasure you begin to take in seeing others who have aged more deplorably than you. The converse resentment against those with whom age has dealt more kindly is just as deplorable but more pointless, there being no pleasure in it. I could not have denied the flush of pleasure that the first sight of Sir David gave me. The stick was not an affectation but a necessity. Without it, he could hardly have made progress. The hand that gripped the stick was clearly itself in the grip of arthritis. The diagnosis was confirmed by the flesh-coloured strapping around his wrist, visible below the cuff of his linen suit. The stooping gait of a man searching for a dropped coin was, presumably, the result of a growing spondylitis. Sir David's morning stroll was slow work. I had no doubt that his doctor had told him that the labour was necessary. He reached the café and lowered himself carefully into a seat in the sun. The waiter's greeting made it clear that he was a regular. There was probably no real need for Sir David to speak his order aloud, but I dare say that 'Un grand crème, s'il vous plait', pronounced with unmodified English vowels, was an unvarying part of the ritual. He took off his panama, put it down on the shiny metal table, and began to rummage in a pocket with arthritic difficulty. Age has stolen away most of my hair, too, but there was something especially worthless and bedraggled about the few wisps that clung to Sir David's liver-spotted skull. He wiped that skull with his handkerchief, and then put his panama back on.

I had long misremembered the name. Dickinson or Davidson was what had come to mind, not quite convincingly, for the grey man in whose company I had taken two, perhaps three tutorials. It was Dennison, of course, though I could not possibly have recognised in the man a few tables away any vestige of the undergraduate of sixty and more years ago. As aged Englishmen are hardly rare birds on this coast, there might have been no real grounds for thinking that this was my man, but I knew I had been spared the labour of finding Rue Bellver de St Cyprien. Indeed the flash of recognition came to me with enough of a poke in the eye almost to make me spill my coffee. Sir David, it was obvious, was a man who could not possibly have arrived anywhere by bicycle. Yet there, around the narrow shins, was a pair of bicycle clips tidying up his trouser-bottoms. It could only be the man I had vaguely remembered from Oxford as Davidson or Dickinson, but who was really called Dennison. Who now turned out to be Sir David Dennison, KCB. I had to choke back what threatened to be an entirely unbecoming guffaw. What I couldn't prevent I disguised as a little choking fit. Coffee gone down the wrong way.

After putting his hat back on, and presumably feeling himself properly turned out for facing company, he looked about the terrace of the café. There were two local women deep in conversation, a man reading the sporting news and me. He nodded to me, probably only because he found that I was already looking his way and smiling apologetically, as if embarassed that my little choking fit had disturbed him. He showed no inclination to engage me any further than with a curt nod. His manner of pulling a small notebook from his pocket and giving it his attention, with adjustments to the set of his reading glasses, suggested that I was beneath any further notice from him. I got up, taking my cup of coffee, and crossed to his table. Without asking his permission, I drew back a chair and sat across from him. He looked up from his notebook with silent, icy, indignation.

'One wonders,' I said, 'in the absence of a bicycle, about the bicycle clips.'

'I'll thank you to mind your own business.'

'Forgive me, but I have been wondering for sixty-odd years. In the end, one has to ask.'

'What are you bloody talking about?'

'Norham Gardens,' I said. 'That's where I first saw you put them on. And you had no bicycle then.'

His face was so entirely blank, and he was silent for so long that I began to wonder if, after all, I hadn't got the wrong chap and that, perhaps, the habit of tidying up one's extremities with clips in this way was more widespread than I had realised. But at last his pink and mottled face began to pucker with incredulity.

'Good God, you're James. You're James.'

'And you are Dennison.'

'Well, good God,' he said. 'Good God, good God.'

A woman about ten years younger than either of us came walking towards the table. Those ten years, at our time of life, can make much difference or none. In the case of Lady Dennison – it took no time at all to make that deduction – it made much. She was one who must have drawn continual pleasure from the decay of others.

'I couldn't park in my usual place. At this time of year, I ask you.'

'My dear, an extraordinary thing. Let me introduce you to Mr James.'

I stood to shake hands while Dennison explained why my presence was an extraordinary thing. His wife was suitably astonished. He and I established ourselves on first name terms for the first time. His wife he introduced as Adelaide.

'Please don't use it,' she said. 'I hate it. Just call me You.'

'Adelaide,' I said, in the German way, to rhyme with 'Aida'. 'Do you know the Beethoven song?'

Her face brightened. 'That's why my parents wished it on me. They were both musicians. If you speak it like that I shan't mind at all. Sing it, even better.'

'I can't manage that, I regret.'

'He knew me by the clips on my trousers, dear.'

'I'm not surprised. You're the only man in the world who can't ride a bicycle and always clips up his trousers.'

'Don't always. Only when it rains, or there's puddles.'

'It's not raining now. There's not a puddle in sight.'

'Well you get puddles when they spray the roads.'

'They haven't sprayed the roads.'

'Well I'm bloody prepared if they do.'

'You usually are, dear.'

He turned to me. 'I don't know why other people don't. It keeps your trouser cuffs from getting wet and filthy. You'll find they don't fray around the bottom, either. It's such a simple thing. Get where you're going, slip 'em off, you're perfectly turned out.'

'But he doesn't slip them off.'

'Well maybe not these days. Too much of a fag. Once they're on.'

'I have to remind him.'

'But they weigh nothing in your pocket. Wonderful invention, which I happen to apply more widely than most. If they had been called trouser preservers – which is what they are – rather than bicycle clips, which, as a piece of English, makes no sense at all, then nobody would think me unusual.'

There is a certain course that conversations take in these circumstances and ours took it. For Dennison, I detected, our fortuitous meeting was a diversion, though not an altogether comfortable one. We both, he clearly felt, had to subscribe to a fiction that we had known each other rather better than was the case. For Lady Dennison, though, it was clear that our meeting came as something closer to a godsend. Her husband must have been constantly on her hands. I took a bet that she would jump at the opportunity to put him into mine for an hour or two and excuse herself.

'Look,' I said, 'why don't I take the pair of you to lunch? There's a little place just over the border. Cheaper over there. Suits my modest purse, but the paella's excellent. What do you say?'

Dennison looked at his wife.

'Why don't you two go together?' she said. 'You will have so much to talk about and you'd only have to keep giving me footnotes.'

'Oh, I insist,' I said, knowing that I had already won. 'Won't you come with us? You really must.'

Which, as an intelligent woman, she correctly interpreted to mean. 'I agree entirely. I'm sure you have something better to do.'

'No, you boys go. I want to go to the shops in Perpignan, anyway, and David simply hates that.'

The road from France to Spain, climbing around the headlands and diving into the bays, is a swooping corniche as exhilarating and beautiful as any in Europe. I drive it more slowly than I used to, but it still demands attention. The passenger gets the best of it. Dennison, however, hardly seemed to take it in.

'I suppose you do this drive often,' I said.

'I think we may have done it once or twice.'

'For me it would be part of the point of living down here.'

'But it leads to such ghastly places. All those tourist beaches.'

'Any road will take you to somewhere you don't want to go, if you follow it far enough.'

'Or any life. Do you find yourself reading the obituaries first? I do.'

'Guilty.'

'I'll be looking out for yours now. You'll be looking out for mine.'

'Doubt if I rate one. Yours comes with KCB, doesn't it?'

He squinted at me sideways.

'I read the honours lists as well,' I said.

'Of course.'

'Astonishing how many deeply second-rate chaps have become lords.'

'Can't say I've ever been astonished by it.'

For the first time since we'd met, he laughed. Briefly.

It is a small bay. In Devon it would be called a cove. The restaurant has the place to itself and is simple to the point of being primitive. Its equivalent in Devon would have culinary pretensions and a garrulous wine list. Here you will eat the dish of the day, take the house wine, eat more or less sitting on the beach and you will not, on any grounds, wish yourself in Devon.

Paella was the inevitable dish of the day and as we waited for it I raised my glass.

'Whom shall we toast?'

'Ourselves, for outlasting so many of the other buggers,' he said. So we did.

'I'll tell you another one we've outlasted. You will not have heard.'

'Who's that?' he asked, perking up.

'Timothy Gray.'

There was a moment of hesitation.

'The fellow who went to Moscow?'

'The same. Old Commie Gray.'

'Where did you read that?'

'Oh, I didn't. I'm not sure it's been reported.'

'How did it come to you?'

'He'd been in touch. To see if I could find a publisher for his memoirs.'

'And have you?'

'No. He died while we were discussing it.'

'Not literally, I hope.'

'Pretty well literally, yes. We talked one evening. Next morning I popped in to see him and he was dead.'

'Had he come back?'

'No, still in Russia.'

'You were in Russia?'

'Oh, not just to see Gray. I had other things to do. He must have heard I was there. On the grapevine.'

I could see Dennison working to assess the information and decide what his response to it ought to be. I was reminded of watching Tim struggle to overcome the effects of the stroke.

'Natural causes, as they say?'

'I think so. I mean they'd clearly come to regard him as a bit of, well, not an embarrassment, more a bit of bric-à-brac they'd collected without really wanting to in the Cold War. But I think they let nature take its course.'

He made a good bit of work out of wiping wine from his lips with his napkin.

'Curious fellow, he must have been,' he said at last. 'Did you know him? Back when, I mean.'

'Oh, about as well as I knew you, really. There you are. Strange. The three of us connected through Dr Kennet. And we all long outlasted her.'

'Did he know her? I wouldn't have assumed . . .'

'Oh, he was hopelessly in love with her. Didn't you know?'

'I had a few tutorials with her, that's all.'

'You didn't stay in touch with her?'

'No. Not at all.'

'Really? I did, rather. She died in the Blitz.'

'Did she?' The arthritic Sir David Dennison could not have been proceeding more carefully had he been walking on ice. 'Did she really?'

'October '40. If you remember, there were some big raids.'

'Long time ago. My recall is not as precise as yours.'

'If you were in the West End at the time, it stays pretty vivid. I was fire-watching. Not far from the one that went in by Jermyn Street. The mine. But no. I think that one was '41. Yes.'

'I think this is our paella.'

It was too obvious that the fuss and interruption that came with the arrival of the food was welcome to him.

'So,' he began, once we had been left to get on with our eating. 'What sort of thing do you fill your time with now?'

'Well, it does become a problem, doesn't it, old man. I've given up most of the committees and the good works, or they've given up me.'

'Same boat. If I were more mobile, I might have kept things up. The Opera House. The United Nations work. But it's a bugger, I'm afraid. More or less house-bound a lot of the time.'

'Memoirs on the go?'

'No. Nothing anybody would want to read, after all. Not like old Gray. Just percolating up the Civil Service in my case, and popping out, at the end of the tunnel, with a K for duty done without up-setting too many apple carts.'

'You do yourself an injustice. People always want to know how it works behind the scenes. The skulduggery. The fell work on the back stairs.'

'Our powers are much exaggerated. What about you? Scribbling away?'

'Oh yes. A pastime, really, like doing puzzles. Or archaeology. Trying to piece together odd bits, seeing the connections. Trying to see the picture.'

'Your life must have been enviably enigmatic. Mine's just laid out in a pile of page-a-day appointment diaries and a mountain of minutes.'

'What about the appointments that were never in any diary?' I looked at him steadily and as amiably as I could.

'I'm not sure what you mean,' he said.

'Most men would, David. The meetings that were never minuted? There must have been some. Some kind of occasional *cinq à sept*? Of one kind or another?'

'Do you know, old man, I'm not sure I care for this paella. Or this conversation. And if *cinq à sept* means what I suppose it to mean, then I take offence. I have never been unfaithful to my wife. '

'I'm sure. How about your country?'

The silence was as hard as a wall. Then he put down his napkin. 'I insist that we leave.'

'The road is a stiff walk for a fit young fellow, David. You've a steep climb in either direction. And I'm not going until I finish my lunch.'

'I shall call a cab.'

It was the sort of thing a man might say in St James's. He tried to turn in his chair to look for *la dueña* or the waiter, but turning was painful and they were, anyway, nowhere to be seen. Playa del Testamen is not at all St James's.

'I know enough about how these things are managed, David, to be fairly sure that you wouldn't necessarily have put all these names on the same list. But try a few.'

I recited the names that Timothy Gray had given me. All that was necessary was that he knew at least one of the others was a spy. It was clear from his pallor and silence that it was so. He stopped trying to shift his chair around so that he could attract attention.

'All Oxford men and one Oxford woman, you might or might not notice. And all heterosexual, by the way. Though not necessarily as monogamous as you claim to have been.'

'I thought you were barmy when you came and sat down uninvited. I should not have revised that opinion.'

'In the world I'm talking about it's hard to meet anybody who isn't barmy, don't you think? Sorry you've gone off the paella. I think it's very good.'

I ate in silence for a while and enjoyed the sparkle of the sun on the small waves. I wondered if Captain Lord Cochrane had ever landed in this cove in one of his beard-singeing attacks on Napoleon's coastal defences. It wasn't quite as random a thought as all that. The author Patrick O'Brian, it occurred to me, who modelled his hero on Cochrane, had lived in Collioure. I wondered if he and Dennison had been acquainted. It seemed quite likely. Dennison had resorted to aggrieved silence as his best tactic. I decided that the blunt instrument was probably mine.

'My mind keeps going back to that air raid. When Mrs Kennet died. She should have been in a shelter. No tube station, of course, in Pimlico, though. Not in those days. She was walking down Lupus Street. I believe you know that. Hit by flying debris. Found in the street apparently. I was terribly infatuated with her. When we had those tutorials. How about you?'

He stared at me without saying anything. It was like peering into the eyes of a fox in its earth.

'A lot of us were sadly disillusioned by then, of course. Stalin signing his pact with Hitler and all that. Especially agonising if you'd been his recruiting sergeant. Which she was in her way. The scales might fall from your eyes, but how do you turn back and not betray the very people you've signed up to the cause? I believe she must have wrestled hard with it. You could almost believe that she'd walked out in the middle of an air raid more than half wanting to be hit. Almost believe it. Almost.'

He started to reach for his stick and to lever himself out of his chair. 'I am going to find the telephone and call a cab.'

I reached out with my foot and shoved the leg of his chair. He needed it for balance and had, briefly, a not altogether governable choice between falling into his uneaten paella or back into his chair. Luckily it was the chair that caught him.

'How many of you met her that night? I'm fairly sure you didn't do it alone. Was it two? Three? Three would be my guess. With three you always have a majority for some course of action. So I guess three of you. You and Reece Meredith and Stanley Hogarth. I'm sure about you and Reece anyway.'

'For Christ's sake. Why are you doing this?'

'The meeting was at your flat. Odd thing, we were practically neighbours. I used to cut along Lupus Street going from my flat to the office in Vincent Square. I'd have passed within spitting distance of your place, wouldn't I?' He said nothing. 'Did you know or did you just fear that it was in her mind to betray you all? Was she surprised to find three of you there? When she was expecting only to see you? Was she alarmed? Right away, I mean. I suppose she would have been. She'd have got the idea straight off, I should think. Being Mrs Kennet. Was it the plan right from the start? To kill her, I mean.'

There was just the beat of the sea for a while.

'Of course, it was,' I said. 'You can't just ask somebody not to betray you. Well you could, but how would you believe them? Would you care to tell me the rest?'

The beat of the sea.

'The sirens must have seemed like a most unwelcome interruption at first, the way they usually did. Until one of you recognised what an opportunity it was. Is that how it went? You can hardly have planned ahead on the air raid. Maybe when you started to hear the bombs falling not so far away, as you might all die anyway, it seemed not so gross an idea. You could all get blown to hell or you could commit the perfect murder. And what I think you did, is that you battered her to death with a brick or something of the kind. Then you dragged her out into the blackout. You'd heard the bombs fall. You knew you didn't have to go far and you could just leave her in the street. If you met an ARP warden, you could say you'd found her lying on the pavement and you were trying to get her to help. Good plan.'

He was rocking slowly back and forth. At length he spoke. It was so quiet I could only just catch the words.

'Please just drive me back to Collioure. Please.'

'Yes, I'll do that. But I just wanted to have it clear, you know. To know I was right.'

He may have been rocking or nodding. It didn't matter that much any more.

'Really, the only job I had to do was pass you the message.'

He looked at me with real fear in his eyes. Until now, at least, he'd known more about what I was talking about than I did. Now he didn't.

'Obviously, HMG has known you were – er – a man of divided loyalties for some time, you know that. But it will, I am afraid, become rather more public knowledge.'

He stopped rocking. His spondylitis took an alarming turn for the worse.

'More Russian politics than ours I'm afraid. Usual case is that both sides want the skeletons firmly locked in their cupboards, but there's a faction in the KGB rather aggrieved, for one reason or another, you see. For their own reasons, they are going to open your particular cupboard to, as they say, selected journalists. I'll settle the bill.'

I found *la dueña* and paid in cash.

There was little conversation in the car as we went climbing back round the headlands towards France. Until suddenly, not far from the old border crossing with its now ghostly checkpoint buildings, Dennison suddenly spoke.

'Hogarth wasn't there. I didn't even know about Hogarth. I'm going to be sick.'

A glance told me that he was already retching. There was a little patch of parking for a viewpoint coming up. I pulled into it and switched off. He opened the door and struggled out of the car. Bending over the metal barrier, he vomited. I walked around the car to stand beside him. The view was impressive. This is the genuine Costa Brava, not the long flat strand of beaches farther south that has usurped the name. This is the Rugged Coast, where the rocky shoulder of the Pyrenees shoves into the sea that I could hear down there, surging against the rocks below us, not loudly enough to cover the sound of retching. It is not a good idea to throw up seawards. The wind brings it back to you.

'Not with a brick, as it happens. With a five-iron.'

A strand of vomit blew about his chin and landed on his shoulder. He rested for a while and then the words came out in the weak, broken voice of a man who has retched.

'I held her down. With a cushion-cover over her head. She didn't even struggle. Not really. One swing. Into the skull.'

He vomited again. I was surprised at how much he had to get rid of. He really had eaten almost nothing of the paella.

'You or Reece?'

'Reece.' The slack-lipped, water-eyed face turned up to me. 'My club. He went and fetched my clubs. Selected the five-iron.'

He threw up again, copiously.

'Of course. Half-blue at golf.'

There was another retch, producing nothing this time but another long strand and a reedy cry to finish with.

'Oh, God. Oh, God.'

He was weak. He was finished. His suit was a mess.

'You'd better clean yourself up. I've got some tissues in the car.'

I walked back round the car, opened the door and fished the pack of tissues from the plastic trough beneath the handle. They didn't look like nearly enough for the job, but you can't be prepared for everything. I should, on the other hand, have been prepared for what I saw as I walked back round the front of the car. A young man might simply have stepped over the metal barrier. For Sir David Dennison it took an extraordinary effort. I saw him just as he stumbled into the coarse growth on the other side and began to claw his way towards the steepening cliff top. His stick was on the ground beside the barrier. I picked it up and reached over. A curl of the wind was blowing his jacket up over his head. I hooked the waist of his trousers. He still struggled to go forwards towards the sea. I could stop him going but I wasn't strong enough to haul him back.

'Let me go! Let me go!'

To get him back, I knew I would have to climb over the barrier. But that was something I could not do if I was holding on to the walking stick. Years earlier I could have done. No longer. I was already at full stretch. Dennison had only a few feet to go to reach the void. I wondered if I could hold him until somebody came driving by. They could hardly fail to see me. I hoped.

'Let me go!'

Nobody came by. You'd have thought he could only get weaker but he seemed to be gaining in strength. He was clawing at the ground. The pain in his arthritic hands must have been ferocious but he kept clawing. Then, all at once he stopped, but by then we were both exhausted. He knelt up on all fours.

'Please,' he said. 'Please. Let me. For Adelaide.'

He pulled again. The stick slipped out of my hand. Or I let it go. I couldn't say which. He took a little awkward bound forward, and suddenly, as if the wind had snatched him, he was gone. The last glimpse I had was of his legs pitching up, the trousers still clipped at his ankles.

The police had come and gone. I had led them back to the scene. The statements had been taken. It was an unfortunate accident. I sat in the house in Bellver de St Cyprien with Lady Adelaide Dennison and we drank tea. I had agreed – it was the least I could do – to stay until the call came that the body had been recovered and she might go to identify it. After a long silence, she looked up from her bone-china cup.

'Was it an accident? Did he really stumble over the barrier?'

'I didn't see him actually cross the barrier. I'd gone for the tissues.'

'I think you may be being disingenuous, Mr James. Probably to be kind to me.'

'I'm not sure I would have any reason to do that.'

'Please, Mr James. In the light of events, I don't think you turned up by chance. I've thought someone might turn up. And I expected that he'd be someone very English. Like you. I thought he might have been a little younger.'

'How long have you known?'

'I didn't. Didn't know. But I began to think. Quite a long time ago. And then I didn't want to know. Didn't want to be sure. You don't want to think your husband is a spy.'

I spared her the rest.

'And now, I suppose I shall be able to go home.'

As the newly widowed Adelaide began to face the things she had to face, I decided to blow the return ticket from Perpignan, and pointed the car back towards the Pyrenees. I headed inland this time and up the road that leads to Llivia, that tiny separated piece of Spain entirely surrounded by France. It still has the apparatus of its border crossings but these days nobody can be bothered to go through the mummery. I drove on into Puigcerda, stopped for a cup of coffee, and then made my way across the Vale of Cerdanya to the town of Seu d'Urgell. I booked into the Parador and then strolled through the town's ancient arcade into the main square, a place I remembered in another time and another mood, when it was filled with men in uniform waiting in trucks. I found myself a bar and sat down outside, where the waiter brought me red wine and a *racion* of polpo.

I had set off more prompted by instinct than by any particular plan, but now I knew why I had come to Seu. Many people had suggested that I should put down an account of certain episodes in my life but I had always hesitated. After all, we have stories to tell only because we are guests in each other's lives, invited or uninvited, and good manners impose a kind of *omertà*. Still, most of the people concerned are now dead and past being offended. For those of us still here, many things that once were of deadly importance – who slept with whom, for instance – have become trivial.

Perhaps there is a need to put things down so that we can see what isn't trivial. The important questions, in the end – or so it seemed to me in the darkening square of Seu – are mostly questions of loyalty.

I was hoping that it was loyalty that had led me to hound down a withered-up old man, and to finish by watching him die. Not that I had wanted to watch. I would have left him back at Collioure, at the gate of 17 Rue Bellver de St Cyprien, with a parting word or two. 'Forewarned is, well, whatever you choose to make of it, old man. But expect to see your dirty linen on the line before too long.' Something like that. And if he'd chosen to take an overdose, I could have borne the news.

When I saw him on the cliff, beyond the barrier, I hooked him back with the stick. He wanted to die. I wanted him to live. Had someone arrived on the scene, they would have thought I was trying to save him. I was, but only because I wanted him to taste the dregs of the anguish he was cutting short. There was no thought involved. It was something visceral that gave my muscles more strength than they should have had. Whatever it was, there was a moment when I felt it in my hands, and felt it with revulsion. I was holding the stick in just the grip that you would take on a five-iron. I hope it didn't slip. I hope I let it go.

It was a very ordinary wine. But it brought back Julia. I didn't drink a toast. I thought I'd done all that loyalty required.